Masks
IN HORROR CINEMA

HORROR STUDIES

Series Editor
Xavier Aldana Reyes, Manchester Metropolitan University

Editorial Board
Stacey Abbott, Roehampton University
Linnie Blake, Manchester Metropolitan University
Harry M. Benshoff, University of North Texas
Fred Botting, Kingston University
Steven Bruhm, Western University
Steffen Hantke, Sogang University
Joan Hawkins, Indiana University
Agnieszka Soltysik Monnet, University of Lausanne
Bernice M. Murphy, Trinity College Dublin
Johnny Walker, Northumbria University

Preface

Horror Studies is the first book series exclusively dedicated to the study of the genre in its various manifestations – from fiction to cinema and television, magazines to comics, and extending to other forms of narrative texts such as video games and music. Horror Studies aims to raise the profile of Horror and to further its academic institutionalisation by providing a publishing home for cutting-edge research. As an exciting new venture within the established Cultural Studies and Literary Criticism programme, Horror Studies will expand the field in innovative and student-friendly ways.

Masks
IN HORROR CINEMA

EYES WITHOUT FACES

ALEXANDRA HELLER-NICHOLAS

UNIVERSITY OF WALES PRESS
2019

© Alexandra Heller-Nicholas, 2019

All rights reserved. No part of this book may be reproduced in any material form (including photocopying or storing it in any medium by electronic means and whether or not transiently or incidentally to some other use of this publication) without the written permission of the copyright owner except in accordance with the provisions of the Copyright, Designs and Patents Act. Applications for the copyright owner's written permission to reproduce any part of this publication should be addressed to the University of Wales Press, University Registry, King Edward VII Avenue, Cardiff, CF10 3NS.

www.uwp.co.uk

British Library Cataloguing-in-Publication Data

A catalogue record for this book is available from the British Library.

ISBN   978-1-78683-496-6
eISBN 978-1-78683-497-3

The right of Alexandra Heller-Nicholas to be identified as author of this work has been asserted in accordance with sections 77 and 79 of the Copyright, Designs and Patents Act 1988.

Typeset by Chris Bell, cbdesign

Printed by CPI Antony Rowe, Melksham

For Casper and Christian

Contents

	Acknowledgements	ix
	Introduction	1
1.	Situating Masks and Horror Cinema	23
Part One: Masks, Horror and Cinema – Towards Codification		**39**
2.	Masks and Horror in Literary and Performance Traditions and Early Cinema	41
3.	Masks in Horror Film before 1970	63
Part Two: Horror Film Masks from 1970 – Case Studies		**87**
4.	Skin Masks: Ritual, Power and Transformation	89
5.	Blank Masks: Ritual, Power and Transformation	111
6.	Animal Masks: Ritual, Power and Transformation	129
7.	Repurposed Masks: Ritual, Power and Transformation	149

**Part Three: Masks as Transformational Technologies –
Moving Forward by Looking Back**   **167**

8. Technological Masks: Ritual, Power and Transformation   169

    Conclusion   191

    Endnotes   197
    Bibliography   239
    Index   267

Acknowledgements

WITH A PROJECT of this scale there are of course many people to thank. First, I must acknowledge Angela Ndalianis without whose practical and emotional support this would never have got off the ground, let alone ever be finished. Many thanks to the Horror Studies series editor Xavier Aldana Reyes and Sarah Lewis at University of Wales Press for the privilege of inviting me to join the series, and for their unceasing warmth, support and encouragement. I would also like to thank Stephen Morgan for his assistance in sourcing the Abel Gance documentation vital to chapter 2, as well as Julien Allen, Franck Boulègue and Samuel Bréan for their translation assistance of this material, and to Kevin Heffernan and Mark Jancovich for their invaluable feedback on the original thesis version of this book. Josh Nelson went well above and beyond the call of duty on pretty much all fronts (including his impressive copy-editing prowess), and I would also like to thank the following for their support: Anton Bitel, Sally Christie, Anna Dzenis, John Edmond, Giles Edwards, Mark Freeman, Lee Gambin, Wendy Haslem, Jade Henshaw, Ian Gouldstone, Anne Marsh, Craig Martin, Jan Napiorkowski, Tim O'Farrell, David Surman and Emma Westwood. As always, thanks to my family, Richard, Lorraine, Max, Fiona and Robert, and with particular love and gratitude to Casper and Christian.

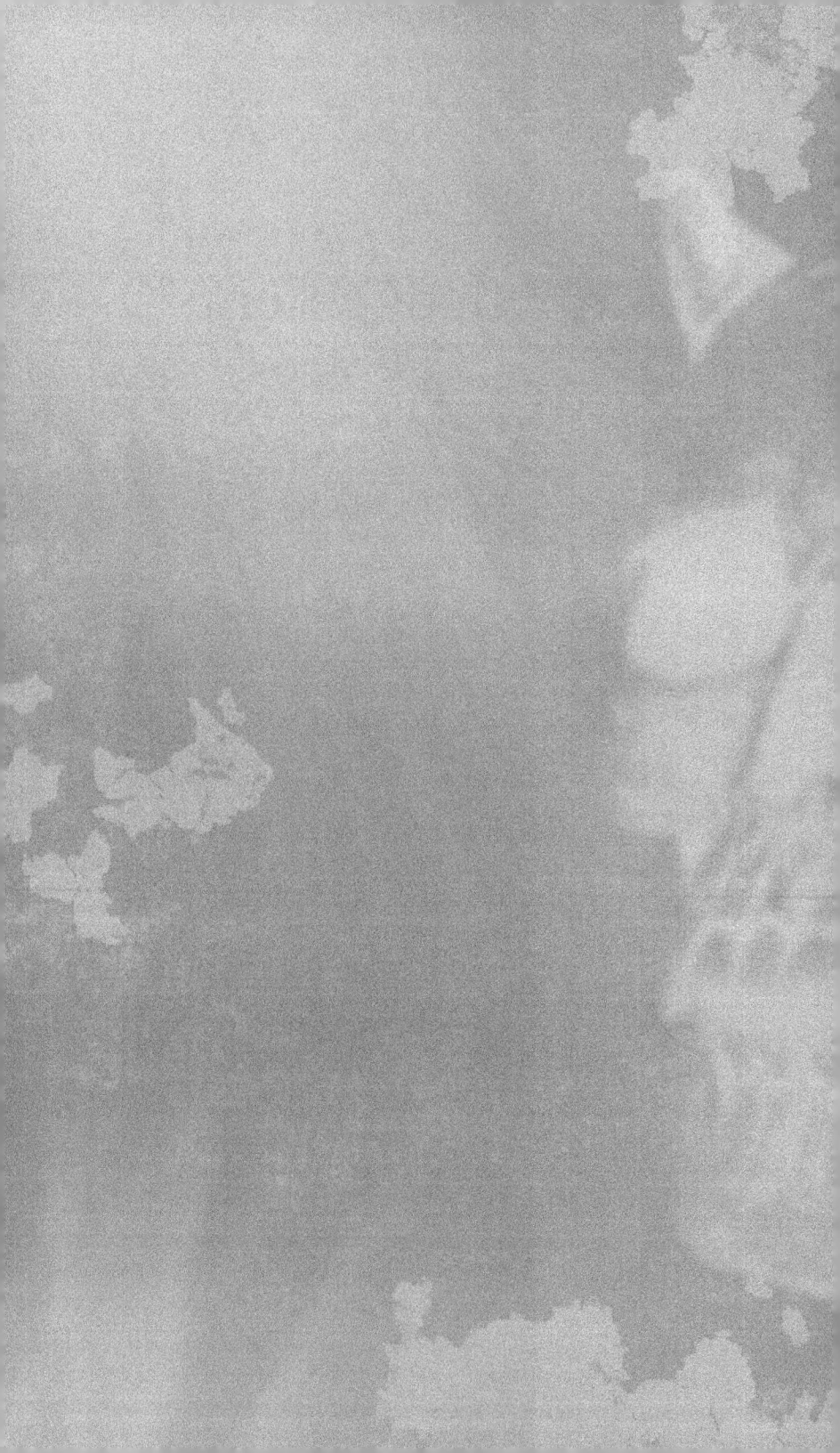

Introduction

LITTLE IS KNOWN of mononymous Belarusian film director Makinov, director of *Come Out and Play*, the 2012 Mexican remake of the Spanish horror classic *Who Can Kill a Child?* (*¿Quién puede matar a un niño?*, Narciso Ibáñez Serrador, 1976). While masks have long been an iconographic staple of horror cinema, Makinov took this generic fascination to its logical extreme: not only did he promote the film wearing a crude red sack mask with eyeholes cut out, but the cast and crew of *Come Out and Play* allegedly never saw his face during the production itself.[1] In a video introduction to a 2012 Toronto International Film Fest screening of *Come Out and Play*, Makinov said 'I wear my mask because through anonymity I can be all I want. As a beloved writer says, I believe in my mask, the man I made up is me. I believe in my dance and my destiny.'[2] Through this reference to Sam Shepard's *The Tooth of Crime* (1972), this horror film-maker made clear his belief that there is a meaningful connection between power, creativity and identity. Whether a publicity stunt or a material manifestation of his aesthetic philosophy, this is a memorable instance of the potency of horror film masks being deployed beyond the fictional constraints of cinema to make a statement.

As a horror film-maker, Makinov's mask consciously evokes a long history. Masks are closely linked to the horror legacies of icons like Lon Chaney Sr. and Vincent Price and in slasher franchises like *Friday the 13th* (1980–2009) and *Halloween* (1978–2018). When used diegetically, horror film masks imply associations with broader notions of identity and there are complexities embedded in how they are both deployed and are understood over time: their symbolic potency as objects linked to ritual, power and transformation has evolved over history. The conceptual force of horror film masks stems from both its generic ubiquity and simultaneous status as a cross-cultural associated with a complex range of historically defined meanings and values. These meanings and values are constantly evolving in horror to reflect new cultural and ideological contexts, rendering masks a persistent and important element of the genre's iconography. There is a crucial tension at play across the history of horror film masks between variation and consistency: while the mask is itself an enduring element of the genre, the meanings and values attached to it are demonstrably dynamic and adaptable.

From the outset, it must be stated that horror masks are not specific to only feature-length horror films, and horror narratives and media experiences across television and videogames are themselves worthy of future discussion and exploration, spanning as they do from a long literary history where masks and horror intersect (that will be discussed elsewhere in this book). The focus here, however, is specifically on horror feature films as they have a much longer history as a screen phenomenon that privileges masks. It thus can inform future examinations of other media, be it in terms of how it overlaps or – just as significantly – how it deviates. Horror film masks are a continuation of a multifaceted historical trajectory, their transformative potential continuing ritualistic and myth-making processes linked both to power, ideology and identity (as seen across myriad cultures with a recorded history of privileging this object) and also to genre itself. Horror film masks provoke associations with disguise and anonymity with a predominantly narrative purpose: to obscure – then possibly expose – the identity of a killer. Yet this reduces the utility of horror film masks to purely one of revelation and occlusion. While not untrue, often in horror movies we *know* the identity of the mask wearer: there is, for instance, no mystery about the *Halloween* franchise's slasher killer Michael Myers or that of the *Friday the 13th* films, Jason Voorhees. To conceive horror film masks solely as anonymity-creating devices undermines the power of the objects themselves. Even in their earliest, supposedly 'primitive' usages, masks were often bestowed with great power in terms of spiritual belief across a range of religious practices. This power is linked closely to masks as transformative devices.

Focusing on the intersection of ritual (be it secular or religious), power and transformation, we can see that horror cinema is a durable forum for the enduring potency of the mask's broader symbolic power to be constantly re-explored, re-imagined and re-invented, continuing key aspects of its cross-cultural and ritual significance that existed long before moving image culture. While there have been numerous critical examinations of horror film masks in specific movies, franchises, national and subgeneric contexts, there remains a broad absence of any substantial critical research dedicated to horror film masks and how they intersect with cultural histories of masks more broadly. We can employ this past research to assist building the foundations of a focused, critical analysis of horror film masks, synthesising and expanding upon these scattered treatments to map a cultural history of horror film masks, focusing specifically on ritual, power and transformation.

Chapter 1 expands on this notion of the shamanic imagination, examining how it plays out in cinema more broadly and how it intersects with traditions surrounding the trickster figure. Rather than attempting to draw a direct (and, as I soon illustrate, ideologically dubious) line between the history of traditionally conceived shamanism with horror film masks, we can more productively opt for a more elastic understanding of this relationship. The shamanic imagination is a cultural sensibility which pertains to how we broadly comprehend the potency of the mask (in horror cinema and elsewhere) beyond any specific anthropological definition or application of shamanism in the more orthodox sense. Rather, the shamanic imagination consists of residual traces of what shamanism 'means' in the broader popular consciousness, manifesting in contemporary horror cinema through a diverse range of rituals, be they explicitly religious or spiritual, or more secular phenomena like birthday parties, family meals or the act of cinema-going itself. The shamanic imagination allows us to think through movement across liminal spaces, linked historically to masks and the supernatural and the closely related figure of the trickster. These are all useful when considering the endurance of masks as a potent cross-cultural iconographic feature of horror cinema.

Part One explores the history of horror film masks as they move increasingly towards codification as a key aspect of the genre's iconographic palate from 1970 onwards. Chapter 2 examines masks in Japanese Noh theatre, the Italian *commedia dell'arte*, in the literary gothic and the work of H. P. Lovecraft and Edgar Allan Poe, and in French theatre in relation to the Grand Guignol and Antonin Artaud's Theatre of Cruelty. Across these we can identify a continuum of sorts through the mask and horror that underscore its affinity for subversion in a manner consistent with Mikhail

Bakhtin's notion of the carnivalesque. This chapter ends considering the intersection of masks and horror in early cinema, moving towards chapter 3 where this loose historical overview continues. Here we explore screen adaptations of Gaston Leroux's novel *The Phantom of the Opera* (1909), the Old Dark House tradition, Universal monster films and cross-generic manifestations through the 1930s, 1940s and 1950s and specific figures linked to masked horror performances such as Vincent Price, Lon Chaney Sr., William Castle and Peter Lorre. We then examine the internationalisation of horror and the rise of masks as a staple of horror iconography in *Eyes without a Face* (Georges Franju, 1960) from France, the El Santo films from Mexico, Mario Bava's *Black Sunday* (1960) with Barbara Steele from Italy and *Onibaba* (Kaneto Shindô, 1964) from Japan.

Part Two focuses on horror mask typologies across four case-study chapters that intersect with ritual, power and transformation in horror films made almost solely after 1970: skin masks, blank masks, animal masks and repurposed masks. Beyond ubiquitous Halloween costume masks (skulls, witches, monsters) whose deployment in horror cinema is tied to their explicit association with that festival, these categories allow a range of examples to be considered that underscore Steve Neale's claim that the longevity of film genres hinge on the interplay of 'repetition . . . difference, variation and change'.[3] Chapter 4 examines skin masks in horror and how they relate in specific instances to a number of rituals and power dynamics, including religion in *The Abominable Dr. Phibes* (Robert Fuest, 1971) and *Alice Sweet Alice* (Albert Sole, 1976), feminine identity in *The Texas Chain Saw Massacre* (Tobe Hooper, 1974) and *Curtains* (Richard Ciupka, 1983), and class in *Happy Birthday to Me* (J. Lee Thompson, 1981) and *Smiley* (Michael Gallagher, 2012). Chapter 5 investigates blank masks in horror in relation to repetition across the *Halloween* franchise and its remakes, to notions of place in *Gurozuka* (Yoichi Noshiyama, 2005) and *Celia* (Ann Turner, 1988), and to masculine identity in *Bruiser* (George A. Romero, 2000) and *Hush* (Mike Flanagan, 2016). Chapter 6 explores animal masks in horror and totemism in *Motel Hell* (Kevin Connor, 1980) and *Bloody Reunion* (*Seuseung-ui eunhye*, Dae-wung Lim, 2006), mythology in *Stagefright* (Michele Soavi, 1987) and *The Conspiracy* (Christopher MacBride, 2012), and note diverse yet simultaneously overlapping spirit of ambivalence to animal masks in Jean Rollin's *The Nude Vampire* (*La Vampire Nue*, 1970) and *You're Next* (Adam Wingard, 2011). Chapter 7 considers repurposed masks (intended for one use but deployed in horror in another way) and untrained labour in *My Bloody Valentine* (George Mihalka, 1981) and *Evidence* (2013) by director Olatunde Osunsanmi, in relation to social play *Friday the 13th Part III* (Steve Miner, 1982) and *Carved: The Slit-Mouthed Woman* (*Kuchisake-onna*, Kōji Shiraishi, 2007) and professional labour (in this case, medicine) in *Dead Ringers* (David Cronenberg, 1988) and *Anatomy* (*Anatomie*, Stefan Ruzowitzky, 2000).

While Part Three continues this focus on how horror movie masks, ritual and transformation intersect, it does so by turning an eye simultaneously towards the future and the past by considering the role of technological masks and temporality itself by looking at two pre-1970 horror films that employ the object specifically to 'move' through time, *Peeping Tom* (Michael Powell, 1960) and *The Mask* (Julian Roffman, 1961). It also considers the relationships between technological masks, ritual and consumerism in *Halloween III: Season of the Witch* (Tommy Lee Wallace, 1982) and *The Den* (Zachary Donohue, 2013) and the broader notion of performance in the Swedish television movie *Månguden* (Jonas Cornell, 1988) and *The Poughkeepsie Tapes* (John Erick Dowdle, 2007). While many of these films might feel distinctly more contemporary in their subgeneric categories and focus on current advances in technology, we can see how technology itself is fundamental to the transformative capacity of masks in horror film. Exploring films made by directors from around the world, through both their differences and similarities they collectively demonstrate the endurance of the object as a key aspect of the genre's iconography. In doing so, we can therefore answer the question at the core of this book: why are masks such a persistent motif in horror cinema?

Why Masks? Ritual, Power and Transformation

Amongst other things, masks are tools of transformation. As objects that facilitate disguise, they encompass dual strategies of revelation and obscuration. This tethers masks to ritual traditions, of which cinema more broadly has a long history: Eric Michael Mazur noted that across film history 'rituals mark transformations', from *Star Wars* (George Lucas, 1977) to *My Fair Lady* (George Cukor, 1964).[4] The scale and significance of this transformative potential, however, cannot be undervalued and as Walter Sorell stated, the belief that masks can transform their wearers – literally or symbolically – is an essential and broadly cross-cultural feature of human civilisation.[5] The transformative capacity of masks is also aligned with heftier questions about being and death and rituals often connected to spiritual and/or religious belief. For N. Ross Crumrine, 'through the dramatization of the generation, communication, transmission and transformation of power, often in relation to the problem of death and the life-death opposition, the mask radiates its own power or transmits power to the masker and or the audience'.[6] This aspect often plays out in horror films in the dynamics between a masked killer and their intended victim. Despite its potential complexity, there are few objects more ubiquitous yet critically underexplored in horror studies. Masks are used in diverse, complex ways that often contain broader socio-political dimensions and are part of a visual language whose transformative capacities are linked in a range of ways to power and ritual.

Framing Horror Masks

Numerous writers have considered the etymology of the word 'mask'. Elizabeth Tonkin noted that the English word 'person' has its origins in the Latin term for mask, 'persona'.[7] John W. Nunley and Cara McCarty also traced its linguistic origins to the Arabic *maskhara* (to transform or falsify), while in Ancient Egypt the word *msk* referred to leather as a 'second skin'.[8] As Laura Makarius noted, subjects of the Rorschach test commonly identify inkblots as masks, prompting Gaston Bachelard to suggest human masks are an integral aspect of a collective human psyche, echoing Carl Jung (discussed in chapter 1).[9] 'Mask' is both a verb and noun: as the former, it pertains to what Crumrine identified 'as the ritual transformation of the human actor into a being of another order'.[10] As a noun, John Mack suggested that masks refer to a singular, specific object, while for Nunley and McCarty, it is an object which covers the head to conceal the face.[11] But it can also imply any aspect of disguise or concealment, often with an element of pretence or deception.[12]

Yet such definitions elide the complexity of their functionality. As W. Anthony Sheppard suggested, the symbolic nature of masks is linked to a neutral duplicitousness: they 'are fundamentally double in function, signification and experience, serving simultaneously as tools for disguise and as markers of identity'.[13] Masks can be disguises, but even this is not a simple process of obscuring identity: its presence implies a potential *un*masking, a moment of revelation. As we explore from chapter 2 onwards, from contemporary horror films back to early examples, masking often activates the power imbued within the object itself. Likewise, there is a process of *de*activation when the mask is removed: in the context of horror, the unmasking of a killer is often (but again, not always) implied to neutralise the power it is implied the mask has granted them. In *Suspension* (Jeffery Scott Lando, 2015), the opening scene shows a young woman in a half-face mask tormenting a man she accuses of being a serial killer. He escapes and before he kills her he removes her mask and places it over his own face. This shift in their power dynamic is defined through the forced exchange of the mask and acts of masking and unmasking are intrinsic to the transformative power associated with the object.

In horror cinema, the presence of a masked villain implies the possibility that their identity will be revealed. This is typical of the *Scooby Doo* scenario: a supposedly all-powerful supernatural monster is exposed as a mere human menace, the act of unmasking removing their power. But in horror, it is often not simply a case of disguising identity as it is disguising certain personality aspects. In horror cinema, the act of masking often allows its wearers to behave in ways they would not otherwise be able to and unmasking can punctuate a return to the status quo. Recalling carnivalesque traditions, masking grants horror antagonists the ability to behave in otherwise unacceptable ways: for Nunley and McCarty, 'the power of anonymity gives us the protection to behave in ways we otherwise might not, to act aggressively or to break rules'.[14] Bakhtin's notion of the carnivalesque will be discussed further shortly.

Yet this is certainly not applicable to *all* horror movies. As noted, in the case of Jason Voorhees and Michael Myers, we know their identities – the faces underneath their masks are subjects of curiosity, but not linked to a revelation of their literal identities. In these instances, masks contain the thrilling possibility of unleashing what lies beneath; even if the wearer's identity is known, masks are understood as obscuring something crucial about the *type* of person who could commit the acts of violence typical of slasher films. Masks transform Jason and Michael from humans into something more powerful, simultaneously concealing something we do not know, while providing an outlet for something to be discovered or strengthened through the mask's transformative capacity and its relation to ritual and power. This echoes Rose Butler's observation that 'We are not just able to project our own fears onto slasher killers because their faces are hidden. The masks used to hide their features can tell us everything about *them*: their traumas and motives.'[15] Similarly, as John Schechter observed, in theatrical history 'the mask hides and reveals at the same time'.[16] This paradox is crucial to the potency of horror film masks.

Mack identified a series of motives for masking from an anthropological perspective, which is useful when considering horror film masks as part of a broader historical tradition of mask-wearing linked to ritual, power and transformation. As Mack noted, they can be found in traditional cultures as part of ceremonies surrounding birth and death:[17] from the surreal surgical masks in the birth flashbacks in Sergio Martino's *All the Colors of the Dark* (1972) to the iconic facial covering of Leatherface in *The Texas Chain Saw Massacre* (discussed in chapter 4), there are many instances of this in horror cinema. Masks can be found in rituals and ceremonies concerning the shift from childhood to adulthood,[18] a tradition brought to the screen in the mud-masks of the seven demon worshipping brothers' intent on impregnating their sister at the onset of menarche in *The Johnsons* (*De Johnsons*, Rudolf van den Berg, 1992). For Mack, masks traditionally mark other significant life changes, again often demonstrated in horror cinema: for instance, shifts in social ranking of an upwardly mobile nature are often formalised through masked rituals, celebrations or performances.[19] Although not technically a horror film, Stanley Kubrick's 1999 film *Eyes Wide Shut* is a dark fantasy that echoes this history. Alternatively, masks were traditionally employed in judicial and legal rituals, recalling the animal mask-wearing jury in Vernon Serwell's 1968 film *Curse of the Crimson Altar* (animal masks in horror are explored in chapter 6). In agricultural cultures, Mack noted that masks were employed during rituals marking seasonal changes, recalling *The Wicker Man* (Robin Hardy, 1973).[20] The relationship between masks and ritual practice is crucial when considering the enduring presence of the former in horror cinema.

Masks and Rituals

The meanings and functions of masks are diverse. They can have practical safety functions in some contexts, while maintaining near-mystical symbolic force in others. As explored in chapter 7, in practical terms mask-wearing is a ubiquitous part of everyday life for surgeons, welders, divers, fencers, hockey players and others, and a wardrobe staple for wrestlers, stage and carnival performers, masquerade ball attendees and children dressing-up for birthday parties or Halloween.[21] As Victor Turner argued, across a range of cultures these latter events in particular require specific customs related to dress, food, song and dance, the decoration or presentation of the event itself, and of course dress including (but not limited to) masks themselves.[22] Ritual practices are diverse and can take a variety of forms.

Ritual is a key concept here and therefore worth clarifying further. Mask-wearing has documented associations with ritual practices. Ronald L. Grimes identified mask-making as a 'ritual gesture',[23] a definition that privileges the embodied nature of mask-wearing: the object is an extension of the wearer's body and a tool for somatic, non-lingual communication. For Richard Schechner, whether 'performance' is conceived in the context of sport, music, theatre or day-to-day living, it fundamentally contains gestures that have a ritualised quality.[24] Horror film from this perspective therefore is conceived as a forum where precisely this kind of mask-centric, ritualistic action takes place.

Performance and ritual have a long, overlapping history. While Schechner challenged assumptions that the performing arts grew directly out of ritual, he conceded that even from very early on there was an overlap between the entertainment aspects of performance and its ritual qualities.[25] Thus, even film star personae can be understood as masks of sorts,[26] while for Paul Coates, the screen is a mask-like membrane between the faces that are filmed and those who are watching those faces across a range of exhibition and reception contexts.[27] Ritual therefore manifests in film in diverse ways and has been approached by numerous critics in relation to horror cinema.[28]

This link between ritual and performance is demonstrated in Lee Strasberg's American method acting, which Michael L. Quinn argued is intrinsically ritualistic in nature, particularly concerning the influence of Polish director and theorist Jerzy Grotowski.[29] These ritual aspects of method acting combine with horror masks in the German horror film *Masks* (Andreas Marschall, 2011), a homage to Dario Argento's *Suspiria* (1977), that follows actor Stella (Susen Ermich) who is granted a place at Berlin's Matteusz Gdula Institute. Stella endures an intense study regime reliant upon method-like masked performance techniques that dehumanise students and indoctrinate them into a death cult. In *Masks*, the surrendering of identity through masked performance rituals that recall method acting techniques are a source of horror.

Even attending the cinema can be considered a contemporary ritual.[30] Michael Richardson observed that the surrealists understood cinema-going itself as a kind of ancient ritual where contemporary dramas could be played out, while Maruša Pušnik noted that from its earliest days cinema-going itself had a whole spectrum of ritualised aspects to it.[31]

James B. Twitchell famously claimed that horror films themselves are rituals governed by strictly coded formulae pertaining to social norms with an almost didactic intent to deliver to its teen audience, drawing parallels to the social learning aspects of traditional fairy tales (especially when it comes to sexuality).[32] Although clearly reductive,[33] at the very least Twitchell's identification of horror film spectatorship as ritual in general terms is noteworthy.

Vera Dika much more successfully saw a connection between horror and ritual in her observation that the return of the killer in stalker or slasher films is frequently associated with the memorialising of an event that triggers the murderer's action.[34] These are often linked to almost always secular social and cultural ritual events,[35] evident in film titles alone: *Black Christmas* (Bob Clark, 1974), *Halloween* (John Carpenter, 1978), *Graduation Day* (Herb Freed, 1981), *April Fool's Day* (Fred Walton, 1986) and *Happy Birthday to Me* and *My Bloody Valentine* (the latter two are discussed at length later in this book). Essential to Dika's and Twitchell's observations is the central role of ritual, supported by a whole array of other horror movies themselves. An obvious case is Lamberto Bava's *Demons* (1985), which uses masks to explore the ritual act of cinemagoing. Set in a cinema, film-goers see a masked figure on display in the foyer who later appears in the horror film they all watch that bleeds into their own reality. In *Demons*, the mask is a contagion, turning those affected into its eponymous monsters. Mask-wearing and cinema-going rituals collide with spectacular, visceral results.

Demons and *Masks* suggest secular rituals and the transformative capacity of masks intersect in ways often highly attuned to horror's broader codes and conventions. For Merrifield, if religious rituals seek to align performers with 'supernatural beings', and if secular, however, the mission is to underscore the value and solidity of the way a given society is organised itself, or to strengthen it even further.[36] Crocker, however, rejected 'the usual doctrine of functionalism, which claims that social customs must contribute to the integrated functioning of society and be meaningful to its members'.[37] This is crucial to the endurance of horror film masks, as Crocker emphasised that particular traditions linked to mask-wearing can endure even when the original context or symbolic meaning has disappeared.[38] One need only consider the use of the beak-nosed mask in *The Poughkeepsie Tapes* (discussed in chapter 8), whose presence is no less disturbing for viewers unaware of its specificity to the Black Death in Europe (1346–53). Whether we know the histories associated with specific masks or not, their transformative capacities are often unaffected in terms of the potency of their impact.

Masks and Identities

Approaching masks as cultural artefacts with material histories widely utilised in horror demands a consideration of further critical aspects. Most immediately, masks must be understood as artefacts in and of themselves. Both mask-wearing and mask-making has manifested across different cultures,[39] and for Nunley and McCarty, their cross-cultural ubiquity often relates to the maintaining of social order.[40] This is a profound observation in regard to horror film masks, as this genre often tests precisely the *limits* of social order and deliberately inverts it (linking it again to Bakhtin's notion of the carnivalesque, discussed shortly). Masks and mask-wearing rituals can therefore be understood as having intrinsic significance to identity, be it for an individual wearer or, as Nunley and McCarty suggested, relating to broader socio-cultural constructions. Efrat Tseëlon defined identity as 'an organising structure around which notions of "self" . . . and "other" are constructed'.[41] In the case of horror film masks, this allows an unpacking of the genre's sometimes radical ideological regimes, particularly in regard to power relations dictated by points of social, economic and cultural difference (class, race, age, gender, etc.), factors considered in many of the films explored later in this book.

That these power relations are so often marked by visible physical difference emphasises how closely masks and associated rituals are to the body, particularly the face. As the communicative source of so much expression and displayed emotion, Sheppard locates the human face as the core of human identity.[42] This communication pertains to language as well as the demonstration of emotion, whose nuance is transmitted through often minute adjustments of facial expression. But the close physical relationship between masks and the face should not belie the broader dynamics of how masked communication manifests, because as Tseëlon noted, the covering of the face transfers attention to the nuances of the body itself: a mask is brought to life not through the face that it covers, but by the actions of the whole body of its wearer.[43] Masks cover the face but by changing identity this affects the entire body; this is vital when considering the mask in Japanese Noh theatre (discussed in chapters 2 and 4) or the white face paint of mime traditions (discussed in chapter 2).

The horror films discussed here are useful for investigating how the *limits* of power can be tested in the fictional, fantastic spaces masked horror film performances allow. While these case studies consider other points of difference in terms of power hierarchies and Otherness, in relation to gender politics a brief acknowledgement of masquerade theory is necessary. Joan Riviere's 1929 essay 'Womanliness as Masquerade' argued from a psychoanalytic position a tendency for some women to use an elevated 'womanliness' as a disguise to hide fears of not being accepted by men and to assuage a sense of failure for not being masculine. In film theory, this was expanded by Claire Johnston (1975) and Mary Ann Doane (1982/1988). Although my specific use of the term 'masquerade' here applies to acts of masking and unmasking, from this approach it importantly functions as a synonym for feminine performance (discussed further in chapter 7 in regard to *Evidence*).

The centrality of psychoanalysis here also recalls another foundational work of feminist film criticism, Barbara Creed's *The Monstrous-Feminine: Film, Feminism, Psychoanalysis* (1993). Applying Julia Kristeva's theory of abjection (1982) to horror cinema, Creed challenges Laura Mulvey's claim that narrative cinema is dominated by a sadistic male gaze (1975).[44] For Kristeva, ritual is the method by which distinctions are made between humans and non-humans, and Creed highlights Kristeva's focus on ritual as pertaining directly to the ways societies simultaneously reaffirm and exclude the abject.[45] Rituals of abjection also evoke associations with dehumanisation, a recurring critical motif when it comes to horror film masks. Nick Haslam argued against a singular, unified definition of dehumanisation as the word can apply to a range of different things, identifying instead a spectrum that runs from 'infrahumanization' to 'dehumanization'.[46] For Haslam, dehumanisation informs a scale of what he calls 'humanness denials': whether explicit or subtle, these can be more productively understood on a spectrum than a binary.[47] As demonstrated throughout this book, Haslam's dehumanisation spectrum model is useful when considering horror film masks. In terms of masks, Thomas Sipos elsewhere observed the dehumanising aspects of masks,[48] and as such humanness and interrelated denials of humanness are inherent to the construction of the monstrous in horror movies beyond slasher, including non-supernatural ones. As Stephen T. Asma noted, 'the term "monster" is often applied to human beings who have, by their own horrific actions, abdicated their humanity'.[49] Haslam's dehumanisation spectrum model allows an appreciation of the range of nuances that the word 'dehumanisation' necessarily demands across the diverse deployments of horror movie masks considered here.

Masks and Histories

The cross-cultural significance of masks is entrenched in their myriad histories. As Walter Sorell observed, 'the mask in its innumerable forms and functions can lay claim to representing the longest chapter in primitive art'.[50] Masks and mask-wearing rituals are potent artefacts in what Nunley and McCarty identified as the way social memory is reconstructed, noting recent revivals in carnival mask-wearing traditions in Europe respond to contemporary anxieties about national borders and cultural identity.[51] As demonstrated through horror film masks, however, these rituals are not bound to national borders: as in the case of Japanese Noh theatre, distinct transnational flows within contemporary horror propel how masks are deployed, how they transform and the influence of this on power dynamics. As discussed in chapter 5, the use of Noh masks in the Australian film *Celia* is a strong example of the scope for this experimentation.

Masks and mask-wearing rituals are a ubiquitous international and historical phenomenon, with evidence of the act spanning every culture from so-called 'primitive' tribal cultures to the technology-oriented Western world of late capitalism.[52] Even in its earliest usage, masks evoke associations with 'performance' at a basic level simply because the wearing of a mask assumes an audience to witness the transformation.[53] Mask-wearing is an intrinsic aspect of shamanic ritual and practice, and rock and cave paintings provide evidence of the value of masks in prehistoric times; masks were a key aspect of ancient theatre, and in Greek Tragedy they represented familiar types and tropes broadly familiar to their audience.[54] Likewise, masks were a central facet of the Italian *commedia dell'arte* that flourished from the sixteenth century onwards, a form crucial to the development of masked performance because they embody distinct, recognisable typologies (discussed further in chapter 2). More recently, masks fascinated both modernists and postmodernists alike, aligned as they are with the modernist fascination of human transformation within the field of the arts.[55] Masks appear throughout modernist art, such as in the work of German-Danish expressionist artist Emil Nolde (discussed in chapter 2) and Belgian artist James Ensor, a strong influence on the surrealist movement. Masks are also closely associated with Spanish artist Pablo Picasso's so-called 'African Period' in 1907.

Russian philosopher and literary theorist Mikhail Bakhtin's focus on *Carnival in Rabelais and His World* (1965) has also been of interest to scholars of modernism and postmodernism.[56] A critical celebration of

François Rabelais's *Gargantua and Pantagruel* (*La vie de Gargantua et de Pantagruel*) pentalogy (1532–64), *Rabelais and His World* examines the Renaissance period in which the novels were written. For Bakhtin, the democratic nature of Renaissance Carnival saw a union of individuals as a singular, culturally defined organism, linked by ideology. Carnival's subversion of social order relies on the body, fuelling Bakhtin's notion of the grotesque. Evoking critical parallels with horror subgenres like splatter and gore, for Bakhtin open, abject bodies allow a process of renewal central to Carnival, where 'people were, so to speak, reborn for new, purely human relations'.[57]

Masks play an important role in how the carnivalesque and grotesque usurp order. As Florent Christol noted, Carnival marked a complex intersection of social and ritual practices where people commonly outside the systems of power were momentarily granted some of the token qualities associated with political dominance.[58] For Katerina Clark and Michael Holquist, masks were key to this ritual, as in Bakhtin's writing as the object symbolised the destabilised, dynamic and multiple identities that were so central to his fascination with Carnival.[59] A central part of Carnival costume, masks for Bakhtin were 'connected with the joy of change and reincarnation, with gay relativity and with the merry negation of uniformity and similarity'.[60] Carnival's ambivalence to dominant social structures renders masks a vital performance tool, whose complexity stems from their transformative capacity. For Bakhtin, 'the mask is related to transition, metamorphosis, the violation of natural boundaries, to mockery and familiar nicknames. It contains the playful elements of life.'[61] Rozaliya Yaneva suggested that the mask is central to Bakhtin's model of Carnival traditions because it functions – like disguise – somewhat ambivalently: both mask-wearing and disguise-wearing more generally are predicated on acts of transformation, an act reliant upon the becoming (or the transformation) into something different from what the wearer is otherwise.[62] Masks, therefore, both transform *and* create simultaneously.

While critical writing on the intersection of Carnival, the carnivalesque and horror cinema is not uncommon,[63] its particular relationship to mask-wearing and rituals such as Halloween is also noteworthy. For Jack Santino, contemporary Halloween celebrations in the United States are intrinsically carnivalesque, originating in festive traditions from the Mediterranean, Africa and Central and South America.[64] Traces of the carnivalesque appear at the intersection of ritual and play: play – like the carnivalesque – provides an opportunity for a culturally sanctioned adventure in subversion, transgression and engaging with taboos otherwise forbidden.[65] For Schechner, ritual and play combined to form a 'second reality', a distinct sphere of cultural and social experience 'separate from ordinary life ... where people can become selves other than their daily selves'.[66] While play and ritual will be expanded in chapter 7, mask-wearing and associated rituals are a concrete, material way of entering this second reality. Horror cinema is a specific cultural forum the carnivalesque can play out through masked transformation.

Masks and the Horrific

Masks are uncanny because they are faces-that-are-not-faces. Defined by Sigmund Freud as 'that class of the frightening which leads back to what is known of old and long familiar', uncanny imagery in gothic horror practically manifests through 'repetitions, returns, *deja vu*, premonitions, ghosts, doppelgangers, animated inanimate objects and severed body parts'.[67] Of particular interest are doppelgängers, crucial to any consideration of masks in horror. Meaning 'double' or 'duplicate' in German, it relates a secondary identity or personality who in the gothic context tends to be a baser or more evil version of the original, more civilised version.[68] The doubling processes that govern the practical split between original/doppelgänger can be created through errors in identification often linked to doubling scenarios that hinge around disguise.[69] Many horror film masks support Paul Fleming's observation that 'the doppelgänger is an effect-machine, generating sensations of the comic, the uncanny and the terrifying for the one confronted with his second self'.[70] Masks transform their wearers into the masked and unmasked.

From this perspective, horror film masks – in their diverse and sometimes perverse replication of the human face – support Georges Bataille's claim that 'the mask is chaos made flesh'.[71] For Bataille, 'the mask communicates incertitude and the menace of unexpected changes, unforeseeable and as insupportable as death. Its irruption liberates that which had been enchained for the maintenance of stability and order.'[72] The capacity for horror within the mask – amplified in this generic context – stems from its destabilising capacity spawned from its status as a transformative device. Death masks are thus worth considering in relation to ritual, masks and horror cinema. The historical origins of death mask traditions unite them with animal masks as prototypes for the kind of masks to come, and they too are a notably cross-cultural phenomenon.[73] Gold death masks date to the Cretan Mycenaean age (second millennium BC)[74] and death masks were used in Roman death rituals – the Mayans, Aztecs and ancient Peruvians also having variations of this ritual.[75] There is evidence of death mask traditions in the Americas, Africa, Asia and Europe.[76] Although diverse, these traditions are underscored by a belief that masks are transformative devices with the ability to transfer power from the deceased.[77]

The utility of masks for horror cinema stems from this provocation of dual, contradictory responses of what Tseëlon has identified as a tension between captivation and repulsion.[78] In language well suited to horror cinema, Tseëlon noted that 'the mask stands in an intermediary position between different worlds . . . Its embodiment of the fragile dividing line between concealment and revelation, truth and artifice, natural and supernatural, life and death is a potent source of the mask's metaphysical power.'[79] This recalls horror icons like the zombie and vampire, as does her observation that 'the mask is simultaneously animated and inanimate, living and dead: an expressionless mass transformed into expressive being'.[80] Others have similarly used language aligned with horror and the supernatural to describe the power and mechanics of the mask, such as Simon Shepherd and Mick Wallis who note that in performance, 'a mask is simply not worn, but is inhabited by the performer', and that while it simultaneously 'inhabits the performer . . . The performer's brain is taken into the attitude of the mask, leaving behind the protocols and constraints of everyday existence.'[81] The idea of a mask 'possessing' its wearer in cinema extends beyond horror in *The Mask* (Chuck Russell, 1994): as the darker aspects of that film's fantasy indicates, there are tensions around possessive-mask and its relationship to power. Although a comedy, the premise of *The Mask* is an anxious one about masked transformation out of control.

Ritual traditions associated with masks have a long history and horror cinema is a site where their symbolic power continues to appear and evolve in ways that continue this history, moving dynamically into new terrain for masked performance. As Nunley and McCarty suggested, masquerades are vital parts of many different societies, many of which have specific 'special areas to play out their myths'.[82] Horror cinema is *precisely* one of these 'special areas', recalling in part Adam Lowenstein's configuration of 'the allegorical moment', defined as a 'shocking collision of film, spectator and history where registers of bodily space and historical time are disrupted, confronted and intertwined'.[83] For Lowenstein, 'These registers of space and time are distributed unevenly across the cinematic text, the film's audience and the historical context.'[84] This allegorical moment is a 'complex process of embodiment, where film, spectator and history compete and collaborate to produce forms of knowing not easily described by conventional delineations of bodily space and historical time'.[85] Recalling Bakhtin's mask-wearing Carnival revellers, horror films that use masks similarly provide a space – a special area – where the film itself, its audience's affective experience of watching it and the long history of masks and masked rituals themselves 'intertwine'. Carnivalesque traditions of mask-wearing are employed in horror to transgress social norms and in horror cinema provide a forum for many social and cultural anxieties to be explored, examined and often subverted: not by wearing masks ourselves, but by watching films *about* the transformative capacities of masks and their relationship to power and ritual.

Masks in Horror Cinema

This is not the first in-depth consideration of horror film masks, but at present British actor Doug Bradley is the author of the only full-length book dedicated to the subject. While a work of pop non-fiction aimed at a fan demographic, *Sacred Monsters: Behind the Mask of the Horror Actor* (1996) provides a number of important connections between horror cinema and the history of the mask; Bradley privileged shamanic traditions in particular (discussed further in chapter 1). His book focuses on actors linked to masked horror film performance, including Lon Chaney Sr., Boris Karloff, Vincent Price, Gunnar Hansen (Leatherface from *The Texas Chain Saw Massacre*), Robert Englund (Freddy Krueger in the *Nightmare on Elm Street* films) and Kane Hodder (who played Jason Voorhees in four *Friday the 13th* films). Bradley weaves through this his own experience as a masked horror actor as iconic Alpha Cenobite Pinhead in the first eight films of the *Hellraiser* series, seeking to discuss masks from the perspective of the masked performer themselves.[86] Horror author and writer/director of the original 1986 *Hellraiser* film Clive Barker provided a foreword to Bradley's book, emphasising the importance of horror film masks and noting that they are 'a means of concealment and one of confession. It covers the human and reveals the *in*human . . . the man disappears and a creature of mythic proportions replaces him: some demon or divinity, a terrible intelligence'.[87] *Sacred*

Monsters is an important predecessor to this book in its emphasis on the dynamics of horror film masks from a performer's perspective.

Beyond this, so ubiquitous are horror film masks that they appear almost too obvious to devote focused critical attention to. The very saturation of the genre with this iconographic element render it for many an uncomplicated cliché rather than a subject worthy of deeper consideration, particularly in terms of Neale's focus on genre longevity being resultant of a process 'dominated by repetition . . . difference, variation and change'.[88] Even books that imply masks might be a central site of focus investigation typify this omission: despite its title, Adam Rockoff's *The Horror of It All: One Moviegoer's Love Affair with Masked Maniacs, Frightened Virgins and the Living Dead . . .* (2015), for example, mentions masks only in passing, rarely attempting any deep critical interrogation of their generic ubiquity. In contrast, academic work tends to focus on film- or franchise-specific contexts. While it is impossible to talk about the *Halloween*, *Texas Chain Saw Massacre* and *Friday the 13th* franchises and not mention masks, these discussions rarely show any broader interest in horror film masks more generally.

There are notable exceptions. Rose Butler too identified an absence of deep, sustained analysis of the horror murderer's mask, which is a notable critical gap, and in the few instances where they have been examined those attempts are frequently reductive in nature.[89] Butler argued for a broad tendency in the little scholarly treatment of horror masks that does exist to assume 'that slasher masks are featureless and emotionless', which she countered in her claim that Canadian slasher films in particular complicate this by 'function[ing] as an outward reflection of the killer's inner trauma or a wider cultural paranoia'.[90] Of the three films she considered – *Terror Train* (Roger Spottiswoode, 1980), *My Bloody Valentine* and *Curtains* – we will look at the latter two in depth later in this book. While Butler focused on Canadian slasher films and masks in this specific subgeneric and national context, we here have the opportunity to look even more broadly.

Butler privileged Sipos's book *Horror Film Aesthetics: Creating the Visual Language of Fear* (2010) for its brief consideration of the role of masks in horror as a notable feature of the genre, where he noted that 'masks have personalities. The hideousness of a mask can heighten its horror and empower its wearer.'[91] Yet earlier research into the subject can be found in Jason Huddleston's 2005 article 'Unmasking the Monster: Hiding and Revealing Male Sexuality in John Carpenter's *Halloween*'. Huddleston

– like Butler and myself – noted that the mask has gone broadly unacknowledged beyond passing reference. In *Halloween*, he argued, the mask is thematically vital as it reflects an aspect of the character who wears it, allowing the audience some insight into a character whose facial covering appears to obscure rather than disclose; as such, for Huddleston 'the mask seems to allow the slasher to hide who he is, compensate for who he is not and enable him to release the anxiety created by his own sexual repression'.[92] The mask does not so much as prompt transformation as it obstructs clarity of vision, a loosely conceived 'truth'.

While Huddleston shares my interest in horror film masks and notes how little critical attention they have received, his article is based on Carol J. Clover's claim that the slasher killer is 'distinctly male'.[93] Yet Clover herself frames this with a clarification: 'On the face of it, the relationship between the sexes in slasher films could hardly be clearer.'[94] Huddleston does not fully acknowledge the importance of Clover's phrase 'on the face of it' here, however, which implies that there is more to it. For, as she continues – which Huddleston effectively ignores – there are further complications of her initial observation, as she notes 'we have in the killer a feminine male and in the main character a masculine female'.[95] That being said, even Clover's text selection process itself has not been without its critics: Tony Williams, for example, suggested she cherry-picked only examples that supported her claims and effectively ignored case studies that did not adhere to her argument.[96] We can see this in Huddleston's argument also: while his case rests on the assumption that the slasher killer is typically biologically male, aside from *Happy Birthday to Me* and *Curtains* (both discussed in chapter 4) and the famous example of *Friday the 13th* (Sean S. Cunningham, 1980), there are *many* slasher movies from North America in the 1980s alone that feature women killers.[97] Consequently, when Huddleston referred to the slasher killer as 'he', much of the subversive potential of what masks in slasher can 'do' in regard to gender and monstrosity is missed, a factor expanded upon in numerous case studies later in this book.

Huddleston was, however, correct in his assertion that horror film masks are critically underexplored, but we can go beyond his claim that 'many of these films that utilize this rather ordinary prop have at least implicitly suggested the significance of its function within the story and have often used the mask itself to capitalize on their slasher-hero's commercial popularity'.[98] To be blunt, both within and beyond the slasher subgenre, despite their ubiquity horror film masks are *anything* but 'ordinary'.

Rather, they have a complex history, both within horror itself and in the broader popular imagination. Horror film masks adapt to social, national and generic requirements, making them recognisably 'horror movies' to audiences despite often widespread experimentation with what masks can or (in some notable cases) cannot do. Through these examples, where horror film masks diverge is just as crucial as where they intersect when it comes to the question at the heart of this book: why are masks such an enduring motif in horror film?

1

Situating Masks and Horror Cinema

THIS CHAPTER considers the endurance of horror film masks as a key aspect of the genre's iconography, including considerations of myth and its relation to genre studies more broadly, shamanism and tricksters. Shamanism is central here for its role in what I like to think of as the 'shamanic imagination', a broader cross-cultural sensibility removed from the specificities of how the term is understood from orthodox anthropological perspectives and rather understood in a looser, more elastic way that accounts for how the power of masks are broadly conceived.

First and foremost, however, masks are 'things' – material objects that can be felt, worn and touched. It is therefore worth considering horror film masks and their material histories when approaching them as an enduring aspect of horror's *mise en scène*. As the study of objects and how they pertain to human culture, for Ian Woodward material culture concerns 'how apparently inanimate things within the environment act on people and are acted upon by people, for the purposes of carrying out social functions, regulating social relations and giving symbolic meaning to human activity'.[1] Objects unite economic and social structures with individuals,[2] and as such there is a tension when considering an object like masks and their place in horror film history: between how they function in diegetic terms and how they are understood by the spectator at any given moment, across a range of exhibition and reception possibilities. For example, the experience of watching John Carpenter's *Halloween* at a British drive-in in 1978, on VHS in Australia in 1988, on television in Japan in 1998, on DVD in France in 2008 or its fortieth anniversary US cinema screenings in 2018, would all be different, even though the text remained the same. This pertains not only to reception and exhibition, but how intertextual reference points may alter in meaning and significance across time and space.

Approaching horror film masks from a material culture perspective offer allows a consideration of both ideological and aesthetic aspects of the object across different contexts. Materiality is significant here, the aesthetic qualities (shape, texture, colour, etc.) we see on screen might be communicated visually, but recalling Vivian Sobchack's essay 'What My Fingers Knew: The Cinesthetic Subject, or Vision in the Flesh', there is far more at stake here than mere 'objective symbolic representation', because 'vision [is] always in cooperation and significant exchange with other sensorial means of access to the world'.[3] Many horror films go to remarkable lengths to provoke multi-sensory responses that imply what the masks might *feel* like: the stretchy peel of the rubber mask off Ann's face in *Happy Birthday to Me* discussed in chapter 4 evokes a clammy stickiness; the heavy breathing that often accompanies Michael Myers's first person point-of-view shots in the *Halloween* franchise arouse a suffocating intimacy. The appearance of these masks is an entry point to other sensorial experiences: they provoke a 'sensual and sense-making experience' *across* our senses, even if the data is visually encoded.[4] Seen from the perspective of material culture, the significance of these factors is heightened when considering the history of horror film masks.

Genre, Myth and Masks

As a film genre, taxonomical factors unite horror with myth and ritual. In his foundational work on the western, John G. Cawelti identified that genre as a 'social and cultural ritual' and 'a means of affirming certain basic cultural values, resolving tension and establishing a sense of continuity between the present and the past'.[5] Christian Metz (1974) and Umberto Eco (1976) were crucial in linking semiotics and structuralist approaches with film studies, but earlier work influenced film and genre studies also. Lévi-Strauss's essay 'The Structural Study of Myth' (originally published in 1955) strongly influenced structuralism and his book *The Way of the Masks* (originally published in 1972) is centred around a mask used amongst tribes on the coast of British Columbia. Lévi-Strauss argues that myths and their representations are not singular, one-off phenomena, and he looks for patterns that demonstrate a historical form of communication between the tribe and those around it. Focusing on patterns in myths spawned from masks, his geographical area of focus expands both spatially and temporally. These patterns are crucial to him, 'as is the case with myths, masks, too, cannot be interpreted in and by themselves as separate objects'.[6] Lévi-Strauss claimed that 'we can perceive, between the origin myths for each type of mask, transformational relations homologous to those that, from a purely plastic point of view, prevail among the masks themselves'.[7] He insisted that 'we must reassemble the data available' for study and that 'it is only after this all-inclusive documentation has been gathered that we may be able to compare it with other records'.[8] In short, he called for intensive close material analysis looking for structural patterns.

Much has been gained by approaching genre in a similar manner. Jim Kitses's (1969) and Will Wright's (1975) work on the western was crucial in the development of genre studies, informed by Lévi-Strauss's structuralist approach to myth. Lévi-Strauss's observation that 'a myth remains the same as long as it is felt as such' was echoed by Andrew Tudor: discussing the 'empiricist's dilemma', he noted a tendency to define genres through what were already broadly assumed to be 'principle characteristics' in the first place, resulting in his famous observation that 'genre is what we collectively believe it to be'.[9] This logic dictates that we need to know the generic characteristics that we are looking for to be able to identify them in the first place. As Mark Jancovich noted, assumptions about horror's formulaic nature are so widespread that they underpin 'meta' horror movies like Wes Craven's *Scream* (1996), a film that for Jancovich 'both draws upon and reproduces in its supposed self-referential play with the "rules" of the horror film'.[10] Thomas Schatz noted that 'in its ritualistic capacity, a film genre transforms certain fundamental cultural contradictions and conflicts into a unique conceptual structure that is familiar and accessible to the mass audience'.[11] While acknowledging this 'genre as myth model is widely influential', as Rick Altman suggested – amongst other issues – Lévi-Strauss's notion of ritual does not fully account for the 'why' of film genre production.[12]

The influence of Lévi-Strauss on genre studies in terms of myth and ritual and his interest in masks position him as an important reference point in this book. However, this risks missing the significance of the mask's materiality, discussed previously: for Angela Ndalianis, while 'a structuralist like Lévi-Strauss may insist that to get to the core of myths it's necessary to strip away the surface' in order to look for these deep structures and patterns, 'horror . . . is as much about the surface as it is about the underlying structure'.[13] Echoing Sobchack, Ndalianis's focus on the sensory aspects of horror is crucial when considering horror film masks, as it is precisely their material qualities in many cases that grant them their potency.

More urgently, the utility of Neale's tension between repetition and variation is also lost when it is only the former that is privileged. In his discussion of Carnival masks, Bakhtin noted that it is all but 'impossible to exhaust the intricate multiform symbolism of the mask' and this is true too of horror film masks.[14] Their very ubiquity makes any attempt to include every mask in the genre practically impossible, so my examples underscore Neale's suggestion that genre is less a rigid system of mimicry as it is a constantly evolving process driven by tensions between repetition and difference. In *Genre and Hollywood* (2000), Neale challenged Thomas Schatz's (1981) privileging of repetition alone as key to generic mechanics, seeking to 'temper the emphasis he places on repetition and sameness as opposed to variation and change'.[15] The endurance of horror film masks reflects this: 'these processes may, for sure, be dominated by repetition, but they are also marked fundamentally by difference, variation and change'.[16] Similarity and difference are crucial when thinking about genres like horror as they maintain their freshness and interest for audiences by experimenting with the tension between originality and mimicry.[17] As the later case studies in this book will indicate, while sharing mask motif, they deploy it in diverse and often sophisticated ways.

We can therefore look towards both intersecting threads and points of diversity as we consider the endurance of horror film masks. It would be difficult to talk about horror film masks and not discuss *The Phantom of the Opera* (1925), for instance, but we might also consider the value of looking towards lesser known films that show how broadly masks have been deployed in horror. As Crocker noted, 'there are . . . many varieties of masking, and it would be very misleading to reduce them to some kind of ur-mask both in form and in social function'.[18] This is true of horror film masks also. Accordingly, while not ignoring trends or disregarding the influence of more well-known horror films that diegetically utilise masks, my case studies include both 'masterpieces' and forgotten television movies. Through horror film masks, we can explore the multifaceted and often complex terrain of their transformative capacities and how they pertain to power and ritual. The shamanic imagination and the associated role of the trickster play a central part in how I suggest we can approach this question.

Masks and the Shamanic Imagination

Central to the enduring symbolic potency of horror film masks, shamanic traditions and practices and rituals of transformation offer a starting place to consider the mask in performance contexts because of widespread historical beliefs in the mask as an object with the capacity to transform, literally or symbolically. Doug Bradley argued that, historically, they had a crucial social function: 'shamans were actors, dancers, singers, poets and storytellers, healers, weathermen, fortune tellers and mystics'.[19] Shamanic ritual for Bradley – like horror film – 'is symbolic theatre of the most powerful, primal kind'.[20] In horror, masked transformations often relate directly to the power of its wearer, be they one of horror's many masked antagonists or – less commonly – those who lack power or who have been victimised, such as in films *Dark Night of the Scarecrow* (Frank De Felitta, 1981), *Black Sunday* (Mario Bava, 1960) and *Eyes without a Face* (both discussed in chapter 3) and *Halloween III* and *The Poughkeepsie Tapes* (both discussed in chapter 8). But even these categories can be complicated: in Jonathan Demme's *Silence of the Lambs* (1991), the mask protects the world from its wearer, its iconic design featuring bars across the mouth, literally imprisoning the offending body part of cannibal Hannibal Lecter (Anthony Hopkins) in a kind of 'mini-jail'. While masks predominantly empower horror antagonists, this is not absolute.

For reasons expanded upon further shortly, I resist positioning horror film masks on a linear continuum from earlier shamanic rituals and traditions as such and rather suggest it is part of a much looser shamanic imagination. This relies less on specific shamanic practices as identified from an orthodox anthropological perspective and on a broader cultural sensibility that frames widespread beliefs that masks – as cultural artefacts – can bestow certain kinds of power (particularly to transform) in cultural arenas such as horror. The shamanic imagination contains residual traces of traditional anthropological considerations of shamanism, but is more elastic, adaptable to contemporary rituals which, in horror, exist both within the films themselves and in rituals that surround cinema spectatorship as previously discussed.

There is of course some overlap between definitions of shamanism from anthropological and/or religious studies perspectives and the shamanic imagination. In 1970, Robin and Tonia Ridington noted that while 'shamanism is usually described as a magical flight into a supernatural realm', it has an integral symbolic aspect: 'The shaman does not really fly up or down, but inside to the meaning of things.'[21] They step away from traditional understandings of shamanism as an institutionalised religious/spiritual practice and argued instead that it is 'a universal human experience'.[22] The shamanic imagination grants a comprehension of new dimensions of movement across symbolic (and in horror, sometimes literal) planes, movement with historically entrenched associations with masks and the supernatural. As discussed later in this chapter, not all horror cinema is supernatural and the shamanic imagination therefore encompasses a range of liminal spaces, natural and/or supernatural, literal and/or symbolic. This logic underscores horror movie masks, rendering them an enduring iconographic feature.

While masks play an important role in shamanic ritual and performance, as Bradley noted they are used in diverse ways across different cultures.[23] For Michael Ripinsky-Naxon, mask-wearing shamans can be traced to the Palaeolithic period in south-western Europe, where animal and bird masks were used into the Neolithic period. For Ripinsky-Naxon, 'when a man puts on a mask, his symbolic position is enhanced, for he assumes the significance of something other than himself'.[24] There are, too, parallels here with horror film masks and their relationship to ritual, power and transformation. I have until now avoided a definition of shamanism as the term risks being misunderstood. From the outset, the ideological volatility of the term must be addressed. Stutley observed that any conception of shamanism as a singular, organised religion denies the diversity of how it was historically practiced.[25] Despite this, she claims shamanism necessarily involves three key factors: a belief in a spiritual world; a belief in a trance state that allows the shaman's spirit to move from the worldly domain into a supernatural one; and that shamans are healers within their communities.[26]

Stutley argued that the label 'shamanism' was applied to a range of practices by Europeans, which Graham Harvey takes issue with.[27] Even down to its assumed etymological roots in the Tungusic language of eastern

Siberia,[28] for Harvey many assumptions about shamanism are debatable: he argued instead for definitional fluidity.[29] Harvey too emphasised the role of European academics in coining the term 'shaman' to reductively collectivise a diverse range of practices and beliefs that *they* assumed belonged together. Shamanism is a product of Western academia, invented 'from indigenous resources' and therefore linked to 'colonial process[es] of appropriation and reification'.[30] In the case of contemporary art, Anne Marsh observed that, 'it is clear that shamanism and ritual are seductive for Western artists looking for alternatives to incorporate, rational systems of being, however this engagement is always fraught due to the appropriation of the "primitive" and/or the "feminine/abject"'.[31] The shamanic imagination in its very terminology seeks to highlight an awareness of and separation from the wholesale appropriation of culturally reductive assumptions borne from biased, Western-centric scholarship.[32] Rather than transplanting a clear-cut usage of 'shamanism' into my examination of horror film masks, I like to deploy the looser term 'shamanic imagination' to frame the concept as explicitly dispatched from a subjective interpretation (one that in my own case is unambiguously grounded in contemporary Western academia). The shamanic imagination allows a conceptualising of symbolic movements and transformations historically understood as spawned from (but not the same as) traditional shamanic rituals and practices, directly linking masked ritual, its transformative capacity and relationships to power with the realm of the supernatural or the other kinds of liminal spaces where horror is so frequently set.

I use the shamanic imagination as a conscious riff on Peter Brooks's notion of the 'melodramatic imagination' and what Leslie J. Moran noted is a parallel concept, the 'Gothic imagination'.[33] Using 'melodrama' as an adjective rather than a noun, Brooks suggested it is 'less a genre than an imaginative mode . . . a coherent mode of imagining and representing'.[34] The melodramatic imagination is a vision of the world 'subsumed by an underlying Manichaeism . . . putting us in contact with the conflict of good and evil played out under the surface of things'.[35] Brooks located the French Revolution as the birthplace of melodrama, pinpointing the transition between the sacred and the secular that saw melodrama spawned 'in a world where the traditional imperatives of truth and ethics have been violently thrown into question, yet where the promulgation of truth and ethics, their instauration as a way of life, is of immediate, daily, political concern'.[36] Melodrama was a secular method of articulating, identifying and proliferating what had previously been encoded in terms of the monarchy or church and was conceived as a result of this crisis. This tension between the sacred and secular is important when constructing the shamanic imagination, because for Brooks, 'a true Sacred is evident, persuasive and compelling, a system of both mythic explanation and implicit ethics'.[37] In the post-sacred context of horror cinema, while the shamanic imagination is less explicitly tied to the Manichean morality of the melodramatic imagination, they are equally united by the sacred: horror film masks often have mystical powers in many cases 'evident, persuasive and compelling', a tangible artefact that represents 'a system of both mythic explanation and implicit ethics'.[38]

The gothic – and the gothic imagination – are a cohesive tissue between melodramatic and shamanic imaginations when applied to horror. A key influence on the horror genre, the gothic for Brooks has much in common with melodrama: 'it is equally preoccupied with nightmare states, with claustration and thwarted escape, with innocence buried alive and unable to voice its claim to recognition'.[39] Mostly, 'it shares the preoccupation with evil as a real, irreducible force in the world, constantly menacing outburst'.[40] Yet they diverge in their outlook: melodrama – unlike the gothic novel – is marked by its 'optimism, its claim that the moral imagination can open up the angelic spheres as well as the demonic depths and can allay the threat of moral chaos'.[41] Like the melodramatic imagination, the gothic has been understood as a 'pervasive cultural mode' rather than a genre as such, and in 1900 John Ruskin used the term 'the gothic imagination' to articulate a 'tendency to delight in fantastic and ludicrous, as well as in sublime, images'.[42] The gothic imagination provides curious overlap – although not direct parallels – with the shamanic imagination, and Maria Beville states that 'the idea of multiple perspectives on reality and the possibility of supernatural or transcendental existence, is in a general sense, the key to the Gothic imagination'.[43] Through masked ritual, these ideas are also crucial to the shamanic imagination. While melodrama and the gothic are obviously not suggested to be synonymous with shamanism, the 'imagination' suffix indicates the potential to remove each from the regimented discursive terrain of their multiple histories and acknowledges these instead explicitly as 'imaginaries'. These are enduring sensibilities that appear across a range of cultural phenomena such as horror cinema. The shamanic imagination is produced by traces of cultural memory that have evolved and morphed over time, culminating today in horror film masks; as I argue, their transformative capacity links them intrinsically to notions of ritual and power.

Cinema, Space and the Shamanic Imagination

Through the shamanic imagination, we can further consider the relationship between masked horror figures and space. An important concept in gothic studies,[44] liminality is crucial here and Charles Ducey noted that shamanic ritual is also closely associated with liminality as a state of in-between-ness.[45] For Victor Turner, shamanic performance occurs in liminal spaces where *communitas* occurs, uniting those involved in the ritual together through the act itself. This has been institutionalised through religious ritual, rendered explicit in the figure of the shaman or the monk.[46] With particular regard to fascinations with gender and sexuality, tensions between the natural and supernatural and general ambient morbidity that mark the horror genre, for Turner, liminality 'is frequently linked to death, to being in the womb, to invisibility, to darkness, to bisexuality, to the wilderness and to the eclipse of the sun and moon'.[47] This is no coincidence, given that producing cultural phenomena is precisely one of its key functions, as 'liminality, marginality and structural inferiority are conditions in which are frequently generated myths, symbols, rituals, philosophical systems and works of art'.[48] In the context of performance, for William S. Haney II, liminality is a '"void of conceptions" ... experienced either intermittently in the spaces between thoughts, or continuously as the screen of consciousness that reflects the mind's phenomenal content'.[49] Sandor Klapcsik's consideration of fantastic fiction refers to a 'constant oscillation, crossing back and forth, between social, textual and cultural positions', referring at the same time to a 'space of continuous transference and infinite process formed by transgressions across evanescent, porous, evasive borderlines'.[50] Liminality and the shamanic imagination are closely linked through horror film masks.

Likewise, Stanley Krippner's examination of contradictory critical approaches to shamans and shamanism is valuable for assessing how the shamanic imagination may be useful when examining horror film masks. Like Harvey, Krippner argued that debates surrounding shamanism are marked less by what they say about beliefs and practices themselves and 'reveal more about the observer than they do about the observed and that the construction of a psychology of shamanism needs to address this challenge'.[51] Krippner identified six often-contradictory categories of shamanism as seen by Western scholars: the Demonic Model, the Charlatan Model, the Schizophrenia Model, the Soul Flight Model, the Degenerative and Crude Technology Model and the Deconstructionist Model.[52]

While aspects of each can be identified in many horror movies that employ masks, Krippner's final model is of particular interest. His Deconstructionist Model links shamanism with postmodernism, an area also of interest to horror studies (as discussed shortly): 'In their efforts to share esoteric knowledge with their community, it is essential for shamans to deconstruct order, especially if a person's or a community's rigidity and inflexibility have blocked adaptation and growth.'[53] But shamanic practice requires a necessary *re*-assembly and can therefore be at odds with postmodernity: the act of putting things back together grants shamans their status as a healer and community advisor.[54] With their frequent acts of physical destruction and social transgression, mask-wearing horror antagonists share this pursuit of deconstruction, but unlike Krippner's model, there is little interest in re-assembly, only chaos.

Krippner's deconstructionist reading informs a preliminary exploration of how residual traces of shamanic practices and beliefs have manifested in horror cinema through the shamanic imagination. Others have used shamanism more as a critical tool to approach film: Cathleen Rountree argued auteurs can be understood as 'contemporary shamans' as both demand a fundamental 'sensitivity to . . . the world of inner vision'.[55] Anthropologist Laurell Kendall approached shamanism and new media, examining how the vivid costuming of contemporary Korean shamans so crucial to their ritual practices has been rendered iconic through a range of self-representations via new media to gain clientele online.[56] Kendall's article pre-dated a powerful depiction of this phenomenon in Na Hong-jin's horror film *The Wailing* (2016), whose shaman combines a mobile phone and colourful ritual robes and Nikki J. Y. Lee also examined shamanism in another South Korean horror film, *Possessed* (Lee Yong-joo, 2006).[57]

Shamanism has been a point of reference in film criticism on subjects as diverse as Peter Weir, Andrei Tarkovsky, Werner Herzog, Raúl Ruiz and George Lucas.[58] There are analyses on films with shaman figures[59] and shamans appear across a range of movies including *Chamane* (Bartabas, 1996), *The Journals of Knud Rasmussen* (Norman Cohn and Zacharias Kunuk, 2006) and *Embrace of the Serpent* (Ciro Guerra, 2015). In horror specifically, films that address shamanism include *The Manitou* (William Girdler, 1978), *Body Count* (Ruggero Deodato, 1986), *The Shaman* (Michael Yakub, 1987), *Szamanka* (Andrzej Żuławski, 1996), *Skinwalker* (Steve Stevens Jr., 2005) and *Mr. Jones* (Karl Mueller, 2013). Tanya Krzywinska has discussed shamanism and werewolf movies, and horror director Richard Stanley has acknowledged a fascination with shamanic traditions.[60]

Jason Horsley utilised shamanism less literally in *The Secret Life of Movies: Schizophrenic and Shamanic Journeys in American Cinema* (2009). Claiming that movies rely on archetypal plots and tropes, Horsley argued for a central consideration of the mythic in film analysis. Horror and science fiction films in particular, he claims, 'are using the same archetypes as ancient myths and that they serve as a kind of psychological blueprint'.[61] Horsley suggested that this mythic aspect is hidden by cinematic realism so even film-makers themselves are often unaware of these subconscious mythic foundations.[62] He continued, 'because we have disconnected from our subconscious, movies have to be more covert in their mythic unfolding', resulting in myths needing to function in less overt ways.[63]

To support this, Horsley examined films where the conscious and the unconscious were explicitly addressed through representations of schizophrenia. There is a disconnection intrinsic to movie-watching that Horsley claimed is itself schizophrenic, because we are 'emotionally involved in a surrogate reality without having to take part in it'.[64] This process of disassociation led him to identify a 'shamanic dimension' of cinema specific to how film configures what we see, opening up a range of different realities.[65] For Horsley, shamanism and schizophrenia are critical concepts which 'allow . . . movies their occult function as collective dreams that, if analysed, provide information in symbolic form on the condition of society and the species'.[66] Describing this methodology somewhat dramatically as 'a psychic blood sample from the collective unconscious', he claimed that 'By looking at movies, we can judge the state of health of the system – our culture and society.'[67] Unlike myths – which he argued were 'consciously designed by sorcerers or shamans to be recognised by others of their kind' – Horsley suggested that films 'are both less and more pure than that', the latter 'shaped by the unconscious', the former through 'conscious agendas of commerce, propaganda, popular taste, etc. . . . which overlay the world, rather like a person who edits his dreams to make them more "wholesome" or entertaining'.[68] In conclusion, he argued that 'movies have been heavily edited and filtered, but the basic components still come from the unconscious'. In short, 'as long as you can sift through the noise and get to the signal, you can still use them to diagnose; even the noise can be diagnosed because it emphasizes the ways in which we block out our unconscious'.[69]

While Horsley offers an important attempt to find a critical intersection between shamanism and film culture, this approach reductively collapses diverse, complex fields like 'culture' and 'society' into a singular, unified body that one single act of critical diagnosis is somehow able to explain. The shamanic imagination is a conceptual tool that seeks to avoid precisely this: it is determinedly *not* diagnostic and consciously acknowledges the subjective biases of Western academic treatments of shamanism in particular and the complexities of colonial politics that accompanies this. It instead incorporates within its very terminology an acknowledgement that this phenomenon is a culturally constructed *imaginary*. The shamanic imagination recognises cultural difference and the subjective biases of its *own* critical history and incorporates this into its conceptual framework. Horsley's symptomatic approach is concerned more with establishing itself as the dominant method of 'genuine' film analysis that solidifies the critic-as-diagnostician, rather than producing an interpretative strategy that acknowledges the nuances and significance of diversity. The shamanic imagination is therefore necessarily unstable, evolving and dynamic and considers 'culture' and 'society' to be the same. As explored throughout this book, this is important when considering the endurance of horror film masks and their relationship to ritual, power and transformation.

More productively, in his identification of a 'shamanic dimension' of cinema itself, Horsley noted how cinema acts as a metaphorical wormhole into different realities.[70] While I hesitate to follow this through to his assumption of a singular collective 'unconsciousness' that can be interpreted to produce a diagnosis of 'society' as a whole, the shamanic imagination overlaps here as part of the complex cultural palette that is understood and re-imagined from a range of diverse and sometimes conflicting positions. In the construction of this palette, the shamanic imagination adheres to 'global folklore', identified by Mark Allen Peterson in his discussion of the Arabic folkloric figure of the *jinn* and its legacies in the globally recognised figure of the genie. For Peterson, 'The transnational circulation of people and media that helps define both contemporary and colonial globalization makes it possible for us to speak of global folklore.'[71] The shamanic imagination allows ideas *surrounding* shamanic traditions – or, more specifically, enduring ideas of what those traditions are popularly conceived to be in the Western cultural imagination – to be explored, while consciously avoiding reducing complex and diverse cultural practices to a singular whole.

Michael Myers from the *Halloween* franchise is significant here. While these films ostensibly take place in the natural world of serial killers[72] rather than the supernatural domain of monsters and demons,[73] the masked Myers demonstrates abilities that do not align with what is conceived as 'normal' human behaviour: his seeming inability to die, his near-supernatural ability to appear suddenly in unlikely places and Dr Samuel Loomis's (Donald Pleasance) insistence that Myers is a 'boogieman'. One of the great clichés of postmodern horror spawned from the series is the trope of the masked villain who almost always returns in the sequel, despite apparently being killed.[74] The shamanic aspects of Michael's mask are significant. As the psychiatrist at Smith's Grove sanatorium where he was committed after the murders that open the film, Loomis and Michael's sister Laurie (Jamie Lee Curtis) struggle against the recently escaped 21-year-old Myers as he rampages through Haddonfield, Illinois. Loomis describes his time with Michael at Smith's Grove as follows: 'I watched him for fifteen years, sitting in a room, staring at a wall, not seeing the wall, looking past the wall – looking at this night, inhumanly patient, waiting for some secret, silent alarm to trigger him off.' Loomis's description of Michael's 'vision' is underscored by the shamanic imagination, made tangible throughout the franchise in large part by the mask itself. Across this series and the genre itself, the symbolic potency of masks often echoes – through the shamanic imagination – beliefs that we broadly associate with mask-related rituals and practices of earlier civilisations.

Tricksters and the Shamanic Imagination

Closely related as they are to the figure of the shaman and a subject of fascination in many disciplines including anthropology, folklore studies, literature and performance studies, tricksters are also of interest to horror studies. Like the shamanic imagination, tricksters are essential when examining the endurance of horror film masks. While not omnipresent, tricksters are not rare in the genre, be it in relation to their desire to transgress and disrupt, their ability to shape-shift, their close relationship to the liminal, or their penchant for tricks and game-play. Lewis Hyde explored diverse manifestations of tricksters, from Ancient Greece to West Africa, North America to India, drawing parallels in the work of twentieth-century artists including Pablo Picasso, Marcel Duchamp, Allan Ginsberg and John Cage.[75] Tricksters are evolving and dynamic, intersecting with shamanism through their relationship to liminality:[76] for Larry Ellis, tricksters are 'shaman[s] of the liminal' and their 'power is rooted in liminality'.[77] This relationship between shamans and tricksters has received much critical attention, Joseph Campbell calling the trickster a 'super-shaman':

as 'the chief mythological character of the Palaeolithic world story', for Campbell while the trickster is the 'epitome of the principle of disorder, he is nevertheless the culture bringer also'.[78] Carl Gustave Jung observed that 'there is something of the Trickster in the character of the shaman and medicine-man, for he, too, often plays malicious jokes on people'.[79] In cinema, tricksters and mask-wearing intersect across examples as diverse as the aforementioned comedy *The Mask* and *The Texas Chain Saw Massacre* franchise (discussed in chapter 4).

Jung is often evoked in critical discourse about tricksters. For Jung, their archetypal quality is demonstrated by their ubiquity across cultures and history: tricksters are a collective shadow that dwells in the unconscious of 'civilised' people, a product of repression. This book is by no means an example of Jungian analysis by any stretch, yet this from 'On the Psychology of the Trickster-Figure' is worth noting: 'The so-called civilized man has forgotten the trickster. He remembers him only figuratively and metaphorically, when, irritated by his own ineptitude, he speaks of fate playing tricks on him or of things being bewitched.'[80] As the language here implies, horror film is a cultural space where tricksters are remembered, often through masks: even the word 'bewitched' echoes associations with the supernatural, so often associated with horror cinema. The transformations and fractured identities that lie at the heart of many films in this book are predominantly propelled by mask-wearing.

Before links between tricksters and horror are expanded further, a more concrete definition is required. For William J. Hynes, there are six traits typical of the trickster, regardless of the culture from which they emerge. These can combine, allowing dynamic, complex re-imaginings to take shape across its vast history. Tricksters are anomalous and ambiguous; they play tricks and are deceptive; they can be shape-shifters; they invert situations; they are messengers and can imitate gods; and they are bricoleurs who engage with both the lewd and the sacred.[81] As will be emphasised throughout the case studies explored in Part Two and Three especially, many of these aspects manifest in mask-wearing horror antagonists. When transposed into cinema, Helena Bassil-Morozow suggested that aspects of traditional trickster narratives appear in powerful new ways. The figure's 'licentiousness, love of freedom, dislike for all types of boundaries, fragmented/flexible body (symbolizing his transformative powers), propensity to lie and general dislike of the truth, lack of stable identity . . . and erratic behaviour'.[82] In horror, she noted one of the trickster's most noteworthy skills is 'the ability to cross the dangerous boundary between the world of the living and the realm of the dead'.[83] The trickster's ability to cross this chasm recalls its shamanic roots and horror movie trickster-villains like Michael Myers and Jason Voorhees straddle similar boundaries, reliant on their function as transformed, destabilised and destabilising forces. While this liminality is intrinsic to manifestations of tricksters in horror, the intersection of tricksters and transition or transformation are of course not specific to horror alone.[84] Yet horror provides a particularly potent forum for trickster activity, and masks are often crucial to that process.

Tricksters and their destabilising transgressions share their origins in the shamanic imagination, where – in horror cinema especially – masks often propel movement across diegetically constructed literal or symbolic planes. The shamanic imagination underpins how this movement and transformation are comprehended, linked frequently to masks. As noted, while its origins may be anthropological, the shamanic imagination is consciously aligned with both the melodramatic imagination and the gothic imagination, the latter in particular prompting associations with liminality that are useful when considering how horror film masks intersect with ritual, power and transformation. Again, no direct line can be drawn between shamanism as it is understood in a traditional anthropological sense and the much looser shamanic imagination. The latter is foundational to my emphasis on ritual, power and transformation in horror movies that diegetically privilege masks, a focus continued in the following chapter as we turn towards a variety of pre-moving image, masked-based performance and literary traditions. These include Japanese Noh theatre that flourished in the fourteenth century, Italian *commedia dell'arte* of the sixteenth century, eighteenth- and nineteenth-century gothic literature and the writing of American genre authors such as Edgar Allan Poe and H. P. Lovecraft, the French Grand Guignol theatre that began in the late nineteenth century and Antonin Artaud's Theatre of Cruelty established soon after. In the rest of the book, we can now apply the critical framework established thus far to my specific focus on horror film masks and their endurance as a key iconographic aspect of horror cinema.

PART ONE

MASKS, HORROR AND CINEMA – TOWARDS CODIFICATION

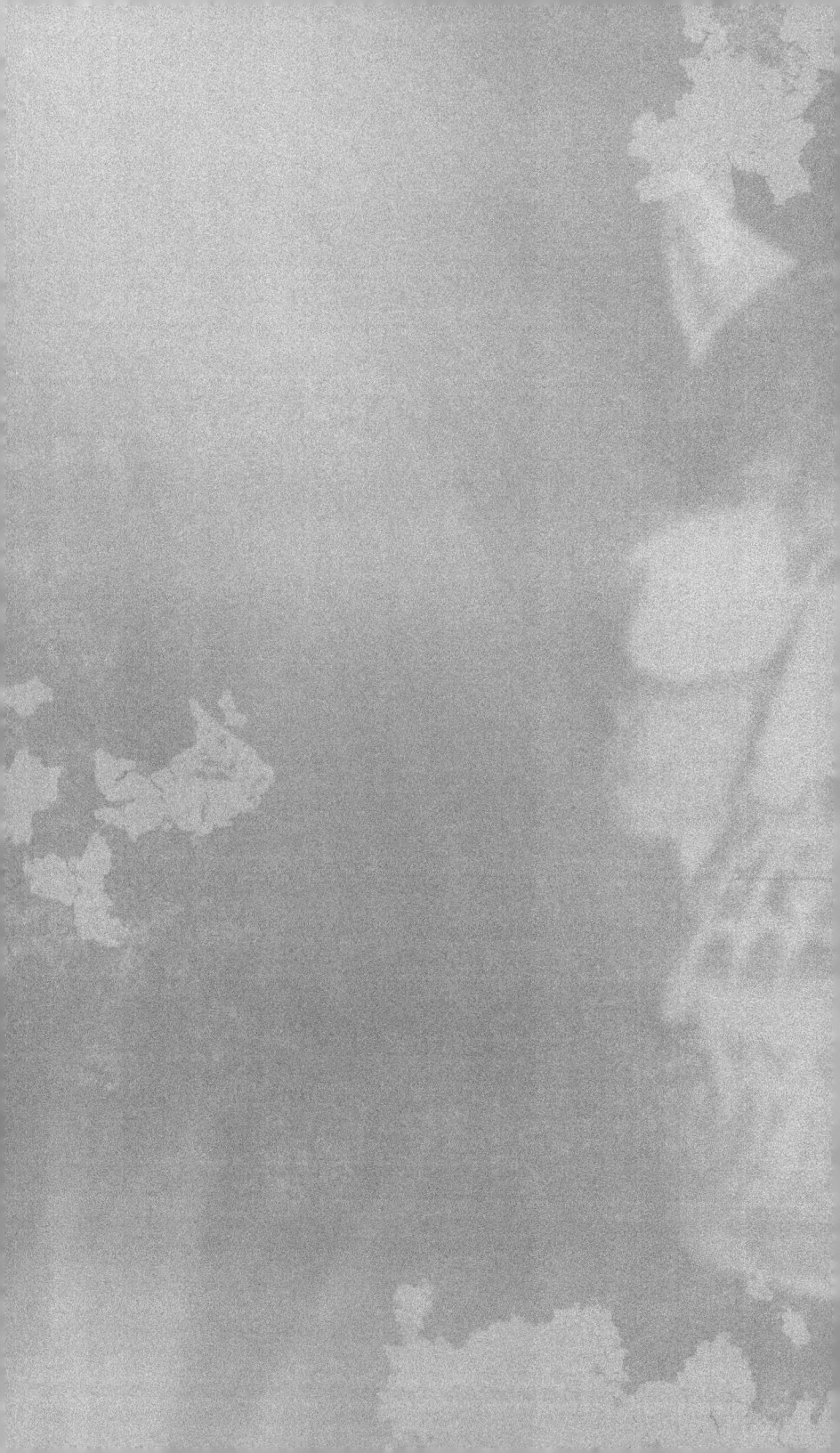

2

Masks and Horror in Literary and Performance Traditions and Early Cinema

MASKS WERE employed across a range of performance and literary traditions well before the rise of screen culture. While loosely chronological, the traditions outlined here do not seek to establish a single linear narrative, but demonstrate how intersecting strands culminated across a range of cultures in rich, diverse ways. This is resultant of the omnipresent shamanic imagination, which played a significant role in the codification of horror film masks as a key iconographic element.

While important mask-based cultural phenomena in their own right, many of the individual legacies outlined here have directly and indirectly bled across time, space and different cultures. For example, the influence of Japanese Noh theatre can be seen through its influence on early twentieth-century modernism and the avant-garde. Sheppard noted that while the influence of Ancient Greek drama has been recognised here, neither Noh nor medieval Christian theatre have been properly acknowledged.[1] Yet their influence on modernist art was notable, stemming from religious ritual performance, formal structures and reliance of symbolism, a rejection of realism, a privileging of movement and music, and their use of masks.[2] Zeami Motokiyo's treatise on Noh aesthetics became widely available in the early twentieth century and also influenced Western scholars and artists.³ Art historian Ernest Fenollosa compared Noh to Greek drama, while Ezra Pound and Jacques Copeau drew parallels between Noh and the religious rituals of early European Christianity.⁴ By the late nineteenth century, American and European artists widely appropriated the aesthetics of Japanese art with little interest in its meaning and Noh influenced Paul Claudel, Jacques Copeau, Gabriel Cousin, Charles Dullin and Jean-Louis Barrault in French theatre alone.⁵ It was also a notable influence on W. B. Yeats and Bertolt Brecht.⁶

The legacy of the Italian *commedia dell'arte* is also important. As an improvisational form, there is little documentation from its golden age in the sixteenth century that has allowed its traditions to have endured with a degree of flexibility. This legacy extends to the contemporary stage⁷ and Rudlin noted that its influence can be found in work by Igor Stravinsky, Sergei Diaghilev, Jean Cocteau and Pablo Picasso.⁸ The influence of *commedia dell'arte* has been observed in early cinema by Duchartre and Rudlin, the latter noting its influence on Charles Chaplin, Buster Keaton, the Marx Brothers and Laurel and Hardy.⁹ From a media history perspective, that these typologies were readapted and reimagined supports my claims for a similar dynamic evolution central to my arguments about the endurance of horror film masks.

Along with the gothic, science fiction and horror literature, ancient theatre, the Grand Guignol and the Theatre of Cruelty, both Noh theatre and the *commedia dell'arte* play an important role in the endurance of horror film masks as a key component of the genre's iconographic palette. Secular performance rituals may have overtaken religious or spiritual rituals in many of these examples, but at their core lies a fundamental recognition that masks can transform through ritual in ways that relate to power in meaningful, diverse ways, often marked by a trickster spirit. The literary and performance traditions outlined here sometimes manifest explicitly in the films discussed in this book's later case studies, such as the centrality of Noh masks in *Celia* and *Gurozuka*, illustrating Neale's intersecting process of 'repetition . . . difference, variation and change'.¹⁰ Via reinvention, appropriation and other cross-cultural borrowings, the diverse range of literary and performance traditions outlined here are crucial to horror film masks and why they have endured.

Masks and Noh Theatre

From a Western perspective, the blank, flat masks broadly associated with Noh theatre were representative of Japan more broadly, Sheppard noting that 'in the Western imagination, Japan was a masked and mysterious nation'.[11] When 'Japanomania' swept the United States and Europe during the late nineteenth and early twentieth centuries, there was a desire to 'unmask' or reveal the until then previously hidden phenomenon of Japanese culture itself.[12] Noh is more than masks: all its elements – including poetry, music and dance as well – work in harmony.[13] But masks and their links to ritual, transformation and shamanism are of particular interest here. David Wiles identified the Noh mask as 'a sacred object', while Benito Ortolani stated that the history of Noh theatre is a direct descendant of Japanese shamanism.[14] For Ortolani, the fourteenth century was the moment where 'popular entertainment and primitive shamanistic ritual transmitted through the *kagura* and *sarugaka* traditions',[15] marking the birth of Noh. Shamanism for Ortolani is a 'folk religion embracing the belief in powerful spirits that can be influenced only by a shaman'.[16] He emphasised that 'shamanistic rituals are an important source of Japanese performing arts', especially Noh, but from the outset, Ortolani noted that Noh theatre itself was not created in a cultural vacuum.[17] Just as English theatre stems from Greco-Roman and Christian traditions, Ortolani argued that Japanese theatre 'find[s] its roots, its inspiration and its inexhaustible resources for regeneration in the two main spiritual forces of Japanese tradition, Shinto and Buddhism'.[18] These two heritages 'assimilated widely different elements of distant origin', identifying additional influences from Confucianism, Taoism and Hinduism.[19]

Noh appeared in fourteenth-century Japan when popular traditions aligned with what Ortolani has identified as highly complex and sophisticated artists.[20] While little is known of the performance history of the era, Ortolani traced the origins of Japanese theatre to the pre-250 BC Jōmon period, based on clay masks that he speculated were used in fertility and well-being rites and rituals.[21] The nomadism of this period was replaced during the Yayoi period from 250BC–300AD with the establishment of farming communities.[22] During this era, magic was an important cultural belief that resulted in rituals that were felt to prompt agricultural prosperity.[23] In the Kofun period (250–710AD), clay images (*haniwa*) of animals and people were linked to burial rites and rituals and *haniwa* of female shamans appeared during this time. By the eighth century, the first indigenous

Japanese historical texts appeared, which – while Ortolani warned of their 'uneven, intricate mixture of myth, native tradition and historical facts'[24] – provide insight into 'contemporary religious rites and dances', such as the myth of Uzme's Trance, which are believed to connect Korean and North Asian shamanic traditions.[25]

As explored in chapter 5, Noh masks are a significant instance of blank horror film masks, used within contemporary Japanese horror cinema and other national contexts. But Noh masks appear in early Japanese horror cinema in ways that acknowledge past traditions while providing insight into its contemporary moment. Teinosuke Kinugasa's *A Page of Madness* (1926) is considered one of the great masterworks of early Japanese cinema, despite only being discovered in 1971 after being assumed lost.[26] There is little debate about the influence and impact of the film. For Aaron Gerow, non-Japanese viewers have considered *A Page of Madness* a 'remarkable masterwork of cinema, an experimental, modernist, avant-garde film', yet many approach it as 'a conventional narrative expression of traditional melodramatic emotionality'.[27] Set inside a psychiatric institution, *A Page of Madness* utilises chaos as a thematic, narrative and stylistic strategy: this is supported not only by its alternate title *A Page Out of Order*, but also by its absence of intertitles and the commentary of a *benshi* actor, typical of the time.[28] Yet despite its historical setting and era of production, the film is also arguably contemporary in a number of aspects, including the iconography of its setting, its preoccupation with mental health as a cipher for social instability and its sophisticated interplay between fantasy and reality. The film blurs this story and a series of hallucinations and dreams, making it difficult to distinguish a clear line between 'reality' and 'fantasy': this and the film's striking formal style are also reminiscent of the German expressionist film *The Cabinet of Dr. Caligari* (Robert Weine, 1920). Like the German doppelgänger film of this period – also including *Metropolis* (Fritz Lang, 1927), *The Head of Janus* (*Der Januskopf*, F. W. Murnau, 1920), *The Blue Angel* (*Der blaue Engel*, Josef von Sternberg, 1930) and *Faust* (F. W. Murnau, 1926) – *A Page of Madness* too is interested in doubling, with the mask splitting individuals into pluralised Others for thematic ends.

The role of masks in *A Page of Madness* is worth considering more closely as it reveals significant aspects of how masks were deployed in Japanese culture at this time. In its final scene, the janitor places Noh masks on the frenzied, rioting inmates which instantly sedates them. For Colette Balmain, 'Central to Nō is transformation from human to ghost or other supernatural entity with the duplicity of being articulated through the use of highly stylised masks.'²⁹ In this scene, transformation is key, but in a different way: masks are a controlling device with the function of a topically applied lobotomy. They are tools of power and dominance. The appearance of the Noh mask is linked intimately to its symbolic power. For Keiko I. McDonald, in Noh performances, actors do not 'create [their] own movement voluntarily', but rather 'follow . . . the formalistic practice of prescribed pattern of bodily movement'.[30] Female Noh masks in particular are often what McDonald described as 'static and almost blank',[31] in this instance effectively wiping the 'psychiatric slate' clean. While 'the static mask is capable of expressing a multitude of emotions',[32] in this scene it is implied that through this mode of 'therapy', new emotions can come to the surface. In these masks, patients have new challenges they can face after their symbolic reprogramming. For David Wiles, 'Noh masks do not have intellectual problems to solve and the Noh brow is characteristically a blank translucent space suggestive of the mind that is ever invisible'. He continued, 'in the Noh mask the pain lies within, leaving no tangible mark upon the flesh'.[33] Faces once manic and deranged have been pacified by the placement of these traditional masks: fresh symbolic canvases for new emotions to be inscribed upon. These masks may also be understood as representative of the smiling social mask of 'healthy' people who hide behind their social masks, disguising their 'true' selves. In the hospital, the masks have an effectively pharmaceutical function: the forced placement of a blank facial expression over what was until then an expression of fury and derangement results in a sedation of sorts, recalling a long history of the mask's transformative potency and frequent associations with power.

Recalling Noh's shamanic origins, there is an implication that the climax in *A Page of Madness* takes place on a different plane to what could be comprehended as diegetically coded 'reality'. For David Sorfa, 'while this is clearly marked as happening in his imagination, the following sequence in which the janitor returns to mopping the floor disturbs the apparent simple delineation between illusion and reality'.[34] The impact of *A Page of Madness* stems from the omnipresent threat of insanity, of which even the janitor is not immune. For Sorfa, 'while ostensibly sane, [he] occupies a rather ambiguous position in the asylum'. He continues, 'there is a suggestion . . . that he is either not there (he sometimes appears as a transparent ghost), or that he himself is insane and therefore his vision, which is the film we see, is entirely untrustworthy'.[35] *A Page of Madness* demands an acknowledgement of liminality and through the mask – a direct reference to Noh traditions – the shamanic imagination is clearly at play.

Yet there are more symptomatic ways to approach insanity in *A Page of Madness*. For Timothy Iles, these Noh traditions and their sedating effect are reflective of the function of Japanese history at the film's contemporary moment. With its Western-style white-coated doctors dominating the insane Japanese patients the film is a metaphor for the shift from 'feudal pre-modernity to the westernised modernity of the Meiji Era'.[36] The scene where the janitor gives the inmates the masks 'mimics the imposition of a traditional and stable identity onto a disturbed and aggressive modernity presented as madness'.[37] There is present in this sequence a potential reading where these symbols of nationalistic traditions are deemed false, hollow disguises, empty signifiers detached from reality. While blank masks will be discussed in chapter 5, *A Page of Madness* is an essential example of how masked performance traditions from centuries ago have manifested in horror cinema – not merely transposed as a referent to an important cultural tradition, but reconfigured as rigorous ideological symbols. Here the mask moves as well as transforms: not only across notions of past/present, but also across other conceptual binaries like healthy/sick and 'Japanese'/'Western'. While different traditions and cultural contexts, the shamanic imagination also allows insight into the transformative potential of the mask of other literary and performance traditions, including the *commedia dell'arte*.

Masks and the *Commedia Dell'Arte*

Like Noh, the *commedia dell'arte* has a vital – albeit indirect – relationship to horror film masks. It demonstrates that popular folkloric typologies were both repeated and generically identifiable long before the appearance of cinema and that the power of masks in horror cinema finds antecedents regarding both its use and function in earlier performance contexts. *Commedia dell'arte* evolved from pre-existing performance traditions like thirteenth-century Sicilian puppetry.[38] For John Rudlin, in the *commedia dell'arte*, 'actors took pre-existing folk forms, improvised masking, music and dance and developed them into a theatrical medium'.[39] These included Carnival, and early *commedia dell'arte* performances were 'of an occasional nature: like fairground showmen, companies . . . would follow an annual celebratory calendar and a complementary touring schedule'.[40] Unlike the *commedia erudite*, the public accessibility of *commedia dell'arte* aligned it with the social rather than the artistic.[41] The history of the iconic *commedia dell'arte* masks themselves lies not only in Carnival, but also street theatre, court entertainment, popular farces and mystery and mummers' plays.[42]

Tricksters were also a key aspect of the *commedia dell'arte*. While tricksters have been identified in Japanese *Kagura* theatre in the character Sanbaso,[43] and also popularly linked to Japanese mythology in the folkloric figure of *kitsune*, the fox,[44] on *commedia dell'arte* tricksters are linked more explicitly to masked theatrical traditions. This is an important stepping stone in understanding how the shamanic imagination developed, playing an important role in the endurance of horror film masks. But in Italy, tricksters are not specific to *commedia dell'arte*: Carlson notes that the thirteenth-century Sicilian wooden puppetry tradition, typical of the *opera dei pupi* influenced early *commedia dell'arte*, was also notable for its tricksters.[45] Christopher Frayling cited this same Sicilian pre-*commedia dell'arte* tradition as a significant influence on twentieth-century Italian westerns: recalling that director Sergio Leone cited the Sicilian *puparri* as an influence, Frayling rejected claims that 'spaghetti westerns' were mere imitators of American westerns and that they have their own histories, particularly in regard to tricksters. Revisiting the *puppari*, Frayling argued he 'discovered a strange fraternity between the *Puparri* and my friends of the Wild West. Their adventures were identical.'[46] Frayling linked Clint Eastwood's character in Leone's *Dollars* films to Italian stage traditions and tricksters, as Eastwood 'leads the audience, like a mercenary version of the traditional "trickster" figure, from one group or "enclosed" space to another'.[47] Identifying these as 'Leone's most marginal characters', this marginality is typical of many horror film monsters, especially those who wear masks.[48]

Tricksters flourished in *commedia dell'arte*. For Rudlin, the trickster Zanni is a *commedia dell'arte* stock character, including Harlequin and Columbina, Harlequin's mistress and Pierrot's wife.[49] The Zanni-trickster is an Italian variation of the charlatan – its Italian variants known as *ciurmadori*, *ciarlatani* and *montimbanchi* – and Rudlin noted that these variations were familiar figures in sixteenth-century Italy, as they drifted between rural and urban fairs and carnivals in places where they could attract an audience.[50] The influence of Carnival can also be seen in *commedia dell'arte* via its shared spirit of defiance, drawing attention to tensions 'between asceticism and artistic licence, censorship and freedom of expression'.[51] Recalling Bakhtin's notion of the carnivalesque, these performances inverted social norms and thus had subversive potential. Along with the marketplace, Carnival and the *opera dei pupi*, other origins can be found in classical Greek and Roman theatre, performance rituals and traditions that similarly took place in close physical proximity to their audiences.[52] Romans began 'to tire of Greek tragedies and turned with relief to pantomime, which the players of Italian comedy were to exploit to such great advantage in a later day'.[53] Again, there is an indication that – like horror and the endurance of masks in the genre – popular forms evolved and were marked by a tension between dynamic changes and adaptations and formulaic patterns and repetitiveness.

The longevity of the *commedia dell'arte* illustrates this. As it travelled across Europe, it needed ways other than language to communicate with broad audiences.[54] Like horror, the masked *commedia dell'arte* tradition often relied on physical spectacle and was a popular dissemination of recognisable typologies. The centrality of masks is undoubtedly a key aspect of *commedia dell'arte* performances: even in its contemporary manifestations, masks have remained a constant.[55] From English pantomime to the harlequinade to the unrecorded continuation of small touring companies in Italy well beyond the late nineteenth century, *commedia dell'arte* continued in a variety of forms.[56] Examples of its legacy endured through tropes, characters and iconography across the twentieth and twenty-first century and, as Ndalianis observed,

> remnants of the carnival tradition persisted . . . in the form of commedia dell'arte, fairs and travelling theatre troupes but were later adjusted to meet the demands of new commercial needs in the form of amusement parks, penny arcades, burlesques and film genres such as comedy and horror.[57]

In comedy, George Kurman noted that the *commedia dell'arte* (and their shared association with Carnival and folk humour) is a strong influence on screen comedies, including *Popeye* (1919–94), *The Road Runner Show* (1948–66) and *Beavis and Butt-head* (1993–2011), while David LeMaster connected both the Marx Brothers and Antonin Artaud's Theatre of Cruelty (discussed shortly) to *commedia dell'arte* traditions.[58] This moves us closer to considering the influence of the *commedia dell'arte* on horror cinema specifically, both in terms of their shared connections to Carnival (and, by association, the carnivalesque) and to the violent comedy that marks slapstick in particular.[59] Jason Marc Harris aligns the *commedia dell'arte* figure of Harlequin to the 'demonic clowns and doomed puppets' in the work of contemporary horror author Thomas Ligotti,[60] a recurrent motif throughout horror cinema as demonstrated by *It!* (Tommy Lee Wallace, 1990/Andrés Muschietti, 2017) and the *Puppet Master* series (1989–2004).[61] A number of critics have explicitly linked the horror genre and *commedia dell'arte* more explicitly[62] and violent death and the *commedia dell'arte* collided in Agatha Christie's first published short story, 'The Affair at the Victory Ball' in 1923, centring around a masquerade party where key participants in the murder mystery are dressed as stock *commedia dell'arte* characters.

Horror and *commedia dell'arte* also intersect through the function and materiality of the masks themselves. As one of the three key groups of *commedia dell'arte* characters,[63] for Schechter the *maschere* ('masks') were at the top of the hierarchy because 'they are deeper in the symbolic or mythological sense because they come straight from the archetype, with all the attendant nuances and intricacies'.[64] These masks contain the features that allow savvy audiences to identify particular characters.[65] *Commedia dell'arte* masks are also traditionally made of leather – the skin of a once-living creature – rather than wood or paper. While in practical terms this allows for greater ease of movement, Schechter noted that leather has a distinct psychophysical effect on the wearer in its status as a living, breathing material.[66] Like Noh, *commedia dell'arte* masks are an extension of the body, a legacy felt both directly and indirectly in horror cinema.

The influence of Harlequin especially foreshadows horror cinema and its use of masks in other ways. In Paris during the reign of Henri III (1574–89), an Italian actor, often considered the creator of the figure, performed as a comic devil known as 'Hellequin'.[67] While John O'Brien noted that others have traced it back to the devil-type character Alichino in *Dante's Inferno*,[68] its origins lie well before *commedia dell'arte* in the 'black-faced devil figures that had been featured in European performances for many generations'.[69] Annette Lust explored the historical relationship between classical mime traditions and *commedia dell'arte*, with James W. Gousseff stating that 'whiteface is the mime's mask'.[70] While Noh is a clear influence on horror's blank masks, in films like *Bruiser* and *Hush* (discussed in chapter 5), mime make-up is also evoked. As noted later in this chapter, the influence of the *commedia dell'arte* and its masks have manifested directly in horror cinema in films like *The Three Masks* (*Les trois masques*, Henry Krauss, 1921/André Hugon, 1929). Yet there are other traditions that demonstrate how diverse typologies culminated through masks and the shamanic imagination, rendering the former an enduring iconographic aspect of the genre.

Horror Masks on Page and Stage

The intersection of masks and the sensation of terror can be identified in ancient theatre, both written and performed. In Ancient Greek theatre, tragedy is often marked by fear, terror and threat: Rush Rehm noted in Euripides' *The Bacchae*, that, while possessed by Dionysus, 'Agave holds what she thinks is the head of a lion she has killed, which is in fact the head of her son, represented by the actor's mask'.[71] Foreshadowing a focus on spectatorship that would become central to horror studies (particularly in relation to gender), Rehm noted that 'in Greek tragedy, both characters and spectators must face what they would rather not, a paradoxical compulsion epitomised by the unflinching stare of the actor's mask'. He continued, 'It is hard to imagine a character looking into the terror and instability of tragedy without the shield of mask, for in real life we would instinctively close our eyes.'[72]

In the Indian Sanskrit epics the *Mahabharata* and the *Ramayana* – tales that incorporate demons and other supernatural entities – masks are a staple performance prop and these stories are performed using masks throughout south-east Asia.[73] John Emigh identified masks as a central part of 'related artistic and psychological strategies found in Hindu iconography and performance' that 'use artistic means to manifest – and partially contain and control – the felt presence of chthonic and, sometimes, demonic forces' in regions of both India and Indonesia.[74] Beelzebub was a regular character-type in British mummer plays stemming back to the eighteenth century that utilised masks and costume for their general spectacular impact.[75] And while masks do not appear in William Shakespeare's *Macbeth* (1611), mask imagery is deployed as one of its central thematic motifs.[76] As noted further shortly, the oft-noted link between French Grand Guignol and horror cinema is another significant predecessor of horror film masks, influenced by *commedia dell'arte* and Carnival traditions.

Just as relevant is gothic literature. Beginning with Horace Walpole's *The Castle of Otranto* (1764), the influence of the gothic has garnered much critical attention. Across the cultural phenomena where the gothic still manifests – fashion, film, music, architecture, painting, youth subcultures and literature – defining the term has prompted much critical activity. Of particular utility here is Dani Cavallaro's notion of 'gothicity' and the facts of which it consists. They are psychological (terror, horror, spectrality, secretiveness, obsession, paranoia, melancholia, persecution and claustrophobia[77]), physical (bestiality, monstrosity, the grotesque, revulsion, pollution and disease), stylistic ('exaggeration, ornamental excess, surrealist effects, dream language . . . [and] tenebrous comedy'[78]) and ideological ('crudeness versus elegance'[79]). Of particular interest to horror cinema, Philip Brophy succinctly encapsulated the gothic spirit in his observation that 'never tragic but always titillating, the Gothic loves death and loves to count the ways a person can die'.[80] Masks and other disguises permeate the gothic as they emphasise this bodily volatility. For Catherine Spooner, 'the body in Gothic fictions is a profoundly unstable concept: continually evoked, nevertheless it is always disappearing beneath the mask or the veil'.[81] Elsewhere she noted, 'Masks and veil simultaneously reveal and conceal: they foreground the interface between inside and outside, the seen and unseen, the self and the world.'[82] Recalling doppelgänger traditions, Spooner noted that if masks and other disguises 'evoke doubleness, their horror frequently lies in its collapse in the control of the mask or the disguise, so that it estranges the bearer from his/her "original" identity, entrapping him/her in a role experienced as alien to the self'.[83] This, she argued, is at stake in the 'split' personae in Robert Louis Stevenson's *Strange Case of Dr Jekyll and Mr Hyde* (1886), a dualism marked by shifts in costume and appearance.[84]

Masks appear frequently throughout gothic literature. In Wilkie Collins's short story 'The Professor's Story of The Yellow Mask' (1856), he revamps the idea of a mask made from a statue employed in his novel *Mr Wray's Cash-Box* (1852). Masks also appear in the work of Sheridan Le Fanu: *Carmilla* (1871) features a masquerade ball where its title character uses the anonymity afforded by her mask to search for victims. For Tammis Elise Thomas, 'Le Fanu depicts the masquerade as a site of initiation into the terrors of the supernatural and the forbidden pleasures of female same-sex desire'.[85] Later, M. R. James employed masks in the short story 'The Rose Garden' (1911), where a real face is so unnatural and frightening that it is mistaken for a mask.

As these examples indicate, masks were well established in the literary gothic by the time horror and science fiction authors such as H. P. Lovecraft and Edgar Allan Poe took to writing in the more recognisable horror genre. Lovecraft wrote as cinema was rising as a popular storytelling and entertainment mode in the United States and masks were a regular – although not exactly signature – aspect of his work. For Lovecraft, masks are an identifying feature of one of the many forms of Nyarlathotep, a figure who appears in many guises across Lovecraft's complex Cthulhu

Mythos. Covered from head to toe in yellow silk, Nyarlathotep is called 'The Thing in the Yellow Mask' in a number of works, including the short stories 'Celephaïs' and 'Nyarlathotep' (both published in 1920) and the sonnet series 'Fungi from Yuggoth' (1943). Masks appear in his short story 'The Festival' (1925), whose protagonist is unable to distinguish between the wax-like skin of a monster and 'a fiendishly cunning mask'. A mask is central to his short story 'Through the Gates of the Silver Key', co-written with E. Hoffmann Price in 1933, and his 1939 short story 'In the Walls of Eryx' (co-written with Kenneth J. Sterling) features a detailed description of an oxygen mask worn by its protagonist. With Adolphe de Castro, Lovecraft co-wrote 'The Electric Executioner' (1929), again featuring a reference to a mask and in the non-fiction essay 'Supernatural Horror in Literature' (1927), Lovecraft praises L. P. Hartley's story 'The Death Mask'. A collection of Lovecraft's work was even called *The Mask of Cthulhu: The Arkham Edition of H. P. Lovecraft* (1971).

Lovecraft's fascination with masks may have stemmed from the influence of Edgar Allan Poe, a legacy acknowledged by Lovecraft himself and his critics.[86] Poe's short story 'The Cask of Amontillado' (1846) is set during Carnival, a tale of revenge told from the perspective of the killer. With his cape and 'mask of black silk', protagonist Montresor adheres to the iconography of a black clad, masked villain soon typical in both horror cinema and pulp fiction. Florent Christol noted the broadly unspoken significance of Poe's 1849 short story 'Hop-Frog' to contemporary horror, a story reliant on masquerade, masked disguise and costume. The masquerade ball is central to another Poe story, 'The Masque of the Red Death' (1842), famously adapted by Roger Corman in 1964 in a film of the same name. As one of the most well-known instances of the mask in horror literature, it relies on an ambivalent deployment of what Tseëlon called 'the enigma of disguise'.[87] The ultimate horror of 'The Masque of the Red Death' is that the masked disguise is all there is: there is no 'other' underneath.

Initially called 'Mask of the Red Death' to emphasise the role of costume, Poe changed it to 'Masque of the Red Death' to shift focus to the ball itself, underscoring masking and unmasking rituals.[88] This does not diminish the centrality of the mask in Corman's screen adaptation, however, which reveals not an empty costume but the face of actor Vincent Price, who played lead character Prince Prospero. As discussed in chapter 4, Price is essential when thinking through horror film masks for this and a number of other roles where his 'stable' identity (linked closely to his broader star persona) is frequently disrupted through masked disguise. Corman's was not the first adaptation of Poe's tale. It inspired the Russian film *A Spectre Haunts Europe* (*Prizrak brodit po Yevrope*, Vladimir Gardin, 1923) and while not an adaptation as such, two years later the story would be famously referenced by Rupert Julian in the classic Universal horror film *The Phantom of the Opera*. Here, during the masked ball sequence, Lon Chaney Sr.'s Erik appears as Poe's Red Death, foreshadowing the monstrosity of his character and solidifying the role of horror film masks in early cinema. This film will be discussed further in chapter 3.

Both Poe and Lovecraft influenced the development of genre fiction, but they too were influenced in part by the so-called 'penny dreadfuls' popular during their respective lifetimes. Pertaining to nineteenth-century British sensational crime and horror serials, variants appeared in the United States referred to by the same name. Paul Roland noted that Lovecraft read penny dreadfuls as a child, while for Shelley Costa Bloomfield the popularity of penny dreadfuls in Britain may have partially inspired Poe's direction into similar generic terrain.[89] For Martyn Colebrook, the rise of the literary Weird Lovecraft represented during this period resulted from the 'collision between modernism and Victoriana . . . accelerated by the rise of penny dreadfuls and mass industrialism'.[90] Penny dreadfuls have been the subject of much critical debate: for some they are understood as a 'sleazy', exploitative by-product of the 'British Gothic fad', marking a shift from highbrow 'literary' gothic fiction to something more lowbrow, appealing to the working class and poor.[91] As such, popular stories by penny dreadful writers like G. W. M. Reynolds depict 'the nobility as vicious and depraved'.[92] Class was crucial to G. K. Chesterton's passionate defence of penny dreadfuls, their assumed 'vulgar[ity]' the result of explicit 'class privilege'.[93] Whatever their politics, their influence on horror film masks is important. Writing in 1862, George Augustus Sala observed that they included 'men with masks and women with daggers' and many other sensational tropes and motifs of late eighteenth-century gothic literature that would later permeate horror cinema.[94]

Pulp literary traditions are more broadly noteworthy here, especially the hard-boiled detective fiction of the early twentieth century. One of the most important pulp magazines was called *Black Mask*, which was essential in popularising hard-boiled fiction.[95] For Peter Stanfield, pulps were defined by their mass production, their focus on working-class readers, their use of low-quality paper and their 'sensational formulaic stories, marked by a high degree of seriality, ensuring that popular characters and situations reappeared with some regularity across issues'.[96] Don Hutchison celebrated the generic diversity of pulps from this era, noting their dedication to detective stories, westerns, science fiction, sports, romance, gang war, horror and jungle and desert adventure stories.[97] Alongside comic book superheroes, other masked figures entered the popular consciousness, such as the Lone Ranger and Zorro.[98] Before the rise of these masked popular figures in the United States, however, there were stage traditions in France in particular during the late nineteenth and early twentieth century that donated significantly to the codification of horror film masks.

Horror Masks and French Theatre

Poe has been identified as a strong influence on Paris's Grand Guignol theatre,[99] whose impact both Tom Gunning and Adam Rockoff amongst others suggest is visible in horror cinema.[100] But this is not the only significant French theatrical movement during this period of interest here: a major figure of the twentieth-century European avant-garde, Antonin Artaud's Theatre of Cruelty appeared later and while it manifested as a distinct cultural phenomenon, both it and the Grand Guignol pivoted around notions of horror and terror and utilised masks in significant ways. While the Theatre of Cruelty was more intellectually driven, as Richard J. Hand and Michael Wilson noted, Grand Guignol plays demanded 'skills more associated with, for example, *commedia dell'arte* than horror theatre'.[101]

During the early 1920s, after working as an actor and collaborating with a number of avant-garde theatrical directors, Artaud joined the Surrealist movement in 1924 and became their 'Director of Surrealist Research', leaving soon after due to a clash with the movement's founder Andre Breton.[102] In 1926, he established the brief yet successful Theatre Alfred-Jarry with Roger Vitrac and Robert Aron and in 1935 he created the Theatre of Cruelty. As a production company, it was short lived, but Artaud's writing that stemmed from it was influential. In *The Theater and its Double* (1938), Artaud outlined a theatrical language established upon the body's supremacy over words: the 'theater of cruelty' configured sensory assault as a political weapon. For Cardullo, 'neither reassuring nor restful, discursive nor detached, Artaud's theater aims at disturbing the senses, pushing the audience's experience to new extremes, revealing our cultural hypocrisies and releasing subconscious as well as anarchic impulses'.[103] Artaud saw theatre as a means to shock the public into radical action and, as Robert

Cunliffe noted, conceptual traces of carnival from a Bakhtinian perspective are visible in Artaud's Theatre of Cruelty,[104] and that many of Artaud's revolutionary social goals continue many aspects of interest to Bakhtin.[105]

Theatrical spectacle – including that pertaining to masks – was crucial to Artaud's ideological mission with the Theatre of Cruelty. His essay 'On the Balinese Theater' was inspired by a Balinese dance performance he saw at Paris's Colonial Exposition in 1931,[106] which Artaud argued consisted of 'a whole collection of ritual gestures to which we do not have the key'.[107] For Artaud 'the Balinese have realized . . . the idea of pure theatre, where everything, conception and realization alike, has value, has existence only in proportion to its degree of objectification on the stage'.[108] In 'The Theater of Cruelty (First Manifesto)', Artaud states that 'every spectacle will contain a physical and objective element, perceptible to all', through 'cries, groans, apparitions, surprises, theatricalities of all kinds, magic beauty of costumes taken from certain ritual models'. Of the latter, he emphasises 'concrete appearances of new and surprising objects, masks, effigies yards high'.[109] Incorporating the ritual power of masks, the Theatre of Cruelty creates a sensory shock – an experience so crucial to horror – with its mystical force and potency aligned with the shamanic imagination.

Although driven by more commercial motivations, the Grand Guignol theatre also recognised the power of masks to create horror. We continue to see a connective tissue associating horror with the traditions outlined thus far: in her discussion of horror cinema in the 1980s, Linda Badley noted that the period marked a 'return . . . to its wellsprings in the theatrical – in the circus side show . . . the phantasmagoria show, the wax museum, the *Theatre du Grand Guignol* of Paris and Theatre of Cruelty'.[110] She linked this to Bakhtin by noting that 'horror is Carnival and is rooted in transgression: norms are inverted, taboos acted out and metamorphosis is celebrated'.[111] In horror cinema this metamorphosis – this transformation – is associated frequently with masks.

Spanning from the late nineteenth century to 1962, the words 'Grand Guignol' are still used to broadly describe any 'display of grotesque violence within the performance media'.[112] Playwright Andre de Lorde was a key figure in the theatre's development and, as discussed shortly, *The Man with Wax Faces* (*Figures de Cire*) was adapted for the screen in 1914 by Maurice Tournear. Victor Emeljanow noted that de Lorde was influenced by Poe and gothic writers Ann Radcliffe and Matthew Lewis amongst others,[113] and the Grand Guignol shares the gothic fascination with body horror, revenge and excess. But as Emeljanow noted, Grand Guignol's origins in the Free Theatre movement meant that it was partially a reaction *against* the nineteenth century 'domestic' melodramas which broadly replaced the gothic in their popularity in England and France.[114] The Free Theatre movement is often linked to André Antoine and his Théâtre Libre *and* sought to escape the restraints of dominant dramatic forms like the gothic and melodrama.[115] Antoine employed Oscar Méténier as a translator, who opened the Grand Guignol.[116]

Méténier's Grand Guignol borrowed Antoine's stylistic approach to naturalism as its core doctrine,[117] while distinguishing itself by maintaining the excesses of melodrama and a flair for gothic excess.[118] This naturalism manifested in the Grand Guignol's notorious fascination with realistic horror effects[119] and this connection to Théâtre Libre's spirit of realism can also be identified in the Grand Guignol's love of re-enacting news stories. Méténier was an ex-police reporter and had underworld contacts who supplied him with 'insider' details,[120] and many of his plays were based on *fait divers*, short news articles and illustrations that vividly described recent crimes.[121] For instance, both Tom Gunning and Adam Lowenstein mentioned the real-world scandal of child murderer Jeanne Weber that inspired de Lorde's play *L'Acquitte* (1919).[122]

Masks were an important aspect of the Grand Guignol. While half-masks were a convention of early nineteenth-century French stage melodrama,[123] in the Grand Guignol masks were more than costume. In many Grand Guignol plays, masks appear as diegetically related to plot in ways that foreshadow horror cinema. Hand and Wilson note that blindfolds and facial bandages in Maurice Level's 1912 play *The Final Kiss* (*Le Basier dans la nuit*) are 'reminiscent of icons of horror . . . films like *The Invisible Man* (James Whale, 1933), *The Fly* (Kurt Neumann, 1958) and *Onibaba* (Kaneto Shindô, 1964)'. Likewise, masks are central to Jean Aragny and Francis Neilson's 1929 play *The Kiss of Blood* (*Le Baiser de sang*).[124] Many titles underscore the potency of masks as an iconographic element of the Grand Guignol, such as Hélène de Zuylen's *The Interrupted Masquerade* (1905) and later works including *The Woman with the Mask* (Alfred Gehri, 1935) and *The Mask of Death* (Claude Orval, 1941).

An important addition is Charles Méré's Grand Guignol play *Les trois masques*, adapted to the screen twice, first in 1921 by Henry Krauss (who would also star in the film) and then in 1929 by André Hugon in a film that was for many years believed to be the first French talkie.[125] Films like Krauss's and Hugon's screen versions of *Les trois masques* and *A Page of*

Madness demonstrate the influence of stage traditions like the *commedia dell'arte* and Noh theatre in early cinema, whose legacies continued in contemporary horror. Across this movement from stage to screen, we see early traces in horror of Neale's process of same-but-different, where tensions between repetition and variation account for the genre's longevity.

Masks in Early Cinema

Masks feature prominently in early cinema, seen in dramas such as Thomas H. Ince's *The Death Mask* (1914), through to the face-covering hood worn by the Klansmen in D. W. Griffiths's *The Birth of a Nation* (1915). While the supposedly 'heroic' Klansman figure in *The Birth of a Nation* may be Griffiths's most well-known deployment of facial covering, masks appeared in his earlier short *The Painted Lady* (1912) in a way closer to horror cinema in this early instance of the masked intruder/home invasion trope (explored in *Hush* in chapter 5 and *You're Next* in chapter 6). Likewise, Griffiths's gothic mystery *One Exciting Night* (1922) also hinges around an ominous masked figure and would influence the Old Dark House subgenre, discussed in chapter 3.

Early European film-makers also experimented with masks during this period. Georges Méliès often appeared as the devil in many of his films – *Le Diable au couvent* (1899), *Les Tresors de Satan* (1902), *Le Chaudron infernal* (1903), *Le Cake-Walk infernal* (1903) and *Le Roi du maquillage* (1904) – wearing a mask of Satan's face.[126] Satan and Hell are also central to films of other early European film-makers such as Segundo de Chomón in *Spectre Rouge* (1907), who like Méliès experimented with the illusionary potential of moving image technology. In his work, masks are elements of spooky costumes in films like *Legend of a Ghost* (*La légende du fantôme*) and *The Haunted House* (*La maison ensorcelée*), both from 1908.

Mask-like visages were also of interest to many early film-makers. In Britain, Walter R. Booth's *The Haunted Curiosity Shop* (1901) shows a floating head appearing as if by magic in its early moments. Horror-comedy finds its roots in this period and in the Harold Lloyd vehicle *Haunted Spooks* (Hal Roach and Alfred J. Goulding, 1920), while not masks per se, facial coverings – particularly sheets worn over the head to represent ghosts – are central to that film's comic climax. In Buster Keaton's *The Haunted House* (1921), villains dressed as skeletons appear in skull masks to torment Keaton's character, who is at one point handed a head that the audience identify as fake, while Keaton's comically terrified character does not. Even in their titles comedies during this period often referenced utilised masks and masquerades,[127] a trend demonstrated in other genres at this time.[128]

Although not featuring masks as such, Robert Weine's *The Cabinet of Dr. Caligari* (1920) is important here. While the make-up of somnambulist Cesare (Conrad Veidt) has been described as looking like a 'deathmask',[129] the original script explicitly referenced masks: at the film's conclusion, Franzis imagines the somnambulist's corpse appearing covered on stretcher, where he says 'Take off the mask. You are Caligari.' Faced with the body, Caligari collapses and is taken away in a straitjacket.[130] As noted in my discussion of *A Page of Madness*, the doppelgänger of German expressionist cinema performs a similar function as the mask in many horror films through its ability to fracture a single identity into numerous (often contradictory) ones. This original reference to masks in *The Cabinet of Dr. Caligari* demonstrates a broader interest in the object across German expressionism, such as artist Emil Nolde who was strongly influenced by the more grotesque aspects of so-called tribal art, seen in his 1911 painting *Masks*.[131] This German expressionist fascination with masks as a source of horror was also arguably to be seen to manifest in the mask-like visage of the robot in Fritz Lang's *Metropolis* (1927), and Ben Morgan suggested that the realities of the production context of films like *Metropolis* required 'almost mask-like makeup . . . necessary for work under the studio lights'.[132]

Eight years before *Caligari*, masks were central to Abel Gance's short film *Le masque d'horreur* (1912). While no copy of this film survived, some materials held at the British Film Institute provide insight into how Gance approached his eponymous 'mask of horror'.[133] This dossier was originally compiled by Jacques Deslandes for issue 5 of the *Revue internationale d'histoire du cinéma*, first published in 1975. In his typewritten introduction, Deslandes stated that while many (including Gance himself) believed that the film was never released because the negative was damaged, an undated issue of *Ciné-Journal* from the time of its release indicates that it was widely advertised and released on 24 May 1912 by Union des Nouvelles Marques Cinématographiques. Deslandes's dossier consists of two documents: Gance's handwritten treatment and a programme distributed during its brief exhibition period. These documents, Deslandes argued, disprove claims that the film is about a mad sculptor who suffocated his son in clay to make a sculpture (Gance published a short story in 1913 also called *Le masque d'horreur* that told this alternate story).[134]

As the film is lost, it is worth detailing what remains known of the film in some detail. According to the synopsis in Deslandes's dossier, the film concerns a psychologically unstable 30-year-old artist called Ermont. His obsession with his art alienated him from everyone except his wife Lucile and their 5-year-old daughter, Estel. As the film begins, it is revealed that he spent ten years obsessed with the creation of a 'mask of horror in its most scary sublimity . . . The day my fellow humans shiver from fright in front of my work . . . people will question no more my genius and glory and fortune will come.' Without this victory in sight, Ermont is frustrated and ridiculed by his peers. The first act sees the arrival of a letter from famous sculptor M. Marcel, who wishes to visit to discuss Ermont's acceptance into his Salon. Marcel is shocked that Ermont is still obsessed with his 'mask of horror' and dismisses him as insane. Devastated by Marcel's rejection, Ermont is struck by inspiration: he himself is the ideal model for his mask, 'Me! yes! me! My face as a living model'. With two days to impress Marcel, he studies himself in the mirror, pulling terrified expressions. His frightened wife runs to get a doctor as he holds Estel, forcing the terrified child to watch him apply clay to his distorted face. The doctor explains the seriousness of Ermont's health to him and drugs him, demanding he rest.

In Act Two, despite Lucile believing his health is returning, Ermont awakens insane. Hallucinating, 'a whole procession of phantasmagories which rode in his brain and compressed his head brings him delight': he sees twenty giant versions of his own contorted head floating before his eyes in red, using hand tinting. Believing red essential to his project, he cuts his wrist and paints his lamp glass with blood so the room is bathed in red light. Spiralling further into insanity, he believes that he will die so poisons himself to use his own agonised face as the ultimate model for his 'mask of terror'. In the red light, 'the poison distorts his face in a scary rictus'. Breaking the lamp that issues this coloured light while in his death throes, blue light from the moon (again using film tinting) fills the room as Ermont forces himself to continue, convinced he is close to achieving his goal: 'By hell! The whole sky of Baudelaire and all the gargoyles of Notre-Dame have an appointment at my place . . . enter, all of you! I am exhibiting!' The noise awakens Estel, who attempts to kiss her sick father. He lifts her up in front of 'the convulsing mask lit by the moon' and she runs terrified to her mother. Lucile finds Ermont dead, but his 'living' mask survives.

As the poster for the Du Theatre Sarah-Bernhardt screening of *Le masque d'horreur* indicates, the spirit of the Grand Guignol was present in early French horror such as this – from its blood-drip style font to the sensational images themselves. Likewise, Maurice Tourneur's *The Man with Wax Faces* (*Figures de Cire*, 1914) was based on a play written by André de Lorde. The second of Tourneur's de Lorde adaptations – the first a reimaging of Poe's *The System of Dr. Tarr and Professor Fether* in 1913[135] – *The Man with Wax Faces* has a simple plot: accepting a bet from Jacques (Emile Tramont), Pierre (Henry Roussel) agrees to spend the evening in a wax museum and inadvertently murders Jacques when driven by terror into a state of insanity. While not about masks as such, when the ominous manager who runs the wax museum (Henri Gouget) appears in the film's credits, a flat white skull figure superimposed over his face, suggesting what remains only implied in the film itself: that he was responsible for the evil that befell Pierre and Jacques. The English-language title emphasises this association between masks and horror.

Recalling the influence of hard-boiled pulps, masks in popular crime serials during the early twentieth century were also not uncommon. French director Louis Feuillade is of interest here, although American serials like *The Trail of the Octopus* (Duke Wome, 1919) and Vitagraph's *The Purple Mask* (Francis Ford and Grace Cunard, 1916) also used masks in significant ways. As indicated in the promotional artwork for Feuillade's crime serials *Fantômas* (1913–14) and *Les Vampires* (1915–16), masks and shadows were key visual motifs. While the title *Les Vampires* might initially imply a horror connection, this serial was less about supernatural bloodsuckers than a cat thief syndicate. Nevertheless, the function of masks in Feuillade's crime serials and their numerous adaptations illustrate how masks were deployed in early twentieth-century screen culture to imply threat and menace, flagging thematic fascinations with identity and disguise. Georges Franju made a feature-length adaptation of Feuillade's 1916 serial *Judex* in 1963 which (like *Eyes without a Face*) is also marked by the presence of masked characters, as is his 1974 film *Nuits Rouges*.

Let's now examine further intersections between masks and what was becoming the more widely identifiable horror genre as we continue to explore the claim that horror is a contemporary manifestation of a popular typology that existed across a range of historical and cultural contexts, spanning ritual practices encompassing religious, spiritual, performance and other secular traditions. This chapter has explored a range of diverse literary and performance traditions (Japanese Noh theatre, Italian *commedia dell'arte*, eighteenth- and nineteenth-century gothic literature and the work of Edgar Allan Poe and H. P. Lovecraft, the French Grand Guignol theatre and Antonin Artaud's Theatre of Cruelty) and early cinema not to suggest a single linear thread running throughout them, but rather to indicate a collective demonstration of the shamanic imagination at work through their diverse fascinations with masks as transformative devices. As we have seen, this sensibility is elastic enough to allow a vast range of re-imaginings, revisions and adaptations across different cultures throughout history. These examples exemplify how the power and potency of the mask has been imagined, both intertwining and diverging to culminate in the codification of masks as an iconographic staple of contemporary horror cinema.

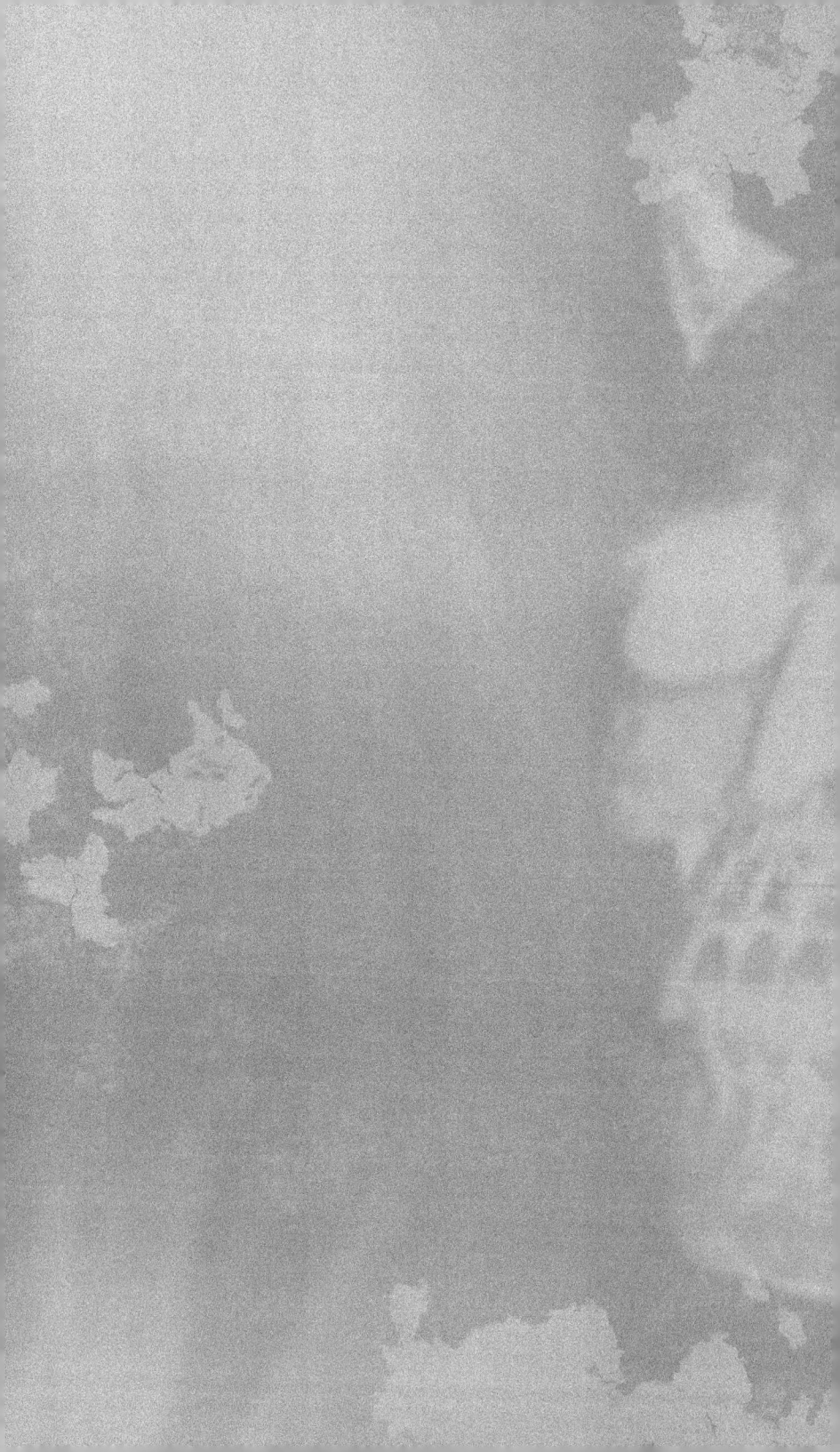

3

Masks in Horror Film before 1970

DIVERSE INFLUENCES played a significant role in establishing masks as a potent recurring motif across many international literary and performance traditions and early cinema. This chapter moves towards the emergence, endurance and codification of masks as a key element of contemporary horror cinema's iconography. Again, the shamanic imagination plays a fundamental role in how the power of masks is broadly conceived in horror cinema, through their ability to transform. The shamanic imagination underscores why we broadly accept that masks allow movement – literal or metaphorically – often (although not essentially) linked to the supernatural, particularly when associated with religious, spiritual or secular rituals. This chapter provides a preliminary background for the case studies that will make up Part Two and Three's focus on specific horror film masks. Each chapter provides a clear indication of how Neale's process of 'repetition . . . difference, variation and change' accounts in part for why and how the mask has endured throughout horror film history.[1] Like the traditions outlined previously, the films explored here maintain the dynamic and symbolic power of the mask, despite their diversity.

Again, films both famous and comparatively unknown are considered in an attempt to demonstrate this diversity, reinforcing the elasticity of the shamanic imagination. Accordingly, many well-known films will be considered in this chapter, including both the 1925 and 1930 releases of Rupert Julian's *The Phantom of the Opera* and *The Iron Mask* (Allan Dwan, 1929), alongside lesser known movies like *The Phantom of Crestwood* (J. Walter Ruben, 1932) and *Scared to Death* (Christy Cabanne, 1947). Across this period, masks would be employed in different ways, while still governed by the shamanic imagination and its fascination with transformation and movement across symbolic (and sometimes even literal) planes. Horror in the 1930s was dominated by the monster movies of Universal Studios, which often featured ritual acts: rituals of seduction, possession and destruction in the case *Dracula* (Tod Browning, 1935), rituals of reanimation and mob justice in regard to *Frankenstein* (James Whale, 1931) and more explicitly configured religious rituals in *The Mummy* (Karl Freund, 1932). As these more famous instances demonstrate, however, while often essential costuming elements, masks were not necessarily a diegetic feature. This is not necessarily true of horror films produced by other studios, however, as many movies explored here demonstrate, including *Mad Love* (Karl Freund, 1935), *The Face behind the Mask* (Robert Florey, 1941), Arthur Lubin's 1943 *Phantom of the Opera* remake, *Flesh and Fantasy* (Julien Duvivier, 1943), *Mr Sardonicus* (William Castle, 1961) and a number of films linked to actor Vincent Price during the 1950s. These films share a fundamental understanding of masks and their power that – through the shamanic imagination – grant them often extraordinary abilities to transform their wearers.

In the second part of this chapter we look beyond the United States towards how masks manifested in France, Mexico, Italy and Japan that marked the genre's internationalisation during the 1960s especially. This continues a consideration of how the mask as a sign – through its increasing repetition across the horror genre – attains a much broader field of signification, which in this last section in particular is closely linked to specific cultural histories. New discourses emerge from masks out of this process of same-but-different, but in a manner still consistent with generic logic, allowing audiences to identify films as still falling under the horror umbrella. Collectively, the horror films in this chapter provide a developing picture of how and why masks have endured as iconographic staple. Across these movies, power, ritual and transformation continue to intersect in significant ways.

The Spectacle of Unmasking: *The Phantom of the Opera* (1925/1930)

Masks and masquerade manifested in cinema from the outset, but if there is a single film that raised the profile of horror masks as a key component of the genre's iconography, it was Rupert Julian's *The Phantom of the Opera* (1925). What remains intriguing about this film is that through the mask, rituals surrounding gender and performance begin to appear in horror even at this early stage of the genre's history. For Harry H. Long, its release marked the precise moment when audiences and exhibitors began to identify this type of movie as a generic trend.[2] There are two different versions of this *The Phantom of the Opera* – the silent original from 1925 and the 1930 re-release with sound – and Chaney himself policed how his image could be replicated in the latter, limiting what Universal could do.[3] Of the new material in the widely viewed 1930 version, the key scene where the phantom's mask is removed was not the same as the original: rather, it was 'derived from a Technicolor take of the scene that Chaney had vetoed due to makeup flaws made visible by the more intense light necessitated by color stock'.[4] Although not up to Chaney's standards, it is arguable that it is the very *frailty* of the disguise that renders its removal so violent. The flimsy materiality of the mask communicates sensorially the delicacy of constructed identities, the mask constructed as a volatile membrane between the 'performed' (controlled) masked phantom and the frightened individual underneath. Rather dehumanising its wearer, this mask recalls Haslam's a spectrum of 'humanness denials'[5] – the Phantom's mask is slightly *less* dehumanised than his own disfigured face.

Audience reactions to Christine's (Mary Philbin) removal of Chaney's mask were passionate at the time of its original release. A 1925 review in the *New York Times* noted 'in the theater last night a woman behind us stifled a scream when this happened'.[6] But this is more than a mere jump scare: for Mark Jancovich, *The Phantom of the Opera* offers an early instance of the horror gaze's sexual politics. Of this unmasking, Jancovich noted that 'since both he and Christine face the camera in a two-shot (with Christine situated behind him) we again see the Phantom's face, this time unmasked, before Christine does'. Because of this, 'the audience thus receives the first shock of the horror even while it can still see the curiosity and desire to see on Christine's face'.[7] Jancovich continued: 'her unmasking of his face reveals the very wounds, the very lack, that the Phantom had hoped her blind love would heal'. This puts the onus on Christine for her experience of horror, as 'it is as if she has become responsible for the horror that her look reveals and is punished by not being allowed the safe distance that ensures the voyeur's pleasure of looking'.[8] Beyond fear, the Phantom's mask is a device that ideologically stabilises and destabilises; for Jancovich, 'clearly the monster's power is one of sexual difference from the normal male' and that 'in this difference he is remarkably like the woman in the eyes of the traumatized male: a biological freak with impossible and threatening appetites that suggest a frightening potency precisely where the normal male would perceive a lack'.[9] This mirrors Sue Ellen Case's reading of the Phantom, where 'the queer is the taboo-breaker, the monstrous, the uncanny. Like the Phantom of the Opera, the queer dwells underground, below the operatic overtones of the dominant; frightening to look at, desiring, as it plays its own organ, producing its own music.'[10] The Phantom is a tragic trickster: through identity-play, he subverts and transgresses the status quo of gender norms, his domain the liminal underground Other space beyond the on-stage/off-stage binary.

In some ways, this foreshadows the blurring of gender binaries that Clover identified in *Men, Women and Chain Saws: Gender in the Modern Horror Film* (1992). Likewise, the abject nature of what lies beneath the Phantom's mask and the instability of gender constructed by his status as Other also recalls Creed's work on monstrous-femininity in horror.[11] Creed suggested this image of monstrosity stems from an awareness of sexual difference and she also draws from Julia Kristeva's work on abjection (itself responding to Sigmund Freud's 1913 work, *Totem and Taboo*). Applying Kristeva's work to horror, Creed stated that abjection 'disturbs identity, system, order', and the divide between human and non-human subjects by the rejection of the abject (non-human).[12] Ritual is key to Kristeva's notion of abjection because it defines the separation between human/non-human and subject/non-subject. Creed contended that horror as a ritual does exactly this: 'the horror film brings about a confrontation with the abject (the corpse, bodily wastes, the monstrous feminine) in order, finally, to eject the abject and re-draw the boundaries between the human and the non-human'.[13] Through rituals of masking and unmasking, *The Phantom of the Opera* functions in this way as the Phantom himself is shunned for the transgression of gendered Otherness. With the mask's removal, the power imbued in it disintegrates. He is defeated and the trickster is exposed.

Masks and Space: *The Iron Mask* (1929) and Old Dark House Films

As *The Phantom of the Opera* indicates, remakes, re-releases and adaptions were already popular during this era; cinema rituals in their own right in their habitual revisitation to past stories with proven success, albeit for commercial reasons. For Mircea Eliade, re-enactment more broadly as a concept is as an essential aspect of religious ritual, and as Anat Zanger argues, film remakes contain ritual components as repetition is fundamentally a ritual act.[14] Between the two different versions of *Phantom of the Opera*, the visual language that marked the development of masks as a key iconographic element of horror cinema evolved in the United States in fundamental ways. Of particular note during this period are a number of films that employ masks to privilege their capacity for horror in regard to particular spaces: prisons in the case of supposedly 'haunted' houses in Old Dark House films. *The Iron Mask* was typical of the romantic adventure film upon which Douglas Fairbanks had built his career and while not horror as such it relied heavily on a gothic sensibility, particularly in its use of the mask. Shadowy aesthetics dominate many scenes that foreshadow imagery which would soon dominate Universal Studios' horror films of the 1930s, yet the use of the mask is noteworthy: rather than a disguise, it is forced upon the kidnapped king as a form of incarceration. At the film's conclusion, this symbolic imprisonment is reversed as the king's evil twin is placed in the mask as punishment. A gothic doppelgänger tale, it demonstrated how gothic and German expressionist aesthetics were becoming mainstream.

Roland West's *The Bat* (1926) is again influenced stylistically by German expressionism. *The Bat* is known primarily as inspiration for Bob Kane's comic *Batman*,[15] yet it spawned two more remakes: West's *The Bat Whispers* (1930) and the Vincent Price vehicle *The Bat* (Crane Wilbur, 1959). Despite being made over thirty years apart, they maintain the basic mask style of the eponymous, enigmatic villain, while also continuing Old Dark House traditions. Peaking in popularity during the 1920s and 1930s, S. T. Joshi located the origins of the Old Dark House films in Mary Roberts Rinehart's 1908 novel *The Circular Staircase*, adapted to the screen in the 1926 version of *The Bat*. Joshi identified the subgenre's key components in Rinehart's novel: 'guests who unwillingly stay overnight because of a broken-down car or nocturnal storm, hidden corridors, sliding panels, spiral staircases and unknown perils'.[16] Alison Peirse noted that they were commonly adapted from plays that focused on families or 'groups of strangers' assembling in 'a creaking and neglected property'.[17] A murder is committed and survivors investigate the crime in the eponymous locale: 'The vision is of old-fashioned creepiness, of property weighted heavily with secrets, cluttered with memories.'[18]

Masks were often deployed in Old Dark House movies to disguise the killer's identity, essential to their whodunnit structure, but they also indicate that the spaces in which their dramas unfold are volatile and potentially haunted (although usually debunked when more human mischief is revealed). Masks are broadly utilised in Old Dark House films such as Michael Curtiz's *Doctor X* (1932) and although lesser known, the use of masks in *The Phantom of Crestwood* (J. Walter Ruben, 1932) is more complex than many Old Dark House films. *The Phantom of Crestwood* concerns the murder of Jenny Wren (Karen Morely), who extorts rich, supposedly respectable ex-lovers. She invites them to a party at the Crestwood estate, but before her demands for more cash can be met, she is killed. Suspicion falls on her ex-lovers and a dubious gang of mobsters and it is revealed that Jenny was haunted just before her death by a much older admirer she believed to be Mister Vayne (Ivan Simpson). Vayne's true identity is Henry T. Herrick, the father of Wren's naive ex-lover Tom (Tom Douglas), who killed himself after Wren rejected his affections. With Herrick Sr. wearing a black cloak and his son's death mask, these sequences are disturbing and the wearing of the young man's death mask by his father – a doppelgänger via genetics as well as the doubling capacity of the death mask itself – prompts power transformations associated with the ability to cross the liminal space between life and death. The mask reanimates the dead, granting extraordinary transformative power to its wearer. Yet the film's conclusion reveals that the real murderer was Faith (Pauline Frederick), aunt of the wealthy Frank (Matty Kemp): Faith mistook Jenny for her intended victim, Jenny's sister Esther (Anita Louise) who she deemed unsuitable to marry Frank. That Faith adopts the mask of the dead Tom Herrick amplifies the film's unspoken fascination with masks as a symbolic vessel for assumed sexual impropriety to be exposed. Masked villains as guardians of puritanical sexuality becomes a staple of the slasher subgenre over forty years later, where Michael Myers and Jason Voorhees garner a reputation for punishing sexually active teenagers. Before this, however, masks and facial transformations appeared during the mainstream spike in the genre's popularity during the 1930s.

Masks and Horror at Universal Studios and Beyond

Although often not diegetically significant, masks were key aspects of costume during the 'golden era' of Universal Studios' 1930s monster films from 1931 to 1936.[19] Boris Karloff's iconic performance as Frankenstein's monster in Whale's *Frankenstein* is an obvious instance, and an important figure in horror history. Evoking doppelgänger traditions, in Mary Shelley's 1818 novel upon which it is based, the monster is broadly interpreted as a double for Dr Frankenstein himself, whose obsessiveness collapses into monstrosity: the monster embodies Victor's own ugliness. As Aija Ozolins argued, 'this motif of a second self constitutes the chief source of the novel's latent power'.[20] Alternatively, the bandages that conceal Karloff's mummified face in *The Mummy* occlude the horrors of what lies underneath: while not 'masked' in the way that we are interested in here, there are regardless echoes of how later horror monsters disguise their monstrosity, such as Jason Voorhees's deformed face under a hockey mask (discussed in chapter 7). But beyond Universal, MGM's *Mad Love* is one of German-émigré Peter Lorre's most enduring cult horror films and reveals its dedication to the genre in its opening moments as a young couple leave a Grand Guignol-style theatre. This is an instance of early 'meta' horror as they discuss their experiences of watching horror as spectators. Outside the theatre, a drunken man flirts with a wax figurine of the theatre's star, Yvonne Orlac (Frances Drake), chiding Lorre's Dr Gogol for being jealous. These opening moments foreshadow a reflexive excursion into genre framed by an awareness of horror's theatrical history, while privileging the visual spectacle of doubles and doppelgängers.

While not a supernatural horror film as such, Gogol's belief in the power of magic (and his obsession with bringing Yvonne's wax figure to life) drives him towards the ominous, transformative power of masked disguise. Like tricksters more generally, Gogol is a master of bricolage;[21] he deploys a neck brace to convince the couple he is the returned killer. Glasses and a hat cover the top half of his face, while this brace covers his bottom jaw and the sides of face, leaving his cheeks, nose and upper mouth visible. While this stands outside the usual way masking manifests in horror (typically a full facial mask) – closer to the aesthetics of pulp fiction – it disguises Gogol and propels the plot, leaving Lorre himself still visible enough to imbue his character with aspects of his broader star persona as a 'strange murderous individual'.[22] While not a traditional mask, in terms of Haslam's spectrum of humanness denials, we see parts of Gogol's human face, but it is obscured by these contraptions. As an example of the repurposed masks we will explore in chapter 7, they collectively present a monstrous image that is effectively a dead man returned to life to torment the living. Shaman-trickster Gogol deceives and transgresses to attain sexual power over Yvonne. His 'mask' grants him power that he could not attain 'unmasked'.

Jacques Tourneur's 1938 short *The Man Behind the Mask* revisits the same source material as *The Iron Mask* and while ostensibly an historical re-enactment/melodrama, Tourneur's flair for the gothic is present with a narrator revelling in the horrors that 'the unknown man still wearing the mask of iron' faced, relishing descriptions of the agony he would suffer if the masked was removed. Tourneur opts for a double-masked deception: when the prisoner arrives at the fortress and removes the fabric hood from over his head, underneath is not his face but the iron mask. Tourneur subverts expectations of how masking and unmasking function: the removal of a mask presents only another layer of deception. The narrator asks, 'who was this man?' and presents three possibilities, implying that it was Louis XIII's own son, a possibility the narrator describes as 'a terrifying answer'. For Tourneur here, masks offer not the capacity for doubling, but for *tripling*: the person behind the mask could be anyone, which is chilling because it denies individuality, again echoing Haslam's suggestion that dehumanisation is not a binary opposite to the state of being human, but rather that 'humanness denials' occur on a spectrum.[23] Identity is a crucial aspect of Tourneur's horror work in films like *Cat People* (1942) and *I Walked with a Zombie* (1943) and this fascination permeates this earlier short.

Masks and Cross-generic Terror

Masks as objects of horror appear outside the genre itself. For example, Lew Landers's film noir *The Mask of Diijon* (1946) starred Erich von Stroheim as a psychotic, abusive husband whose villainy and power were granted a supernatural aspect through his mastery of magic and hypnotism. While the 'mask' of the title refers to his deceptive identity, the potency of the word is linked to the film's dark, mystical content and the object's broader associations with power and transformation. Likewise, Anthony Mann's film noir *Strange Impersonation* (1946) hinged upon a deceptive identity resultant of plastic surgery, its promotional materials relying on the implicit horror of masks themselves. Masks were also used in more explicitly horror contexts during this period. *The Woman Who Came Back* (Walter Colmes, 1945) concerns Lorna Webster (Nancy Kelly), the descendant of a witch-hunter who believes a witch has possessed her and is causing her to do harm. Early in the film, Lorna is confronted by a group of children wearing Halloween masks; while a mother dismisses this as 'foolishness', Lorna is shaken. Masks here recall archaic, transformative powers; their potential is unleashed through supernatural possession.

In 1941, Peter Lorre's star persona and facial transformation would again be pivotal, this time in Robert Florey's *The Face Behind the Mask*. Although ostensibly a crime film, the association of Lorre and masks suggests an attempt to rekindle the power of *Mad Love*.[24] Here, Lorre plays sympathetic immigrant Janos Szabo, burnt beyond recognition and forced into crime to afford a lifelike mask of his previous face. A strong sense of the uncanny dominates scenes where the masked Lorre's face has an unhuman, waxy sheen under the thin latex. Lorre was typecast as a horror actor by this stage and despite the absence of the horror monsters typical of the Universal films of the previous decade, the combination of Lorre himself with the mask is directly relevant to my interest in horror masks, ritual, power and transformation.

Arthur Lubin's 1943 horror musical remake of *The Phantom of the Opera* starred Claude Rains who, despite appearing in romantic dramas *Casablanca* (Michael Curtiz, 1942) and *Now, Voyager* (Irving Rapper, 1942), had significant horror form with Universal due to appearances in *The Wolf Man* (George Waggner, 1941) and *The Invisible Man* (James Whale, 1933). Rains's performance in *Phantom of the Opera* unites both these previous generic strands. As Ron Backer noted, 'a screen adaptation of *The Phantom of the Opera* can emphasize one of two elements – the phantom or the opera'[25] and as such is considered more musical than horror,[26] despite sitting in the canon of Universal's monster films. In converting Gaston Leroux's story from horror to musical, a distinct softening occurs in how the mask is reconfigured in this new generic context. Backer voiced disappointment in the absence in the 1943 version of the scene in the 1925 film where Mary Philbin removes Chaney's mask, which suggests that what lay beneath the mask was less a source of horror and more a sympathetically presented Rains.[27] The film's climax takes place at a performance of Mozart's 1787 opera *Don Giovanni*, which includes a number of masked characters. This creates dramatic tension when the police realise that one of their men has been killed by the Phantom and that Rains's Erique is amongst the masked cast of the opera, hidden in plain view.

That there are *multiple* masked characters drains the force from the object: their ubiquity *reduces* their power. After Erique is killed in an accident, the film ends on an image of his mask and violin: the mask is ultimately decorative, and acts of masking and unmasking no longer denote transformations relating to power or ritual.

Flesh and Fantasy (Julien Duvivier, 1943) develops its interest in the transformative capacity of masks through what are presented explicitly as Carnival rituals. The first story in this horror anthology hinges on masked transformation and power relations regarding gender and the supernatural potential contained within the object itself. Set in New Orleans Mardi Gras, Henrietta (Betty Field) is a bitter young woman, disillusioned by her physical 'plainness'. Nursing an unrequited affection for handsome Michael (Robert Cummings), her sense that she is out of his league fuels her anger and isolation. Evoking Cinderella, Henrietta discovers a mask shop where the enigmatic owner (Edgar Barrier) gives her a beautiful mask to wear to Carnival, under the proviso that she returns it at midnight. Michael falls instantly in love with the masked Henrietta, but she is resistant to remove the mask despite his insistence as she feels he loves the mask, not her. Returning to the mask shop, the owner has vanished and said never to exist. Removing the mask, Henrietta's face is transformed to reflect the beautiful face of the mask itself, leaving her and Michael happily embracing. Here the mask transforms not merely in the moment of its wearing; its magic lingers, allowing Henrietta to transition from bitter isolation to normative heterosexual monogamy. The common logic of the horror mask is reversed: the mask resolves transgression, rather than propels it. Regardless, it is a ritual that still grants her power, and of particular interest is how the magical object of the mask triggers a mystical alteration in the wearer. For better or for worse, the relationship between her outer appearance and her inner emotional status is governed by the act of masking.

Masks were by now becoming a staple in horror and horror-tinged cinema, an identifiable visual cue to provoke particular kinds of affective and intellectual responses. While the examples discussed thus far utilise different masks in different ways, they simultaneously recall Neale's process – driven by a tension between similarity and difference – where this repeated iconographic element continues to move towards codification: an old object is given new life (and, more importantly, new meanings) in what audiences recognise as the generically appropriate context of horror. This is visible in *Scared to Death* (Christy Cabanne, 1947), where again the mask is privileged in promotional material to highlight the centrality of enigmatic identities. Through flashback, *Scared to Death* reveals how Laura (Molly Lamont) died, a stubborn racist who refuses to divorce her husband out of spite. The arrival of Professor Leonide (Bela Lugosi) discloses through hypnosis that Laura deliberately informed the Nazis that her husband was a spy, leading to what she believed was his murder. Unbeknownst to her, he survived and planned his revenge with Leonide: the appearance of his floating death mask at the window when she comes out of her confession-inducing hypnosis triggers her being – as the title indicates – 'scared to death'. The presence of both trickster and doppelgänger traditions are evident here and Laura's shock at seeing the death mask speaks of the object's power to transgress the liminal spaces between life and death. The power of masks to shock and disorient in the context of genre cinema would only continue to solidify in the films of Vincent Price.

Vincent Price, William Castle and the 'Crisis of Identity'

Masks that appear diegetically in horror movies were by now becoming a generic convention that granted an expanded potential for signification to the already much-utilised artefact. While masks as elements of costume were also crucial to horror/sci-fi hybrids like Jack Arnold's film *The Creature from the Black Lagoon* (1954), *Invasion of the Saucer Men* (Edward L. Cahn, 1957) and *Invaders from Mars* (William Cameron Menzies, 1953), they were also used diegetically during this period. As Mark Jancovich noted, the 1950s are assumed to deviate from horror's status as a site for ideological subversion and instead was a decade of supposed conservatism.[28] A position typified by Robin Wood, for Jancovich this assumption relied on a reductive tendency to dismiss the decade's genre films as 'all the same'.[29] Arguing against this, he identified a turn from gothic horror 'towards a preoccupation with the modern world' where 'the threats which distinguish 1950s horror do not come from the past or even from the actions of a lone individual, but are associated with the processes of social development and modernisation'.[30] During this period, 'horror texts were at least as concerned with developments within American society as they were with threats from without'.[31] Arguing for a rethinking of 1950s horror, Jancovich identified three areas that mark the decade's genre output: invasion narratives, outsider narratives and 'narratives concerned with "crises of identity"'.[32] While the first two are fascinating, the third is of particular interest when considering horror film masks. Examining films that anticipated Hitchcock's *Psycho*, Jancovich noted their emphasis on identity crises rather than specific attacks on the American nuclear family. Although locating this crisis of identity active within the science fiction/horror hybrid *Forbidden Planet* (Fred M. Wilcox, 1956), he also noted that American horror during this period was marked as a gothic revival, inspired by Britain's Hammer Horror films and television broadcasts of Universal's classic monster films of the 1930s.[33] Key to this renaissance was Roger Corman, particularly his Edgar Allan Poe cycle – including *The Masque of the Red Death* (1964), discussed previously – which Jancovich argued was 'directly concerned with crises of identity'. For Jancovich, characters (often played by Vincent Price) 'are not only aware of their vulnerability, but often seem to actually desire their own destruction'.[34]

The Masque of the Red Death was not Vincent Price's first venture into mask-based horror, and his horror status was established with films including mask-centric horror films such as *House of Wax* (1953) and *The Mad Magician* (1954). These films demonstrate the crisis of identity that Jancovich suggested permeated American horror during this period. *House of Wax* was a remake of the Michael Curtiz's 1933 film *Mystery of the Wax Museum*, loyal to the original in its retelling of a sculptor disfigured in a fire lit by a greedy partner, who later opts for the macabre craft of wax-embalming human victims to maintain the success of his new professional venture, the eponymous *House of Wax*. The major difference between *The Mystery of the Wax Museum* and *House of Wax* was the utilisation of 3D film technology.[35] As explored in Part Three, 3D horror films about masks are often highly reflexive, where the placement of an object on the face is essential to perceiving the technological spectacle. Yet masking and associated rituals are significant in *House of Wax* in purely diegetic terms, as they necessitate a complex process of 'double' masking. The plot requires Price's character Professor Henry Jarrod to wear a mask the audience recognise as the character's pre-injury face (the face of Vincent Price). As we see throughout the film, however – most spectacularly when his mask is ripped off, echoing the 1925 *Phantom of the Opera* – underneath that 'normal' face lies one disfigured by fire (constructed within the film as 'monstrous'). In the scene where Price's 'normal' mask is ripped off, he was in practical terms wearing *two* masks – a plastic one over the top of the disfigured make-up and prosthetics that lay underneath.[36] Transgressive and deceptive, Price here (and elsewhere, discussed in chapter 4) is a trickster, his characters dominated by the power of transformation and the unstable, playful identities of his many masks.

Directed by cult horror figure William Castle, *The Tingler* (1959) includes a brief but memorable inclusion of a mask, essential to its narrative. Following Price's Dr Warren Chapin and his research into a strange insect-like creature that responds to terror in the human body ('The Tingler' of the title), his deaf-mute patient Ollie Higgins (Philip Coolidge) is scared to death (with the help of the 'terror bug' triggered by her husband who torments her by wearing a monster mask). A key scene in terms of plot development and spectacle, while not central to the overriding story, *The Tingler* demonstrates Castle's and Price's continuing interest in horror film masks.

While Castle had previously employed masks in both *The Tingler* and his film noir *When Strangers Marry* (1944), it is in *Mr Sardonicus* (1961) that he deployed it most centrally. Here the mask is a symbolic membrane between two identities linked to one man, the tragic, impoverished Marek (Guy Rolfe) who – by digging up his father's corpse to recover a winning lottery ticket becomes a ghoul, his face instantly petrified into a macabre grin – takes on another identity, the rich Baron Sardonicus. Covering his face with an immovable mask, Sardonicus's mask typifies its transgressive, uncanny status as a face-that-is-not-a-face, demonstrating Tseëlon's previous observation that the mask is alluring due to a tension between 'fascination and avoidance', standing 'in an intermediary position between different worlds' and marked by binaries of concealment/revelation, truth/ artifice, natural/supernatural and life/death.[37]

Through the shamanic imagination – the residual traces of traditional, anthropologically conceived shamanism that resonate throughout the popular consciousness – Sardonicus's mask allows him to move across these spaces, binaries which physically demarcate the divisions that mark Marek and the baron. Using the object to hide the disfiguring paralysis caused by a moral transgression (grave robbing), the baron's mask is a transformative device. While superficially disguising his face, it also marks his ethical deterioration, a symbol of his corrupted morals and the total change in his personality from innocent, brow-beaten Marek to violent and cruel Sardonicus. The mask dehumanises Marek: it represents his lack of humanity and his loss of compassion and empathy. The mask in *Mr Sardonicus* is therefore fundamental to the film's thematic and narrative trajectory and – through acts of masking and unmasking and the building of tension around the question 'what lies underneath?' – provides many of its thrills. Castle's film is not unique in this way but, through the mask, he mines the historical potency of the object inherent to the shamanic imagination. The horror of *Mr Sardonicus* is explicitly linked to the baron's transgressive disconnection between his face, ethics and identity.

Masks and the Internationalisation of Horror

Moving towards the major case studies that comprise the last two parts of this book, we continue to underscore Neale's identification of a same-but-different process that marks the codification of the mask as an iconographic staple of horror. We now consider the internationalisation of horror during the 1960s to emphasise the further codification that was broadly solidified in films from a diverse range of countries from the 1970s onwards. This repetition creates a productive tension through variation in a process that sees this popular form – like Carnival, *commedia dell'arte*, the gothic, Grand Guignol theatre and many other cultural forms before it – updated to a new cultural context. The function and meaning of the mask-as-artefact is therefore once again adapted to particular ideological or social functions that are specific to its historical and cultural contexts.

Masks appeared in horror films from around the world since cinema's earliest days, but a range of films have survived since the 1960s, that are now relatively accessible, demonstrating just how global this scope was.[38] In the United States, the expansion of art houses during the 1950s saw the market for foreign films increase, benefitting in both exhibition and distribution terms from rapid industrial changes with the decline of the classical Hollywood production model. The decrease of B-picture production saw many cinemas seeking alternatives, switching to foreign films to keep businesses open.[39] Television also challenged the traditional dominance of Hollywood, compounded by the fact that foreign films were generally more cheaply made and considered more risqué than what was made under the strict production code.[40] Peter Hutchings noted that from the 1950s onwards, a 'growing internationalization of horror production' flourished and for Tim Bergfelder, international co-productions increased from the mid-1950s in particular.[41]

With the codification of masks from the 1970s onwards, many emerging American horror film-makers surely would have been exposed to foreign cinema, not only in art house cinemas and television but in grindhouses.[42] We now examine some notable instances of horror film masks from France, Mexico, Italy and Japan during this period of rapid internationalisation to demonstrate the increasing codification of masks as a central element of horror iconography. While masks are deployed in notably diverse ways across these different cultural contexts, collectively they illustrate how pervasively masks were employed as both narrative devices and an element of horror iconography imbued with great symbolic power.

France, masks and *Eyes without a Face* (1960)

From Grand Guignol theatre to the legend of 'The Man in the Iron Mask' to films like *Le masque d'horreur* (1912) and *Les trois masques* (1921/1929), masks have a long history in French tales of terror that have proven influential beyond its own national boundaries. The same can be said of Georges Franju's *Eyes without a Face*. The mask was a logical artefact for Franju to employ his pursuit of 'anguish' – a term he himself privileged over 'horror'[43] – due to the production pressures of making a film that would appeal to a number of international markets.[44] *Eyes without a Face* extends the mad scientist trope from Mary Shelley's *Frankenstein* (1818) and H. G. Wells's *The Island of Doctor Moreau* (1896), bringing again a kind of double masking into play. Often disguised by surgical masks, goggles or other facial coverings, mad scientists embody mistrust in science, where transformations of power through the surgical mask in particular create a space to harm instead of heal (discussed in chapter 7). The surgical mask transforms the mad doctor through surgical rituals into sadistic tricksters; they are deceptive, believe in their own god-like capacities and invert scenarios where they are meant to heal into ones where they seek actively to harm.[45] There are echoes of the shaman in the mad scientist: for David J. Skal, 'The mad scientist . . . is a restless synthesizer, scuttling around his laboratory, stitching together our central schisms, digging into graves while pulling down the energy of the sky.'[46]

Eyes without a Face also recalls the figure of the doppelgänger. As Kate Ince noted, even the title implies myriad interpretations: it appears to refer to the protagonist Christiane (Édith Scob), forced to wear the blank white mask over the scar tissue caused by an accident as her deranged father Dr Génessier (Pierre Brasseur) attempts to master facial transplants, kidnapping young women with his accomplice Louise (Alida Valli), who is indebted to him for his successful reconstruction of her own face. Yet there are other eyes without faces: not only, notes Ince, 'the alarming close up on Edna's (an early victim of Dr Génessier, played by Juliette Mayniel) bandaged face and staring eyes after she has jumped from an upstairs window', but in the very masked faces of Génessier himself, hidden as it is behind a surgical mask. For Ince, 'in all these instances, facelessness signifies inhumanity, either imposed and innocently suffered or consciously assumed. Eyes retain their traditional meaning of a window onto the soul: her undamaged eyes glimmering through her mask are a major contributor to the pathos of Christiane's character.'[47]

As expanded on in chapter 5, it is the very blankness of Christiane's mask that renders it a neutral canvas upon which a variety of identities (and interpretations of those identities) can be inscribed. Both Joan Hawkins (2000) and Adam Lowenstein (2005) have argued that Franju's film can be read through post-war France and its involvement in the Second World War. For Hawkins, 'Doctor Génessier's painstaking removal of female skin is reminiscent of the horror stories about lampshades made from the bodies of concentration camp victims'.[48] That it is women who are punished in the film – both Christiane and those murdered in attempts restore her identity – is crucial, and Hawkins notes that 'French guilt over all French collaboration was initially mapped onto women's bodies and it was women who bore the brunt of the punishment for most of the quotidian traffic in German commerce'.[49]

For Lowenstein, the construction (and destruction) of identity is also political in *Eyes without a Face*. For him, the film's moral ambiguity stems from the fact that 'the roles of Christiane as victimized and Génessier as victimizer include complex, double-edged connotations';[50] while we may feel for Christiane, we simultaneously know that she is aware that young women are murdered for her benefit. Although monstrous, Génessier too 'is also granted brief but significant moments of humanity'.[51] For Lowenstein, Franju rejects 'any easy, one-to-one index for his allegories of the Occupation and the Holocaust reflects a commitment to engaging history as a complicated force to be struggled with by the audience, rather than spoon-fed to them'.[52] Franju's ambivalence in the ethical construction of his protagonists is important, the blankness of Christiane's mask providing a metaphorical space for ideological anxieties to be projected onto. This is a strong example of how a variation of traditional mask-wearing rituals (here surgery) can be refashioned through horror to reflect culturally specific ideological debates: it presents old traditions and objects in new contexts to provide social commentary. Identities are destabilised in *Eyes without a Face* and Christiane's blank visage is less a cypher for innocence as it is a slate wiped clean: an identity purified of any traces of a horrible and horrifying 'truth' that lies hidden underneath. Typifying Lowenstein's powerful claim that horror cinema is a 'return to history through the gut', the mask here 'speaks' of what many struggled to articulate about French guilt and complicity during the war.[53] Yet even for audiences who watch the film untethered from the film's historical moment, as a stand-alone horror movie – through the presence and deployment of the mask – its impact is nevertheless still memorable.

Mexico, masks and El Santo

The significance of masks in Mexican culture cannot be understated when considering the El Santo films. For Octavia Paz, masks are the defining metaphor of Mexican identity, arguing that for all Mexicans – regardless of social status or background – 'his face is a mask and so is his smile'.[54] From this perspective, masks govern specifically 'Mexican' behaviours, framing all interactions through this symbolic distancing device. While Paz acknowledged a spirit of nihilism to these metaphorical masks – resultant in large part to a national identity caught between its pre-Columbian origins and the influx of Spanish cultural influences that came with the colonialisation of the Aztecs in the sixteenth century – an awareness of this masking tendency in the Mexican psyche is essential to Mexican culture. Paz identified the Día de los Muertos carnival or fiesta as a significant moment where the dominant 'mask' is exchanged for another, bringing otherwise isolated ('masked') participants – stranded as they are, according to Paz, between two powerful cultural/historical influences – together in a communal experience that privileges death as the ultimate symbol of solitude.

Masks played a crucial role in Mesoamerican culture long before Spanish colonialism. As Alexandra Mendoza Covarrubias noted, Día de los Muertos spans back at least 3,000 years, its origins stemming from both pre-Columbian and Spanish-Catholic cultural influences.[55] Tseëlon traced Mesoamerican masquerade rituals to the pre-classic period during the first millennium BC.[56] Masks have a lengthy tradition in Mexican folk art and anthropologists have explored how pre-colonial traditions have evolved and endured across a range of cultural practices in different regions.[57] Walter Sorell acknowledged the artistry of Aztec death masks, whose very materiality contained potent symbolic and religious force in cremation ceremonies.[58]

The El Santo films offer a significant example of how masking traditions have endured throughout Mexican culture. Doyle Greene noted that these movies dominated the market from 1957 to 1977, combining another popular contemporary Mexican masking tradition – *lucha libre*, or Mexican professional wrestling – with 'films featuring an array of vampires, Aztec mummies, mad scientists, ape-men and various other macabre menace[s]'.[59] Alongside these monsters were *luchadores*, the most famous of which was Santo, *El Santo, el Enmascarado de Plata* or 'The Saint, the Silver-Masked Man'.[60] A more elaborately choreographed adaptation of North American professional wrestling from the 1930s, *lucha libre* is marked by acrobatics, colourful costumes (including iconic full-face masks) and explicitly moral narratives. For Gabrielle Murray, there are intrinsically ritualistic aspects to *lucha libre*, as it 're-enacts a story – a mythic battle between good and evil'.[61] *Lucha libre* 'permits an official transgression whereby members of the audience chant and shout what they cannot voice in "normal" circumstances'.[62] From this perspective, *lucha libre* and the Santo films are twentieth-century incarnations of carnivalesque traditions, emphasised through masks which have a distinct historical significance in Mexican cultural history.

The low-budget Santo films were tremendously popular in Mexico, attracting predominantly working-class audiences.[63] For Evan Lieberman, when *lucha libre* was banned on television in 1954, it found an alternative outlet in film.[64] The success of José Cruz's El Santo *fotonovellas*[65] led to Santo's film career in 1942, the *luchador* never credited by his real name, Rodolfo Guzman Huerta.[66] According to Lieberman, Cruz's *fotonovellas* 'offered the first construction of Santo as the hero of the Mexican people, endowed with superior intelligence, morality and almost superhuman powers'.[67] His mask echoes Mesoamerican religious beliefs, where Peter T. Markman and Roberta H. Markman noted that 'the wearer of the ritual mask almost literally becomes the god; he is, for the ritual moment, the animating force within the otherwise lifeless mask'.[68] Santo's 'super powers' are explicit, and Murray emphasises that he is never seen without his mask: while 'he is "super" in the eyes of his audience but apart from the traits of a champion wrestler – strength, fitness and agility – he has no magical or science based super-powers'. Murray noted that through the mask 'he is a transformed persona . . . capable of creating control, yet due to his human skills, he is also an emphatic figure'.[69] This allows him to straddle 'the strange and fantastic world of the films' and the more traditionally recognisable domain of *lucha libre* wrestling, 'a singular persona who lives in dual worlds and never without his mask'.[70]

Santo's mask historically grounds him as a horror-superhero. For Murray, 'a profound transformation occurs in which the individual withdraws from the everyday and a new a "super" persona is presented'.[71] While undoubtedly 'super' and 'heroic', the construction of Santo's 'superhero-ness' is distinct to that of North American counterparts like Bruce Wayne/Batman, Clark Kent/Superman and Peter Parker/Spiderman: there is no binary persona and no distinction between a public and private face. As Greene suggested, 'Santo, as a real-life *luchador* and a mythic superhero in a horror film, occupies two thoroughly public roles in Mexican society'.[72] On this level, El Santo deviates from the Eurocentric doppelgänger traditions often linked to horror film masks.

The popularity of Santo during this period rose during the international rise of superheroes, while still remaining rooted in *lucha libra* culture and Mexico's cultural history privileging masks. The Santo films maintain this through an object with long-held associations to Mexico's past and through genre render their use and meanings fresh and dynamic. While the label '*luchador* film' emphasises the wrestling aspects of these movies, as their titles indicate, horror was also central:[73] Greene identified *Santo vs. the Vampire Women* (*Santo vs. las Mujeres Vampiro*, Alfonso Corona Blake, 1962) as typical of 'Mexploitation' films that demonstrate a 'simultaneous reliance on and borrowing from classic Hollywood horror films, as well as its disregard for cinematic convention'.[74] Likewise, in *Santo in the Wax Museum* (*Santo en el Museo de Cera*, Alfonso Corona Blake, 1963), Greene suggested that it did not 'merely parod[y] generic horror film conventions, but incorporated key elements from a number of specific classic horror films', such as *Mystery of the Wax Museum* (Michael Curtiz, 1933), *Island of Lost Souls* (Erle C. Kenton, 1933), *Frankenstein* (James Whale, 1931) and *Dracula* (Tod Browning, 1931).[75] Lieberman outlined the relationship between horror and wrestling, emphasizing Santo's background in *fotonovellas* because 'the films [are] . . . comic book fantasies in which wrestling is essentially the day job of the superhero whose true focus is on fighting vampires, mummies and Martians'.[76] These films have little interest in cohesively suturing the wrestling sequences into their otherwise horror plots and, as Murray indicated, 'the films literally intercut large sections of recorded and sometimes staged footage of often complete *lucha libre* matches'.[77]

Like the Santo films themselves, these matches are marked by the presence of mask-wearing heroes and villains. Masks link the Santo films to broader traditions of mask-wearing in Mexican culture and, echoing Paz, Lieberman notes that 'the mask might well be considered the defining icon of Mexican culture'.[78] Santo's *luchador* mask brings Mexico's history of masked ritual traditions into its contemporary moment, Murray noting it allows Santo to enter the realm of the mythic, as it 'not only affects the perception of the wearer but also the audience's perception of the wearer'.[79] The iconic *lucha libra* costume shifts the forum for mask-wearing rituals from the past to the present and the centrality of horror in these films grants a space for the power attained through masked transformation to play out in a continually evolving, slowly codifying generic context. Horror masks adapt to social, national and generic needs.

Italy, masks and *Black Sunday* (1960)

As noted previously, masks are closely linked to Italian cultural history, from Venetian Carnival to the *commedia dell'arte*. Masks appear in Italian films as diverse as Pier Paolo Pasolini's documentary *Love Meetings* (*Comizi d'amore*, 1965) to the romance *The Mask* (*La Maschera*, Fiorella Infascelli, 1988). Masks were not uncommon in Italian peplum or sword-and-sandal films, as indicated by many of their titles alone.[80] But in terms of horror, masks are most explicit in *giallo* cinema, Mikel Koven noting that along with black coats, hats and gloves, masks were 'the *sine qua non* of giallo-killer disguises'.[81] Mario Bava's 1963 film *The Girl Who Knew Too Much* (*La ragazza che sapeva troppo*) is considered 'the first true Italian *giallo*', refined into a more recognisable *giallo* formula the following year with *Blood and Black Lace* (*Sei donne per l'assassino*, 1964).[82] Koven has identified the classic *gialli* period as 1970–5, which would form such a huge influence on the North American slasher cycle of the late 1970s and 1980s that Koven would label the latter 'North American *gialli*'.[83] These include *Happy Birthday to Me*, discussed in chapter 4, a film centring on a black-gloved killer and a masked reveal.

Masks in *Blood and Black Lace* introduce the object as a staple of *giallo* iconography. While blank masks are discussed further in chapter 5, in *Blood and Black Lace* the killer's blank mask does more than simply obscure their identity. As Leon Hunt observed, in *gialli*, 'the mask can conceal gender and point as well in a quite reflexive way to the killer as a function within the text'.[84] In *Blood and Black Lace*, 'the white featureless mask . . . is worn by two different characters and can thus perpetrate a seemingly impossible chain of killings'.[85] While the killers are revealed to be a man and a woman, Hunt observed that even though the mask that means they look the same – rendering gender more fluid (foreshadowing Carol J. Clover's notion of gender fluidity in modern horror, as discussed in the introduction) – their killing methods are themselves gendered: 'the male killer (Cameron Mitchell) scars, burns and disfigures his victims, [while] the female killer (Eva Bartok) suffocates them'.[86]

Blood and Black Lace was not Mario Bava's first use of masks in horror, as indicated by the original Italian title of his 1960 film *Le Maschera del demonio* (*The Mask of Satan*), released internationally as *Black Sunday*. Peter Bondanella suggested that the placement of the mask onto Asa's (Barbara Steele) face is crucial: shot from the victim's perspective, for Bondanella it is 'one of Bava's most famous shots' and while initially 'Bava shoots the mask and its metal prongs from the executioner's point of view . . . he then reverses the perspective in a seamless transition, moving the camera through the apertures and transferring the point of view from that of the executioner to that of the victim'.[87] Martyn Conterio later also identified a similar association between the mask and gender, foreshadowing the meaning of the mask in *Blood and Black Lace*. For Conterio, 'the mask, as well as functioning as a cruel and unusual torture device, also plays a deeply misogynistic role'.[88] Conterio suggests that, in *Black Sunday*, Prince Vafja (Ivo Garrani) 'wants to destroy and deny the woman her own face and substitute it with the mask',whereby 'beyond its use as an instrument of torture and wrecker of beauty, the mask is a supernatural talisman imbued with abilities to ward off evil'.[89] The failure of the mask to do so is emphasised by the film's most iconic image: Steele's pierced face. While many of the film's posters privilege the mask, it is the visible evidence of the mask's damage to Asa's face rather than the mask itself that is key. The significance of the mask and its transformative potential is again inextricably linked to ritual, power and transformation.

Japan, masks and *Onibaba* (1964)

Like France, Mexico and Italy, Japanese horror cinema recalls its own mask heritage while simultaneously using its generic logic to engage with and adhere to international trends. As noted earlier, *A Page of Madness* suggests a complex historical relationship between masks and Japanese horror cinema (see previous chapter). For Zvika Serper, two Japanese horror films from the 1960s by Kaneto Shindô – *Onibaba* (1964) and *Kuroneko* (1968) – are both historical supernatural drama films that share a similar premise: a woman and her mother-in-law target and kill samurai.[90] In the former, the film's climactic action is centred around a demon mask, providing one of the most enduring images of Japanese horror cinema. Both *Kuroneko* and *Onibaba* represent a conscious effort on Shindô's part to represent the determination of 'common people for survival', and to do so he harnessed aspects of traditional Japanese theatre and literature to 'constitute a very important performative embodiment of the ritualistic demonic pattern, borrowed from the traditional aristocratic Noh and popular kabuki theatre'.[91] This is crucial both in terms of Japanese horror cinema and to histories of horror film masks more generally. This is far more complex than appropriation; rather, it is a dynamic process of evolution where meanings and values ascribed to masks throughout history and across different cultures provide ways of conceiving the power of the object through its transformative potential. The mask in *Onibaba* and its relationship to Japanese performance traditions demonstrates this potency.

The exact type of mask used in *Onibaba* is important. In Noh, the two distinct types of demons are understood through a taxonomy outlined by Noh master Zeami Motokiyo as being defined as either powerful (*rikidofu*) or unstable (*saidofu*) demons. In the case of the latter, for Serper 'the extent of the demonic aspect manifested in the human being is varied in the plays through different kinds of demonic masks and through the modes of performance'.[92] It is through this distinction that both *Kuroneko* and *Onibaba* mark a radical departure from Noh because, as Serper notes, these two rarely overlap or intersect. By combining them, Shindô 'created very original and complex narratives of the quintessential Japanese ritualistic embodiment of vanquishing a demonic threat'.[93] Further observing that the mask in *Onibaba* was a *hannya* mask – rarely used in Noh plays – it uniquely represents two types of ritualistic embodiment: female jealousy and revealing the true nature of a demon in human disguise.[94]

But the use of the mask – and the disfigurement caused by the act of unmasking – has for Colette Balmain and Adam Lowenstein far greater significance than this connection to Noh traditions. For Balmain, *Onibaba* was a logical progression from Shindô's previous films that dealt with the atomic attack on Japan (such as *Children of Hiroshima* (1952) and 1959's *Lucky Dragon No. 5*), noting that '*Onibaba* also makes explicit disfigurement as metonymic signifier of war trauma'.[95] For Lowenstein, even the make-up on the mother-in-law's face when the mask was removed was based on wounds of actual nuclear attack survivors (*Hibakusha*).[96] Similar to his analysis of *Eyes without a Face*, for Lowenstein the use of the mask here also pertains to the ethical status of the mask-wearer themselves: the older woman is both villain and victim, the very component 'that unlocks the film's ambivalent presentation of victimization and war responsibility, as well as the anchor for the film's recasting of traditional gender iconography surrounding these issues).[97] Here lies the difficulty in unequivocally defining the mother-in-law as either human or demon: 'The film's conclusion exists between the two terms, both thematically and cinematically', noted Lowenstein. While the younger woman successfully jumps over the hole, it is unclear what happens to the older woman when she follows, which Lowenstein suggested prompts 'questions central to rethinking discourses of victimization and war responsibility in relation to Hiroshima'.[98] *Onibaba* is therefore less of a *continuation* of Noh traditions, but rather a conscious *rupturing* of them. Recalling Barbara Steele in *Black Sunday* and its corruption of Carnival and *commedia dell'arte* traditions, for Lowenstein the mask in *Onibaba* 'does not celebrate the classical Japanese theatrical tradition; instead, it functions as an affliction'.[99] Although historical in context, *Onibaba* speaks of a new Japan faced with a post-war crisis of identity, brought to life through a mask whose transformative power renders it both corrupted and corrupting.

As seen across these different national contexts throughout the 1960s, although masks were used in horror in a range of different ways, together they demonstrate the symbolic force of the mask and how it was becoming codified as a key aspect of horror cinema's iconography. These films illustrate how combining older histories and traditions linked to masks with the new symbolic possibilities the horror genre afforded them provided a way to allegorically articulate often profound social or ideological commentary. While the previous chapter explored the development of how masks were used in cinema and the various aspects that were incorporated into pre-cinema and early film history, this chapter has more closely considered horror as it became more widely identifiable as a genre, from *The Phantom of the Opera* onwards, through the 1930s, 1940s and 1950s, towards the growing internationalisation of horror in the 1960s. In Part Two and Three – across the categories of skin masks, blank masks, animal masks, repurposed masks and technological masks – we can explore precisely how horror film masks rely on Neale's process of 'repetition . . . difference, variation and change' to largely account for their longevity as a key iconographic element of the genre.[100] Across these case studies, ritual, power and transformation continue to intersect in ways that account for the object's endurance as a compelling motif in horror cinema.

PART TWO

HORROR FILM MASKS FROM 1970 – CASE STUDIES

4

Skin Masks
Ritual, Power and Transformation

PART ONE explored a range of literary and performance traditions, specific films and other cultural phenomena that led to the codification of masks as a key iconographic element of horror cinema from the 1970s onwards. This culminated most visibly in the explosion of slasher films popular during this period with films like John Carpenter's *Halloween* and Tobe Hooper's *The Texas Chain Saw Massacre*, both of which privilege masks. While masks are a notable iconographic aspect of the slasher subgenre, they permeated a range of horror films globally, especially from 1970 onwards. Part Two offers case studies that employ masks in diverse ways that simultaneously still maintain a fascination with ritual, power and transformation through horror film masks in some way. The following four chapters are loosely themed under the taxonomical umbrellas skin masks, blank masks, animal masks and repurposed masks accounting for the most typically deployed masks beyond the relatively self-explanatory Halloween style 'fright' masks (skulls, monsters, etc.). Part Three will then turn towards what might be easy to conceive as a more contemporary category – technological masks – but this will itself be revealed to have significant history as well as simultaneously giving us an idea of the future territory masked horror films may continue to take. To underscore diversity as well as similarity, we will explore movies made by film-makers from Argentina, Australia, Canada, France, Italy, Japan, Nigeria, South Korea, Sweden, the United Kingdom and the United States.

Skin masks as they are conceived here refer simply to masks that replicate the human face: regardless of their materiality (flesh-coloured latex, fibreglass, etc.), the wearing of these masks denotes overt performativity, where wearers either attempt to disguise themselves as someone else (*Happy Birthday to Me*), to present reconstructed versions of the wearer (*The Abominable Dr. Phibes*), to provide an ominous, synthetic subversion of 'humanness' (*Alice Sweet Alice* and *Curtains*) or – as in *The Texas Chain Saw Massacre* and *Smiley* – to offer performances that dehumanise their wearers through the corruption of human skin itself, literally detaching and re-stitching the organ in grotesque replication of perceptibly 'natural' faces. The performativity associated with skin masks is crucial to the ideological force of these films, selected because each in their own way critique patriarchy, in particular in their often-explicit engagements with class, gender, age and other points of difference. Echoing Neale, they are each driven by a process of similarity and difference, overlapping to maintain their status as recognisably horror films, yet diverging in fresh – and sometimes challenging – ways.

Across both shamanic[1] and performance traditions like the *commedia dell'arte*,[2] leather face-like masks were common in transformation rituals. Through the shamanic imagination, traces of this remain in horror film skin masks. Skin masks are also aligned with shaman-as-trickster traditions, the films here offering different instances of transgressive playfulness: in Dr Phibes's elaborate murders that rely heavily on the predictable behaviour of his victims; in the perverse corruption of First Communion in *Alice Sweet Alice*; in the logic-defying movement of the killer in *Curtains*; in the famous dinner table sequence in *The Texas Chain Saw Massacre* that subverts the quotidian act to darkly comic cannibalistic ritual; in the grisly birthday party/murder scene vignette in *Happy Birthday to Me*; and in the excessive intersection of meme-aligned 'lulz' with serial killing in *Smiley*. If, as Ricki Stefanie Tannen notes, tricksters are defined by 'a playful energy which has the capacity to produce humor that can trigger transformation', that 'playful energy' in this chapter takes a dark shape, reliant on transformations that, through skin masks, engage with both ritual and power.[3]

Recalling doppelgänger traditions, implicit in skin masks are notions of authenticity and duplicity: the 'second face' of the mask must be distinct from the supposedly 'real' face underneath. In mystery horror films with skin masks that narratively hinge on revelation, the function of this doubling is clear: in *Tourist Trap* (David Schmoeller, 1979) and *New Year's Evil* (Emmett Alston, 1980), the mask obscures the identity of the individual underneath, the revelation of which is the dénouement. Yet this is not always the case: in *Mr Sardonicus*, *The Frankenstein Syndrome* (Scott Tretta, 2010) and Fuest's *Dr. Phibes* films (1971/1972), human face skin masks cover wounds or scars: it is not the wearer's identity that sparks curiosity, but the *severity* of their injuries (in these examples, all explicitly framed as monstrous 'deformations'). Yet even within the category, skin masks that replicate human faces demonstrate notable diversity: for example, the masks in *Happy Death Day* (Christopher B. Landon, 2017) and *The Spearhead Effect* (Brandon Moore and Caleb Smith, 2017) are explicitly cartoony (echoing Warner Bros. vintage cartoons and anime respectively) while the masks in *Kill Game* (Robert Mearns, 2017) and *Terror Train* (Roger Spottiswoode, 1980) subvert the star images of Marilyn Monroe in the former and Groucho Marx in the latter into something far more malign.

The films explored here use skin masks to critique or subvert patriarchal norms, with varying success. For William Anthony Sheppard, some masked traditions encourage a similar gender fluidity that Carol J. Clover identifies in horror more generally (as discussed earlier), the former noting 'a mask that is relatively naturalistic in appearance often functions as a device for gender reversal – an additional form of concealment and transformation'.[4] Traditionally, masks allowed male performers to adopt female identities through performance rituals and that 'the prevalent use of masks for gender disguise in exotic – particularly Asian – theater traditions reinforced Euro-American dreams of the East as a sexually open paradise'.[5] Some horror films invert shamanic mask traditions by rendering them tools against patriarchy, continuing their subversive, carnivalesque potential. In the films here, skin masks complicate assumptions about the gender, identity and/or the age of the wearer (*Alice Sweet Alice*, *Curtains*, *The Texas Chain Saw Massacre*, *Happy Birthday to Me*), or collapse distinctions between the human and monstrous altogether (*The Abominable Dr. Phibes*, *Smiley*). Despite their diversity, these films utilise skin masks to critique, mock and interrogate patriarchy through transformation and ritual.

Skin Masks and Religion: *The Abominable Dr. Phibes* (1971) and *Alice Sweet Alice* (1976)

Robert Fuest's British/American co-production *The Abominable Dr. Phibes* provides a useful point to begin my case study component for a number of reasons, most notably in its casting of Vincent Price, a key figure in masked horror film as discussed previously. Just as important, however, are the centrality of religious and other rituals in the film and the centrality of masks to them. The ritualistic nature of Phibes's serial murders as he kills those he holds responsible for the death of his late wife Victoria (Caroline Munro) transcends their explicit reliance on biblical text. Phibes does not seek to reaffirm Christian ritual, but rather – in true trickster fashion – to mock and subvert it. As John E. Parnum noted, at each death scene Phibes 'ritualistically drapes an amulet around a clay bust of the victim and sprays the statue with a blow torch'.[6] In *The Abominable Dr. Phibes*, it is not only the frog mask murder device in the second killing that privileges masks within the film, but more crucially that worn by Phibes himself. As revealed at the climax, the 'human' Vincent Price-faced skin-like mask is worn by Phibes to hide the scarred remains of his face, burnt in a car accident as he rushed towards the hospital where Victoria died. This is itself an inversion of sorts, as Phibes's actual face of sinew and bone is hidden beneath his 'true' mask-face. Facial damage is part of Phibes's criminal modus operandi: his first victim is disfigured by bats, a nurse's face has the flesh removed by locusts and an off-screen murder by bee sting is also mentioned in terms of a specifically facial assault. To further emphasise the face, Phibes uses a blow torch to melt wax busts of his victims.

While the biblical references to the Ten Plagues of Egypt that structure Phibes's murders offer an explicit link to religious ritual, masks themselves are also used ritualistically. As Rick Worland noted, this includes intertextual nods to earlier horror movie masks, including *The Phantom of the Opera* (1925/1930) and Price's earlier *House of Wax* (André de Toth, 1953).[7] Like Erik in *The Phantom of the Opera*, Phibes is both monstrous and sympathetic; Patricia MacCormack observes that his 'revenge comes from the tender love for his dead wife'.[8] The film is also marked by excessive campness, and Steve Chibnall notes that it is 'saturated . . . with Gothic excess, self-satire and ironic quotation'.[9] Like *House of Wax*, Price 'portrays a character whose face has been horribly burned . . . [who] must wear a "Vincent Price" disguise to cover his disfigurement'.[10] Whether the film is understood as a dark love story or a parody of earlier horror movies, Phibes subjectivity is crucial: his status as hero-villain is linked to Price's broader star persona and as Schechner noted, these personae are themselves 'masks' of sorts.[11] The 'Phibes mask' – understood through the actor's star persona as a 'Price mask' also – is central to both the film's narrative and spectacle, the complex dynamics of the mask itself replicating doppelgänger-like identities. The mask-wearing Price aligns this film intertextually with his previous horror masked roles: we 'read' Phibes and the meaning of his masks alongside movies like *House of Wax*, *The Masque of the Red Death* and *The Oblong Box*. In all these films, masked, transformed Price is deranged and traumatised, leading to abuses of power.

Straddling life and death and empowered through rituals of masked performance, Phibes typifies Larry Ellis's description of the trickster as a 'shaman of the liminal'.[12] Phibes adheres almost completely to William J. Hynes's trickster definition checklist: he is ambiguous, deceptive and plays tricks, and his behaviour encompasses the sacred and the profane in his imitation of God.[13] Price's casting as masked trickster Phibes is essential to this subversion of religiosity in particular. For Karen Hollinger, stars 'serve as totems or gods and goddesses in a pseudoreligion of fandom', Phibes's *own* mask – that of Price's face – holds additional 'religious' significance in the film on top of its biblical references.[14] The latter is of course notable: in their comparative analysis of Phibes and Jigsaw from the *Saw* franchise, Fernando G. Pagnoni Berns and Amy M. Davis identified a God-like aspect in the former as he 'literally takes on this role when he unleashes the ten plagues of Egypt on his unsuspecting victims'.[15] The meticulous execution of his plans implies infallibility and this contains 'divine aspects'.[16] For Pagnoni Berns and Davis, Phibes's mask is essential because 'most of the victims of Phibes' reenactment of divine punishment never have the opportunity to see Phibes' actual face'.[17] The obscuration of Phibes's real face by a mask suggests therefore that 'if humans are an imperfect copy of a divine creator, Phibes takes refuge in human skin to hide the 'true' face of humanity, the true face of God'.[18] The use of skin masks in *The Abominable Dr. Phibes* is thus connected to religion and ritual in overlapping ways: first, how masks intersect with biblical references and, more significantly, to these theological aspects of Price/Phibes as 'god-like' himself. Phibes affirms the link to the divine near the film's conclusion where he cries: 'Don't cry upon God . . . he is on my side. *He* led me, showed me the way in *my* quest for vengeance.'

Phibes's mask can also be understood as a subversive demasculinisation of the deity. Drawing comparisons between Phibes and Baron Otto von Kleist (played by *Phibes* co-star Joseph Cotton) in *Baron Blood* (Mario Bava, 1972), MacCormack notes that the stripping away of their skin removes them from an otherwise assumed gender binary: 'the perception of their living skull-heads present, like zombies, an ambivalent definition of "life" and particularly because the facialized upright head is the grand symbol of "the human" theirs are inhuman heads'.[19] Although biologically male, 'they appear simultaneously anatomically generic, gender neutral, their heads both raw defleshed wounds and primitive canvasses upon which new faces are worn as masks'.[20] When applied to *Phibes*, masking contributes to the radical and pronounced deconstruction of identity and power. In *The Abominable Dr. Phibes*, ritual, power and transformation intersect with masks in complex, myriad ways.

The skin-like face mask in *Alice Sweet Alice* also reconfigures recognisable religious rituals to interrogate gender performativity, here regarding women and age. For Victor Turner, the very difference that marks women's bodies from men render them subversive, not for their potential *capacity* for subversion, but simply by not being male:

> The danger . . . is not simply that of female 'unruliness'. This unruliness itself is the mark of . . . the perilous realm of possibility of 'anything may go' which threatens any social order and seems more threatening, the more that order seems rigorous and secure.

He continued, 'The subversive potential of the carnivalized feminine principle becomes evident in times of social change when its manifestations move out of the liminal world of Mardi Gras into the political arena itself.'[21] Through its evocation of the shamanic imagination – a cultural imaginary spawned from (but distinct to) orthodox, anthropologically defined visions of shamanism – like masked Carnival play, the mask here is granted an unspoken power to not merely disguise the identity of the murderer, but to reductively transform those who wear it (a young girl and an older woman) into a literally synthetic state of idealised womanhood. Turner's 'subversive potential of the carnivalized feminine principle' that these women embody is marked as much by gender as it is their actions. Alice's transformation in the liminal space of adolescence – between girlhood and womanhood – is configured as an inescapably violent transition. The mask is fundamental to the gender politics of *Alice Sweet Alice* through its association with ritual, power and transformation, as Alice indulges in a transgressive, trickster-like desire for deception, subversion and play.

While the mask in *Alice Sweet Alice* appears to simply obscure the killer's identity, its function is more complex. Initially, the film suggests that Alice herself (Paula E. Sheppard) is the killer because we see her wearing it and the mask belongs to her. But the killer is later revealed to be Mrs Tredoni (Mildred Clinton) – the housekeeper of Alice's family priest, Father Tom (Rudolph Willrich) – who wears an identical mask and yellow raincoat to Alice to cast suspicion onto the young girl. Like *The Abominable Dr. Phibes*, religion and ritual are central to *Alice Sweet Alice*, but while Phibes's mask subverts gender assumptions about divine power, in *Alice Sweet Alice*, the mask is a tool to explore feminine identities beyond adult womanhood, exposing the complex and difficult spaces of adolescent girls and older women within the patriarchal constructs of Roman Catholicism.

The opening credits foreshadow this with a subversion of Roman Catholic imagery where assumptions about gender and facial disguise are central. A silhouette of a girl in First Holy Communion garb prays as a veil obscures her face. She holds a large crucifix, revealed at the end of the sequence to also be a knife. Symbolic religious innocence is subverted through the corruption of sacred religious ritual, reconfiguring the symbol of girlhood purity as violent and deceptive (a contradiction echoed in the film's title: although not a killer, Alice is far from 'sweet'). From the outset, relationships between women are privileged – not only between Alice, her mother Catherine (Linda Miller) and spoilt younger sister Karen (Brooke Shields), but also between Alice and Mrs Tredoni. The latter is established as Alice – jealous of Karen – wears a cheap plastic Halloween mask to frighten Mrs Tredoni. Returning home, disgraced Alice seeks refuge in the basement where she performs a strange ritual with Karen's favourite doll, the plastic mask looking down on her from the wall where she has reverently placed it.

When Karen is murdered at her First Holy Communion ceremony by a figure wearing this mask, Alice is the implied perpetrator: through ritual, the mask is central to her violent transformation. Despite the killer being Mrs Tredoni – driven by a repressed sexual jealousy of Catherine's relationship with Father Tom (Rudolph Willrich) – the two women representing early and later womanhood (the younger Alice, the older Mrs Tredoni) remain symbolically connected through the mask. At the film's conclusion, despite her innocence, Alice is neither vindicated, nor configured as innocent. Having witnessed Mrs Tredoni kill Father Tom at the church altar in a ritualistic embrace blurring the maternal and sexual, Alice picks up her knife and leaves the church, looking directly at the camera as the film freezes on an image of her face. This look is important: accusatory in nature, there is an unspoken suggestion that the audience who has just enjoyed the film's perverse spectacle are themselves partially culpable for maintaining cultural assumptions about gender and age that have driven both Alice and Mrs Tredoni over the edge. While the utility of the mask blurred Mrs Tredoni and Alice's identities to create suspense surrounding the killer's identity, despite Mrs Tredoni being the guilty party, the film implies that Alice may continue Mrs Tredoni's violent legacy. The patriarchal hegemony of the Roman Catholic Church is fundamental to the film's exploration of gender identity and violence associated with the mask. As Tony Williams noted, 'although Alice ends with community realization of Alice's innocence she, too, becomes polluted by the social system'.[22] For Claire Sisco King, the 'sacrificial masculinity' of Father Tom is central to *Alice Sweet Alice*, placing particular emphasis upon 'the cinematic performance of ritual sacrifice and gender performativity' as 'a key regulatory practice within the performative matrix of hegemonic masculinity'.[23]

But there are non-religious rituals where the mask is central in the film also. The type of mask is important because it deliberately obscures the *age* of its wearer: its cheap plastic surface creates smooth skin and blue eye shadow and red lipstick imply excessive femininity. This mask represents the forced neutralisation and eradication of female difference regarding age. The style of make-up would be inappropriate for either 12-year-old Alice or the older Mrs Tredoni: it is the make-up of idealised femininity, that of an adult woman in her twenties, thirties or forties and not deemed culturally 'appropriate' for an older woman or a child. Gender performativity is thus flagged through this mask, whose very materiality denotes an overtly staged 'plastic' or synthetic transformation. Recalling Judith Butler's work on gender performativity, the film demonstrates that 'There is no gender identity behind the expressions of gender ... identity is performatively constituted by the very "expressions" that are said to be its results.'[24] In *Alice Sweet Alice*, through the idealised adult woman mask and the subsequent implied demonisation of the non-idealised women who wear it – Alice in the liminal space between birth and womanhood and Mrs Tredoni in the liminal space between menopause and death – these characters subvert rituals of gender performance through trickster-like play with representations of womanhood culturally out of synch with their own ages. Through the mask, 'corrupted' performances of femininity by both Alice and Mrs Tredoni are rendered insane and violent. For Alice, this tension stems from her transitional status as not-girl and not-woman:

in the film's opening scene, Catherine reprimands her for frightening Mrs Tredoni with the mask by saying 'try to act like a lady', pressuring Alice to 'perform' womanhood. More troubling is the scene where Alice is questioned by police, male officers asking each other 'did you see her tits?' – offensive to a woman of any age, but particularly uncomfortable with a female character just beginning puberty. This is complicated further by the fact that actor Paula E. Sheppard who played Alice was 19-years-old, significantly more 'womanly' than the character herself.[25]

Alice Sweet Alice reflexively manipulates mask-wearing traditions, employing this now-codified iconographic element of horror cinema to subvert and critique patriarchy. *Alice Sweet Alice* reveals how patriarchal power endures through Roman Catholic ritual in particular. Through the mask, both Mrs Tredoni and Alice use the tools of traditional religious ritual to undermine masculine power: recalling the carnivalesque, they invert rules and rupture the dominant order. The passing on of the mask at the end of the film is a symbolic ellipsis suggesting that this rupturing will continue, this seriality as much a codified aspect of contemporary horror as the use of masks themselves.[26] Mrs Tredoni and Alice ultimately represent what Ricki Stefanie Tannen identified as the postmodern female trickster because their embodied playfulness has a concrete mission to thwart patriarchal dominance. The sadism of both characters are extreme manifestations of the 'social work' Tannen considered central to this figure, 'part of the transformed ethical orientation . . . which results in the construction of an identity which refuses to be a victim'.[27] As now revealed in *The Texas Chain Saw Massacre* and *Curtains*, the intersection of masks, ritual, power, transformation and gender performativity are not specific to *Alice Sweet Alice* and *The Abominable Dr. Phibes*.

Skin Masks and Feminine Identity: *The Texas Chain Saw Massacre* (1974) and *Curtains* (1983)

Gender performativity also provides insight into the role of masks in *The Texas Chain Saw Massacre*. While often cited as a key film in the history of the slasher subgenre,[28] for Christopher Sharrett this undermines its broader importance as it 'represents a crucial moment in the history of the horror genre, when the form develops a specific relationship to the historical and cultural tendencies of America . . . and to a distinct period of discontent in American society'.[29] While *The Texas Chain Saw*

Massacre engages with ritual in a number of ways, we here focus primarily on that related to masks. So essential are skin masks in the film that its central antagonist is famously credited as Leatherface (Gunnar Hansen). Leatherface has been a durable figure for adaptation, his legacy spanning from the formal (in the many remakes and sequels) to imitators whose films hinge around similar (sometimes identical) masks, such as *Mask Maker* (Griff Furst, 2010), *XII* (Michael A. Nickles, 2008) and *Two: Thirteen* (Charles Adelman, 2009).

Leatherface's mask is linked to ritual in ways that fluctuate between the sacred and secular. The film playfully acknowledges – even mocks – these ritualistic elements: astrology is introduced early as a continuing motif, inverting Pagnoni Berns and Davis's observation that Phibes – who, through the wearing of a face mask and his role as a controlling force in the bulk of the film's action, can be considered 'the "King Sun", the center of the cosmic system'[30] – represents order. But in *The Texas Chain Saw Massacre*, the evocation of astrology implies collapse. As Robin Wood suggests, 'we infer near the opening of *Massacre* that the Age of Aquarius . . . has already passed, giving way to the Age of Saturn and universal malevolence'.[31] While astrology suggests cosmic order, within the film it is mocked, undermined and maligned. Even before arriving at the house where the film's horrific action is set, ritual is linked to violence and chaos, such as when the hitchhiker (Edwin Neal) cuts his hand to curse the young travellers. Ritual is further emphasised through the vast numbers of corpses and bones used to decorate Leatherface and his family's home, implying that they have gone more successfully through the grizzly routine we witness many times beforehand. Even John Laroquette's documentary-style voice-over at the beginning claiming it is a 'true story' infers a conscious restaging of past events; however tenuous, this claim of authenticity again recalls Eliade's privileging of re-enactment as an essential aspect of religious ritual.[32] As Sharrett noted of the socio-political turmoil in the United States at the time of production, the film's 'ritual violence . . . has important implications when considered against the backdrop of repetition on a broad social level, as a form of collective experience denying the foundations of crisis'.[33] Here ritual implies a desperate clinging to the fragmented remains of traditional order that once marked patriarchal control, now reduced to chaos.

Of the numerous rituals in *The Texas Chain Saw Massacre*, cannibalism may have received the most critical attention.[34] While not explicit, it is strongly implied and as Rose noted it is critically often linked to economic themes: 'consumer has turned upon consumer and, quite literally, consumed them. Cannibalism has become not just a breaking of a taboo but simply the basest and most extreme form of consumerism.'[35] For Sharrett, 'Leatherface and his family are products of oppression by industrial capitalism', and cannibalism is central to his reading of the film, citing it as key to its primal-mythic focus.[36] Leatherface and his family excessively evoke 'primitivism', from the connection between mask-wearing and shamanism to their dedication to anachronistic rituals and the film's allusions to cannibalism. As critics have noted, associations between cannibalism and shamanism are not uncommon, despite the lack of evidence to suggest such claims.[37]

Ritual also relates to Leatherface's masks themselves. He has three masks, each given a different name by the cast and crew relating to how they understood the character had transformed when a different mask was worn: the 'Pretty Woman', the 'Old Lady' and the 'Killing Mask'.[38] As Leatherface actor Gunnar Hansen noted, in the dinner scene he wore 'the pretty woman . . . because we had company and he was getting all dressed up for dinner, so he put on the pretty face'.[39] In the presence of the now-feminised Leatherface, a crude nuclear family takes shape with abusive husband (Jim Siedow), hitchhiker son and the barely human grandfather (John Dugan). 'Pretty woman' Leatherface is abused by the family's patriarch, transforming Leatherface into a gendered victim of male violence through the ritualistic wearing of this mask, underscoring the family's perception of what 'woman' means. Marked by the absence of biologically defined women, so complete is their commitment to a ritualistic performance of excessive patriarchal domesticity that Leatherface is forced to fill the gaps in their 'cast'. That this 'performance' is staged for Sally (Marilyn Burns) – the embodiment of the modern woman in the film – and that she survives suggests a strengthening of progressive, civilised order: the film suggests that patriarchy has cannibalised itself. On an unconscious level, the construction of the masks themselves supports this: shamanic traditions of east Greenland required that 'skin masks were sewn by women, whereas the wooden masks were carved by men',[40] and sewing is understood traditionally in the West at least as 'woman's work'.[41] The materiality and production of Leatherface's masks link him to gendered craft traditions.

Leatherface's masked transformations continue after Sally's escape. While the hitchhiker immediately pursues her after she leaps through a window, Leatherface stops long enough at least to change out of feminised clothing and back into his (male) killer outfit. As evidence of the film's critique of capitalism, Johan Höglund notes here that he is dressed 'in the uniform of the middle-class: the suit, the white shirt and the tie',[42] which stands in contrast to Leatherface's re-gendering and feminisation during masked and costumed transformation in the ritualistic reconstruction of the dinner scene, subverting idealised domesticity. Rather than consolidating a single, traditional gendered identity, this symbolic rejection of stable gender identities in a fictional world seemingly dominated by binaries of 'male' and 'female' roles fracture Leatherface to the point where, as Rose notes, Leatherface is marked if anything by a significant *nothingness*.[43] This echoes Hansen's own observation that 'the mask reflected who he was now – my feeling was that under the mask there was nothing – if you take the mask away there's no face there'.[44]

Sally's survival thus exposes the monstrous family's performance for what it is: a perverse simulation rather than an actual example of functional domesticity. Leatherface's failure to control Sally undermines the historicised rituals linked to patriarchal power, rituals that are depicted in excessive, darkly comic ways as anachronistic. Masked transformations and rituals are therefore unstable, and Sharrett notes that 'Leatherface's mask does not have the social function of some ritual acts; it merely serves to cover up and terrorise by reminding the spectator of corruption, the degradation of the flesh, disease, insanity. Death.'[45] This renders *The Texas Chainsaw Massacre* so profoundly emblematic of the despair synonymous with independent American horror cinema during this period.[46]

The Canadian slasher film *Curtains* also utilises masks in a manner that speaks to gendered performance, transformation, ritual and power. Like *Alice Sweet Alice*, *Curtains* focuses on gender performativity in specific regard to women and age. The film begins as actor Samantha Sherwood (Samantha Eggar) feigns a psychological collapse so her director and partner Jonathan Stryker (John Vernon) can have her committed to a psychiatric institution for her to research her starring role as a mentally unstable woman called Audra in Stryker's upcoming film of the same name. While incarcerated, Samantha discovers Stryker has cast the role without her, leaving her institutionalised while he 'auditions' a series of younger women on the casting couch. Outraged, she escapes and joins Stryker and the young women at an isolated house and as a series of murders begins it is implied that Sherwood has genuine mental health issues that culminate in extreme violence.

Samantha's assumed guilt is linked to the implication within the film that she is too old to play Audra, reflected by the extreme, caricature-like representation of older women depicted in the killer's mask. In one scene, this – and Stryker's awareness of Samantha's sensitivity to her age and fears of professional and sexual redundancy – is made explicit.[47] In a group performance workshop, Stryker tells Samantha 'make yourself ugly for us' and throws her the same mask that the killer has worn, a grotesque parody of an older woman's face. Removing the mask, he forces her look at her own distorted reflection in a broken mirror as he squeezes her face, saying 'This is a mask, too.' At the film's conclusion, Samantha confesses to young comedian and aspiring actor Patti (Lynne Griffin) that she shot Stryker and one of the girls, Brooke (Linda Thorson) after discovering them post-coitus and explains her fury at Stryker abandoning her. Importantly, Rose Butler links Patti's occupation as a comic to the 'clown trope of horror cinema', which in turn allows an association with broader trickster traditions and their relationship to masks and the shamanic imagination as outlined previously.[48] Patti admits that she killed everyone else so as to attain the role of Audra and then stabs Samantha. The film concludes with the institutionalised Patti performing Audra on stage in a psychiatric hospital to a room of disinterested fellow patients.

The skin mask in *Curtains* not only obscures the killers' identities, but is also deployed explicitly within the diegesis as a performance tool. Recalling Judith Butler's observation that 'gender is always a doing', the overt theatricality of the mask highlights the professional imbalances that exist for women over certain ages.[49] This mask exemplifies Barbara Creed's notion of the monstrous-feminine, typical of the witch who is configured as 'an old, ugly crone who is capable of monstrous acts'.[50] In her analysis of late medieval literature, Sarah Allison Miller noted that in France, England and Italy there is evidence of 'clear concerns about female destructive powers' in women of a certain age – of the 60,000 women executed for witchcraft from the fourteenth to sixteenth centuries, the bulk were women in the later stages of life.[51]

Because of her age, Samantha is Othered by her younger colleagues, who Stryker considers more desirable because of their youth. This drives the aforementioned scene where Stryker uses a mask to sexually and professionally humiliate Samantha, forcing upon her through the mask the 'performance' of monstrous older womanhood. Stryker and the broader patriarchy he represents are therefore by the film's own logic responsible for her violent tendencies via his active process of dehumanisation (she is 'old', therefore monstrous, therefore explicitly denied humanness). Unable to escape the socially assumed role of 'killer crone' because of her gender and age, like Alice and Mrs Tredoni in *Alice Sweet Alice*, through the mask Samantha struggles with preconceived performance templates of what and how the category of 'woman' means for women at different ages, resulting in a mental health collapse.

At play are pressures that circulate around what Miriam Bernard, Pat Chambers and Gillian Granville have identified as the symbolic invisibility of women 'in mid-life and beyond', not just culturally but even as subjects of academic research.[52] Samantha seeks professional visibility, but her forced monstrosity typifies Deborah Jermyn and Su Holmes's observation that 'in a youth-obsessed culture the everyday lives and appearances of older people remain "Other"', reliant upon assumptions 'of ageing being scary, the stuff of horror films and frightening folklore'.[53] The mask in *Curtains* renders Samantha's difference excessive, therefore continuing 'historical, reflexive accounts of the damaging machinery of fame and its particularly punishing ramifications for older women' alongside films like *Sunset Boulevard* (Billy Wilder, 1950) and *What Ever Happened to Baby Jane* (Robert Aldrich, 1962).[54]

As Patti demonstrates in *Curtains*, however, even for women who adhere to what Stryker and the masculine authority he represents consider desirable, the human life cycle render it a necessarily fleeting stage. For Jermyn and Holmes, the question 'When does a woman become an "old woman?"' is challenging because 'we are all, by the simple virtue of living and breathing, becoming "older" all the time'.[55] Patti understands this when Stryker tells mask-wearing Samantha in the improvisation scene, 'What if your face were different? It could be one day, you know. Hideous, repulsive.' Stryker's cruelty articulates patriarchal assumptions that age determines feminine 'redundancy'. Knowing that she cannot escape her own propensity to age, Patti – through the mask – adopts the role of 'old woman' as a weapon, embracing what Stryker configured as Othered monstrosity in a transformative act of transgression and aggression.

Like *The Texas Chain Saw Massacre*, *Curtains* interrogates gender performativity, patriarchal dominance and ritual practices related to capitalism through human face skin masks. With a narrative that relies on the so-called 'casting couch' phenomenon that has plagued film industries around the world, as noted by figures including Roger Ebert, Ann Hornaday and Deborah Martinson it contains fundamentally ritual aspects.[56] For Jim Rutenberg, Rachel Abrams and Melena Ryzikoct, the casting couch is 'the symbol of ritualized abuse that studio chiefs meted out in trading roles for sexual favors'.[57] In *Curtains*, casting couch rituals of workplace harassment intersect spectacularly through the mask via rituals of masked performance and the familiar structures of the slasher film to reveal institutionalised discrimination.[58]

While the transformative blurring of gender skin masks is central to *The Abominable Dr. Phibes* and *The Texas Chain Saw Massacre*, in *Alice Sweet Alice* and *Curtains* the pressure of maintaining unsustainable performances of idealised womanhood drive its women trapped in hegemonic systems of harassment and abuse to psychological collapse. As we now explore in *Happy Birthday to Me* and *Smiley*, class is also a point of difference that marks power inequalities worthy of critical examination when considering ritual in relation to the transformative capacity of skin masks in horror cinema.

Skin Masks and Class: *Happy Birthday to Me* (1981) and *Smiley* (2012)

While the emphasis here is on class difference in *Happy Birthday to Me* and *Smiley*, again – like the previous four examples – these films simultaneously address differences relating to gender and power. As a transformative device, skin masks here once more transcend simple disguise/revelation functions and their power dynamics are closely aligned with a range of cultural rituals linked to masks or mask-wearing. Class difference has been a subject of horror at least since Robert Louis Stevenson's *Strange Case of Dr Jekyll and Mr. Hyde* (1886), Reynold Humphries noting that in Rouben Mamoulian's 1931 screen adaptation, *Dr. Jekyll and Mr. Hyde*, Hyde functions 'as a signifier of class conflict'.[59] Class is central in horror films as diverse as *King Kong* (Merian C. Cooper, 1933), *Driller Killer* (Abel Ferrara, 1979) and *My Bloody Valentine*, the latter discussed in chapter 7, and for Humphries the genre's ubiquitous town/country binary is analogous with discourse surrounding class.[60]

Consumer rituals dominate slasher films in particular across secular festivals where participation is linked to wealth: buying dresses, hosting parties, driving cars. As noted in the introduction, film titles alone are often linked to social festivals and rituals – *Graduation Day*, *Happy Birthday to Me*, *Halloween*, *Prom Night* (Paul Lynch, 1980) – who in name at least flag associations with consumer rituals understood as 'performative events that are often planned, repeated over time within a social group or culture and characterized by intensive use of goods and services'.[61] *Happy Birthday to Me* follows Ginny (Melissa Sue Anderson) – a member of the popular, wealthy 'Top Ten' seniors clique at the Crawford Academy – whose members are being executed. Over the course of the film, it is revealed that at some point in the past Ginny had brain surgery and requires ongoing care by psychiatrist Dr David Faraday (Glenn Ford). As noted by Hendershot and Midelfort, excessive representations of mental health disorders broadly categorised as 'madness' have historically been gendered female and, like Samantha in *Curtains*, Ginny's mental health history actively undermines the audience's faith in her ability to distinguish right from wrong.[62] Although the film shows Ginny killing one of her peers, it is revealed that the killer is her friend Ann (Tracey E. Bregman), who wore a convincing mask of Ginny's face to shift the blame onto her. Ann's hatred of Ginny is class-based: as a lower-class girl who became upwardly mobile, Ann felt Ginny was an interloper, her anger complicated by the revelation that Ginny's deceased mother had an affair with Ann's father. Linked through both the mask itself (they both look like Ginny) and that both have mental health issues concretely locates the violent activity that propels the film's action as explicitly feminised. Regressively, there is a consistent implication that it is the 'madness' of women that forces them to reconcile difference in this way, manifesting in both women as gendered 'hysteria'.

While *Happy Birthday to Me* is typical of the ritualistic countdown execution structure of the slasher film reminiscent of Agatha Christie's 1939 novel *And Then There Were None*, it also deviates from the standard slasher in crucial ways.[63] In her analysis of slasher films, Sorcha Ní Fhlainn concluded that 'in this period of excess, overindulgence and increasing greed among the middle and upper classes, the victims of the slasher in these violent, visceral films are construed as the intended inheritors of Reaganomics'.[64] Typically, said Fhlainn, the slasher killer 'is usually depicted as sidelined due to issues of social class and Reagan's abandonment of necessarily social policies'.[65] In the slasher film, being scared or targeted by the killer

> recognises both the victims' class and the victims' security within their class prior to their onscreen destruction and allows them the position of being both secure in their assured politics while perpetually afraid of its loss at the hands of the 'other'.[66]

With both Ginny and Ann, these tendencies are explored explicitly through the film's diegetic focus on privilege, class and wealth. Ginny's instability actively fosters doubt in the spectator and through the mask we see a person we believe is Ginny commit murder. For Ann, Ginny is a fraudulent poor girl who became rich, rather than being 'naturally' dispossessed to wealth and privilege. Her past exclusion and invisibility to her new best friends in the Top Ten is a constant source of anxiety for both Ginny and, more urgently, to Ann, who considers Ginny a disruptive outsider and punishes her accordingly.

Vera Dika therefore considered the film 'ambitious' in terms of its intersection of class, privilege and violence.[67] 'The children of the upper class are mean-spirited, cruel and immoral,' Dika observed, 'apparently like their capitalist parents, they are out only for themselves.'[68] It is their privilege that 'cut[s them] off from the rest of the elite school and the suburban community'.[69] While not unusual for slasher films to focus on unlikable teens, protagonists at least – especially the typical Final Girl – are generally required to be a point of some sympathetic identification, as previously noted in regard to Clover's examination of cross-gender identification in horror. Ginny does not fit this description: as Dika noted, she is 'untrustworthy, selfish and unkind', and the film 'uses . . . these qualities and Ginny's nasty disposition and psychiatric history to raise the viewer's suspicions against her'.[70] We not only see Ginny revel in her superiority as part of the Top Ten, but also watch her seduce her friend's boyfriends and – most memorably – appear to murder fellow clique member Steve (Matt Craven) mid-seduction as she spectacularly impales him with a shish-kebab skewer.

Importantly, the murderer is not Ginny, but Ann *disguised* as Ginny, who peels off her Ginny-like skin mask in a cartoonish reveal. This transformation occurs in gruesome tableaux where the corpses of her friends have been placed around a festively decorated birthday party table, recalling the film's title. This consciously disrupts ubiquitous Western birthday party rituals – commonly involving cake, candles and a specific song[71] – and the very words 'Happy Birthday to Me' subverts the traditional 'Happy Birthday to You' song lyrics, implying loneliness and isolation rather than communal goodwill. But its pronoun subversion collapses Ann and Ginny's identities: through the mask, their identities have merged. 'In the final confrontational moment we are presented with two identical but antagonistic images of Ginny', said Dika. 'With the use of editing and optical effects, the image of the double is created . . . In *Birthday*, then, the close connection between the killer and the heroine is literalized by means of this visual image.'[72] For Dika, this underscores 'the tension between two opposing aspects of a symbolic single self':[73] again, as in many movies that incorporate horror film masks, doppelgängers and tricksters, ritual, power and transformation are central.

Implicit in the film's final thematic punch, however, when Ginny kills Ann in a struggle as the police arrive, the film ends with the implication that Ginny will be assumed guilty of all the murders. This renders Ginny herself a victim, despite surviving Ann's attempts to kill her. Ann is a bourgeois trickster-shaman who transforms through mask-wearing at its extreme: through her macabre sense of play, she employs a masked disguise to gain power and manipulate and destroy Ginny. But rather than seeking to *subvert* order she desires to return it to an archaic, regressive norm that maintains class distinctions and reinforces her privilege. The film's conclusion is a powerful critique of social order: that formal institutional forces like the police support Ann's mission implies that there remain deeply embedded social factors equally determined to maintain the status quo.

Michael Gallagher's 2012 film *Smiley* also centres around rituals involving human face skin masks, class difference and notions of dehumanisation taken to extremes with its total reconstruction of human head flesh to replicate a crude smiling face emoticon. The film seeks to profit on the moral panic surrounding Anonymous at the time, the relationship between Anonymous and its emblematic Guy Fawkes mask from *V for Vendetta* (James McTeigue, 2005) already briefly addressed in the introduction. When released in 2012, Anonymous were at the forefront of public discourse, evidenced by their being awarded one of *Time* magazine's People of the Year.[74] Jason L. Jarvis noted that the nature of the group render it difficult to define: as its name suggests, Anonymous is unstable and ambiguous and its meanings are variable.[75] Regardless, its origins are part of popular Internet mythology as a 'hacktivist' movement originating on 4chan, 'a place where thousands of people gather for cheap thrills: porn, gore and spontaneous collaborative pranks that range from the harmlessly goofy to insidiously dangerous'.[76] For Cole Stryker, this activity is linked to informality and leisure: 'for the most part, 4chan's users just want to kill time shooting the shit with other geeks'.[77] The online rituals of 4chan activity – such as meme creation and trolling – stand in contrast to Anonymous's high-profile activism.[78] Anonymous's intersection of trolling and mask-wearing again recall shaman-trickster traditions: like many of the mask-wearing horror antagonists in this book, subversive masked play seeks to disrupt and Internet trolling itself, for E. Gabriella Coleman, is a noteworthy contemporary manifestation of the trickster tradition.[79]

Explicitly casting Anonymous as the villain, *Smiley* presents them as a bratty college clique, spoilt by privilege and too much leisure time (recalling the Crawford Top Ten in *Happy Birthday to Me*). But trolling in the film is presented as ritualistic, an act identified as such by Bettina Kluge.[80] By aligning Anonymous with drug- and alcohol-fuelled house parties rather than virtual spaces, the film's representation of the movement is more closely aligned with Whitney Phillips's identification of 4chan and Anonymous as having triggered a 'moral panic', mining public anxieties about Anonymous's post-2006 'ominous refrain that "none of us is as cruel as all of us"'.[81] In privileging ritualised trolling, *Smiley* necessarily ignores that the victim-selection of this trolling is often politically motivated: 'religious cults, white supremacists, scam artists, pedophiles and animal abusers'.[82]

In terms of its use of masks, the most striking factor in *Smiley* is that the characters representing Anonymous are not anonymous at all: they have names, such as their leader Zane (Andrew James Allen). The film denies Anonymous any broader social or ideological motivation beyond cyberbullying – another moral panic at the time of its production[83] – as they attempt to drive protagonist Ashley (Caitlin Gerard) to her death 'for the lulz'. Online communication as a site of horror is configured as an explicit threat to young people, as demonstrated in a range of horror movies including *Megan is Missing* (Michael Goi, 2011), *Unfriended* (Leo Gabriadze, 2014) and *The Den* (discussed in chapter 8): central to all these films is an assumption that 'online communication is a daily ritual for just about everyone'.[84]

Yet, despite reducing real-world Anonymous networks to a gang of bored killer rich kids, the use of skin masks in *Smiley* in many ways is just as complex as the other examples in this chapter. In its climax – again like *Happy Birthday to Me* – what is assumed to be a 'real' face is revealed to be a mask. Throughout the film, Smiley is understood to be the physical manifestation of the eponymous urban legend, a murderous online stalker who sewed his eyes and mouth closed, his facial tissue, sinew and muscle swelling grotesquely. This uncanny turning of flesh into a grim parody of the eponymous emoticon is part of the disturbing materiality of the Smiley face itself. By restricting his ability to both see and speak, the visual iconography implies that he attained alternate, less human powers, granting him unspoken powers to move across the Internet's liminal virtuality.

The film's 'twist' reveals that Ashley has been taunted by Zane and his Anonymous friends wearing Smiley masks. Instead of stalked and driven to her death by an online bogeyman, she has been cyberbullied by her peers. Like *Happy Birthday to Me*, *Smiley* highlights its protagonist's mental health issues (like Ginny, Ashley is traumatised by the death of her mother): there is an implication that Ashley is a suitable victim precisely because she is unstable to begin with, recalling Lizbeth Goodman's observation that in literature 'at the most basic level, it is often females who are called mad and males who make them so'.[85] After her death, the masks are removed, making literal the notion of 'two-facedness' (especially in the case of Ashley's seemingly sympathetic housemate). Yet the film's conclusion reveals the 'real' Smiley just before the end credits as Ashley's killers discuss online the ethics of what they have done. Although a pedestrian twist, conceptually the existence of a 'real' Smiley invites a rethinking of the doubling process integral to the film's reveal: what remains is the knowledge that underneath the 'real' Smiley's face, a similar kind of doubling remains. Masked transformation and online communication rituals intersect in *Smiley* to render monstrous its representation of Anonymous: because of their class privilege, they represent a murderous moral bankruptcy constructed to profit directly from moral panics surrounding cyberbullying, Anonymous and 4chan.

This chapter has explored six horror films that employ skin masks as transformative devices, intersecting with a range of rituals to explore (however ambivalently) power dynamics relating to religion, class and gender in particular. As evidenced by *The Abominable Dr. Phibes*, *Alice Sweet Alice*, *The Texas Chain Saw Massacre*, *Happy Birthday to Me*, *Curtains* and *Smiley*, these rituals deviate and intersect in significant ways: instead of arguing for a singular, unified way that skin masks are deployed in contemporary horror, these films illustrate pluralism regarding how they explore broader social, cultural and ideological questions. Whether the emphasis is (like *Dr. Phibes* and *Alice Sweet Alice*) on explicitly religious rituals or – as in *The Texas Chain Saw Massacre*, *Happy Birthday to Me*, *Curtains* and *Smiley* – more informal or secular ones, the privileging of skin masks allows an exploration of patriarchal dominance in particular. Like Dr Phibes, Alice, Mrs Tredoni and Ann, these trickster-shamans subvert dominant structures through masked transformation. Like Leatherface, they can evoke supposedly 'primitive' masked ritual traditions in order to return to a regressive past, or – like the masks in *Smiley* and *Curtains* – they can replicate grotesque extremes where monstrosity results from a denial of humanness altogether. Masked transformations and rituals converge in these films to explore power imbalances, the shamanic imagination underscoring the immense symbolic potency of masks themselves is granted. We shift now to the intersection of ritual, power and transformation in horror films that feature blank masks.

5

Blank Masks

Ritual, Power and Transformation

LIKE SKIN MASKS, blank masks in horror cinema have their own often complex histories, particularly in relation to the intersection of ritual, power and transformation. This chapter explores blank masks in horror cinema after 1970, particularly those similar to the iconic white blank mask prominent throughout the *Halloween* franchise (1978–2018) that simultaneously recalls older performance traditions such as Japanese Noh theatre. This mask typology is distinguished by the various ways these films use 'blankness' to explore not only notions of identity, but also as a symbolic canvas upon which viewers can inscribe meaning. Masks in horror demand a level of cultural work on the part of their audiences who must negotiate the multiple identities and meanings often at play in the transformative acts of masking and unmasking visible within the genre. In thinking about the potential for transformation and movement across either symbolically or literal transitional spaces, the shamanic imagination – a residual cultural memory of orthodox, anthropologically defined shamanism that underscores an unspoken yet widespread belief in the power of masked ritual – reveals that horror film masks often require this precise kind of labour. This is arguably nowhere more explicit than in the blank mask, as its defining absence of information demands the audience work to locate meaning in a space defined by its very lack of visual information. Blank masks simultaneously erase identity and create spaces to project new meanings onto, prompting another dimension to the visual iconography of horror film masks.

While this chapter focuses on the blank white face mask, there are other methods of deleting or 'blanking' faces through masks in horror cinema. The stocking mask often deployed in home invasion films and robbery-based thriller or crime films is a ubiquitous alternative, contorting the wearer's face, obscuring their features and impeding identification. Beyond cinema, Elizabeth Tonkin found images of the stocking-masked terrorist 'the most frightening' and 'inhuman because they are faceless'.[1] Stocking masks are both blank masks and repurposed masks (the latter explored in chapter 7), as are similarly ubiquitous ski masks, other staples of both horror and crime thrillers that grant their wearers a transformative blankness.[2] Blank masks deny the humanness of their wearer by deleting the features that render them identifiable as individual humans, and there are similar mechanics at play in horror films that employ sack masks like *The Town that Dreaded Sundown* (Charles B. Pierce, 1976/Alfonso Gomez-Rejon, 2015), *Nightbreed* (Clive Barker, 1990), *The Orphanage* (J. A. Bayona, 2007) and *Trick R' Treat* (Michael Dougherty, 2007). As well as deleting identifying facial features, the placing of the head in a bag also implies an association with waste, refuse and abjection: trash films about literal human rubbish.

The blank white face has a long history in performance traditions which continue throughout contemporary horror cinema. Through the success of John Carpenter's original *Halloween* in 1978 in particular, the blank mask has played an important role in the codification of horror film masks from that decade onwards, again supporting Neale's notion of repetition and difference as a process that accounts for the endurance of the genre more broadly.

Echoing Neale, the blank mask in *Eyes without a Face* has been adopted and adapted throughout the horror genre (in films by Jesús Franco and Pedro Almodóvar, for example[3]), increasingly codified through its repetition as it is reimagined and redeployed in diverse ways. This chapter explores a number of blank horror film masks to demonstrate this process of same-but-different, illustrating how the codification of these masks is underscored by important deviations that often thwart or subvert expectations. Again, of central interest is the transformative capacity of masks themselves and how they intersect with ritual and power. In the first section, we explore masks, ritual and repetition across the *Halloween* franchise, from John Carpenter's original to Rob Zombie's 2007/2009 re-imaginings to the official franchise reboot in 2018. This section positions the repetition of the blank mask motif throughout *Halloween* alongside the very rituals of similarity and difference that dominate film sequels and remakes more broadly. This section concludes by exploring vital tensions not only in the differences but also the similarities that govern the use and aesthetics of masks across the *Halloween* films and how they reflect a broader tendency across horror for reflexivity. This reflexivity is particularly important in the films explored in this chapter: film-makers often rely on audiences to have a preconceived understanding of how masks gain their power when worn in association with a broad range of what can be loosely conceived as 'ritual' acts. This power is understood through the shamanic imagination as granting masks and their wearers abilities that they would not have access to otherwise. However, while this knowledge recalls beliefs about masks that transcend film history, as the mask became codified in horror it could be reconfigured in a range of new contexts that – while still recognisable as 'horror' – simultaneously spoke to new ideological and social contexts and concerns.

Following this, we turn to Japan and Australia with two films that privilege Noh masks in different ways. While not as well known as J-horror peers like Hideo Nakata's *Ringu* (1998), *Gurozuka* too evokes traditional Japanese theatrical traditions (here the Noh mask instead of *Ringu*'s contemporising of the *onryō* figure from Kabuki theatre). Like *Ringu*, *Gurozuka* explores tensions surrounding then contemporary ubiquitous media technologies, but like *A Page of Madness* it strategically deploys the blankness of the mask as a space to project new meanings. In contrast, Ann Turner's Australian film *Celia* does not mention Noh or even Japan, but through its story of the psychological collapse of its eponymous traumatised young protagonist as she attempts to navigate the fraught world of adulthood, the mask represents a broader symbolic transformation accessible through the child's simplistic embrace of homogenised cultural Otherness.

Finally, the relationship between masks, ritual, power and transformation is explored in George A. Romero's *Bruiser* (2000) and Mike Flanagan's *Hush* (2016). In surrendering to capitalist ideals and ambitions, Romero's protagonist loses his identity by literally becoming faceless, the director using this metaphor in his critique of the dehumanising nature of Western corporate culture. *Hush* too addresses the intersection of male violence and anonymity, but through an early unmasking it complicates notions of identity by rejecting the mythology of the enigmatic masked killer. Erasing some identities while complicating others, in a variety of different ways – confirming and diverging, same and yet different – blank masks in this chapter demonstrate how ritual, power and transformation intersect with the empty facial canvases these films offer.

Blank Masks and Repetition: The *Halloween* Franchise

Rituals of repetition take various forms in horror, such as the widespread use of horror film masks and the sequel-heavy nature of its most well-known franchises, from *Friday the 13th* to *Saw* (2003–17), *Ring* (*Ringu*, 1998–2017) to *A Nightmare on Elm Street* (1984–2010). The *Halloween* franchise is a poignant subject on both fronts, as it not only has been made and remade with ritualistic frequency, but the films diegetically deploy Michael Myers's iconic mask in a repetitive, ritualistic way. Film sequels and remakes contain ritual aspects, Catherine Russell noting of action franchises such as *Death Wish* (1974–94) and *Lethal Weapon* (1987–2016) that 'the endless regeneration of sequels of these movies indicates their ritualistic impetus and also the failure of the ritual to stem the tide of violence'.[4] As discussed in the introduction, Thomas Schatz's work on intersection of ritual and genre film is significant, where he observes that 'as we repeatedly undergo the same type of experience we develop expectations which, as they are continually reinforced, tend to harden into "rules"'.[5] The *Halloween* franchise illustrates that as 'expectations' about horror film sequels 'are continually reinforced' and thus 'harden into "rules"', so too the codification of masks themselves in terms of both how they are narratively deployed and their affective impact on the audience, themselves engaging in what we noted previously can be understood as acts of ritualised spectatorship.

In sequels and remakes, the relationship between ritual, repetition and pleasure is fragile. Andrew Scahill noted that while in horror, 'a sequel *may* provide the pleasure of recognition by echoing a familiar narrative event', there is the risk – as Charles Derry claimed of the *Saw* franchise – that horror sequels can become 'more mercenary than visionary, offering repetition and not elaboration'.[6] This is not specific to film genre, and Christina Pratt notes that even shamanic rituals traditionally have a tendency to 'lose their efficacy when simply repeated or imitated'.[7] Mircea Eliade was a key figure in articulating the role of repetition in shamanic ritual, arguing for its importance as 'a fundamental conception in archaic religions – the repetition of a ritual founded by Divine Beings implies the re-actualization of the original Time when the rite was first performed'.[8] The sacred aspects of repetition manifested in a shaman's ability to recall through ritual their community's cultural and spiritual history. There is a tension, therefore, between what Eliade identified as sacred rituals of repetition and what Pratt and Derry argued is hollow repetition-for-repetition's sake.

Repetition has also been considered in terms of secularist aesthetics, and for Umberto Eco postmodern aesthetics are perpetually rejuvenated through repetition.[9] Citing Eco in her work on repetition and ritual in horror film, Zanger suggested that 'any remake of a film is . . . the retelling of a previously successful story' and that 'since repetition and difference function in mutual interdependence, the economy of cinematic versions is that of difference in repetition'.[10] Echoing Neale, this tension between repetition and difference is central to the *Halloween* franchise, but the iconic Myers mask has historical precedence. Argentine horror director Emilio Vieyra's *Feast of Flesh* (*Placer sangriento*, 1967) follows a masked serial killer who injects young women with heroin, luring them to his beach house where he hypnotises them with his organ-playing prowess. His mask is privileged in the opening credit sequence, where it is shown next to silhouettes of syringes. The mask itself is disturbing: while in close-up appearing to be that of an older man, when shot in high contrast black-and-white and from below in one of the film's most climactic scenes it is rendered blank and flat. From a contemporary perspective, this mask immediately recalls Michael Myers from the *Halloween* franchise, the first entry of which would appear over ten years later.

While unclear if Carpenter saw this film or was indirectly influenced by it, this mask in *Feast of Flesh* regardless suggests a process of same-but-different, recalling Neale's identification of how repetition and variation intersect to assure the endurance of film genres. Looking at the *Halloween* franchise, this is brought vividly to life through the dynamic centrality of masks themselves: while adult Myers's blank mask has been the film's most enduring visual icon from the first film onwards, the clown mask worn by the young Myers in its opening scene also returns in *Halloween IV: The Return of Michael Myers*, where it is worn by his niece Jamie (Danielle Harris). While the use of masks in *Halloween III: Season of the Witch* will be discussed in chapter 9, that film's broad commercial and critical failure has been understood as a too severed divergence from the earlier films.

As noted in chapter 1, in the first *Halloween* film Dr Loomis (Donald Pleasance) at one point reflects upon his time as Michael's psychiatrist during the killer's time at the Smith's Grove sanatorium where he was incarcerated after killing his older sister. Loomis describes Myers as having mystical visions, these shamanic qualities ascribed to Myers echoed in Kendall R. Phillips's description of not merely as a crazed killer but 'a kind of cosmic force'.[11] Adopting the famous blank mask on his escape from Smith's Grove, it would become synonymous with the genre more broadly and its iconographic impact saw it endure across the sequels and their remakes. As Reynold Humphries noted, this mask is therefore not so much a means for disguise – his sister Laurie (Jamie Lee Curtis), for instance, recognises Michael specifically *by* his mask – but rather functions as an Othering device to separate him from his human prey as it 'symbolizes Michael's refusal to be looked at, to become the object of the other's look, to recognize the other as having the same rights and desires as himself'.[12] For J. P. Telotte, 'the almost luminous white mask' itself 'is neither grotesquely distorted nor natural, but more resembling the face of a dead man'. Consequently, it 'functions not only to cloak his human features, but also to effectively divorce him from the world of the living, his victims'.[13] For Murray Leeder, 'the mask, which both resembles but is clearly not a human face, works to winnow away the human factor from Michael Myers. Like an actor in a Greek drama, Michael wears his villainy plainly on his face.'[14] The mask suggests both an erasure of identity while simultaneously allowing the audience to 'read' their own experience of Myers's presence 'into' the blankness itself, encouraged to imagine the horrors he is capable of because more usual communication systems – language, facial expression, emotion – are simply not there.

The creation of Myers's blank mask has itself attained an aspect of cult film legend. As told by Leeder, while the screenplay requested a mask that depicted the 'pale, neutral features of a man weirdly distorted by the rubber', production designer Tommy Lee Wallace (director of *Halloween III*) modified and painted white a mask of William Shatner's *Star Trek* character to give Myers his disturbing look.[15] David Roche compared Michael's mask to the *commedia dell'arte*'s Pierrot, which, when combined with its *Star Trek* origins, 'literally distorts and defamiliarises the reassuring face of an iconic hero'.[16] Across the *Halloween* sequels and its remakes, rituals of repetition manifest not only in the numerous reiterations simultaneously aligned with and deviating from each other, but through the repeated, ritualistic act of masking itself. Rob Zombie's 2007 remake and its 2009 sequel take significant liberties, expanding the narrative and symbolic functionality of the mask. While in the original film Myers is catatonic in hospital for fifteen years, in Zombie's 2007 version he busies himself with mask making. Expanding the five-minute introduction of the original, child Myers (Daeg Faerch) is obsessed with masks and – in a crucial deviation from the original's opening – he picks up the mask when his sister Judith's (Hannah R. Hall) boyfriend drops it on the floor after pulling it out of a bag and putting it on while they are making out as a joke. Here the mask has a distinctly adult look and on Michael's body it suggests that he is a child capable of committing 'adult' crimes. There is, like Carpenter's original (and other films in the franchise), the capacity for transformation: he puts on the mask and becomes a killer. Yet, in contrast with the original, Zombie's adult Myers's (Tyler Mane) crude papier mâché masks are shown to decorate his cell.

Masks and masked transformations are how Myers negotiates his own identity as both a child and adult: child Myers wears an adult mask and becomes a killer, while adult Myers – obsessed with masks – uses them in his return to violence. The transformative capacity of the mask is linked to his fundamental moral and social mis-wiring: it is only after returning to his childhood home in search of his now teenage sister Laurie (Scout Taylor Compton) that he finds the original mask that marks the beginning of his murderous rampage as he seeks a reunion. The blankness of the mask does not function in the same way that it had previously – rather, through the franchise's ritualised process of repetition, the significance of the mask is not reliant on its blankness as such, but in its intertextual echoes of the 'adult' crimes Zombie knows that the audience are aware of, their knowledge of the preceding films informing their experience and understanding of the events in his remake. As discussed in the introduction, this reflexivity in horror spectatorship itself has a ritualistic aspect, and this conscious game-playing feature of slasher film in particular will be expanded on in chapter 7.

While the earlier films included rare moments of Michael's exposed face, in Zombie's 2007 remake, his unmasked face as a child is privileged throughout, emphasising his humanity. In *Halloween II* – the 2009 sequel to his 2007 remake – Zombie continues to refer to earlier moments in the franchise's history (again same-but-different) by the important final turn to mask-wearing by Compton's Laurie, the film's Final Girl. This explicitly references the ending of *Halloween IV: The Return of Michael Myers* where the child-Final Girl Jamie puts on Michael's clown mask and (apparently) murders her aunt off-screen. Most recently, David Gordon Green's 2018 reboot of the series rejects the broader mythology from *Halloween II* (Rick Rosenthal, 1981) onwards (notably rejecting any family connection between Michael and Laurie) but still maintains the centrality of the mask; when Michael is revealed in high-security medical care at the beginning of the film he is shown from behind, maskless. After his escape he has the capacity to kill but his first goal is to retrieve his iconic mask, an act which – when he places it back on his face – appears in many senses to formalise his return as the legendary killer. Across the *Halloween* franchise, ritual and repetition intersect through the constant reconfiguration of the mask, especially the blank mask of the adult Myers. Key here is the tension between difference and repetition: the blank mask is not only a disguise or an empty canvas for a range of new (and often conflicting) meanings to be projected upon, but a tangible forum for a critical, reflexive consideration of the role of ritual and repetition in horror more broadly. As indicated in the next two case studies, even the use of near identical masks in different cultural contexts allows space for notable diversity.

Blank Masks and Place: *Celia* (1988) and *Gurozuka* (2005)

Although both featuring Noh masks, *Celia* and *Gurozuka* appear to have little in common beyond their surface affiliation with the horror genre. *Celia* is a hybrid drama that employs horror iconography to replicate the intense Manichean imaginary of its titular child protagonist, who (seemingly suffering from a form of post-traumatic stress disorder) must find her place in an increasingly ugly adult world during 1950s Melbourne. With its jump frights and fascination with the intersection of technology, vengeance and the supernatural, *Gurozuka* is typical of contemporary J-horror. But through their shared use of Noh masks, both films in different ways are tied to a sense of place (or, just as importantly, placeless-ness). While *Onibaba* and *A Page of Madness* demonstrated that mask-wearing traditions in Japanese horror cinema are not rare, they continue in contemporary J-horror, sparked by the phenomenal success of *Ringu*.[17]

While the *onryō* is synonymous with J-horror through *Ringu*'s antagonist Sadako, other contemporary Japanese horror films have engaged with Japanese theatrical traditions in different ways. Yoichi Noshiyama's 2005 *Gurozuka* continues mask-wearing practices closely associated with Noh as it follows a group of young women who visit the isolated lodge Yuai House. They plan to make a movie under the guidance of Ai (Chisato Morishita) and Maki (Yôko Mitsuya) to revive a film society that was shut down seven years previously when a member went missing. Their project is a remake of the final film made by the society before it was disbanded, a short horror film called *Gurozuka*. As Maki explains, the film was based on a Noh play called *Kurozuka* about a demonic woman who lived isolated, deep in the mountains. Visited by travelling monks, she gave them orders to not look in a certain room in her house. They disobeyed and discovered the remains of previous travellers that she had devoured.

Translated as 'Black Mound', *Kurozuka* was written by Noh playwright and actor Zeami Motokiyo (discussed in chapter 3). As Lowenstein noted, it is a famous example of a play centring around the *Hannya* mask, denoting a female demon driven by jealousy.[18] Watching the original film on a videotape they discovered before they arrived at the lodge, the girls see in the diegetic short *Gurozuka* a masked woman beat another character to death before walking towards the screen – covered in blood – her hand reaching out towards the camera (this is an image curiously repeated almost exactly in the found footage central to another film we discuss in chapter 8, *Månguden*). Here, the girls identify the Noh mask as that of a *Deigan*, identifiable via her plain blank face and the whites of the eyes painted gold to denote the supernatural.[19] Reviving the figure of the *Deigan* and its connection to feminine monstrosity, one of the girls begins to kill her peers, eventually revealed to be Maki who is 'possessed' by the videotape and driven by obsessive, murderous desire for Ai. Again, the mask is not merely a disguise, but a blank slate upon which new identities may be written. Like *Halloween*, the blankness renders its wearer's actions unknowable, symbolised by the absence of facial expression – one fame-hungry character is even reluctant to wear the mask because it will obscure her face and reduce her potential visibility.

Yet, despite the use of this Noh mask in the film, *Gurozuka* seems less concerned with Noh theatre itself than with the convention established by *Ringu* that requires J-horror films to reference Japanese performance traditions in some way. There is a strong aspect of reflexivity at play as we watch a horror film about characters who watch a horror film: like *Ringu*, *Gurozuka* consciously constructs the act of watching scary movies from within its own diegesis as a ritual closely associated with horror spectatorship. With its film-within-a-film structure, much is made in

Gurozuka of the internal diegetic short and its capacity to 'infect' the present: influenced by *Ringu*'s haunted technology plot, as Colette Balmain noted, this is a general tendency in contemporary J-horror.[20] The utilisation of Noh traditions – particularly the blank mask – may be an attempt to follow the conventions established by *Ringu* to garner the same international success for *Gurozuka*. While the past is consciously echoed through the deliberate deployment of this Noh mask, *Gurozuka* is in fact influenced to a greater extent by more recently established generic traditions. The Noh mask here re-writes on its blank space a new Japanese horror narrative of masked transformations, responding to trends active within its contemporary moment. The blank mask allows for a play of identity across a range of texts associated with Japanese cultural history – traditional Noh theatre, experimental analogue film[21] and J-horror films about haunted videotapes – that exist both within the diegesis and intertextually beyond it. The blank Noh mask is therefore the perfect symbol for *Gurozuka*: like *A Page of Madness* and – in a very different way and a very different cultural and historical context – *Celia*, it uses the object as a blank canvas upon which new meanings can be inscribed.

Although conceived as a drama, *Celia* was released outside Australia with horror-style artwork as *Celia: Child of Darkness*, underplaying the film's genre hybridity.[22] *Celia* aligns with horror most explicitly through its employment of the Scottish folktale *The Hobyahs*, but this relationship is consolidated through the unspoken importance of masks in the film as a transformative device that Celia believes grant her ancient powers when used in ritual. *The Hobyahs* are central to both Celia's nightmares and her moral vision: through these folkloric monsters and the threat that they embody, she understands order and disorder being maintained through varying degrees of violence and displays of body horror. Celia's obsession with *The Hobyahs* indoctrinates her with the belief that ritual violence is essential to establishing and maintaining order in what she sees as a corrupt adult world.

In *Celia*, the 'Japanese-ness' of the mask itself is never mentioned and its Noh origins are not acknowledged. But the instability of faces and the identities associated with them are rendered visually in *Celia*'s opening credits, where images of her face distort and blur on top of each other until they solidify into a single image of actor Rebecca Smart looking directly at the camera – an act that challenges the viewer to consciously identify a 'true', singular Celia. The fragility of Celia's face – and her entire identity

– continues through her use of the mask. The role of ritual is most explicit in the 'primitive' masked ceremonies she and her neighbouring friends, the Tanner children, undertake in a deserted quarry, a carnivalesque space where the logic of play dominates the otherwise banal oppression of their everyday lives. But social rituals are also ubiquitous, manifesting from the very outset in schoolyard rituals like passing notes or writing repeated lines on a blackboard as punishment. The parental gifting of an iconic Australian Malvern Star brand bicycle is a localised rite of passage and in an anti-Communist church sermon, religious ritual is explicitly granted a political dimension. The film even includes a book-burning sequence – a ritual typically associated with extreme ideological sentiment – where Celia's father burns her deceased grandmother's Lenin and Marx books, Celia rescuing the Noh mask from the flames and hiding it in a waterproof box in a local creek.

The Noh mask is a sacred object for Celia, yet she indicates no knowledge of its cultural heritage beyond its association with her grandmother. Its unspecified Otherness for her is representative of a world beyond her stifling suburban existence. As she and the Tanner children sit in a deserted shed in the quarry, she passes it to each child who places it on their face, Celia explaining reverently that 'it has secret powers'. Bully Stephanie (Amelia Frid) uses the mask to torment Celia, stealing it and mocking her with it. Bonding with the Tanner children through a ritualistic blood exchange through their pricked thumbs, this is another ritual that mobilises Celia and her gang against Stephanie to rescue the sacred mask. Their pursuit leads them to a cinema, where Stephanie continues to taunt Celia with the mask: for her, its power stems only from the importance Celia has invested in it, granting Stephanie control over Celia. The mask ritualistically represents a way to negotiate life and death to the latter, with its link to her deceased grandmother and the unspoken role it plays in Celia's increasing proximity to death (of both her pet rabbit and her ultimate killing of Stephanie's father, Inspector Burke, played by William Zappa).

When Celia regains the mask, tensions escalate: Celia is forbidden to play with the Tanner children and together they enact mock-primitive rituals cobbled together from their collective knowledge of what such ceremonies might necessitate to seek revenge. With her mask, Celia and the Tanner children return to the quarry where the masked Celia chants and dances around a fire, making voodoo dolls of her father, Stephanie and Inspector Burke. When the Tanners are forced to move to Sydney because Inspector Burke and Celia's father reported Mr Tanner's political status to his employer, the children throw a voodoo doll of Inspector Burke onto a fire, chanting 'Death! Death! Death!' In both ceremonies, mask-wearing Celia is the central controlling power, performing mock-tribal dances in childlike imitation of shamanic ritual wholly dependent on what she believes the transformative potential of her sacred mask affords. Although not seen again, the mask mobilises Celia's destructive power and grants her the power to fulfil her wish for Inspector Burke's death: at the film's climax, she and friend Heather (Clair Couttie) shoot him when Celia – now unable to distinguish reality from fantasy – mistakes him for a Hobyah.

Crucially, the film's coda employs another blank facial covering: playing at the quarry with Stephanie and other children, Celia convenes a mock trial against Inspector Burke's killer, stringing Heather up in a white cloth sack mask reminiscent of a lynching. As Celia jokingly screams 'guilty!', the frightened Heather falls to the ground unharmed and the children run away, laughing. The Noh mask and its strongly ritualised yet unattributed Otherness is replaced with a blank mask of more ominous cultural origins: echoing images of the Ku Klux Klan lynching African Americans in the United States, the Noh mask is superseded by a more menacing blank mask whose iconography evokes associations with horrendous real-world atrocities. If *Celia* is about a traumatised child negotiating the corrupt adult logic of 1950s suburban Australia, that her interest in masks evolves from Noh to this speaks powerfully of the symbolic potency of masks and how meaning is inscribed upon them.

Celia's use of the Noh mask – wholly untethered from its specificity to Japanese cultural history – exemplifies the shamanic imagination and the often subconsciously perceived power imbued within masks, especially when deployed in association with behaviours configured and performed as consciously 'ritualistic', as impromptu and informal as they may be. Celia's DIY approach to masked ritual shows how 'old' things can be reimagined to attain fresh meanings and power in 'new' contexts. The very blankness of the mask grants it the quality of a floating signifier: Celia creates new meaning to suit her needs, indifferent or at least unaware of any possible alternate (traditional) meanings. While the potency of masks in *Celia* and *Gurozuka* are ultimately tied to specific cultural and historical moments, as the final two case studies explore, blank masks can also relate to tensions between subjective experiences of individuality, masculinity and anonymity.

Blank Masks and Masculine Identity: *Bruiser* (2000) and *Hush* (2016)

Although released sixteen years apart, the masks in George A. Romero's *Bruiser* and Mike Flanagan's *Hush* are notably similar. Recalling Michael Myers's emotionless expression across the *Halloween* franchise, these masks mimic its blankness but experiment in different ways with the expressive facial nuances that reflect their wearers' identities. Inspired by Franju's *Eyes without a Face*,[23] in *Bruiser* Romero employs the mask in his story of Henry Creedlow (Jason Flemyng) whose face suddenly adopts a solid white covering at the revelation that his demanding wife Janine (Nina Garbiras) and bullying boss Milo (Peter Stormare) are having an affair. Masked Henry is liberated and transformed, empowered to enact the violent fantasies that filled his internal life in an increasingly vicious killing spree.

Utilising this blank mask to examine the vulnerability of identity in the context of contemporary capitalism, Romero depicts the dehumanising nature of the corporate environment. This culture is embodied by Milo, his racism and misogyny implied to be representative of the entire corporate demographic. That this is a culture Henry aspired to succeed in and – at the discovery of Janine and Milo's affair – is revealed as morally toxic, Henry descends into violence. With its focus on white-collar masculinity, *Bruiser* superficially adheres to Barry Keith Grant's identification of the 'yuppie horror film', which 'specifically addresses the anxieties of an affluent culture in an era of prolonged recession'.[24] For Grant, 'in yuppie horror films, it would seem that to be underfunded is more frightening than being undead', defining the subgenre as one where late capitalism itself is deemed the ultimate monster.[25]

Yet, while Grant identified the yuppie horror film cycle with a series of films predominantly produced in the United States in the late 1980s and early 1990s, made in 2000, *Bruiser* is potentially a retrospective deconstruction of this cycle.[26] Through the blank mask, Henry's monstrosity does not denote an eradication of his identity as such, but a transformation of it. Romero renders Henry's previous invisibility explicit before the mask appears: ignored and demeaned at work and home, the only person who 'saw' Henry was Milo's unhappy wife Rosemary (Leslie Hope). That Rosemary is a mask-maker positions her as a representative of a world beyond corporate life and a literal creator of new identities through her creative practice. Rosemary grants Henry a method of building a new identity – through the ritual of mask-making. Henry, however, awakens with a more fantastic kind of mask: his mask does not delete his identity as much as it grants a fresh slate upon which he can construct a new one. Henry's face becomes a battleground between different aspects of his own personality – the 'real' face that is effectively invisible, or the 'blank' face that he can use to allow new emotions and desires to flourish. As Kendall R. Phillips suggested, *Bruiser* 'explicitly employs the body as a site of struggle and it is ultimately these bodily urges that the protagonists must resist'.[27]

Henry's mask does not conceal his identity from the police for any great length of time and it does not take them – or Rosemary – long to connect Henry's disappearance to the spate of crimes linked to the 'faceless' man. For Phillips,

> it is noteworthy that Henry's blank face does not actually equate to any real sense of invisibility or stealth. He can be seen by others and leaves fingerprints and other evidence at the crime scenes so that his blank visage actually does little to facilitate his crimes.

What is crucial is 'that Henry's blank face releases something murderous within him'.[28] Again, the power of the mask – one that endures through the shamanic imagination – continues, but it is reshaped to create new meanings in this specific cultural context, again recalling Neale's process of 'repetition . . . difference, variation and change'.[29] Henry's mask is a mystical trigger that sets in motion a vital transformation, granting him power that he did not have previously. In the construction of his new identity there is a shift to what the film frames as violent 'primitivism' that consciously rejects the yuppie ethos embodied by Milo. Henry's 'normal' face returns only after he has killed Milo. This underscores the de/re-humanising dynamics that underlie Romero's politics of identity, corporate masculinity and the transformative power of the mask.[30] Here masks undermine the social capacity of identity, replacing it with something altogether inhuman.

Like *Bruiser*, the blank white mask in home invasion film *Hush* (2016) represents the absence of emotions within a man capable of committing extreme, violent crime. Played by John Gallagher Jr., the assailant in *Hush* is credited simply as 'Man', suggesting that he is representative of a ubiquitous brand of white male violence, representing a capacity for violence against women within many men, not just one fictional character. Following deaf-mute author Maddy (Kate Siegel), who is recovering from a heartbreak in her rural home, Man murders her neighbour on Maddy's doorstep and is fascinated with terrorising Maddy when he realises that she has not heard her neighbour's scream. Influenced by Terence Young's *Wait Until Dark* (1967)[31] – a home-invasion movie about a blind woman – *Hush*'s tension builds around audience assumptions regarding ability and disability: in both films, the women are marked by a perceived lack and the drama of each film is driven by their ability to survive.

In *Hush*, Man's mask complicates this relationship. Although an iconographic aspect used heavily to promote the film, he only wears the mask for the first twenty-three minutes of the film when he is stationed almost solely outside the house. With the threat he represents to Maddy's safety clear, she writes a message in lipstick on her living room window telling him that she will not reveal his identity because she does not know it: she has not seen his face. Accepting this as a challenge, he removes the mask, revealing his face and voiding her argument. The film's action escalates into a heavily ritualised repetition of a familiar cat-and-mouse-style pursuit typical of home invasion horror narratives. Although the mask is not seen again, its centrality in this opening quarter offers a complex reimagining of the role and function of horror film masks in terms of its potency as an almost mystical object bestowed with certain powers.

The most striking feature of Man when he wears the mask is that – like Maddy – he too does not speak. The acts that instigate the film's action all occur with no spoken communication between them, recalling Peter Brooks's definition of melodrama as a 'text of muteness'.[32] This puts the onus for communication and meaning on other aspects because 'words . . . appear to be not wholly adequate to the representation of meanings and the melodramatic message must be formulated through other registers of the sign'.[33] While *Hush* obviously does not fit the generic definition of melodrama per se, in its confrontation between clearly delineated personifications of good and evil and a combination of what Linda Williams has identified as melodrama's defining factors of 'action and pathos', it supports Christine Gledhill's claim that melodrama is less a genre than 'a genre-producing machine'.[34] What renders *Hush*'s utilisation of muteness so complex in this opening is how diversely it configures muteness in relation to power: while for Maddy this renders her vulnerable (especially when combined with deafness), for Man – when combined with the mask – it intensifies his power and enigmatic force.[35] Largely this is due to his mythic appearance, not only by wearing the uncanny mask (human yet not human), but by his weapon of choice: bow and arrows.

When his mask is removed, this mythic aspect vanishes – not merely because it reveals his face, but other elements that collapse the vaguely supernatural, mythic aspects of his appearance. He has neck-tattoos, emblematic of certain class and subcultural affiliations specific to the time and place of the film's production. The effectiveness of his mask as a tool to create fear – in Maddy and the audience – is its tangible fluctuation between blankness (manifesting in the mask itself) and its slight smile, indicating a degree of emotionality the blank mask seeks to otherwise deny. This tension comes to the fore at moments where the smile can be understood as sadistic: when killing Maddy's neighbour, he sexually thrusts a knife into her stomach long after she is dead, his mask's facial expression implying a perverse degree of pleasure. Similarly, when masked Man plays with Maddy's deafness and muteness, his smile adds a further degree of cruelty than would an expressionless mask. Masked man is a trickster: his is a disruptive playfulness and his adoption of the mask aligns this behaviour with the shamanic imagination via the power the object grants him.

But only to begin with. That Man voluntarily removes his mask early on recalls how the deployment of the horror film mask practically executes Neale's process of same-but-different, the tension between expectation and surprise propelling the genre and stopping it from becoming stagnant. Generic conventions dictate that Man's mask would not be removed until the end of the film (if even then) and certainly not casually by the wearer himself: this is the antithesis of the climactic reveals of *Halloween*, *The Abominable Dr. Phibes* and *Happy Birthday to Me*. That he does so – consciously expunging not just myth but the ritualistic wearing of masks in horror and the rejection of the enigmatic power that comes with it – speaks of ambivalence here towards what masks actually do. Fascinatingly, the revelation of the unmasked face means nothing in terms of the killer's identity. He is, ultimately, still 'no one': he is, quite literally, just a Man. But *Hush* simultaneously maintains assumptions about the power of the mask as a transformative device, because when Man is masked, he is silent, mythic and undefeatable. His 'no-one-ness' renders him vaguely supernatural, unlike the mortal, maskless and ultimately defeatable man. When the mask is removed, he is granted the ability to speak and – combined by the revelation of his still identity-less face – is rendered more human and thus able to be conquered.

A similar ambivalence regarding masking and unmasking can be found in another recent home invasion horror film explored in the next chapter, Adam Wingard's *You're Next* (2011). In *Hush*, the blank mask recalls a long horror tradition where the denial of identity rendered in the mask's very blankness offers the viewer a canvas upon which they can project their own meanings. In *Hush* and *Bruiser*, issues of masculinity, power and identity drive this process, while in *Celia* and *Gurozuka*, Noh masks speak through ritual in different ways to culturally specific notions of place, placeless-ness, power and identity. The *Halloween* franchise is one of the most immediately recognisable instances of masks in horror cinema and, as such, the repetition of the mask across the sequels and remakes reflects the process of replication and deviation that Neale contends is so vital to the longevity of genre cinema more broadly. These examples demand a degree of labour on the part of the spectator as their frequent reflexivity suggests that film-makers themselves are aware (however subconsciously) of how deeply embedded the shamanic imagination is: these films assume that we identify masks as objects with enormous potential to unleash great power, be it literally or symbolically. This allows the meaning of masks to evolve, adapt and transform according to new contexts, addressing a range of social and ideological issues yet remaining recognisable to audiences as a now codified, familiar horror convention. The blankness of these masks encourages us to fill in the space through the shamanic imagination that dominates how we comprehend and value the intersection of ritual, power and transformation. Just as blank masks erase identities and demand new ones, animal masks in horror also share the belief that masking and unmasking in horror cinema are acts imbued with extraordinary transformative power.

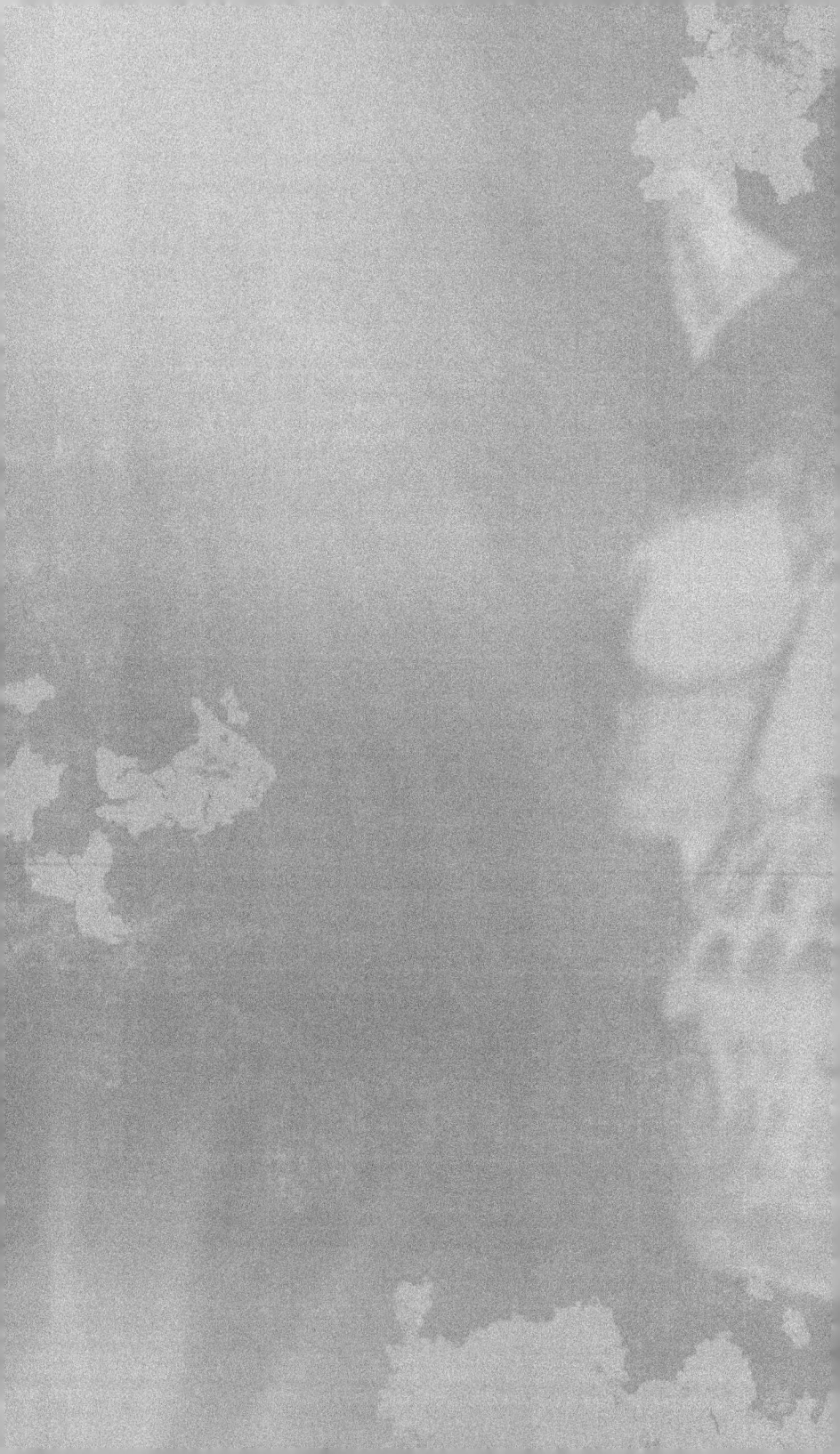

6

Animal Masks
Ritual, Power and Transformation

IF THERE IS a single mask typology that appears throughout horror cinema that indicates its long history, it is animal masks. As Walter Sorell noted, outside body painting, animal masks 'were among the first and most logical images and disguises for man, whose major and immediate experiences were with the animal world'.[1] Since the dog masks of Dionysian festivals, for Sorell 'the animal mask has never lost its imaginative hold' and animal masks in horror cinema support this claim.[2] This chapter examines six films that demonstrate how this 'imaginative hold' is maintained in contemporary horror: the South Korean film *Bloody Reunion*, the Italian neo-*giallo Stagefright*, French art-horror auteur Jean Rollin's *The Nude Vampire*, the Canadian found-footage horror film *The Conspiracy* and the US movies *Motel Hell* and *You're Next*.

In horror films whose spectacle includes the iconography of the animal mask there is sometimes an implied 'primitivism', a return to a state beyond that of assumed contemporary civility. In these examples, animal masks symbolically transform their wearers into something less-than-human: they dehumanise through the mask into an animalised state. From an anthropological perspective, this transformation can have positive practical utility: as Nunley and McCarty noted, in 'earlier times the Cherokee made animal masks for use in prehunting rituals to bring success to the hunters' – masked ceremonies and rituals aligning the hunter with the animal they seek.[3] Animal masks do not suggest a blanket primal reversion, as there are well-documented spiritual aspects crucial to their longevity and cross-cultural ubiquity: for Tonkin, animal masks have a broader spiritual function as 'very often . . . are spirits in a community's cosmology, mythical beasts or monsters'.[4] This echoes Bataille's observation that 'the mask in truth divinizes rather than humanizes the world' as 'the presence that it introduces is no longer the reassuring presence of the sage: a divine force issues from the depths of natural animality and is evident when it suddenly erupts'.[5] This again recalls shamanism's traditionally conceived ties to animism and totemism; as Schechner noted, it is 'clear that people identify themselves with animals, dress in animal skins and heads and develop specific ceremonies and observations to keep intact links connecting animal species to humans', a tendency he identifies in both European Palaeolithic and Asiatic Palaeo-Siberian shamanism.[6]

The granting of human qualities onto animals is not rare in screen culture, from *Babe* (Chris Noonan, 1995) to the television series *Mr Ed* (1958–66). In horror, parallels can be drawn between the unrelenting drive to kill between the shark in *Jaws* (Steven Spielberg, 1975) and slasher killers like Michael Myers and Jason Voorhees,[7] a correlation that simultaneously constructs the monstrosity of the latter as somehow animal-like and the former as almost monstrously human in its determination and cognitive skill. Anthropomorphism – what Michel Weemans and Bertrand Prévost defined as 'the projection of the human form onto aspects of the world'[8] – is historically linked to pre-modern and primitive religious belief and practices, falling out of vogue with the rise of rationalism in the seventeenth and eighteenth centuries with Galileo Galilei, Isaac Newton, Immanuel Kant and René Descartes, resulting in anthropomorphic religious beliefs becoming 'stigmatized'.[9] And yet in the obvious case of children's literature, anthropomorphism has endured as what William Wynn Yarbrough identified as a 'mainstay . . . exciting the child's mind with magic and uncertainty that animals bring to a human-centred consciousness while simultaneously portraying human foibles and characteristics'.[10]

From werewolves to vampires, horror tends more readily towards the opposite: it beastialises and renders humans beast-like. Filippo Menozzi referred to this as a 'reverse anthropomorphism in which it is not animals who behave like humans or take human form but rather humans who are perceived through the looking glass of a . . . "bestiary"'.[11] When cross-species representation works in this direction – animal qualities applied to humans – in horror at least similar critical concerns come to the fore: just as Weemans and Prévost identify a fundamental set of tensions inherent to anthropomorphic representation 'between the magical and the rational, the speculative and the practical, the literal and the metaphorical', so too this chapter demonstrates similar binaries underscoring mask-centric human-to-beast transformations in the films discussed here.[12]

These case studies are not the only examples of animal masks in horror cinema – one need only think of brief yet memorable images from movies like *The Shining* (Stanley Kubrick, 1980) or *The Wicker Man* (Robin Hardy, 1973). Animal masks of different 'species' appear in horror films including *The Mephisto Waltz* (Paul Wendkos, 1971), *Phantom of the Paradise* (Brian De Palma, 1974), *Screams of a Winter Night* (James L. Wilson, 1979), *Terror Train* (Roger Spottiswoode, 1980), *Berserker: The Nordic Curse* (Jefferson Richard, 1987), *Hideous!* (Charles Band, 1997), *Death Stop Holocaust* (Justin Russell, 2009), *Necromentia* (Pearry Reginald Teo, 2009), *Santeria: The Soul Possessed* (Benny Mathews, 2012), *Torment* (Jordan Barker, 2013), *Creep* and its sequel *Creep 2* (Patrick Brice, 2014/2017) and *Jackals* (Kevin Greutert, 2017). Animal masks are not specific to North American cinema and appear in the Japanese films *Black Rat* (Kenta Fukasaku, 2010) and *Museum* (Keishi Ohtomo, 2016), the Australian horror-thriller *Fortress* (Arch Nicholson, 1985) and British horror films *Satan's Slave* (David McGillivray, 1976), *White Settlers* (Simeon Halligan, 2014), *Curse of the Crimson Altar* (Vernon Sewell, 1968) and *The Abominable Dr. Phibes*, discussed in chapter 4.

The films in this chapter reveal many dimensions of animal masks in horror cinema, particularly in regard to ritual, power and transformation. *Motel Hell* and *Bloody Reunion* utilise pigs and rabbits respectively to draw direct associations between their fictional contexts and the broader culturally specific meaning of these animals. *Stagefright* and *The Conspiracy* – implicitly in the former and explicitly in the latter – deploy animal masks in reference to ancient mythology, reconfiguring their meanings in contemporary horror scenarios. Finally, both *The Nude Vampire* and *You're Next* present a number of different animal masks, deliberately neutralising the specificity of each animal away and relying instead on a transformative process that broadly dehumanises their wearers, with specific thematic motivations. These case studies illustrate the diversity of animal masks in horror, particularly in relation to ritual, power and transformation.

Animal Masks and Totemism: *Motel Hell* (1980) and *Bloody Reunion* (2006)

Pigs have long been rendered symbolically across a range of cultures as objects of disgust and transgression. Islam and Judaism explicitly forbid the eating of pork in accordance with the Quran and Hebrew scripture respectively, the latter stating that 'because it parts the hoof and is cloven-footed but does not chew the cud, [the pig] is unclean'.[13] In *The Politics and Poetics of Transgression*, Peter Stallybrass and Allon White highlight the pig's historical association with abjection, noting its role in Carnival: along with the rat, the pig is 'symbolically base and abject'.[14] Films like *Carrie* (Brian De Palma, 1976) and *Daddy's Deadly Darling* (Marc Lawrence, 1972) connect pigs and abjection in the centrepieces of their respective narratives and spectacles and pig masks in horror are not rare: Benjamin Christensen's *Häxan* (1929) includes pig masks and they are worn by a range of horror antagonists in films including *The People Who Own the Dark* (León Klimovsky, 1976), *The Butcher* (Kim Jin-won, 2007), *Death Stop Holocaust* (Justin Russell, 2009), *Porkchop* (Eamon Hardiman, 2010), *Torment* (Jordan Barker, 2013), *White Settlers* (Simeon Halligan, 2015) and throughout the *Saw* franchise (2004–17). The pig mask as a visual signifier of transgression transcends horror, from Pier Paolo Pasolini's *Porcile* (1969) to Nelson Lyon's adult art film *The Telephone Book* (1971).

The pig mask in *Motel Hell* is limited in terms of actual screen time, but its impact surpasses temporal duration, evidenced by its ubiquity in the film's promotional materials. For Clover, *Motel Hell* is 'a send-up of modern horror with special reference to *Psycho* and [*Texas*] *Chain Saw* [*Massacre*] *II*', noting its pig mask-wearing villain Farmer Vincent (Rory Calhoun) is typical of the 'sexually disturbed' killer of the slasher film.[15] For John Kenneth Muir, it is 'a black comedy about hypocrisy, about the way in which every person, even serial killers like Farmer Vincent, tell themselves little lies to get through the day'.[16] Wearing his pig-head mask and wielding a chainsaw, Vincent's pig mask appears mostly in the film's climax, when his brother – Sheriff Bruce Smith (Paul Linke) – confronts him in the meat-processing shed as he seeks to rescue Vincent's victim/ fiancé Terry (Nina Axelrod). Vincent's wears the pig mask to punctuate moments where he has the greatest levels of power and control – frightening children who visit the eponymous motel, or menacing the innocent Terry. Notably, he does not wear it when tending the human 'crop' that he farms in his garden to produce his highly sought after small goods:

these for him at least are not him flexing his dominance, but rather he speaks explicitly of 'humane' farming practices. He wants their deaths to be spiritually fulfilling, as 'they're good animals, they're not like chickens or hogs', bragging about his refusal to use preservatives. Capturing his victims with bear traps, he turns them into meat-producing stock, but in his mind the wearing of the pig mask reduces himself to an 'animal' too, the mask constructing *Motel Hell* as a film about 'animals' farming humans. As such, it typifies Shaun Kimber's 'food horror' category, 'texts within which food and eating are its central focus'.[17] Because of his 'humane' farming practices, Vincent considers himself an environmentalist, noting that 'there's too many people in the world and not enough food. I'm just trying to help out.' When Vincent is killed in his final showdown, normative eating regimes are reinstated: the 'animal' is slaughtered, people are no longer turned into jerky and human dominance of the food chain returns. But not just any 'animal': as Vincent notes earlier, 'hogs' are not 'good animals', recalling Islamic and Hebrew food laws that consider the animal 'unclean'. This implies a degree of self-awareness on his part that belies his stated belief that he is an ethical farmer (underscored by the hypocrisy of his dying confession: 'I used preservatives'). Vincent's adoption of the pig mask subconsciously aligns him with a 'bad' animal; deep down, he considers *himself* abject.

Farming itself has been considered a ritual practice across a range of cultures and histories, reflected in the heavily regimented practices governing Vincent's cultivation of his human crop.[18] More broadly, Vincent's pig mask recalls Sigmund Freud's work on totemism: while Freud's associating it with 'savage' people from Australian First Nations make its origins ideologically biased from a contemporary perspective,[19] it is undeniably applicable to *Motel Hell*: 'The totem is first of all the tribal ancestor of the clan, as well as its tutelary spirit and protector.'[20] While Freud spoke of First Nations Australians, Christina Pratt identified broader global traditions of totem animal spirits (including clans on the Pacific coast of North America), stating that 'the connection of a clan or family to a totem animal is based on the recognition of a common nature (qualities, skills, talents)'. The ways these connections are made through ritual, however, are diverse:

> in some cultures eating the animal in ordinary reality is a way to directly assimilate the animal's power and teaching (while) in other cultures a shaman must observing [*sic*] a strict taboo against eating the flesh of the animal to maintain a relationship with the animal.[21]

In relation to Vincent's pig mask, Pratt's writing on totem animals is particularly poignant:

> In most cultures the relationship with the totem animal is honored through animal-like dancing that occurs when the individual merges with the spirit of the animal and allows that animal to dance through his or her body during ritual or ceremony.[22]

In *Motel Hell*, slaughter itself is ritualistic and Vincent's totem animal – the pig – is privileged through that most traditional of shamanic practices: the wearing of a mask. Vincent's transformation from friendly yokel to malign human-farming psychopath is marked explicitly by transformations and rituals associated with his pig mask.

Animal masks are also used in Dae-wung Lim's 2006 South Korean slasher film *Bloody Reunion*. Again, rabbit masks are not unique in horror, famously associated with *Donnie Darko* (Richard Kelly, 2001) and films including *Easter Bunny, Kill! Kill!* (Chad Ferrin, 2006), *Rabitto horâ* (Takashi Shimizu, 2011) and *Dhogs* (Andrés Goteira, 2017). In these films, the supposedly cute, harmless nature of rabbits is manipulated to subversive (and sometimes comic) effect. Like *Motel Hell*, this particular animal is adopted as a totem by the film's killer, revealing as much about the wearer's self-image as the animal's broader cultural meaning. Through the rituals of the slasher film scenario – the sequential murder vignettes that structure the film and mark the killer's modus operandi – the deployment of the rabbit mask in the movie's final revelation of the killer's identity suggests a softer side that contrasts with the brutality of the crimes depicted. Rather than an inhuman monster, the killer is a psychologically damaged individual irreversibly harmed by childhood trauma. The vulnerability of the rabbit is not ironic, but tragically appropriate.

Daniel Martin identified *Bloody Reunion* as a 'slasher-melodrama', which is useful as it privileges Linda Williams's previously noted defining intersection of action and pathos as much as slashers' more spectacular codes and conventions.[23] The film tracks a group of young adults visiting their dying, wheelchair-bound school teacher Mrs Park (Oh Mi-hee) at the invitation of their former schoolmate, Mi-Ja (Seo Young-hee). But a range of abuses they experienced at Mrs Park's hands are revealed as they are each killed off by a killer in a crude rabbit mask. The film implies that the mask is worn by Mrs Park's intellectually disabled son, who she has locked in her basement, away from broader community. The film's final twist reveals this entire narrative was a fabrication by its unreliable, guilty narrator, Mi-Ja herself (really named Jung-Won). The traumas she falsely ascribed to her school peers instead happened to her: mocked by Mrs Park for her poverty, she is humiliated when she accidentally defecated in class with the onset of menarche. The death of her mother triggered a mental health collapse and she massacred those who humiliated her, leaving only her teacher to hear her confession.

Bloody Reunion provokes a disturbing contrast between the cute, childlike bunny mask with the extreme acts of violence committed by its wearer. An early, portentous shot of a decaying rabbit near Mrs Park's home begins a conscious strategy of flagging the literal and symbolic decay of 'softness' itself. In Jung-Won's fabricated story, the killer wears both a rabbit mask and teams it with a jumper embossed with a cute bunny motif. Told through flashback to an investigating detective, even though made up, from Jung-Won's perspective the emphasis on rabbit symbolism is revealing. This is confirmed when investigators raid Jung-Won's home and discover a wall covered in her hand-made rabbit masks, similar to Michael Myers's cell in Rob Zombie's 2007 *Halloween* remake, discussed previously.

While Martin emphasised the film's generic hybridisation and its significance in the global reach of contemporary South Korean horror, he ignored the rabbit mask itself. As he noted, 'the film's "Final Girl" is thus actually its killer and she represents the ultimate outcast', but her tragic story makes her highly sympathetic, despite the violence that preceded her confession.[24] Typifying the film's melodramatic aspects, Mi-Ja/Jung-Won's soliloquy at the film's conclusion adheres to Ben Singer's definition of pathos as 'the elicitation of a powerful feeling of pity', aligning her with Williams's 'victim-hero' of action melodramas.[25] For Williams, 'the suffering of the victim-hero is important for the establishing of moral legitimacy'[26] yet, rather than excusing her for the massacre, *Bloody Reunion* instead seeks to position her victimhood as a result of broader social injustices linked to class: the mistreatment of those living in poverty by those in privileged positions of power.

The cuteness of the rabbit and Mi-Ja/Jung-Won's adoption of it as her totem animal is vital. One need only look at the popularity of Dutch illustrator Dick Bruna's 'Miffy' character in Korea[27] to identify the iconographic origins of the mask design in *Bloody Reunion*, its overt associations with a broader childhood imaginary underscoring Mi-Ja/Jung-Won's tragically stunted emotional development that resulted from childhood trauma. Like Vincent in *Motel Hell*, the executions that make up the visceral spectacles of Mi-Ja/Jung-Won's diegetically fictional account of the story are ritualised, the careful placement of the bodies in the basement where Mrs Park's son was supposedly imprisoned echoing the final tableaux in *Happy Birthday to Me*, discussed in chapter 4. Mi-Ja/Jung-Won's identification with the rabbit and its placement in murder scenes were foreshadowed by the early shot of the rotting rabbit: Mi-Ja/Jung-Won sees her own story as one of innocence corrupted. Cuteness is rendered abject and the symbolic potency of the rabbit mask reflects what she sees as her own transformation from softness into a monstrous, abjected Other.

As we move towards the next section, however, the folkloric status of the rabbit in South Korea specifically is worth of note. The folktale 'Tale of Rabbit and Tortoise' is described as a Korean version of 'The Tortoise and the Hare', which reflects the deceptive power dynamics between assumed positions of strength and weakness in *Bloody Reunion*.[28] Likewise, the folktale 'Tiger Gets its Tail Cut Off' – where a rabbit uses a tiger's greed against it to trick it into getting its tail frozen off in icy water – has two possible interpretations: 'it can be read as a fool's tale from the tiger's point of view, but from the perspective of the rabbit, who is the weaker party, the focus is on the scheme that eventually leads to triumph'.[29] Neither wholly weak nor ineffectual, rabbits in Korea from a folkloric perspective have a traditionally violent streak, seen elsewhere in the self-explanatory 'Rabbit Throws Baby in Cauldron Before Running Away'.[30] While this section has focused on the adoption of totem animals by mask-wearing killers, we now consider the intersection of ritual, power, transformation and mythology in horror film animal masks, examining owls in Michel Soavi's *Stagefright* and bulls in Christopher MacBride's *The Conspiracy*.

Animal Masks and Mythology: *Stagefright* (1987) and *The Conspiracy* (2012)

While the symbolic potency of specific animals is key to *Motel Hell* and *Bloody Reunion* regarding how they symbolically represent particular characters, this section explores the mythological deployment of animals through masks in *Stagefright* and *The Conspiracy* respectively. While *Bloody Reunion*'s rabbit evokes connections to Korean folklore, although they intersect it is worth emphasising that folklore and mythology are distinct categories: as Danielle Kirby noted, while 'notoriously difficult to articulate' the difference hinges on issues of temporality: 'Myth . . . tends to occur outside of linear time, in sacred time', while 'folklore can be situated in any time, either mundane or sacred'.[31] The films in this section engage with diegetic urban legends and the use of masks also contain mythological aspects regarding owls and bulls respectively. Human transformation through masked rituals here intersect with ancient mythologies.

In *Stagefright*, masked performance is central to its diegetically staged theatrical performance that provides the film's primary setting. An opening scene where a woman is chased by an owl-masked killer is revealed to be a dress rehearsal for a play as the participants begin dancing. The lines between this performance and the film's 'real' action surrounds escaped serial killer and ex-actor Irving Wallace (Clain Parker) who adopts the owl mask and kills off the cast and crew, leaving only Final Girl Alicia (Barbra Cupisti) and caretaker Willy (James Sampson) alive. With its theatrical setting and the professional aspirations of its villain André Loiselle considered *Stagefright* typical of the 'actor as psycho-without-psychology' trope, as it makes no attempt to provide a motive: 'there is no explanation whatsoever as to why this fugitive from an insane asylum chooses to slaughter actors'.[32] Wallace seems driven only by a desire to 'appear centre stage and indulge in a performance of sadistic carnage', manifesting in the climactic tableaux where he sits on stage in a throne-like armchair, surrounded by the carefully positioned bodies he has systematically butchered throughout the film (similar to ritualised spectacles at the end of both *Happy Birthday to Me* and *Bloody Reunion*).[33] It is, for Loiselle, a hollow victory: 'the psycho-killer is but a poor player who slashes and slaughters his hour upon the stage and then is heard no more'.[34]

Yet, like *Motel Hell* and *Bloody Reunion*, the specific animal central to the masked performance is significant. *Stagefright*'s play-within-a-film is called *The Night Owl*, uniting the bird's nocturnal alertness with horror's generic tendency to present night as a period for sinister activity. *Stagefright*'s use of an owl mask also has mythological connotations: in Italy, there is a widespread superstition that owls are harbingers of bad luck.[35] In ancient Rome, Desmond Morris noted that 'some Romans were so convinced that the cry of an owl heralded an imminent death that they would do their utmost to capture the bird and kill it, hoping this would neutralize the prophecy'.[36] Yet even after death, the owl still held unique power, for 'there were fears that it would have supernatural powers that would enable it to come to life again, so its body was cremated and its ashes thrown into the River Tiber'.[37] As a slasher killer, Wallace's utilisation of an owl mask specifically contains profound mythological significance in the context of Italian cultural history. While his ritualistic slaughter recalls broader traditions of slasher and neo-*giallo* cinema, the symbolic potency of the owl itself in ancient Roman mythology is just as important. Through the owl mask, Wallace is transformed into something symbolically far grander than his character's reality suggests, aligned with ancient Roman myths about the ominous, immortal power of the bird itself. *Stagefright* plays out performance rituals that straddle both the codes and conventions of neo-*gialli*, while simultaneously framing them in the broader framework of ancient Roman mythology that underscores the owl's symbolic potency.

The intersection between ritual, power, transformation and mythology is more explicit in the mockumentary *The Conspiracy*. Following film-makers Aaron (Aaron Poole) and Jim (James Gilbert), the movie tracks their descent into conspiracy theory subculture, their investigations leading to the Tarsus Club, a secret society of the global power elite based on the ancient religion of Mithraism. The film privileges Mithraic ritual practice and the word 'Tarsus' strategically links it to actual mythological origins. In the film's climax when Aaron and Jim successfully sneak into a Tarsus Club meeting as initiates, the forced placement of a bull mask on Aaron offers the film's central horror spectacle, marking him as the victim of the club's ancient ritualistic 'bull', targeting him as the victim of ritualistic human sacrifice.

The Conspiracy deliberately manipulates this myth to provide ideological commentary on its contemporary moment. Like its use of masks and the power they bring with them through the force of the shamanic imagination, it is another example of a horror film that reconfigures the 'old' to speak to 'new' cultural contexts, and *The Conspiracy* explicitly defines the mythological mechanics governing the Tarsus Club's human sacrifice ritual. Discussing Mithraic religious beliefs and practices central to *The Conspiracy*, Michael Rice notes that it reached its popular peak during the Roman Empire and that the 'central myth' upon which Mithraism was based concerns a young god (originally the Persian god Mithra or Mitra): 'The journey is symbolic, for the god suffers almost as much as the bull as he is dragged over the rough ground by the bull's furious flight to his cave shelter.'[38] Practised from Scotland to India during its peak, as a 'mystery cult', Mithraic rituals were secret. In terms of its initiation rites, a number of known elements are directly referenced in *The Conspiracy*: like the real cult, followers in the film refer to each other as 'brothers'[39] and identify each other on an animal hierarchy, including 'ravens' and 'dogs'.[40]

While Mithraic rites conclude with the eating of the bull in a 'ritual feast',[41] the explicit reference to Tarsian Mithraism in the name the Tarsus Club indicates an engagement with a specific historical variation of Mithraicism. While dominant Mithraism originated in Iran, Tarsian Mithraism – as the name suggests – originated in the Anatolian city of Tarsus. This variant was also specific to a power elite and the conquest of the bull was executed by Perseus, a mythological figure with long historical associations with Tarsus itself.[42] This informs how Mithraic rituals are reconfigured in *The Conspiracy*. For Rice, the most visible remaining traces of Mithraism and religious rituals of their bull-sacrifice manifest in contemporary bull-fighting; but in *The Conspiracy*, its legacy is more literal.[43] By emphasising the historical intersection of Tarsian Mithraism with the power elite, it provides the mythological foundations for a fictional secret society with great global power. *The Conspiracy* therefore engages broadly with the post-9/11 conspiratorial imagination of people like Alex Jones and David Icke, and one of the most striking features of the film is its ambivalence to this: it is often difficult to decipher if the film is a critique of conspiracy theory culture or a vindication of it.

From this perspective, this 'fictional' aspect is itself unstable as writer/director Christopher MacBride positioned his eponymous 'conspiracy' as not wholly limited by purely fictional constraints. This is accomplished through the inclusion of the Zapruder film, arguably one of the most privileged documents for conspiracy theorists. MacBride also included interviews with real conspiracy theorists to highlight that this is 'what it's like when you're looking into a conspiracy theory: It's so hard to discern fact from fiction'.[44] MacBride himself seemed convinced of the veracity of some conspiracy theories, such as that of the Bohemian Club and their 'pagan ritual[s]': 'People would be shocked if they knew the types of ultra-powerful people that are a part of this organization . . . Whether they are up to anything nefarious or are just a secretive and exclusive club is up for debate.'[45] Identifying the Bohemian Club as an inspiration for the film,[46] MacBride's Tarsus Club reimagines this real-life group of whom many US presidents were members, haunted by rumours of 'pseudo-Druidic rituals'[47] and even claims that Ronald Reagan sacrificed a goat to protect him from assassination.[48]

This conspiracy theory that members of the Bohemian Club participated in human sacrifice during 'Cremation of Care' ceremonies in a 'lavish pyrotechnic display by men dressed in priests in front of a large owl sculpture, which is the symbol of the Grove' is reconstructed in the climax of *The Conspiracy* where Aaron is forced to wear a bull mask.[49] With their paranoid belief that the Tarsus Club is behind a 'new world order' driven by the power elite, Aaron and Jim infiltrate the initiation ritual. As revealed on hidden camera footage, while Jim is welcomed into the Tarsus Club as a new member (with implied threats to his family if he does not pledge), Aaron is unknowingly transformed into the symbolic bull figure, which he only discovers when he looks in a mirror. Re-enacting Mithraic ritual, the members of the Tarsus Club pursue 'bull' Aaron through the woods, until he is captured and his camera stops recording. While his fate remains unclear, the final moments of the 'documentary' reveal Aaron's footage has been recrafted into a pro-Tarsus Club propaganda film: his footage is retrospectively framed as a warning to other interlopers. While accepted into the club, it is implied Jim and his wife are under pressure to appear happy about this. The film finishes with the indication that Aaron's wearing of the bull mask rendered him the human victim of the ritualistic Tarsus Club 'bull' hunt. He is effectively erased as a human player in the film, and reduced to sacrificial animal.

Through the bull mask, *The Conspiracy* renders Aaron the (probable) victim of ritualistic human sacrifice in an explicitly Mithraic context, configured through the film's evocation of contemporary conspiracy theories as implicitly linked to the real-world Bohemian Club and the dominant ideological 'new world order'. Ritualised mask-wearing transformed Aaron into an animal to be hunted and he is punished for his willingness to interfere or question the dominant order. The bull mask is a ritual tool that allows the re-enactment of key Mithraic initiation rites and the bull is slaughtered, allowing young (and old) gods to retain their power. Masked transformation enacted through ancient ritual is necessary for the maintaining of hegemonic, patriarchal control: *The Conspiracy* renders the endurance of this system emphatically horrific.

Animal Masks and Ambivalence: *The Nude Vampire* (1970) and *You're Next* (2011)

The final case studies in this chapter shift towards masked menageries in horror cinema: a horse, bull, reindeer, frog, rabbit and pig in Jean Rollin's *The Nude Vampire* and a lamb, tiger and fox in Adam Wingard's *You're Next*. While collectively the imagery of these masked groups is visually striking, in terms of narrative function and screen time they are effectively negligible. It would be impossible, for instance, to draw parallels between the specific kinds of animal masks worn in these films as has been done with the pig in *Motel Hell*, the rabbit in *Bloody Reunion*, the owl in *Stagefright* or the bull in *The Conspiracy*. Yet it is precisely the sparsity of their symbolic specificity that renders them significant: both films are ambivalent regarding these animals beyond their status as uncanny and inhuman for different thematic reasons.

The uncanny is a key concept when considering Jean Rollin in particular. In 2011, Tim Lucas christened Rollin the 'screen's most important surrealist of the past quarter century',[50] while Marcelline Block – a contributor to the 2017 all-woman written collection *Lost Girls: The Phantasmagorical Cinema of Jean Rollin* – has also emphasised the centrality of surrealism to Rollins's practice, noting that 'he was personally influenced by painters such as Magritte and the Surrealism movement', and that he has 'often been called a poet of the cinema whose fantastique films express a melancholy, romantic aesthetic imbued with Surrealism and/or Dadaism.'[51]

For Hal Foster, surrealism was marked by its association with the uncanny through its fascination with how 'repressed material returns in ways that disrupt unitary identity, aesthetic norms and social order'.[52] Defined by Freud as 'that class of the frightening which leads us back to what is known of old and long familiar', his use of the term is linked to the German word *heimlich* that simultaneously refers both to 'what is familiar and agreeable' and 'what is concealed and kept out of sight'.[53] This tension evokes the *unheimlich*, which for Freud 'is what was once *heimlich*, familiar; the prefix "un" is the token of repression'.[54] The uncanny hinges on this merger of familiar and unfamiliar, the perception of something familiar as emphatically strange. For David Bate, 'the uncanny is something repressed which recurs', which was 'a habit already noted in surrealism'.[55]

Writing of his relationship to cinema in 2004, Rollin championed 'an illogical and nonsensical European cinema'.[56] For Rollin, 'the images and dialogues of my films, like the images and texts of my books, attach themselves to the idea that they can become, or are, a cinema of the imaginary'.[57] Recalling earlier masked horror performance traditions, Rollin was not just aware of the heritage of the Grand Guignol theatre but shot scenes from both his first and last feature films there: 1968's *Rape of the Vampire* and 2009's *The Mask of Medusa* respectively.[58] Championing Franju's *Judex* (1963), for Rollin the 'cinema which permits these meanderings is the only real cinema. It is the European cinema I want to make and write about.'[59] The use of animal masks in *The Nude Vampire* was clearly influenced by the animal masks in *Judex* and while peripheral to the film's central action, Rollin deploys both animal masks and masks more generally at the beginning of the film to uncanny effect. The opening shot shows an unidentified figure in a lab coat with a black leather horned hood. A door opens and reveals other figures in lab coats wearing red fabric hoods with eye holes cut out and a woman in a blue fabric hood. The red masked figures strip the woman, apply a tourniquet and draw a blood sample that is placed into a contraption that splits the blood into distinct, rainbow-coloured liquids. Even before the opening credits, Rollin presents a familiar scenario – a blood test in the clinical context of a scientific laboratory – yet defamiliarises it through an unintelligible, unfamiliar ritual. After the credits, a young woman in an orange gown ethereally prowls city streets, pursued by black-clad figures in leather animal masks: a horse, a bull, a reindeer, a rabbit, a pig and a frog. Encountering the film's protagonist Pierre Radamante (Olivier Martin), he helps her elude her pursuers, but she is shot by the reindeer masked figure and carried to a property Pierre recognises as a private club run by his father. What follows focuses on Rollin's defining erotic spectacle over coherent plot and while masks are no longer central, they certainly fulfil Rollin's attempt to move towards a 'meandering' cinema, where potent images leave lasting impressions over character and plot development.

The masks – be they fabric or animal-shaped – protect their wearers from the (possibly) dangerous gaze of the (possibly) vampire-like woman in orange, yet at no point is the specificity of the animals brought into play. But the masks both transform their wearers from human to uncanny, animalised Others and protect those who look at them from (possibly) vampiric transformation. These animal masks are uncanny in their rendering of something strangely familiar, disturbing in their status as animals and non-animals, humans and non-humans. The masks are privileged in ritual contexts, such as a staged performance where the woman in orange is first implied to be a vampire. In an opulent room, an audience of expensively dressed onlookers watch as a woman walks before them and smilingly shoots herself in the head, falling to her death. Blue fabric masks are placed on both the corpse and the audience as the woman in the orange gown appears from behind theatre curtains and walks towards the body, placed on a bed-like altar by two animal-masked figures. She approaches the corpse, is drawn to the blood and begins to lick it. The role of these animal masks is again vague, yet clearly central to a ritual whose meaning is beyond our comprehension. This is in keeping with Rollin's broader aesthetics and tone: of the opening scene where Pierre first meets the woman, Rollin called it 'Nothing special, only elements of everyday . . . but the bizarre atmosphere is there. Why? Which? What? I don't know but the mystery is there.'[60] *The Nude Vampire* is ambivalent to the specific transformations occurring to the wearers of these animal masks, but their involvement in the rituals that are privileged spectacles in the film are clearly crucial ceremonial aspects, part of the Othering strategies that marks the community as existing beyond what the film implies is mainstream society. Rollin's fascination is with the power of cinema itself as a forum for ritual and myth-creation, and masks play an intrinsic part in how this is constructed.

If the menagerie of animal masks were deployed here according to Jean Rollin's surrealist practice, then mumblegore home invasion film *You're Next*'s three masked villains – a tiger, fox and lamb – are deployed even more ambivalently. What in the traditional horror film might be a key enigma linked to masked villains – who is underneath the mask? – in *You're Next* is consciously undermined, similar to the previously discussed *Hush* five years later. While *The Nude Vampire* evokes the shamanic imagination to imply something ritually powerful – albeit vague and undefined – about its animal masks, both *Hush* and *You're Next* in fact effectively subvert and undermine the power that the shamanic imagination has historically imbued in the object: in these films, we *assume* masks are powerful, but they are not. In *Hush*, while associations with the trickster spirit continue even after Man's mask is removed, this is not the case in *You're Next*. As discussed here, capitalist greed destroys everything, not just families but even powerful, enduring legacies like the shamanic imagination. Masks here are revealed to be hollow signifiers.

You're Next's real villains are indifferent to the human wearers of the animal masks and rather consider them Othered subordinates hired to execute their family with the systematic, ritualistic violence of the slasher film. The often-privileged unmasking moment is consciously downplayed, the wearers revealed – like *Hush* – to be 'nobodies': even when their humanness (and, briefly, humanity) is revealed, they are animals to the slaughter. Yet it is precisely this which grants them an ethical and ideological aspect in terms of the film's broader politics. By considering them disposable and less-than-human, the culpability of those truly responsible for the film's atrocities is exposed. *You're Next* is a home-invasion slasher film framed around a family reunion – itself a bourgeois social ritual – as the adult children of Aubrey (Barbara Crampton) and Paul (Rob Moran) join them at their isolated holiday home in rural Missouri. Family members and their partners are killed in increasingly elaborate ways and it is revealed that Felix (Nicholas Tucci), Zee (Wendy Glenn) and Crispian (A. J. Bowen) hired animal-masked assassins to gain the large inheritance remaining after everyone else's deaths. Their plans are thwarted when it is revealed that Crispian's girlfriend Erin (Sharni Vinson) was raised in an Australian survivalist compound, dispatching both the animal-masked assassins and those who hired them.

The processes that Other the three animal intruders – fox-masked Tom (Lane Hughes), lamb-masked Craig (L. C. Holt) and tiger-masked Dave (Simon Barrett, also the screenwriter) – are visible from the outset. The film forbids any attempt to ascribe meaning to the specific masks, unlike the masks in the first four films discussed in this chapter: while traditional readings would suggest the lamb mask represents meekness or innocence, the tiger mask strength or wildness, or the fox cunningness and ferocity, the film denies any evidence to support such interpretations. Like Rollin's *The Nude Vampire*, these animal masks represent only non-human Otherness as they do not seek associations with specific animals and their traditional meanings. Rather, their broader non-humanness indicates a symbolic fracture that is defined in relation to class differences. On screen, the light-coloured animal masks worn by black-clothed characters in dark rooms create the impression of abstracted heads floating in space, implying a supernatural aspect to their crimes: these actions are executed with a precision deemed well beyond the standard capabilities of most people. Formally constructed in this way, they are disembodied presences rather than characters as such and while not spiritual or divine, their (initial) indestructibility aligns them with forces not wholly of the natural realm. The *absence* of character that can be attributed to their blank, unmasked faces (and – like *Hush* – the lack of fanfare accompanying the removal of these masks) recalls Coates's observation that 'the face becomes a mask that fails, a surface haunted by intimations of concealment, interiority and exteriority'.[61] As Jeanne Dubino noted, that animals were once 'closely intertwined' with humans shifted with the rise of modernity, 'marked by the increasing disappearance of animals'.[62] *You're Next* makes this explicit: the traditional relationship between animals and animal masks (as seen in the earlier examples in this chapter) is severed.

This assumed 'primal' Otherness is central to how those who hired the masked assailants view the assassins. To them, these paid killers are amoral animals and they show genuine surprise when one masked character expresses emotion at the death of another: the man in the lamb mask screams and flips a table when he learns the man in the fox mask has been killed. He mentions his brother is the man in the tiger mask, which shocks Felix: that these men could have their own familial relationships bewilders him. This is a rare moment where we gain insight into the men behind the masks: 'unlike you, I liked my brother', the unnamed man tells Felix. Felix's response offers further backstory: while unaware that they were related, he knew that they 'served together'. The animal masked intruders are therefore implied to be returned military veterans of some type and Felix's offer of more cash if they kill Erin suggests that they have turned to this line of work out of financial necessity, their experience with death stemming from their experience as 'legitimate' servicemen.

Felix's grievances voiced to the masked killers when their plan unravels are consumer complaints: from his and Crispian's perspective, some can kill and some cannot and despite masterminding the scheme, they consider themselves above such 'animal' actions. *You're Next* critiques the hypocrisy of 'soft' liberal masculinity, typified when Felix kills his brother Drake (Joe Swanberg) with his own hands and saying without irony 'could you just die already, this is hard enough for me'. From the brothers' perspective, their wealth and privilege make it impossible for them to commit violence, while the comparative poverty of their hired assassins renders them in their mind – literally, through the deployment of the tiger, fox and lamb masks – simply animals. Notably, the lamb-masked man has a southern accent: he is a poor outsider and as such Felix and Crispian have no issue seeing him as a guilty party, despite his only being there at the request of more affluent brothers. Although Felix and Zee are revealed early in the film as being responsible for driving the murder conspiracy, Crispian's involvement is the plot twist. That Crispian came up with the plan, yet still identifies as a pacifist reveals the liberal hypocrisy the film attacks: through their social privilege, Crispian and Felix believe that they are effectively innocent of murders which they themselves commissioned.

Zee and Erin stand in contrast to the 'soft' liberal masculinity Crispian represents and reveal its failures. Although a minor character, Zee's calm perversion exposes the murderous Felix's hypocrisy especially: sitting on a bed next to Aubrey's dead body, Felix is horrified when Zee asks him to 'fuck me next to your dead mom'. While perverse, Zee is self-aware: her involvement with the murder was undertaken with full knowledge of her culpability, knowledge she finds sexually titillating. Final Girl Erin too exhibits a frankness that the men lack and she counteracts Zee, Felix and Crispian's conspiracy through what is configured in the film as a distinctly feminist act of mobilisation. While the tiger-, lamb- and fox-masked men are driven by a need for money, Erin is driven by a need to survive. Yet Erin and the masked intruders are united in their Otherness – the former as monstrous 'animals', the latter (as is mentioned throughout the film) by her status as a non-American Outsider (her 'abrasive' accent is mentioned earlier in passing). That the film ends so ambivalently in regard to Erin's future as the police arrive and mistakenly believe she is responsible for the massacre (echoing the conclusion of *Happy Birthday to Me*), suggests a pessimistic view of how the violent, hypocritical and privileged masculinity the film documents will be punished. The ambivalence with which the film deploys its animal masks permeates the entire movie with forceful ideological intent.

This chapter has explored the intersection of ritual, power and transformation with animal horror masks. While these masks broadly imply transformations from human to an often 'primitive' state of animality, these six films underscore the diversity with which animal masks have been deployed in the genre. In *Motel Hell* and *Bloody Reunion*, masks are used in ritualised contexts to provoke associations with the symbolic meaning of specific animals to engage with the central themes of each film. In *Stagefright* and *The Conspiracy*, animal masks are (implicitly in the former and explicitly in the latter) utilised with an eye towards each animal's mythological histories. But in *The Nude Vampire* and *You're Next*, groups of mixed animal mask-wearing characters undermine this exact specificity, presented collectively as an uncanny collective of non-human Others, deployed with different yet potent thematic intent. Animal masks in post-1970 horror underscore yet again the dynamic, evolving ways that horror film masks have endured as a central iconographic element of the genre. As explored in the next chapter, the same is true of horror films that feature repurposed masks, where masks intended for a specific use are redeployed in a new, different way.

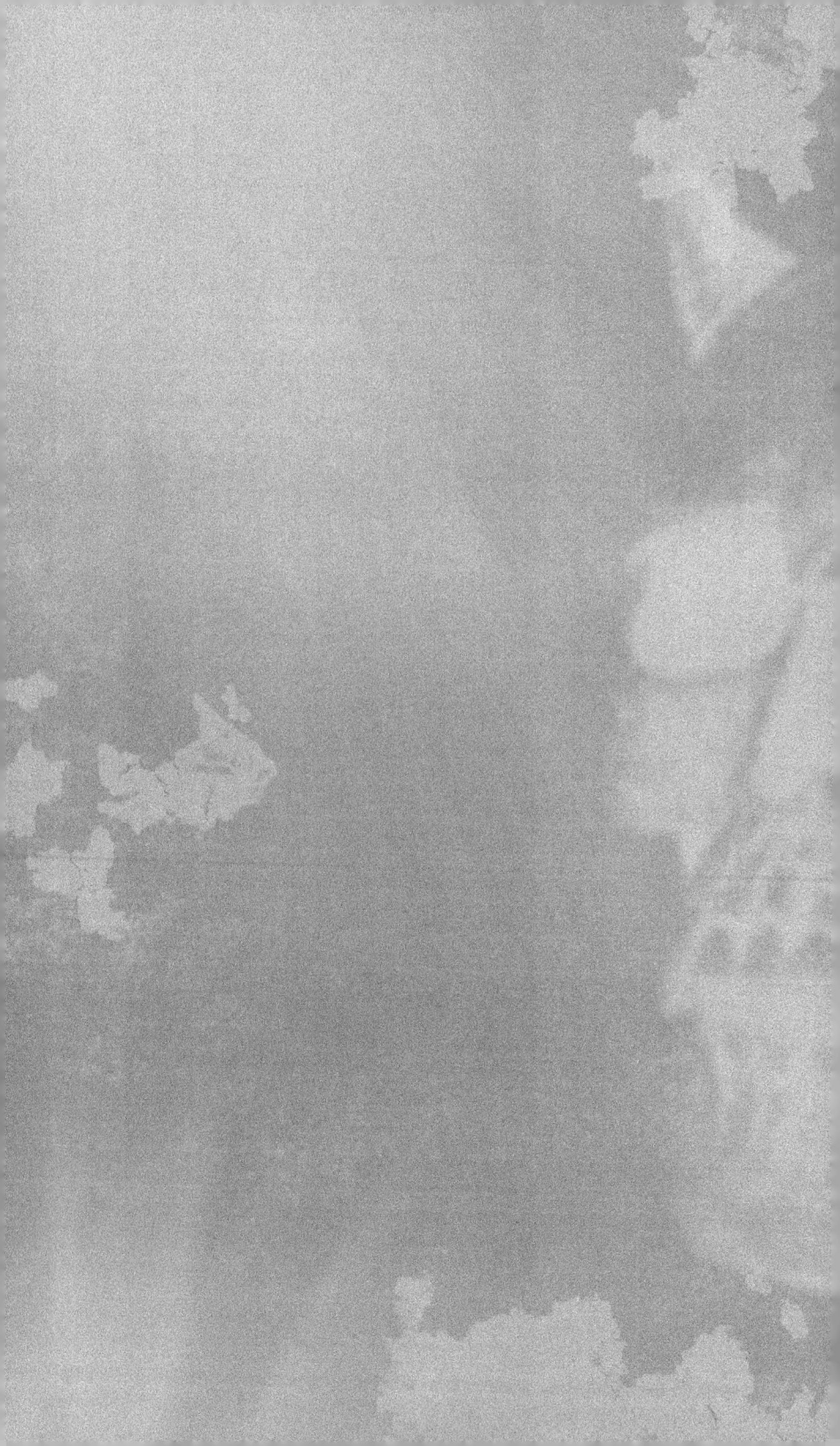

7

Repurposed Masks
Ritual, Power and Transformation

HAVING EXPLORED horror film masks with distant historical origins in the previous three chapters, we now turn to horror mask typologies with more contemporary roots. Here we examine repurposed masks, understood as objects whose initial, intended functions are redeployed in horror to create new cultural meanings. In *My Bloody Valentine*, *Evidence*, *Friday the 13th Part III*, *Carved: The Slit-Mouthed Woman*, *Dead Ringers* and *Anatomy*, different masked transformations intersect with ritual and power in a range of ways to demonstrate the durability and dynamism of repurposed horror masks. These films reveal that even if the original intended function of certain masks is benign or even helpful (such as, for instance, safety masks), the heft of their symbolic presences is broadly transferable, even if their specific meanings are not. For John Mack, 'it is precisely because . . . masks have an authority and power in one context that they are meaningful in another'.[1] For instance, as explored shortly, gas masks have rich historical significance and while that specific history may not be immediately relevant to *My Bloody Valentine*, its symbolic presence is underscored by the *force* of its broader iconographic power. Even in their original contexts, masks can serve a number of functions: the executioner's mask, for instance, shields its wearer from blood splatter, but as Laura Makarius noted, it also fulfils a moral and psychological function as it 'allows him to disappear, as it were and cease to be the specific person he is'.[2]

The masks examined in this chapter – gas masks, welding masks, surgical masks and hockey masks – all likewise conceal and protect. On a narrative level, repurposed masks hide the identity of the wearer, but at the same time still loosely fulfil their original purpose as protective garb. While therefore relatively contemporary when compared to mask typologies explored in previous chapters, again the broader shamanic imagination is at work here through parallels between repurposed masks in horror films and those worn traditionally by shamans. 'Shamans use masks and costumes as a kind of armor that helps protect them while negotiating with evil forces of the spirit world', noted Nunley and McCarty.[3] In horror cinema, when worn by villains, this is frequently subverted: rather than seeking *protection* from evil forces, it predominantly *aligns* the wearer with those powers. Like the executioner's mask, in some instances they both disguise the wearer and protect them from the visceral spray of their violent acts. For Nunley and McCarty, the shaman's mask is part of their 'armour' to 'do battle with the spiritual forces, influencing them through ritual'.[4] This can be seen in contemporary industrial cultures, where we 'wear protective masks to negotiate with competitors or forces that threaten our survival'.[5] In horror film, these masks are repurposed to create fear in the audience, reliant on the endurance of the mask as a key aspect of horror cinema's iconographic palette. These six films do not represent all horror films that use repurposed masks;[6] however they collectively present an overview of the different ways that repurposed masks can be employed in horror and how they intersect with ritual, power and transformation.

Repurposed Masks and Untrained Labour: *My Bloody Valentine* (1981) and *Evidence* (2013)

While broadly dismissed at the time as a weak *Halloween* imitator,[7] unlike Patrick Lussier's US-made 2009 remake, George Mihalka's *My Bloody Valentine* was a distinctly Canadian film. Caelum Vatnsdal emphasised this point, calling it 'almost without rival . . . the most Canadian horror movie ever made'.[8] Set in the fictitious mining town of Valentine's Bluff on Cape Breton Island in Nova Scotia, for Vatnsdal 'the film gives us at least as enlightening and realistic a portrait of Maritime economic depression as *Goin' Down the Road* [Donald Shebib, 1970], making it perhaps the single most successful synthesis of the Canadian documentary tradition with pure genre cinema'.[9] This socio-economic context is crucial to any reading of the mask in the film: as Rose Butler argues, '*My Bloody Valentine*'s masked killer is representative of sociocultural concerns related to deindustrialization and the demise of working-class communities in Canada.'[10]

Loosely structured around a love triangle between TJ (Paul Kelman), Axel (Neil Affleck) and Sarah (Lori Hallier), *My Bloody Valentine* follows a series of murders assumed to be committed by a miner called Harry Warden. As the only survivor of a work accident where excitement about the annual St Valentine's Day dance led to negligence, Harry sought vengeance against the town. Memories of Warden's murders were rekindled twenty years later when a new generation attempted to revive the long-banned social ritual of the dance. The killings begin again, but the culprit is revealed not to be Warden, but Axel, who adopted the former's persona after seeing his father murdered in the original massacre. Unlike many North American teen slashers from this period, *My Bloody Valentine* is distinguished by its focus on a rural working-class community rather than suburban middle-class high schools or universities.[11] The Otherness of the killer therefore does not stem from his working-class status: everyone here is roughly from the same social strata. Importantly, the killer is not the only character who wears a gas mask and helmet, another deviation from traditional slasher films: set in a mining town, the enigma of the killer's identity stems from the fact that many characters wear the same masks.

While not all mask-wearing characters in *My Bloody Valentine* are monstrous, when deployed to commit murders, the mask – frequently shown in close-up from the perspective of his victims – is essential to what makes this figure so terrifying. This pertains to the cultural history of gas masks themselves, adding to the symbolic force of his monstrosity. As Nunley and McCarty noted, through their association with modern warfare, gas masks 'are devastating affirmations of our aggressive nature and are a very real and terrifying reminder of our society's worst fears' and 'the modern icon associated with some of the most horrific acts of the 20th century'.[12] Finis Dunaway traced the rise of the gas mask from the late 1960s as 'a suggestive emblem of the environmental crisis . . . [and] ubiquitous in the visual discourse of pollution'.[13] Its symbolic power stems from prior association with the First World War, where – although protective – became 'a symbol of the dehumanizing effects of modern warfare'.[14] In horror, although these specific meanings of the gas mask are often unstable, the intensity of its dehumanising power remains.

These aspects of gas masks are not actively at play in *My Bloody Valentine*, but it demonstrates Mack's previously cited observation that it is 'precisely because the masks have an authority and power in one context that they are meaningful in another'.[15] *My Bloody Valentine* jettisons this specificity of the masks' broader history and instead fuses its symbolic potency with these ambient associations to dehumanisation and threat, supporting Dunaway's claim that 'the gas mask would often circulate as a symbol detached from place, removed from the particularities of local conditions to represent the notion of universal vulnerability'.[16] In *My Bloody Valentine*, it is the victim of the gas-masked figure who is vulnerable, the mask indicating from the wearer's subjective perspective that they require 'protection' from what its wearer perceives as their abjection. This is explicit in the film's opening moments, where two gas-masked androgynous figures enter a deserted mine. What at first appears to be professional activity is a sexual rendezvous, as one removes her mask and overalls. Suggestively stroking the other's phallic breathing tube, she is murdered and the credits begin. The mask not only transforms the wearer from a young, troubled man into an enigmatic serial killer, but in the context of a horror film transforms the object itself from part of a miner's standard protective gear to an unknown killer's disguise.

This mask therefore has a dual function in terms of what can loosely be conceived as labour rituals in terms of the industrial necessity of wearing certain items and in its repetition and maintaining of slasher cinema's affinity for masked killers. But other social and work-place rituals also permeate the film: initiation rites for trainees, the singing of familiar folk songs, masculinity rituals like stabscotch and the reintroduction of the Valentine's Day dance itself, a return to a lost cultural festival. By disrupting these rituals, the gas-masked figure represents a physical threat to the community and, by repurposing the symbol of the very industry that forms the town's foundations, exposes the vulnerability of their social, economic and cultural infrastructure, like that of the real towns that suffered from the decline of mining as a viable industry after the Second World War.[17] In *My Bloody Valentine*, untrained labour, economic and social instability, ritual and masked transformation intersect to reveal a more sophisticated thematic core than this film is often credited with.

Nigerian director Olatunde Osunsanmi's US production *Evidence* also features a repurposed mask commonly linked to working-class labour. Its underlying manipulation of gender, class and monstrosity – and how they are linked to the welding mask – make it a useful film to consider in relation to ritual, power and transformation. Just as the youth and mainstream prettiness of LeAnn (Torrey DeVitto) and Rachel (Caitlin Stasey) imply their innocence, so too the welding mask frames its wearer's violence as a product of working-class masculinity. The film's 'twist' collapses these assumptions with the revelation that the entirety of the video footage police discover at the site of a massacre the girls survive was a conscious, carefully executed plan by the girls to attain fame and notoriety. LeAnn and Rachel – like Mrs Tredoni and Alice in *Alice Sweet Alice* – again adhere to Ricki Stefanie Tannen's postmodern female trickster category because they consciously play with assumptions about working-class masculinity in order to mock and destroy broader patriarchal structures and logic.[18] The use of the welding mask here is governed by the shamanic imagination – the residual traces of orthodox, anthropologically defined shamanism that, while jettisoning its historical specificity, maintains its historical associations between masks, ritual, power and transformation.

The welding mask in *Evidence* is heavily mediated: we never see the mask in the diegetic 'real' world of the film's narrative, but only in what is framed from within the film itself as amateur video footage. The first shot of the killer wearing the mask appears as investigators watch a recording of a woman murdered with a blow torch, and, when replaying it, they reverse an image and see a reflection of the masked face. 'That's the mask we found at the scene', one investigator notes. Subsequent shots of the mask-wearing killer are similarly indirect: they appear on videotapes that the investigators watch, often shown as reflections. A 'hall of mirrors' process of identity distortion permeate *Evidence*, with the mask playing a central role. That the entirety of the video evidence upon which the police attempt to investigate the case is revealed as a constructed performance by LeAnn and Rachel is foreshadowed by the former's early recognition of the performative nature of what they are watching. When the mask is shown reflected in a mirror with the words 'fear me as you fear god' written in blood on it, Detective Burquez (Rahda Mitchell) explicitly articulates that the mask plays a role in 'some sort of fantasy, a ritual'. With the revelation of LeAnn and Rachel's guilt, the film is on one hand little more than a flimsy critique of contemporary celebrity culture and a misogynist attack on the perceived vanity of fame-hungry young women. But what renders

Evidence so curious is how clearly it articulates the performative potency of masks as gendered objects in horror, in this case – like *My Bloody Valentine* – through its association with an occupation linked broadly to working-class masculinity.

Like the gas mask in *My Bloody Valentine*, the welding mask both hides its wearer's identity and protects them from the blood splatter caused during their violent murders. Yet, as Nunley and McCarty noted, 'in addition to their protective function, modern industrial masks have the same psychological impact as their predecessors: they intimidate, mystify and can transform the wearer's behaviour'.[19] Assumptions about gender performativity further complicate the use of this particular mask in *Evidence*. For Anne Balay, associations between welding and masculinity are made explicit in her interview with Isabel, a steel worker's daughter, who says 'it'd be really weird if someone took off their welding mask and it was a girl, they'd be like "unh unh, that's not right"'.[20] Yet in one of the most iconic moments of 1980s cinema, this is precisely what happens when Alex (Jennifer Beals) removes her welding mask in Adrian Lyne's *Flashdance* (1983). The symbolic presence of the masculinised welding mask and the hyper-feminine performance ambitions that drive the women protagonists in both *Evidence* and *Flashdance* is a notable overlap. Kimberly Monteyne provided a rare interrogation of the importance of the welding mask in the latter, suggesting that it granted Alex *masculine* power: 'Alex is . . . physically strong enough to perform a man's job: welding in the gritty mills of the Pittsburgh steel industry'.[21] Alex is therefore not a 'normal' woman, but an 'extraordinary' one, physically strong and symbolically powerful enough to move fluidly across identities and qualities aligned with otherwise immobile definitions of masculine and feminine.

Performed gender identities, masks and disguises also recall Mary Ann Doane's notion of feminine masquerade. Expanding on Joan Riviere's 'Womanliness as Masquerade' (1929) mentioned briefly in the introduction, for Doane masquerade 'constitutes an acknowledgement that it is femininity itself which is constructed as a mask – as the decorative layer which conceals a non-identity'.[22] As Doane later noted, 'masquerade suggests a "glitch" in the system', allowing space to 'read . . . femininity differently'.[23] *Evidence* complicates the relationship between femininity and masquerade with the addition of class difference. LeAnn and Rachel's assumed innocence is knowingly prompted through a genteel masquerade of femininity: they are young, beautiful aspiring artists. The vision of violent masculinity that they deploy through their use of the welding mask as a red herring is hardened, grizzled and dehumanised, a construction reliant on a mask with strong associations to working-class men and masculinity.

As violent, ambitious women, Rachel and LeAnn utilise masks and masquerade on two levels: literally in the deceptive deployment of the masculinised welding mask (successfully triggering assumptions that the killer is a man) and also through feminine masquerade. LeAnn and Rachel are exposed as vicious killers who knowingly utilise assumptions about gender and class to get away with murder and, alongside films Hilary Neroni explored like *Terminator* (James Cameron, 1985), *Terminator 2* (James Cameron, 1991), *Thelma and Louise* (Ridley Scott, 1991) and *The Last Seduction* (John Dahl, 1994) – while not horror but still about violent women – 'each of these cases reveals feminine identity as something that can be removed because it is not intrinsic to the characters'.[24] What is so important to Rachel and LeAnn's masking strategies is how detached and unknown their true identities remain: they take feminine masquerade to violent, identity-obliterating extremes. *Evidence* thus presents a significant instance where repurposed masks, transformation, performance rituals and ideological assumptions about gender and untrained labour intersect to result in a fascinating conclusion.

Repurposed Masks and Social Play: *Friday the 13th Part III* (1982) and *Carved: The Slit-Mouthed Woman* (2007)

While masks can denote specific occupations, they are also associated with many social activities, behaviours and rituals. This section considers two horror films that, despite employing masks in different ways, unite through their repurposing of each with the specific intent of disturbing their audiences. In the *Friday the 13th* franchise, Jason Voorhees's hockey mask is one of the most iconic symbols of 1980s horror, yet at no time is it implied that Jason was a hockey enthusiast. Modern sport is, for Kath Woodward, 'organized structured play' and as such has been understood as a ritual practice:[25] Susan Birrell noted 'the significance of sport as a ritual is based on the status of the athlete as exemplary role incumbent with power to mediate between the individuals who compromise the audience and the moral order of the community'.[26] For Kendall Blanchard, 'sport often assumes a ritual-like character' and 'has its roots in ritual performance',[27] while Jason's quasi-supernatural indestructibility[28] links sport and ritual through Anne Bolin and Jane Granskog's observation that 'sport, as well as play in its broader manifestations, can be viewed as ritual: an enactment of myths that serve to validate or justify cultural beliefs and practices; a symbolic validation of a group of norms by individuals whose very participation in ritual acts may constitute, under some circumstances, a transcendental sacred experience'.[29] The iconographic potency of Jason's hockey mask stems in part from its macabre subversion of the complex relationship between sport, culture and ritual.[30]

The *Friday the 13th* series was not the first exploitation film to employ a villain in a hockey mask, with Bob Kelljan's rape-revenge movie *Act of Vengeance* (1974) centred around the 'Jingle Bells Rapist' who wore the disguise during his assaults.[31] But *Friday the 13th* made the object synonymous with horror, referenced and appropriated for sinister effect in movies like *Asylum of Terror* (George Demick, 1998), *Bloody Murder* (2000) and *The Unravelling* (Thomas Jakobsen, 2015). Although the hockey mask does not appear in the franchise until *Friday the 13th Part III*, masks do appear in earlier films, rendering its later mask-centricism a somewhat logical progression. In Sean S. Cunningham's original *Friday the 13th* (1980), the first half hour includes a comic 'fake scare' sequence where one character puts on a mask with an old, grizzled non-white face and – with clearly racist overtones – wields a spear to frighten another character (this same mask appears later on the steps to a cabin flagging an impending murder vignette). In *Friday the 13th Part II* (Steve Miner, 1981), Jason wears a sack mask: a pillow-slip with eyes cut out and a rope tied around his neck. Worn with a plaid shirt and overalls, there is an emphasis on class difference between the urban teens who work at Camp Crystal Lake and 'hillbilly' Jason. This difference is established in the first film through Jason's physical and intellectual Otherness, crucial to the film's final revelation: that it is not Jason but his mother Pamela (Betsy Palmer) who committed the murders, seeking revenge for what she believed to be the drowning death of her son in 1957. Rising from the lake in that film's final moments, Jason continues his mother's killing spree in the sequel. There, in the climactic confrontation between Jason and Final Girl Ginny (Amy Steel), costume-centric transformation is central: wearing Jason's mother's jumper, Ginny confuses Jason, who imagines that Ginny has morphed into Pamela. Ginny accidentally reveals Jason's makeshift altar to his dead mother (replete with mummified head). Upon seeing this, Ginny's true identity is revealed and Jason attacks her.

With the introduction of the hockey mask in *Friday the 13th Part III*, however, masks become more central. For audiences who experienced the film on its original release, the notion of masking had dual meaning: seeking to profit on the rebooted trend of 3D films during this period,[32] the viewing experience required 3D glasses to fully experience the special effects (horror film masks and 3D are discussed further in the next chapter). The introduction of the hockey mask 'was an innocent thing, just something that looked really good', director Miner told David Grove. 'The script called for a mask and obviously, we had to have Jason wear something.'[33] The film's technical advisor Terry Ballard brought an old 1950s leather hockey mask to the set and it caught the attention of Miner and SFX artist Douglas J. White.[34] After some adjustments, this mask became a key symbol for Jason and the franchise more broadly.

The introduction of the hockey mask is a transitional moment in constructing what makes Jason a monster. Opening with a repetition of the final scene from the previous film, Jason is revealed to have survived Ginny's machete attack and in the first stages of the third film he appears maskless and shadowy. But masks are foreshadowed: when a group of frisky teens gather to travel to Camp Crystal Lake, nerdy Shelley (Larry Zerner) fails to amuse his peers in a tasteless gag where he wears a mask, mock-stabbing them. Notably, Jason first adopts the hockey mask after killing mask-wearing prankster Shelley: while sporting a different mask to that worn by Shelley earlier, something of a trickster spirit lies within Jason with his malign playfulness (particularly his flair for cat-and-mouse-like encounters) and broader mission of disrupting the status quo. Combined with his signature penchant for mask-wearing, Jason's strength relies again emphatically on a broader shamanic imagination that governs assumptions that these masks hold specific kinds of transformative power when combined with ritual.

The appearance of the hockey mask at this stage of the franchise as Jason evolves from a disturbed man-child with mother issues to a less human force of chaos and destruction is significant. As a dual symbol of threat and protection, this mask is worn in a sport where – in regard to the rules of the game – the wearer is simultaneously defensive and on the attack. As Nunley and McCarty noted without referencing this franchise, even the basic design of the hockey mask is unnerving, 'resemble[ing] . . . the battle scars one is apt to incur in the physically intense and often very violent game'.[35] As a sport, hockey therefore further complicates Jason's motives. By *Friday the 13th Part III*, he appears to kill now not for revenge, but for sport: it is for him now – to reference the title of Vera Dika's book on films like *Halloween* and *Friday the 13th* – a 'game of terror'.[36]

This spirit of play lies at the heart of Kōji Shiraishi's *Carved: The Slit-Mouthed Woman*, based on the Japanese urban legend *Kuchisake-onna*. This tale triggered a notorious moral panic in Japan in the late 1970s and Shiraishi offers the first explicit feature film exploration of the phenomenon to interrogate the intersection of motherhood and domestic violence. The urban legend upon which *Carved* is based follows a ritualised 'game' structure and while Michael Dylan Foster[37] and Yoki Inagi noted regional nuances, the latter outlined it as follows:

> A tall woman with long black hair in a trench coat wearing a large white mask would walk up and ask a person, 'Am I Pretty?'. . . If the person replied 'Yes', the woman would take off her mask and reveal her mouth widely slit all the way up to her ears, asking, 'even with this?' And she would slit the person's mouth and/or stab the person to death with a sickle.[38]

Like horror film masks themselves, for Foster 'the story of the Kuchi-sake-onna is characterised by variation over time and space; it is reinvented with each telling',[39] and regional variations altered the type of weapon *Kuchisake-onna* would carry, her wardrobe, the cause of her injury and strategies to survive the encounter.[40] Peaking in 1979 with the widespread yet unproven belief that there was a hidden coroner's report about a woman resembling *Kuchisake-onna* who died when hit by a car as she chased potential victims,[41] children in Ibaraki Prefecture were warned to keep their distance from anyone wearing a mask.[42] Foster notes that 'the rumor had a profound effect on Japanese life' resulting from anxieties linking it to 'rapid urbanization and the breakdown of traditional village communities'.[43] For Western viewers, *Kuchisake-onna* recalls Bloody Mary or Mary Worth rituals, which – although again demonstrating regional and generational variations[44] – 'involve the ritual summoning of a witch in a mirror'.[45] Just as the Bloody Mary 'game' is defined as a ritual practice,[46] parallels between *Kuchisake-onna* and Bloody Mary can – despite their cultural difference – allow the former to also be considered ritualistic.

In *Carved*, Shiraishi reconfigures the urban legend and rituals surrounding *Kuchisake-onna* to explore the phenomenon of abusive mothers. The film begins with the game outlined above: a group of young girls tell each other that if the slit-mouthed woman catches them she will cut them with scissors. Shifting to a scene of domestic abuse, Mayumi Sasaki (Chiharu Kawai) torments her traumatised daughter Mika (Rie Kuwana), threatening her with a visit from the 'slit-mouthed woman'. Two children in the area soon disappear and an informal investigation is undertaken by two teachers at Mika's school: Kyôko Yamashita (Eriko Sato), an abusive mother of a young daughter herself and Noboru Matsuzaki (Haruhiko Kato), who was the victim of physical and emotional violence as a child, his mother revealed to be *Kuchisake-onna*. This intersection of the supernatural *Kuchisake-onna* urban legend with the reality of family violence grants Shiraishi's film its impact: as Inagi noted, 'perhaps the storyline suggests that just as the tale of the *Kuchisake Onna* is horrifying, it can be equally horrifying in real life when a person who is supposed to be a guardian turns abusive and harmful'.[47] Shocking audiences with its scenes of child abuse and provoking censors internationally, these scenes are arguably far more disturbing than its supernatural components.[48]

Kuchisake-onna's surgical mask in *Carved* is significant here. With community panic rising about the missing children, when Kazuko Toshida (Ryoko Takizawa) – the mother of one of Mika's schoolmates – wears a surgical mask due to a cold, her children grow suspicious that she is hiding *Kuchisake-onna*'s identifying slashed mouth underneath and Kazuko is soon revealed to be involved in the disappearances. Suggesting that the desire to abuse children is spread virally amongst mothers as the *Kuchisake-onna* seeks new hosts, a flashback reveals that the surgical mask is not only to disguise her facial disfigurement, but to protect other women from being 'infected'. While the next section will explore the use of surgical masks in explicitly professional contexts (worn by surgeons in both *Dead Ringers* and *Anatomy* respectively), in relation to *Carved*'s production context, the mask has a distinct cultural and social meaning. Across Asia during this period, so ubiquitous were surgical masks that for Thy Phu they became 'the most prominent feature of the etiquette of hygiene during the SARS crisis' and 'one of the most recognizable symbols of contagion in the twenty-first century'.[49] Adam Burgess and Mitsutoshi Horii argued that surgical mask-wearing in Japan had become common, originating in a public health response to the Spanish flu in 1919 and 'reson[ating] . . . with folk assumptions as making a barrier between purity and pollution'.[50] The wearing of surgical masks in Japan became 'socially embedded as a general protective practice during the 1990s through a combination of commercial, corporate and political pressures that responsibilised individual health protection'.[51]

In *Carved*, *Kuchisake-onna* recalls all of these aspects of the Japanese social ritual of surgical mask-wearing. Issues of risk, danger and public health come to the fore and parallels can be made between the dual function of the surgical mask in *Carved* that both hides *Kuchisake-onna*'s mutilated face and simultaneously protects others from being 'infected'. There is in the mask a tragic aspect of self-awareness: *Kuchisake-onna* and women 'like' her know what they are doing and what they have become, and the film suggests that some of its abusive mothers are themselves survivors of domestic violence. The mask therefore acts not only as an iconographic marker of horror, but also renders tangible the tragedy upon which the film concludes with its emphasis on Kyôko's relationship with her estranged daughter and husband, their family destroyed by Kyôko's struggle to control her own violence. Underscoring the subjective experience of abused children, issues of violent transformation lie at the heart of *Carved*: Shiraishi employs the fantastic parameters of horror and the transformative potency of the mask as an enduring element of the genre's iconography (and its specific meaning in this cultural and historical context) to provide an explicit commentary on a very real social issue.

Repurposed Masks and Professional Labour: *Dead Ringers* (1988) and *Anatomy* (2000)

While *Carved* utilises the symbolic power of the surgical mask in the ritual context of social play, *Dead Ringers* and *Anatomy* demonstrate the potent – although distinct – force of masks when utilised in horror films about their professional usage in medicine. If Burgess and Horii's research emphasises the cultural aspects of surgical masks in Japan, in the medical profession others have raised issues about their own specific symbolic meanings. In a letter to the editor in the *British Journal of Anaesthesia* in 2007, Dr Azriel Perel recalled a colleague who told him that 'there is no evidence that wearing a mask decreases the incidence of infection', rendering them optional for anaesthetists in the United Kingdom. Criticising the rule, he argued that the absence of the surgical mask risked undermining 'the anaesthetist's public image', as many patients would not consider anaesthetists to be qualified medical professionals without them.[52] The editor confirmed that professional culture had changed 'so that now few, other than the operating surgeon, wear them', emphasising that 'there has been no increase in the incidence of wound infection'.[53] Yet Perel's concerns about the 'public image' of the anaesthetists reveals much about the real-world power of the mask as a symbol of professionalism and superior knowledge.

This is a useful starting place to think through surgical masks as symbols, crucial to both *Dead Ringers* and *Anatomy*. *Dead Ringers* is an addiction horror film that hinges on the nightmare of degenerative psychological transformation. It pivots around the *idea* of body horror with its twin mad scientist protagonists (obsessed as they are with 'mutant women') far more than the explicit spectacle of body horror typical of Cronenberg's earlier films like *Shivers* (1975), *Rabid* (1977), *The Brood* (1979), *Scanners* (1981), *Videodrome* (1983) and *The Fly* (1986). As Lowenstein noted, *Dead Ringers* is the first Cronenberg film that reverses his previous tendency towards making 'genre films that utilize art film devices to complicate their generic structures', and rather is an 'art films whose structures are challenged by the injection of genre elements'. What runs throughout, Lowenstein argued, is 'the presence of deliberate friction between genre and art elements geared to strain viewer expectations and frustrate genre/art categorizations'.[54]

Dead Ringers follows the downfall of doctors Beverly and Elliot Mantle (both played by Jeremy Irons) as they collapse into madness and substance abuse, their loss of professional power paralleled directly with their increasingly destructive relationship dynamics. This propels the film towards the seemingly inevitable tragedy of their deaths. That the two main protagonists are twins and the consequent blurring of their identities again recalls doppelgänger traditions and the mask has played a crucial role in the long history of horror's various tales of doubling and fractured identities. Throughout the film, it is often difficult to tell the twins apart; both for the audience and for Claire Niveau (Geneviève Bujold), the third participant in the film's central love triangle.

In the surgery scenes throughout the film (each marking a point of decreasing control as the twins descend into insanity), their costumes contain a distinctly sacred aspect, 'astounding red gowns with flowing robes, copes and mantles (the name affinity is surely not accidental) whose Catholic-religious overtones are daringly obvious'.[55] Aspects of religious ceremony are heightened by the heavily ritualistic gestures and tone of the surgical 'performances' themselves: the sacred-medical rituals of the Mantle brothers reconfigured their professional capacity as surgeons with religious ritual to underscore their own godliness, a central thematic pillar of the film discussed further momentarily. These rituals are performed consciously for an audience (both the film audience and characters in the operating theatre) and as such *Dead Ringers* exemplifies Lowenstein's observation that 'Cronenberg's cinema crystallizes the fraught translation of a private, embodied self into a public, abstracted social body'.[56] In the first surgical scene, Bev – the (initially) more confident brother – instructs students from his position of authority. As he describes what is happening, the patient on the operating table is laid out like a sacrifice on an altar, emphasising the heavily ritualistic aspects of the scene's construction.

This intersection of professional authority and ritual drives the deterioration of its protagonists. The troubled, arrogant brothers who configure themselves as surgeon-as-deity figures is made explicit when Claire screams during sex with Bev, 'Oh Doctor, Oh God'. But the ritualistic construction of the surgery scenes make this just as clear, for instance where Elliot strikes a Christ-like pose in his red robes, his 'sacrifice' reflected in the window before him, waiting on the 'altar' of the operating table. Beard describes Bev here as 'the Chief Priest or Cardinal' being 'ritually vested by his acolytes'.[57] At the end of the film, the symbolic power of this costuming is rejected, where Bev ritually disembowels his brother in their apartment. For Steven Shaviro, 'the hieratic red robes that Beverly dons when performing operations give way to the Caravaggiesque nudity of the two brothers in the final shot of the film', as 'the rituals of medical power and prestige are turned back against the selves that they had previously confirmed and inflated'.[58] Recalling Catholicism-imbued ritual acts of self-sacrifice, the surgical masks so central to their performance as god-doctors mark a transformation often overtly linked to power and ritual. The mask is symbolically linked to the power they felt they gained from their roles as urban, professional shaman-healers. The shamanic imagination imbues these scenes of masked surgical ritual with immense power that through the collapse of their identities in a number of ways ultimately destroys them.

In Stefan Ruzowitzky's *Anatomy*, masked medical rituals are driven by more explicitly ideological and historical motivations unique to its country of production. In many ways, *Anatomy* is a key example of Adam Lowenstein's identification of the 'allegorical moment' discussed in my introduction that relies on a 'complex process of embodiment, where film, spectator and history compete and collaborate to produce forms of knowing not easily described by conventional delineations of bodily space and historical time', particularly in regard to national trauma.[59] Following aspiring surgeon Paula (Franke Potente), who is accepted into the prestigious surgery school at the University of Heidelberg, she uncovers there a secret association – the Anti-Hippocratics – who undertake mercenary covert medical experiments in their pursuit of greater knowledge. With explicit references to Nazism and notorious German SS officer Josef

Mengele, *Anatomy* mines national anxieties about Germany's past active within its contemporary moment. For Steffen Hantke, *Anatomy* 'draws on Germany's failure to come to terms with its Nazi past',[60] while for Alexandra Ludegwig, it 'deals with Nazism not as a discrete period of history but rather as an ever-present tendency in any civil society'.[61] *Anatomy* exemplifies Linnie Blake's claim that 'by focusing on the sites where ideologically dominant models of individual and group identity are sequentially formed, dismantled by trauma and finally re-formed in a post-traumatic context', horror movies can

> demand not only a willingness . . . to undertake a fundamental questioning of those ideologically dominant models of individual, collective and national identity that can be seen to be deployed across post-traumatic cultures, as a means of binding (hence isolating and concealing) the wounds of the past in a manner directly antithetical to their healing.[62]

While surgical masks play a more explicit role in the promotional material for Ruzowitzky's less explicitly political 2003 sequel *Anatomy 2*, in both films surgical masks denote the susceptibility of patient-victims, powerless at the hands of medical professionals.

Anatomy's neo-Nazi conspiracy is part of a small but notable trend in some contemporary European genre films concentrating on neo-fascism, eugenics and racial purity.[63] The return to horror in German-language cinema is significant: as Ludegwig noted, despite early achievements in the genre by directors like Robert Wiene and F. W. Murnau, a general distaste grew after the Second World War against horror that – consolidated by Siegfried Kracauer's *From Caligari to Hitler: A Psychological History of the German Film* (1947) – saw horror as 'an unnecessary reminder of the "bad German"'.[64] Aside from the spike of Rialto Film's Edgar Wallace-inspired *Krimi* films from the late 1950s to the early 1970s, Ludegwig claims it took more than sixty years for German-speaking directors to stage a horror revival, privileging Austrian Ruzowitzky and Oliver Hirschbiegel's *Das Experiment* (2001).[65] For Ludegwig, these directors explicitly 'fuse . . . historical references with elements of popular genre', in a contemporary context to launch 'a new school of film, as they reveal a novel perspective on Nazi crimes, not only because of their setting in twenty-first-century society, but also due to their choice of genre'.[66] This is demonstrated by the use of surgical masks in *Anatomy* which foreshadow impending acts of violence.

The power of mask-wearing surgeons and the powerlessness of their patient-victims are used in a horror context explicitly framed in reference to Germany's Nazi past. The first murder vignette uses music, narrative context and pacing to foreshadow a spectacular death scene. A man opens his eyes on an operating table and sees bright surgical lights shining above him. The scene is riddled with abstractions, denoting his subjective viewpoint as he struggles to comprehend his surroundings. We see from his perspective figures in surgical masks casually talking about the patient in the third person, ignoring his questions as sinister music intensifies. He sees his own organs removed from his body as the surgeons chat excitedly about Paula's arrival. He looks down to discover that most of the skin and flesh has been removed from his hands, shifting his gaze towards a Dissecting Room sign. In a later scene, a young man with a rare disease Paula met earlier on a train awakens in a similar scenario: he again sees masked figures talking and he pretends to be unconscious. He grabs a scalpel and attempts to fight them, but they retaliate and kill him, disappointed: 'too bad, he's dead . . . we can't use him anymore'. Both scenes contrast the vulnerability of the victims with the inhumane 'experiments' and professional dominance of the masked figures. Surgical masks are crucial in the transformative dynamic in *Anatomy* as seemingly 'normal' medical students become faceless monsters.

This combination of professionalism with monstrosity materialises symbolically in the doctors' masked faces through the ritualised space of the surgical theatre. With its references to Mengele, as Ludegwig noted, these surgical horror scenarios 'evoke . . . connotations of the horrors of the Holocaust, especially as the viewer is visually reminded of the similarities between the cruel operations being depicted and Nazi medical experiments'.[67] This is emphasised in the film's setting at the University of Heidelberg specifically, an institution openly supportive of the Third Reich who eagerly enacted some of that regime's most shocking medical programmes.[68] In *Anatomy*, surgical masks symbolise the transformation of human to monster and, located as they are at this explicit location, the film draws direct parallels between the atrocities of the past with the Germany of the present, offering Paula and her generation as an idealised generational force of resistance.

The films explored in this chapter demonstrate how repurposed horror masks overlap and deviate in terms of their functionality and symbolic specificity. Repurposed masks can manipulate assumptions about class and gender in the genre (*My Bloody Valentine* and *Evidence*), can imply a perverse sense of play when sports masks are deployed in a film like *Friday the 13th Part III*, and in the case of surgical masks, their use in the Japanese urban legend ritual game *Kuchisake-onna* is the starting place of unflinching interrogation of domestic violence in *Carved: The Slit-Mouthed Woman*. The professionalised sphere of medicine incorporates surgical masks in different ways in *Dead Ringers* and *Anatomy*, in their respective tales of ritual, power and transformation, pertaining to the personal in the former and the national in the latter. Collectively, these films demonstrate how the symbolic potency of masks linked to one function – hockey masks, surgical masks, welding masks, gas masks – is broadly transferrable in horror cinema. Simultaneously protective and menacing, the generic potential of repurposed masks is again largely reliant on myriad intersections of transformation, ritual and power, but as demonstrated here – and throughout this book – these elements frequently manifest in dynamic, original ways. I now extend this argument in my final case study as we move away from a chronological, post-1970s period of codification and towards a more elastic view of how technology and temporality intersect in horror movie masks, providing some insight into the potential future of the object in the genre to come.

PART THREE

MASKS AS TRANSFORMATIONAL TECHNOLOGIES – MOVING FORWARD BY LOOKING BACK

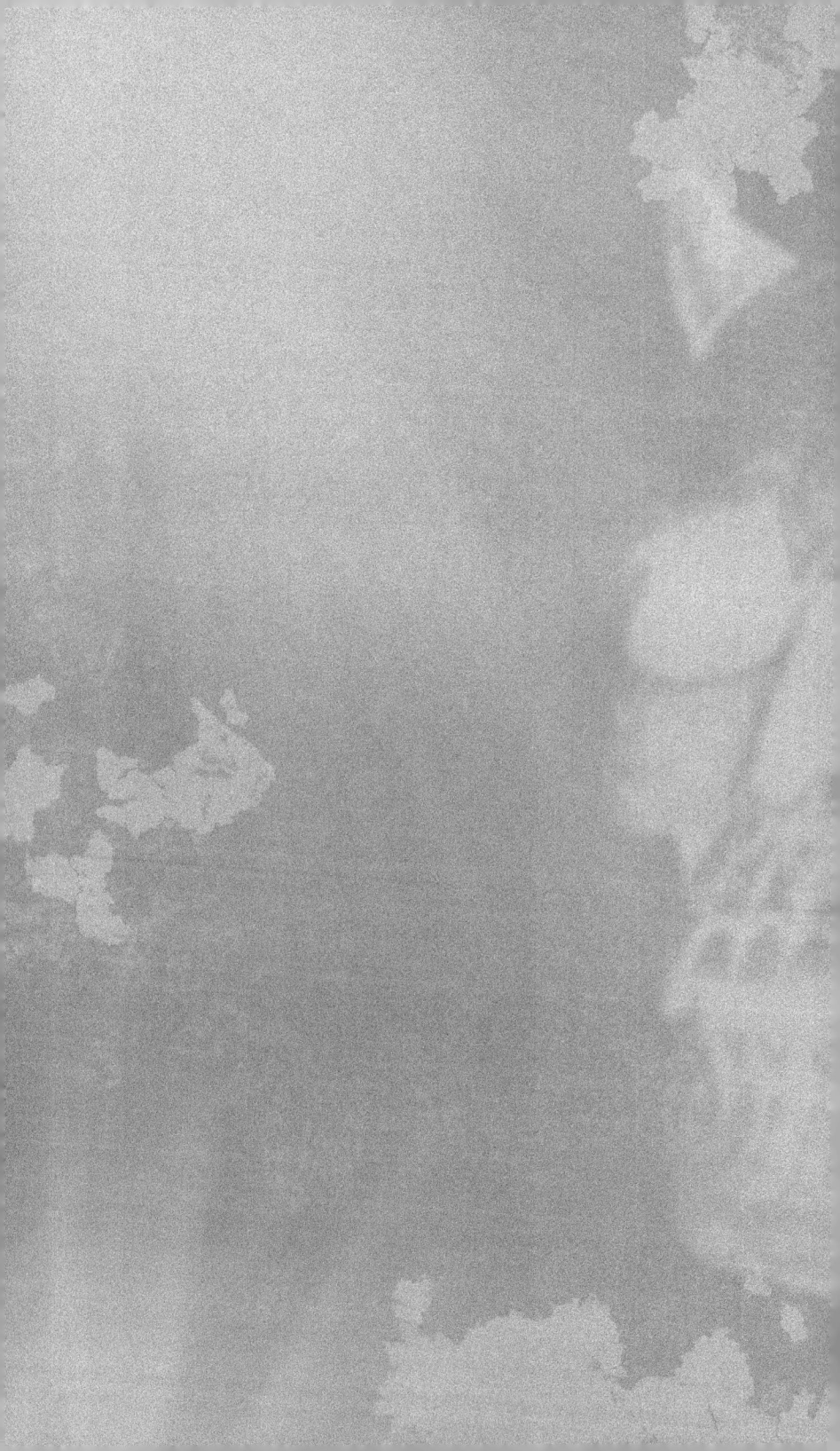

8

Technological Masks
Ritual, Power and Transformation

THE FINAL SECTION of this book steps away from the post-codification period after 1970 and takes a more elastic approach in considering how masks in horror movies function at the seemingly very contemporary intersection of technology, transformation, power and ritual in horror film masks. While the bulk of the films here are also made after 1970, two key films – *The Mask* (Julian Roffman, 1961) and *Peeping Tom* (Michael Powell, 1960) clearly pre-date that period, yet are hugely useful case studies when attempting to recontextualise the relationship between masks and the concept of transformational technologies. As will be elaborated shortly, these two films are of interest here precisely because of their anachronistic relationship to masks, technology, ritual, power and temporality itself; if approached through the key arguments of this book, they provide perhaps surprising ways that we can rethink the role of the mask in horror film today, and in the future.

The word 'technology' might suggest from a contemporary perspective 'non-human, mechanical instrumentalities, in confrontation with human, rational and organic attributes', but as Montserrat Ginés Gibert noted, '"Technology" evokes a broader, more inclusive type of knowledge beyond the technical artefact itself'.[1] While we often think of 'technology' in this mechanical sense (especially in regard to cameras, screens and other moving image technologies), in the case studies here, we employ this more elastic definition of 'technology' to this preliminary consideration to consider its interplay with ritual, power and transformation through horror film masks.

Horror masks are often closely aligned with technology and ritual. As Heather Margaret-Louise Miller argued, if 'rituals can be defined as stereotyped patterned behavior or activities of any kind, whether religious, political, social, or a mixture', they can be conceived 'within the context of an overall technological system' that can focus on 'the social and cultural context in which these rituals are occurring'.[2] For Crumrine:

> In co-ordination with other items of material apparatus, masks act as elements within human systems, systems that also include charters or explanatory myths, personnel occupying differing social positions or statuses and sets of rules or norms that structure the roles of status-holders. Generating co-operation, such systems focus upon sets of activities and ultimately fulfil certain functions useful in achieving continuity in human groups.[3]

Christina Pratt noted that shamans have historically employed the 'technology' of action – 'drumming, singing, rattling, making offerings and dancing' – as part of their healing rituals.[4] As part of the shaman's toolkit, masks are a significant part of this technology-based ritual, a tradition that has evolved in a dynamic way to manifest anew across the horror films we will now explore: *Peeping Tom*, *The Mask*, *Halloween III: Season of the Witch*, *The Den*, *Månguden* and *The Poughkeepsie Tapes*.

Technology played a significant role in literary horror, long before the rise of moving image culture. For John Bowen, gothic horror traditionally 'loves modern technology almost as much as it does ghosts . . . which is why a novel like *Dracula* is as full of the modern technology of its period – typewriters, shorthand, recording machines – as it is of vampires, destruction and death'.[5] For Jeffrey Sconce, contemporaneous discourse about once new media technologies (radio, television, virtual reality, etc.) has historically leant itself to supernatural metaphors. For example, he argues that Orson Welles's 1938 Halloween radio play of H. G. Wells's *War of the Worlds* (1898) that was famously misinterpreted by some of its audience as a live broadcast of an actual alien invasion 'was as much a panic over the new and rather suffocating presence of mass communication as it was a panic over extraterrestrial invasion'.[6] For Sconce, 'tales of paranormal media are important . . . not as timeless expressions of some underlying electronic superstition, but as a permeable language in which to express a culture's changing social relationship to a historical sequence of technologies'.[7] Gothic, horror and supernatural stories have long demonstrated a complex relationship with technology.

From an archaeological perspective, the broad ways that 'technology' has been conceived is useful when thinking through the endurance of horror film masks. As transformative devices, masks have a technological capacity. For Miller, technology is 'an outwardly expanding, nested set of actions and relationships: from production itself, to the organization of the production process, to the entire cultural system of processes and practices associated with production and consumption'.[8] This consideration of technology as a 'set of actions and relationships' evokes associations with another primary concern of this book: ritual. Technology and ritual are closely aligned, as indicated by Miller's identification of technology as an 'active system of interconnections between people and objects during the creation of an object, its distribution and to some extent its use and disposal'.[9] Across the six films considered in this chapter, the way that masks function and intersect with technology reveal a range of transformative possibilities, reliant in each case on ritual practices that speak to diverse power relations.

Technological Masks and Temporality: *Peeping Tom* (1960) and *The Mask* (1961)

As noted, the most obvious deviation in this chapter from those in Part Two concerns the era of production of its first two case studies, Michael Powell's *Peeping Tom* and Julian Roffman's *The Mask*. While Part Two focused on films made after 1970, these films are explored here because their relationship between masks, ritual, power and transformation relate directly to histories of perception themselves: both in terms of technological history (in the sense of the 'mechanical instrumentalities') and from the broader archaeological perspective as outlined above. Apart from being 'historical' in the sense that these films pre-date 1970, I privilege them because they employ masks-as-technology through ritual to grant their wearers' mastery, knowledge or control both literally and figuratively in ways that refers specifically to time: through the shamanic imagination, these two films hinge on the wearing of technological masks in diverse ways that allow their antagonists to move across time itself. While *Peeping Tom* has received much critical attention in terms of its relationship to both the dominance of the male gaze and the camera, I explore how its camera-weapon is itself worn as a facial covering, pressed close to its antagonist's skin, with a conscious goal of both hiding his face and transforming him into a powerful monster. In *The Mask*, the technological aspects of its eponymous object are privileged in two distinct yet intersecting ways. First, the ancient mask in question is worn by characters in the film as a psychiatric device that exposes them to the darker elements of their subconscious. Yet in its status as Canada's first 3D film, it also explicitly invites the viewer at certain points to 'put the mask on' – a demand to place their magenta-and-cyan lensed 'mask' – so they can experience the film's technological spectacle of 3D.

In *Peeping Tom*, Mark (Karlheinz Böhm) is a young film cameraman employed at a film studio who shoots pornography on the side, and is also a serial killer. He equips a camera with a large mirror, light and a tripod-embedded-knife to force women to watch their own terrified faces as they die while he films them. For Shohini Chaudhuri, *Peeping Tom* offers an 'extreme example' of Mulvey's identification of cinema's dominant and sadistic male gaze. Chaudhuri noted that the title alone 'effectively positions its spectators as Peeping Toms: the darkened auditorium gives each spectator the illusion of being a privileged voyeur, peeping in on a private world, separate from the rest of the audience'.[10] With its power dynamics hinging on a man-with-a-killer-camera and women-as-objects of that camera's violent look, *Peeping Tom* is a near literal manifestation of Mulvey's theory.

Peeping Tom's meditation on the culpability of the camera and the moral responsibility of the person wielding it for some feminist film theorists aligns it with overt reflexivity. For Clover, 'the self-reflexive dimension of *Peeping Tom* . . . has led to its reevaluation . . . as first and foremost a sustained reflection on the nature of cinematic vision'.[11] For Michele Aaron, films like this 'remind . . . spectators that they are watching a film, they are made aware of themselves as spectators'.[12] This is essential to the film's gender politics for Kaja Silverman, because 'not only does it foreground the workings of the apparatus and the place given there to voyeurism and sadism', but it ultimately renders the film through its film-within-a-film structure 'a device for dramatizing the displacement of lack from the male to the female subject'.[13] It is, for Clover, a horror movie 'that has as its task to expose the psychodynamics of specularity and *fear*'.[14] Clover offers *Peeping Tom* as further evidence of her broader claims for gender fluidity active within horror spectatorship, an approach to the film shared by later critics.[15]

While many critical considerations on *Peeping Tom* have been concerned with its intersection of the gaze, spectatorship and reflexivity, other critical lines of enquiry are also available. Elana Del Ray identified the film's 'pervasive articulation of a discourse of touch and the provocative ways this discourse is intertwined with the general thematics of vision for which the film is so acclaimed'.[16] In her claim for Mark's 'embodied voyeurism', Del Ray recalled Silverman by stating that with his contraption, 'Mark tries to erect [a barrier] between himself and his victims so as to dissociate himself from them and thereby consolidate his own claim to the paternal legacy'.[17] This barrier denotes a literal space between Mark and his victims, separating him both physically and morally from the pain he is inflicting and thus constructing technologically mediated vision itself as a literal mask. As mentioned in chapter 1, the sensory dimension of horror cinema spectatorship is significant, regarding the often intensively constructed sense of materiality that permeates the genre and provokes what Sobchack described as a 'sensual and sense-making experience'.[18] As a transformative device with a clear ritual function, Mark places a physical object between his own face and the events occurring before him, and as an audience we have a sensory awareness of this 'barrier' even if it is not registered consciously.

Del Ray's argument thus allows a rethinking of Mark's relationship to technology through the iconographic potency of horror film masks. 'Technology' here can be understood in multiple ways: not only in terms of the camera as moving image technology, but the bespoke murder contraption Mark has crafted to ritually execute women. The actual object is therefore worth further consideration in terms of both its construction and functionality. Throughout much of the film, Mark approaches his victims holding the camera close to his face. For me at least, there is a sensory awareness when Mark raises the camera to begin filming: the tightness of his grasp is superseded by the sheer force and determination with which he presses the object against his face. While his purpose is to film a murder, the ritual-like repetition that marks this act indicates that it is arguably even more than the 'barrier' Silverman and Del Rio suggest. Rather, Mark *wears* the camera: aside from granting him the simultaneous ability to film and kill, by 'wearing' it in this manner, the object is granted an important place in the history of horror film masks. He executes these murders as masked rituals that are emphatically transformative: through his camera-mask, he is granted new powers.

This is of course not the only function of his camera-mask. Mark has grafted other attachments to service his needs: a bright light and what is revealed at the film's conclusion to be a tripod leg with a knife attached and a large, distorting mirror that forces his victims to watch their own murders. In terms of the intersection of masks, technology, transformation, power and ritual, these two acts – the filming of the murders and forcing his victims to witness their own deaths – are, while occurring simultaneously, executed with distinct goals in relation to time and space. Mark films the murders so that he can watch them later, for use in his ongoing 'documentary' project that Clover notes was 'begun by his father and continued by Mark himself (through the filming of his murders and of the public reaction that attends them) and finally completed by him as well, as he films his own suicide with and by the same "magic camera"'.[19] But the mirror is as much about his victims at the moment of their deaths as it is to Mark documenting their murders for later use. Powell himself has called Mark 'a technician of emotion':[20] he refers here not only to Mark's emotions but also to those of his victims. These two experiences exist in distinct temporal moments.

When worn on his face, the camera-mask distances man-child Mark (who is rendered sympathetic by the lengthy descriptions of his experience of child abuse) from the crimes against women we see him commit. It is not sympathetic, survivor-Mark who commits these crimes, but rather the camera-masked Mark: he has transformed from victim into aggressor through the ritualised wearing of his hand-crafted 'mask'. While the image-making technology of the camera-mask records events for later reference, the mirror acts both as part of that filmed spectacle, while simultaneously – and crucially – linked to the immediacy of the moment of death. The camera-mask in *Peeping Tom* may be intrinsically linked to oft-cited notions of the gaze, gender and power, but its effectiveness as an object of horror is simultaneously dependent on its transformative power as an object worn on his face. Although not commonly recognised as such, *Peeping Tom* is an important and highly sophisticated reimagining of horror's mask-wearing traditions.

Julian Roffman's *The Mask* also explores the transformative possibilities of the mask to allow symbolic movement between the past and present in explicit relation to acts of masking. Like *Friday the 13th Part III*, it too required its audience to wear mask-like 3D glasses upon its initial cinema release. The film is therefore not only about characters wearing a mask, but about the audience knowing that same sensation: to experience the film fully, the audience is forced to mimic its title action. By doing so, it reflexively collapses the conceptual distance between the audience and the film's diegesis. *The Mask* begins with archaeologist Michael (Martin Lavut) haunted by violent dreams after acquiring an 'Indian burial mask'. Telling psychiatrist Dr Allan Barnes (Paul Stevens) that he is possessed by the 'evil' of the mask, he dies by suicide and leaves the mask to his sceptical doctor. Describing it to his girlfriend Pam (Claudette Nevins) as a 'horrible looking thing, unearthly', through a number of 3D nightmare sequences it is revealed that the mask has the same influence on Barnes as it did on Michael. The conclusion reveals that the mask will only make those already with a proclivity to violence susceptible to its power, Professor Quincey (Norman Ettlinger) explaining the cross-cultural belief that masks can transform the personalities of those who wear them. While there are undeniable issues surrounding the fact that the eponymous artefact hinges on an undesirable Othering of non-Western cultures (thus granting them access to what is coded unambiguously as dark, 'primitive' magic), the film uses masked transformation, ritual and technology to interrogate masculinity and violence.

Discussing *The Mask* and David Cronenberg's *Shivers* (1975), Caelum Vatnsdal suggests that both films reveal that 'it only takes a single alien element for the house-of-cards society we've constructed to fall down around us'.[21] In *The Mask*, that 'alien element' is explicitly foreign – an Aztec mask – but the film is clear in its final revelation that the demonic forces unleashed through the mask do not work on everyone: the transformation from 'civilised' westerner to violent 'primal' sex criminal is triggered (and not created) by the mask – that desire must already lie repressed within its wearer. The mask, Dr Allen realises early in the film, reveals deep subconscious desires and thus he considers it a powerful psychological technology with research potential. These fantasy scenarios are brought spectacularly to life through 3D anaglyph sequences – in the opening scene with Martin and then two lengthier scenes when worn by Dr Barnes. But as Ray Zone noted, the movie is largely a 'black-and-white horror film' and these more traditional aspects are just as significant when considering the transformative potential of the mask and its intersection with ritual.[22] While the bulk of the film set in suburban 1960s Canada presents a world of rational civility governed by logic and order, the wearing of the mask – both by

Martin and Dr Allen and the audience in the form of their 3D glasses – presents a primal world rendered in 3D, riddled with stereotypical horror iconography (skulls, snakes, skeletons, etc.). The centrepieces of these masked-induced fantasy scenarios are acts of sexual violence, in Dr Allen's case against a blonde mask-wearing woman, reminiscent of his secretary Miss Goodrich (Anne Collings). These sequences are heavily ritualistic, suggesting ancient ceremonies far from the moral propriety of supposedly 'civilised' suburbia.

The monstrous past Dr Allen and Martin return to through masked transformation grants them a subconscious space to indulge in their pre-existing violent sexual desires. These masked transformations collapse civility through these hallucinations and render tangible distinctions between the suburban/normalised/'contemporary' present (presented in black and white) and a spectacular/fantastic/ 'primitive' past, witnessed by both the film's diegetic mask wearers and the 3D mask-wearing audience. The audience too are likewise compelled to 'put the mask on' by a voice in the film, simply because it is essential for experiencing the 3D spectacles of the film itself. The unquestioning acceptance with which the audience wear the mask in order to transform their vision is subtly acknowledged from within the film to mimic what it codes as a dangerous addiction to mask technologies: numerous characters refer to the mask as a drug, addiction and curse. The lure of the mask – to both the male protagonist and the audience who accept the demand to 'put the mask on' – emphasises the intersection of masks and ritual, manifesting in the audiences' compulsion to reflexively mimic the precise behaviours they see problematised on screen.

Technological Masks and Consumerism: *Halloween III: Season of the Witch* (1982) and *The Den* (2013)

When adapted into new contexts, masks intersect in myriad ways with rituals, themselves old and new. Of these, a more overtly contemporary ritual is that of consumerism. As noted in chapter 5, *Halloween III: Season of the Witch* notoriously deviated from the Michael Myers narrative that marks the rest of the *Halloween* franchise, a stand-alone story that concerned a popular brand of children's Halloween masks designed to trigger a mass human sacrifice. *The Den* presents a different critique of technology and its relationship to consumerism, turning to social media usage and the role of masks, transformation, power and ritual in the commodification of users themselves as physical products to be bought and sold online.

Martin Harris suggests that while critical treatments of horror franchises like *Halloween* emphasise postmodern aspects like open narratives that are ambivalent about closure and unmoving narrative truths, he argued that *Halloween III* is a significant case study because of 'the way the complicated, extratextual narrative of the conflict between commercialism and art surrounding the film is reflected in the film itself'.[23] Replacing Myers's slasher killer figure are the monstrous witches led by Conal Cochran (Dan O'Herlihy), a deranged practical joker who runs the Halloween mask company Silver Shamrock. He embeds his popular masks with computer chips and fragments of Stonehenge itself (explicitly evoking rituals past and present), to be activated on Halloween eve when the Silver Shamrock ad plays on television and slaughtering its child-wearers *en masse*. The story was conceived by British screenwriter Nigel Kneale, who had previously united technology, horror and history in the cult British horror teleplay *The Stone Tape* (Peter Sasdy, 1972). While Kneale left the project,[24] *Halloween III* echoes *The Stone Tape*'s fascination with the ability of technology to bridge old and new: here, technology unites ancient and modern through masks themselves.

Eschewing the Michael Myers storyline that otherwise defines the franchise, masks remain central in *Halloween III*. The Silver Shamrock masks are aggressively marketed and therefore popular with children, configuring them according to the film's own logic as therefore already potentially ominous and linked to mind control. In *Halloween III*, the wearers of these masks are victims, not antagonists. For Tony Williams, *Halloween III* thus shares *Halloween II*'s focus on sacrifice 'and post-1960s ambivalent feelings towards childhood', describing Cochran as a 'ritual "monster"' with the privileging of Stonehenge in his murderous plan.[25] Cochran also seeks to replace humans with a corporate robot-army as part of his planned technological utopia, resulting in what Williams called 'the destruction of children and the victory of patriarchal corporate control'.[26] But the method Cochran uses to execute his plan is notable: while Harris called Cochran a 'prankster',[27] he is in fact a contemporary trickster, fitting Hynes's definition of a figure who is anomalous and ambiguous, who plays tricks and is deceptive, who imitates gods, who inverts situations and who engages with both the lewd and the sacred.[28] Most of all, Cochran evokes associations between trickster traditions and shamanism through his 'ability to cross the dangerous boundary between the world of the living and the realm of the dead':[29] the shamanic imagination is again here crucial in providing the conceptual foundations that account for why we as audiences assume masks contain great power, especially when combined with ritual.

The focus on technology and consumerism is alluded to in *Halloween III*'s opening credits. Rolling static appears alongside Carpenter and Howarth's minimalist synth soundtrack and its visual aesthetics recall a monochrome CRT computer monitor, colour treated to be in black and orange. This defines the screen as a consciously mediated space, marked by technological presence. As lines appear and disappear, the camera pulls back to reveal a computer-generated image of a digitally rendered pumpkin vector. The centrality of the pumpkin continues an opening credit tradition established in *Halloween* and *Halloween II*, but this screen-centric construction is crucial to *Halloween III*'s broader critique of technology, foreshadowing the use of television to trigger mass murder via the Silver Shamrock masks. Cochran's company offer three models for sale: a witch, a skull and a jack-o'-lantern. The Silver Shamrock ad is played on high rotation throughout the film, a musical countdown with structural functionality leading to the moment Cochran executes his plan ('six more nights till Halloween'). The ad is ubiquitous: children (even those of the film's protagonist Dr Dan Challis, played by Tom Atkins) flock to their televisions to watch the commercial, their susceptibility to advertising the cornerstone of Cochran's plans.

This self-reflexive consideration of the commercialisation of horror itself is emphasised by the fact that Carpenter's original *Halloween* is screening on one of the channels within the diegetic world of *Halloween III*. Scepticism about the marketing strategies that are narratively central to *Halloween III* are expressed by Thomas M. Sipos's in his dismissal of the mask in Wes Craven's *Scream* (1996): 'The *Scream* mask is popular not on the film's merits, but due to Miramax's heavily bankrolled, Halloween merchandising machine, trying to do by design what *Halloween*'s "shape" mask did by serendipity.'[30] Released fourteen years before *Scream*, *Halloween III* certainly complicates Sipos's observation through its central employment of a killer television transmission signal: at play is the assumption that children are now fully controlled by the mask (and by the commercial powers that seek to control them). As consumer objects, masks in trickster-Cochran's hands become weapons to use against those that paid for the privilege of wearing them, allowing him 'to punish America for its commercialization of the holiday'.[31] *Halloween III* is therefore, as Harris suggested, 'a sustained satire targeting American consumer culture', which it achieves through the explicit emphasis of masks themselves as commercial products.[32] Sold through television commercials, controlled by computer chips and activated as weapons of mass destruction via analogue television signals, the masks in *Halloween III* transform their wearers – lacking self-control through the paralysing effects of television advertising – through the ritual of Halloween mask-wearing itself.

Horror masks, technology and consumerism combine in a different way in *The Den*. Closely related to the found-footage horror subgenre, *The Den* is typical of the much smaller sub-subgenre I previously identified as 'interface horror' – horror films diegetically and formally implied to be playing out on a computer screen, where characters are computer users who participate in a range of horror scenarios that unfold in online social spaces.[33] *The Den* follows grad student Elizabeth (Melanie Papalia, who appeared also in *Smiley*) through her research project on a video-chat website similar to ChatRoulette called The Den. Recording encounters with random strangers as a psychology experiment to document 'human behaviour in its most transparent form', there is a degree of hubris to her project as she feels protected by her researcher status from the perils of her unrestricted consumption of the website's services. The film reveals that she has been placed in extreme danger through her exposure to an organisation of masked users who torture and murder young people like Elizabeth, selling footage of their crimes on another website as snuff films.

This plot intersects thematically with tensions between visibility and invisibility, rendered most coherently through the film's focus on surveillance technologies and Elizabeth's willing submission to them. *The Den* exposes what it considers the dangers of unchecked social media usage, where the practices Elizabeth wishes to study enable her own dangerous engagement with strangers on the site. Surveillance culture rose significantly after the terrorist attacks in the United States on 11 September 2001,[34] with tensions between paranoias about being watched and a desire to be watched triggering broader cultural anxieties that manifest in horror films like *The Den*. Both David Lyon and Adam L. Penenberg emphasised the ubiquity of surveillance technologies through mobile phones and surveillance cameras, peaking in what Penenberg suggested is the 'round-the-clock surveillance as entertainment' phenomena of reality television.[35] *The Den* both critiques and – in its status as 'surveillance as entertainment' itself – promotes these surveillance anxieties as a rich source of inspiration for horror. *The Den* seeks to both profit from and critique these anxieties, and commercial gain is itself integral to the conclusion of *The Den*, where Elizabeth's murder becomes a commodity on a pay-to-view website.

Like the business-suited robots in *Halloween III*, the ominous corporate figures in *The Den* are literally and symbolically faceless: in *Halloween III* they are inhuman, whereas in The Den they wear sack masks. Importantly, these figures symbolise larger structures – corporations, governments, etc. – who oversee real-world, global surveillance agendas. But transformations via masking and unmasking appear earlier on in the film: the more spectacular aspects of *The Den* represented by these masked figures stand in contrast to more banal moments as Elizabeth clicks endlessly through random faces, looking for people to talk to. If Elizabeth's initial experience on *The Den* reveals anything, it is how deeply embedded casual sexual harassment is within her everyday experience online: these encounters at first are presented comically and as an assumed norm of what women should expect in online spaces, positioned between a stream of more innocuous scenes of cats licking their stomachs and giggling Japanese schoolgirls. Elizabeth scrolls through these scenarios like she is channel surfing – under the guise of research, Elizabeth finds pleasure in acts mirroring Penenberg's 'round-the-clock surveillance as entertainment' observation.

What Elizabeth witnesses on The Den are framed as micro-performances and the rare encounters where she appears to make sincere connections are atypical. Trevor J. Blank used the term 'digital performance' in relation to the Internet 'to indicate the process of aesthetic production, reception and response in digital environments', and these are brought to life in *The Den* as Elizabeth searches through a seemingly endless parade of 'digital performer[s]'.[36] The identities presented on The Den can in this way be understood as digital masks akin to what Harold Bell referred to as 'social media masquerade', hinging on 'the underlying assumption . . . that . . . user profiles, personify the lives that people live', when 'the reality is quite the opposite'.[37] For Armina Dinescu, 'the striking lack of rules apparent on the web' render it a prime space for misrepresentation as one may 'represent oneself as wildly inaccurately as one pleases', an observation reliant on social media spaces being a forum for often radical transformation.[38] As Dinescu noted, 'In the case of ChatRoulette, identity play can be as obvious as masking one's webcam with photos of famous people, to literal masks, or as subtle as "lying" about one's geographical location, gender or age.'[39] *The Den* is a horror movie about the potential threat inherent to this 'identity play'.

The potency of deceptive transformations as acts of figurative masking first becomes overt when Elizabeth encounters a user who claims their video is not working, so they materialise on her screen as a still photograph of a young woman and communicate only via written text. Elizabeth assumes an indexical relationship between the user with whom she is communicating and the girl in the photograph, but it is later revealed that this young woman has been murdered to make a snuff film to be sold online, a fate that will also befall Elizabeth. But it is the uniqueness of this still image that initially attracts Elizabeth and brings her to the attention of the film's ominous commercial powers. Elizabeth's assumption that there is a correlation between the user and the image presented is proven incorrect, as the image was bait that resulted in Elizabeth's own death. After the mysterious group behind the snuff film business hack Elizabeth's computer and contact people as Elizabeth without her knowledge (another kind of transformative 'masking'), her friends and family are soon also targets for the literally masked villains. Despite her friends' desperate pleas with her to stay offline, she cannot and is drawn fatally towards the group's headquarters. There she discovers an entire community of masked killers; she is tortured and killed, the footage sold in the final scene to an eager consumer.

The sack masks that prove so central to *The Den* provide a direct parallel between the history of horror film masks and the violent potential of online anonymity and 'digital masks'. This act of masking has a dual representational function, acting as ciphers for both the faceless, organised bodies that control surveillance (corporations, governments, etc.) and the performed masks of social media users. In the horror-fantasy world of *The Den*, online surveillance technologies and social media are tools for commercial control in the creation taboo (and highly priced) snuff film commodities. The horror of *The Den* is consciously configured around the mask as a cipher for anonymity, governed as much by sadism as commercialism. In both *The Den* and *Halloween III*, masks, ritual and transformation intersect as moral warnings for audiences who unquestioningly consume technology.

Technological Masks and Performance: *Månguden* (1988) and *The Poughkeepsie Tapes* (2007)

The last section of this chapter – and the final case studies of this book – examines the Swedish television horror movie *Månguden* and the US found-footage horror film *The Poughkeepsie Tapes*. These both reveal how filmed performance and masked transformations (diegetically coded as existing within each film) are reflexively incorporated through masked rituals and film-making technologies themselves; celluloid and videotape respectively. In both films, masked performance and technology intersect again in ways that render the screen itself as a kind of mask, their killers taking on a consciously 'screened' disguise, parallels both emphasised and gestured towards by their wearing of more traditional horror masks.

While this focus on the intersection of masks with digital technology will be revisited shortly in my discussion of *The Poughkeepsie Tapes*, it is important to not conflate this intersection as pertaining *only* to digital technology. Jonas Cornell's *Månguden* interrogates the relationship between technology, masks, ritual, power and transformation in horror through a focus on analogue moving image technologies. While little writing exists in English on the film, amongst horror fan communities it is a privileged cult artefact due to its scarcity until a Swedish-language DVD was released in 2010.[40] According to the *Cinezilla* blog, the film's status as 'a holy grail amongst enthusiastic collectors' with a reputation as 'one of the bloodiest Swedish TV productions to the most nightmare inducing TV movie ever shown on the tube' in Sweden stems from its revisiting of the still unsolved Appojaure murders in 1984, where a couple were murdered in their sleep while camping.[41] This context is ignored by Pidde Andersson who, without this real-world association, dismissed it as 'an utterly strange film which in the weirdest of ways combines traditional, stiff, old-fashioned TV drama with the slashers of the 80s'.[42] Yet, according to the *Cinezilla* blog, so strong was the public reaction to the September 1988 broadcast of *Månguden* that people cancelled their camping holidays and complained to channel SVT in large numbers.[43]

Issues of reception are crucial to *Månguden* because spectatorship lies at its core both thematically and diegetically. Superficially a standard police procedural, *Månguden* is based on the discovery of a series of home movies that depict a figure in a 'primitive' Moon God mask (the *Månguden* of the title) as he murders camping families in wooded areas. His most extreme acts – performed through elaborate masked ritual – like *Peeping Tom* focus on fathers and the murders are consciously constructed for the camera. Troubled police investigator John Vinge (Tomas Laustiola) has little luck with the case and is forced to collaborate with Erland Salander (Per Myrberg), a neuropsychologist with past successes in assisting the police on serial killer cases. As Vinge investigates the history of the mask he meets anthropologist Rebecka Nordenskiöld (Agneta Ekmanner), the film's climax revealing that she is the spirit of Salander's mother, returned to comfort her son who is revealed to be the masked 'Moon God' killer. Ritually re-enacting the murder of his parents Erick and Anna Van Meer as they plundered the African villages during the 1930s, Salander seeks vengeance against all fathers as he held his father Erick responsible for his orphan status.

The filming of the ritual murder 'performances' in *Månguden* is thematically central. Walid El Khachab argued that 'cinema bears the traces of the Sacred simply because the physical film – particularly during the celluloid era – and the flattening of the image projected on the screen act like sympathetic equivalents of the world'. He suggested that 'film fulfils the same sacred function as the ritual engravings on temple walls, or in prehistoric caves'.[44] Growing up in isolated African villages that suffered at the hands of Erick's colonial exploitation and witnessing his parents murdered when his father's mass theft of tribal relics was revealed, Salander uses film to re-empower himself, restaging his childhood trauma. But now – through masked transformation – he recasts himself as the powerful aggressor-deity (the Månguden), rather than child victim-survivor. By making these films, Salander assumes a highly engaged diegetic audience in police investigating the case (of which he is included). Through film-making technology and masked performance ritual, Erick seeks to rewrite history to address his own trauma. Evoking the shamanic imagination, this recalls El Khachab's claim that

> The act of viewing a film is therefore a ritual that is based on 'recollection' not just in the sense of piecing together images and fragments of past experience into the stream we usually call memory, but also in the sense of 'rememorating' a time when one can argue that the decisive distinctions between the Human and Nature, or between the Human and the Animal were not yet accepted wisdoms.[45]

While *Månguden* recalls Freud's return-of-the-repressed and Oedipal anxieties, it is the relationship between moving image technology, ritual, power and the horror mask itself that renders the film of particular interest.

Månguden's status as a film-about-film is visible in its opening credit sequence that shows strips of celluloid film rushing through machinery in slow motion, defamiliarised until the location is revealed as a film processing laboratory. Moving to the first crime scene, the ritualised nature of the murder and the investigation surrounding it are emphasised. The

Månguden mask first appears in close-up as it is handled by police technicians who make a model from an imprint at the crime scene. Throughout the film, the passing of time and the importance of transformation is highlighted by repeated shots of the moon in different lunar phases, which also indicates to the investigators when the next crime is likely to occur (all eight murders ritualistically occur under a full moon). Of the mask itself, Nordenskiöld tells Vinge that when worn by the killer 'the face isn't just hidden for others, but also for the wearer . . . perhaps he protects himself against a part that he won't accept'. Implicit in retrospect is Nordenskiöld's belief that Salander is unaware of his crimes and Salander's statements that the killer makes the films because 'he wants to see what he has done' and that 'the murderer is trying to reproduce an underlying trauma' are implied to be honest diagnoses rather than conscious deceptions.

With the revelation that Erland is the killer – transformed by the mask into Månguden – Nordenskiöld vanishes, leaving no trace in the contemporary moment. Just as Erland uses the mask and film-performance as a wormhole back through time to restage childhood trauma, the cinematic object *Månguden* – the television movie the audience have been watching – has reflexively provided a space for his mother Nordenskiöld (really Anna Van Meer) to return also, in an attempt to stop Erland and to soothe his suffering. In the film's climax, Vinge chases Erland across a rooftop, the latter wearing the Moon God mask. When removed, he is far from the typical horror villain. Unmasked and weeping, he is sympathetic and tragic, rather than a monster. As the mask falls and shatters on the ground in slow motion, the masked transformation Erland maintained throughout the film ends and he is taken into custody. But near the film's final moments, the footage of Nordenskiöld/Anna Van Meer is shown running through a projector. As Vinge pauses the film to reveal her unaged face in the 1930s footage, the celluloid burns in the projector and the image is destroyed. 'She has left,' says Vinge and she too becomes faceless, transformed into a memory that now exists diegetically beyond cinema and yet materially etched within the movie *Månguden* itself.

Technology, ritual, power, performance and masked transformation merge in a different way in the 2007 found-footage horror film *The Poughkeepsie Tapes*. Like *Månguden*, murder scenarios are configured diegetically as being performed specifically for a film camera: this is both central to the plot and to the pleasures the films offers as a horror movie. Like *The Den*, there is also a conscious parallel between on-screen anonymity and the wearing of literal masks. *The Poughkeepsie Tapes* concerns analogue videocassette technology – rather than *The Den*'s streaming digital video or *Månguden*'s celluloid home movies – but while the film-making technology differs, it emphasises and extends the confluence of masks, technology, ritual and power as seen across these other horror movies. A mockumentary that tracks the criminal history of an unidentified, uncaptured serial killer after he allowed 2,400 hours of archived videotape footage of his crimes to be discovered in a house in Poughkeepsie, New Jersey, *The Poughkeepsie Tapes* combines this footage with interviews with investigators, other law enforcement officials and families and friends of his victims to structure the film's elaborate horror vignettes, marked as much by their synthetically deteriorated (thus materially implied 'authentic') VHS aesthetics as by the violent sadism of the acts recorded.

Like *The Den*, masking functions in two ways in *The Poughkeepsie Tapes*. First, the videotapes are a conscious attempt by the killer to disguise his identity while simultaneously revealing the heinousness of the crimes he has successfully avoided punishment for. At one point, FBI agent Simon Alray (Michael Lawson) describes how the killer must have practised a particular movement when he held the camera in front of himself and a victim in a car, drugging her while simultaneously obscuring his face from the camera. At another point, the killer holds his hand over his face in surveillance video from a petrol station that he knows the police will retrospectively view after the discovery of the tapes. But, unlike *The Den*, the scenes where he murders and tortures his victims are explicitly masked performances of a more overtly theatrical nature, conceived with the camera in mind. One investigator acknowledges his 'bizarre sense of theatricality – you know the costumes and what not', offering it as evidence that he 'is extremely mentally ill'.

Recalling the previous chapter's focus on repurposed masks, at times in *The Poughkeepsie Tapes* the killer wears a gas mask while he hacks away at often-unidentifiable body parts, evoking associations with toxicity and abjectness. Yet the most disturbing images are arguably those he has clearly gone to some effort to stage in terms of blocking and the crude *mise en scène* of his torture chamber. Here, the technological mask of the videos themselves merge with another kind of mask: he wears a traditional plague doctor mask, worn by medieval doctors during the Black Death. As Mack noted, 'The dominant visual feature, the exaggerated nose, was not developed the more completely to conceal the masker; stuffed full of sweet-smelling herbs, it acted rather to conceal the stench of death and was intended to prevent the spread of contagion.'[46] Today, however, it has been 'recycled to cohere with contemporary expectations' and is little more than 'part of the fun and spectacle of medieval pageant'.[47] *The Poughkeepsie Tapes* both supports and complicates these usages: in the context of the elaborate, theatrical and ritualistic sequences, this particular mask appears to be consciously used as a prop in a perverse pantomime, knowingly engaging with the carnivalesque aspects of costume and subversion that have marked the history of horror film masks. This is in striking tension with the macabre specificity of the mask's original functionality as summarised by Mack: while medieval plague doctors wore the masks as a practical means of diffusing the smell of dying bodies and protecting themselves from infection, by wearing this mask in *The Poughkeepsie Tapes*, the killer acknowledges the intensity of what a room that has seen so much carnage must smell like. And, like the gas mask, the notion of protection – that the mask will filter out diseased air – only adds to the dehumanisation of his victims, reduced in his eyes to diseased, abject meat. Often teamed with a long black cape and a ruff, he has put great effort into his costume, adding evidence to the construction of these videos as much ritualised performances. These echoes of European history in particular recall Carnival traditions – this mask is still a popular costume at the Carnival of Venice[48] – and the power this unnamed killer attains through myriad acts of mask-wearing (especially when combined with his destructive penchant for perverse, trickster-like play) reveal again the influence of the shamanic imagination.

This killer's understanding of masks as related to power, transformation and ritual is far more sophisticated here than in almost any of the other films explored in this book. For, as depicted so memorably in his victim Cheryl Dempsey (Stacy Chbosky), he does not merely wear the mask himself, but forces his victims to wear them in deliberate strategies of dehumanisation and submission. Abducted from her home at the age of nineteen, Dempsey was believed dead until her masked body was found alive in a makeshift plywood coffin in the house in Poughkeepsie where the tapes were discovered. Suffering from Stockholm Syndrome, Dempsey was so disoriented by her return to her previous life that – missing the approval of her captor she so craved during her years of physical, sexual and psychological abuse – she died from suicide soon after her release. The plague mask first appears in scenes of Dempsey's torture, far more intricately constructed vignettes than with any other victim. Dempsey is, therefore, grotesquely privileged and she is shown as the victim of a gruelling range of torture acts, both psychological and physical. At one point, he offers to remove her ball gag, replacing her costume with a fetishistic PVC maid costume and a generic plastic mask of a woman's face (recalling that of *Alice Sweet Alice*, again emphasising idealised 'plastic' femininity). While this further reduces her in his eyes to an everywoman-as-submissive-victim symbol, there is no indication that at any point during her captivity Dempsey would have been able to see her own reflection: from her point of view it would simply have felt like a restrictive plastic facial covering. Dempsey's horrific experience would have therefore resulted not only from the physical sensation of suffocation, but the psychological detachment of not knowing what she looked like.

As his killings intensify in violence and theatricality, the killer changes his modus operandi to avoid detection. At the film's conclusion, one FBI investigator acknowledges that their future strategy to locate and identify the killer is hoping that he turns up to screenings of *The Poughkeepsie Tapes*, diegetically coded from within as an 'authentic' documentary: they assume that he will be incapable of resisting seeing his own performance on a cinema screen. This feeds back into carefully constructed tensions between technology, transformation, power, ritual and masked performance, both literal (in the case of the gas mask and plague doctor mask and the mask he forces upon Dempsey) and symbolic (in terms of the titular tapes themselves being a 'disguise' or method of hiding his own identity). The tapes present an empowered self, transformed through ritual and masked performance into a seemingly omnipotent and extremely powerful, sadistic force.

The six films examined here underscore both the simultaneously diverse yet overlapping ways that technological masks, ritual, power and transformation function across contemporary horror cinema. The notion of performance runs through many of these explorations, particularly in instances where masked transformations are diegetically presented as consciously staged. This is clear in *Peeping Tom*, where killer Mark's iconic camera-weapon is rethought in terms of the mask, with the duel functionality of capturing movie footage for his later viewing, while simultaneously revealing to his victims their own terror as they are murdered. Temporality is just as significant in *The Mask*, where the wearing of a so-called 'primitive' mask acts as a catalyst of the regressive, violent fantasies of its wearers. This runs in tandem with *The Mask*'s own status as a 3D film, its audience compelled to 'put the mask on' to fully experience the film's special visual effects. Both *Halloween III: Season of the Witch* and *The Den* explore anxieties about technology and consumerism through ritual and masked transformations to critique in different ways two historically distinct screen technologies: television in the former and social media in the latter. Lastly, *Månguden* and *The Poughkeepsie Tapes* explore transformative masked performances at the intersection of screen culture and identity, pivoting around home movies. Like the other case studies in this book, these examples demonstrate the broad ways that ritual, power and transformation intersect, overlapping and diverging, to account for the endurance of horror film masks. But they also do something much more: they give us an insight into the way that masks in horror respond to advances in technology, which in turn might allow some useful context for mask-centric horror cinema to come in future years.

Conclusion

THIS BOOK HAS surveyed a range of horror film masks in order to answer a central driving question: why has the mask been such an enduring generic motif in horror cinema? The answer lies in a combination of the object's potency as a transhistorical, transnational artefact and the horror genre's status as a contemporary forum where this power can evolve and adapt to new aesthetic, ideological and national contexts while adhering to the genre's broader codes and conventions (making them recognisably 'horror movies'). As outlined throughout, the transformative potential of horror film masks continues the object's broader complex cross-cultural history and intersects in a multitude of ways with myth-making capacities often inherently aligned with ritual, power and transformation.

By focusing on this intersection of ritual, power and transformation in particular, through the mask we have seen that horror is a durable contemporary space for the symbolic force of the object to endure through its unique adaptability to new contexts and to align its intrinsic power with new meanings. At its core, this relies on what we can now understand as the shamanic imagination, less a reference to orthodox, anthropologically defined shamanism as it is to a much looser cultural sensibility. The shamanic imagination consists of lingering yet often unspoken residual traces of the mask's importance to long-forgotten rituals and cultural festivals, beginning in tribal communities and continuing across history through a range of masked cultural events, performance traditions and literary movements such as Renaissance Carnival, the *commedia dell'arte*, Japanese

Noh theatre, gothic literature, the Grand Guignol theatre and the Theatre of Cruelty, before manifesting in cinema from its earliest days, codifying as a key iconographic element of the genre from the 1970s onwards. As noted throughout, Neale's articulation of genre as an evolving process governed by a tension between repetition and difference is demonstrated through the history of horror film masks. While masks have appeared in horror movies from cinema's earliest days, this process of same-but-different underscores the generic logic that resulted in both its codification and its longevity. Horror film masks are not new, but they have been frequently deployed in new ways that adapt and engage with what are in many cases often urgent and significant ideological concerns specific to certain cultural, social and historical contexts.

As we saw in chapter 1, the materiality of horror film masks is crucial and while communicated visually they often provoke the identification of sympathetic sensory experiences – of suffocating, of occluding vision, etc. This materiality in turn is widely linked to horror film masks as transformative devices and their relationship to ritual and power. Likewise, genre studies itself has previously identified ritual aspects that link horror to the broader myth-making capacities likewise inherent in the object of the mask itself. The shamanic imagination allows us to further elaborate on its significance to horror film masks and their close conceptual proximity to ritual, power and transformation, while also considering the closely related figure of the trickster, whose legacy is frequently aligned particularly with the mask-wearing antagonists of horror film history.

Taking our minds back to Part One, we can recall how we examined the history of the mask in particular relation to performance and literary traditions as it moved towards codification in the horror genre from the 1970s onwards. Beginning with Japanese Noh theatre, chapter 2 explores the role and function of the mask in the Italian *commedia dell'arte*, gothic literature and French theatre such as the Grand Guignol and the Theatre of Cruelty, identifying a loose continuum where the mask and its intersection with horror is in many ways consistent with Mikhail Bakhtin's notion of the carnivalesque. This chapter concluded by looking at the earliest examples of masks deployed in horror and tonally similar contexts in early cinema, a focus continued in chapter 3 as we discussed mask-centric horror films such as the 1925/1930 versions of *The Phantom of the Opera*, the Old Dark House movies, Universal Studios' famous monster films of the 1930s and how masks began to show early signs of codification – recalling Neale's process of same-but-different – from the 1940s and

1950s in particular. In closing, we explored the significance of the rising internationalisation of the horror genre during the 1960s with a focus on France, Mexico, Italy and Japan, and how these culturally specific strands of mask-centric horror cinema would influence the genre more broadly as exhibition and distribution structures garnered them a wider audience beyond their own national borders.

Part Two and Three saw us put our broader theories to work as we examined over thirty individual case studies to demonstrate my central claims about horror film masks and how their relationship to ritual, transformation and power manifest in specific instances. The four chapters that made up Part Two were brought together by dominant horror film mask typologies made after codification from 1970 onwards: skin masks, blank masks, animal masks and repurposed masks, while Part Three looked at technological masks – spanning back to the early 1960s – to examine the contemporary role and function of how technology, temporality and masked transformation and ritual can intersect to tell us more about the future of mask-centred horror films to come. Considering movies made by film-makers from countries including Australia, Britain, Canada, France, Germany, Italy, Japan, Nigeria, South Korea, Sweden and the United States, across these case studies Neale's process of repetition and difference is mapped out to illustrate precisely how the deployment of the same object can be re-imagined and re-deployed, adapting to new, culturally specific contexts and creating new meanings by interpreting this familiar iconographic element into something often unique, creative and ideologically significant. While these categories do not account for every single type of mask ever deployed in horror cinema, they certainly demonstrate their scope and amongst them illustrate precisely why and how the mask has been such an enduring aspect of horror's generic iconography.

Horror film masks are powerful ideological tools, but crucially they do not have a stable political 'meaning' – they can be used in different ways. Masks are not in themselves inherently progressive or reactionary, but rather – and more significantly – we can now begin to value the diverse, varied and multiple ways that their meanings can shift and be adapted to suit certain contexts and support specific (and often competing) ideological positions. Yet, for the primary claims of this book to have any effect outside the immediate cultural field addressed herein, it is important in closing to step back from the specific terrain of horror cinema and consider the wider implications of masks as transformative devices with a demonstrable relationship to ritual and power. Despite their ubiquity and associations with the childhood play in forums such as fancy dress parties or Halloween, there is today great political urgency to the conceptual mechanics of masks, their significance as a material object and their cultural potency. From Pussy Riot to the appropriation of the *V for Vendetta* Guy Fawkes mask by Anonymous, international debates about the so-called 'Burka ban' to the current rise of the 'alt-Right' and its iconographic association with the hooded figures of the Ku Klux Klan, the politics and power of facial coverings are as widespread as they are important. While these much broader debates are clearly beyond the purview of this book, this politics does find its way into horror movies (and has done for a long time), with masks in the many case studies we have explored playing a crucial role in providing the conceptual punch for how that meaning is played out so engagingly on screen. There is now and throughout history a fundamental politics about the human face and the power dynamics of occluding it, and horror film masks – through the intersection of transformation, ritual and power – play a long, fascinating and, until now, broadly unexplored role in continuing enduring traditions that speak to this precise power.

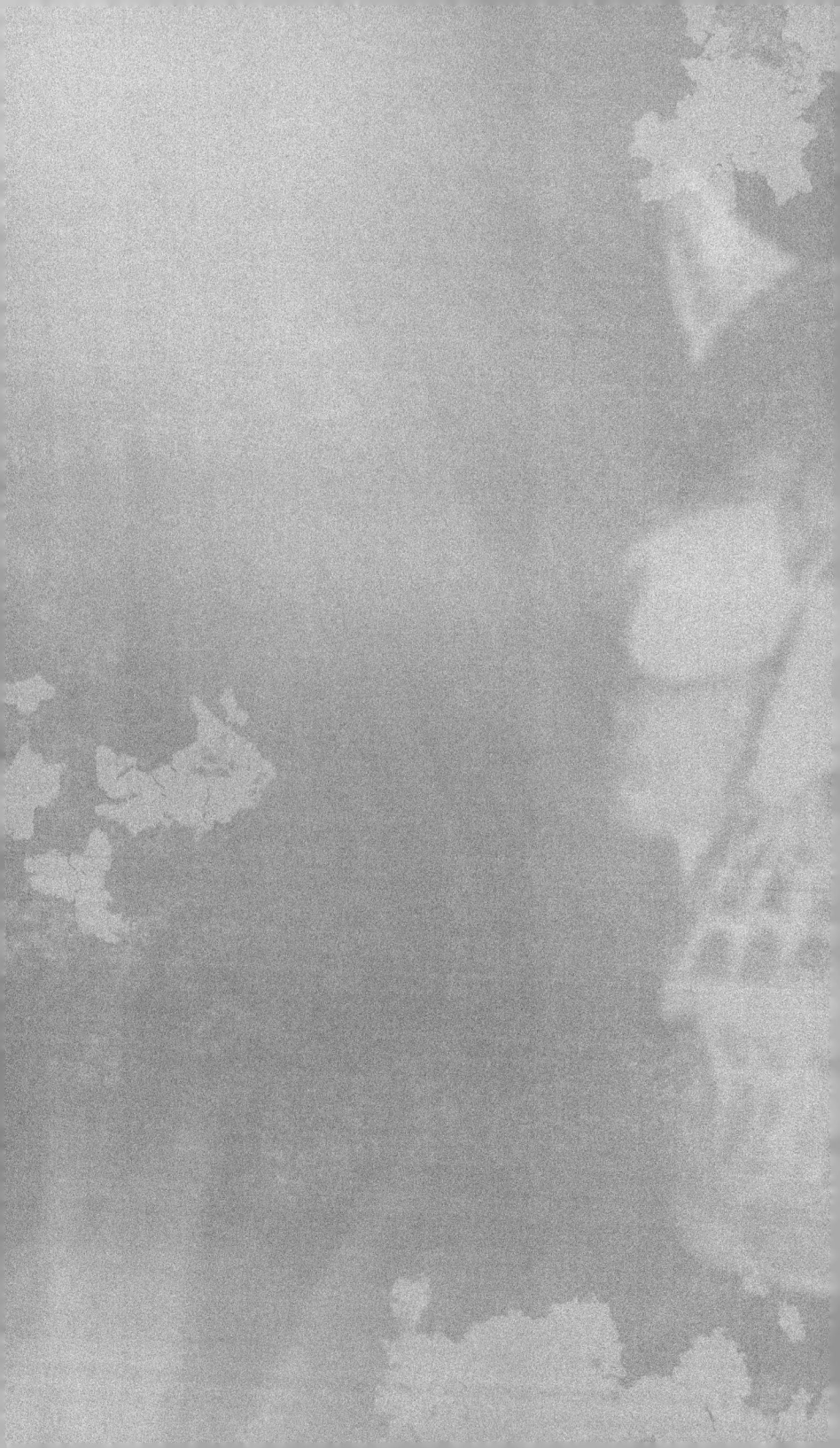

Endnotes

Introduction

1. Jonathan James, 'Q&A with *Come Out and Play* Director Makinov', *Daily Dead*, at *https://dailydead.com/qa-with-come-out-and-play-director-makinov/* (accessed 22 February 2019).
2. Clark Collis, '*Come Out and Play*: The Mystery of the Masked Director', *Entertainment Weekly*, 25 March 2013, at *ew.com/article/2013/03/25/makinov-come-out-and-play-diego-luna/* (accessed 22 February 2019).
3. Steve Neale, 'Questions of Genre', *Screen*, 31/1 (1990), 45–66 (56).
4. Eric Michael Mazur (ed.), *Encyclopedia of Religion and Film* (Santa Barbara: ABC-CLIO, 2011), p. 369.
5. Walter Sorell, *The Other Face: The Mask in the Arts* (London: Thames and Hudson, 1973), p. 16.
6. N. Ross Crumrine, 'Masks, Participants, and Audience', in N. Ross Crumrine and Marjorie Halpin (eds), *The Power of Symbols: Masks and Masquerade in the Americas* (Vancouver: University of British Columbia Press, 1983), p. 11.
7. Elizabeth Tonkin, 'Mask', in Richard Bauman (ed.), *Folklore, Cultural Performances, and Popular Entertainments – A Communications-centered Handbook* (New York: Oxford University Press, 1992), p. 225.
8. John W. Nunley and Cara McCarty, *Masks: Faces of Culture* (New York: Harry N. Abrams, Inc. Publishers, 1999), p. 15.
9. Laura Makarius, 'The Mask and the Violation of Taboo', in N. Ross Crumrine and Marjorie Halpin (eds), *The Power of Symbols: Masks and Masquerade*

in the Americas (Vancouver: University of British Columbia Press, 1983), p. 201.
10. Crumrine, 'Masks, Participants, and Audience', p. 1.
11. John Mack, 'Introduction', in John Mack (ed.), *Masks: The Art of Expression* (London: British Museum Press, 1994), p. 9; Nunley and McCarty, *Masks: Faces of Culture*, p. 15.
12. Mack, 'Introduction', p. 12.
13. W. Anthony Sheppard, *Revealing Masks: Exotic Influences and Ritualized Performance in Modernist Music Theater* (Berkeley: University of California Press, 2001), p. 25.
14. Nunley and McCarty, *Masks: Faces of Culture*, p. 17.
15. Rose Butler, 'Faces of Rage: Masks, Murderers, and Motives in the Canadian Slasher Film', in Julia Petrov and Gudrun D. Whitehead (eds), *Fashioning Horror: Dressing to Kill on Screen and in Literature* (London: Bloomsbury, 2017), pp. 211–12.
16. John Schechter, *Popular Theatre: A Sourcebook* (Hoboken: Taylor and Francis, 2013), p. 88.
17. Mack, 'Introduction', p. 20.
18. Mack, 'Introduction', p. 20.
19. Mack, 'Introduction', p. 20.
20. Mack, 'Introduction', p. 20.
21. Mack, 'Introduction', p. 10.
22. Victor Turner, 'Introduction', in Victor Turner (ed.), *Celebration: Studies in Festivity and Ritual* (Washington: Smithsonian Institution Press, 1982), p. 12.
23. Ronald L. Grimes, 'Masking: Toward a Phenomenology of Exteriorization', *Journal of the American Academy of Religion*, 43/3 (September 1975), 508–16 (508).
24. Richard Schechner, *Performance Theory* (London: Routledge, 2003), p. 52.
25. Schechner, *Performance Theory*, p. 87.
26. Schechner, *Performance Theory*, p. 45.
27. Paul Coates, *Screening the Face* (Basingstoke: Palgrave Macmillan, 2012), p. 6.
28. See Linda Badley, *Film, Horror, and the Body Fantastic* (Westport: Greenwood Press, 1995); James Twitchell, *Dreadful Pleasures: An Anatomy of Modern Horror* (New York: Oxford University Press, 1985); Bill Van Wert, '*The Exorcist*: Radical Therapy', *Jump Cut: A Review of Contemporary Media*, 1/4–5 (1974), *www.ejumpcut.org/archive/onlinessays/JC01folder/exorcist.html* (accessed 28 February 2019).

29 Michael L. Quinn, 'Self-Reliance and Ritual Renewal: Anti-theatrical Ideology in American Method Acting', *Journal of Dramatic Theory and Criticism*, 10/1 (fall 1995), 5–20 (12).
30 Arthur Knight, Clara Pafort-Overduin and Deb Verhoeven, 'Senses of Cinema-Going: Brief Reports on Going to the Movies around the World', *Senses of Cinema*, 58 (March 2011), sensesofcinema.com/2011/feature-articles/senses-of-cinema-going-brief-reports-on-going-to-the-movies-around-the-world/ (accessed 28 February 2019).
31 Michael Richardson, *Surrealism and Cinema* (Oxford: Berg, 2006), p. 8; Maruša Pušnik, 'Cinema Culture and Audience Rituals: Early Mediatisation of Society', *Anthropological Notebooks*, 21/3 (2015), 51–74 (52).
32 Twitchell, *Dreadful Pleasures*, p. 84.
33 Carol Senf, *The Vampire in Nineteenth Century English Literature* (Madison: University of Wisconsin Press, 1988), p. 167.
34 Vera Dika, *Games of Terror: Halloween, Friday the 13th and the Films of the Stalker Cycle* (Rutherford: Fairleigh Dickinson University Press, 1990), p. 58.
35 Dika, *Games of Terror*, p. 99.
36 Ralph Merrifield, *The Archeology of Ritual and Magic* (London: B. T. Batsford, 1987), p. 6.
37 J. C. Crocker, 'Ceremonial Masks', in Victor Turner (ed.), *Celebration: Studies in Festivity and Ritual* (Washington: Smithsonian Institution Press, 1982), p. 78.
38 Crocker, 'Ceremonial Masks', p. 80.
39 Mack, 'Introduction', p. 9.
40 Nunley and McCarty, *Masks: Faces of Culture*, p. 15.
41 Efrat Tseëlon, 'Reflections on Mask and Carnival', in Efrat Tseëlon (ed.), *Masquerade and Identities: Essays on Gender, Sexuality and Marginality* (London: Routledge, 2001), p. 3.
42 Sheppard, *Revealing Masks*, p. 27.
43 Tseëlon, 'Reflections on Mask and Carnival', p. 22.
44 Laura Mulvey, 'Visual Pleasure and Narrative Cinema', *Screen*, 3/1 (1975), 6–18.
45 Julia Kristeva, *Powers of Horror: An Essay on Abjection* (New York: Columbia University Press, 1982), pp. 63–4; Barbara Creed, *The Monstrous-Feminine: Film, Feminism, Psychoanalysis* (New York: Routledge, 1993), p. 8.
46 Nick Haslam, 'What Is Dehumanization?', in J. Vaes, P. G. Bain and J. P. Leyens (eds), *Humanness and Dehumanization* (London: Taylor and Francis, 2013), p. 34.
47 Haslam, 'What Is Dehumanization?', p. 38.

48 Thomas Sipos, *Horror Film Aesthetics: Creating the Visual Language of Fear* (Jefferson: McFarland & Co., 2010), p. 63.
49 Stephen T. Asma, *On Monsters: An Unnatural History of Our Worst Fears* (Oxford: Oxford University Press, 2009), p. 8.
50 Sorell, *The Other Face*, p. 10.
51 Nunley and McCarty, *Masks: Faces of Culture*, p. 17.
52 Tseëlon, 'Reflections on Mask and Carnival', p. 18.
53 Nunley and McCarty, *Masks: Faces of Culture*, p. 15.
54 Nunley and McCarty, *Masks: Faces of Culture*, pp. 16, 24.
55 Sheppard, *Revealing Masks*, p. 25.
56 See Julia Kristeva, *Desire in Language: A Semiotic Approach to Literature and Art* (New York: Columbia University Press, 1980); Stacy Burton, 'Paradoxical Relations: Bakhtin and Modernism', *Modern Language Quarterly: A Journal of Literary History*, 61/3 (2000), 519–43 (519); Anker Gemzøe, 'Modernism, Narrativity and Bakhtinian Theory', in Astradur Eysteinsson and Vivian Liska (eds), *Modernism* (Amsterdam: John Benjamins Publishing Company, 2007), p. 126; Terry Eagleton, 'I Contain Multitudes', *London Review of Books*, 29/12 (21 June 2007), 13–15, *https://www.lrb.co.uk/v29/n12/terry-eagleton/i-contain-multitudes* (accessed 28 February 2019).
57 Mikhail Bakhtin, *Rabelais and His World* (Cambridge: MIT Press, 1965; Bloomington: Indiana University Press, 1984), p. 10.
58 Florent Christol, 'Massacres and Masquerades: Costume in the American Slasher Film and the Cultural Myth of the "Foolkiller"', in Julia Petrov and Gudrun D. Whitehead (eds), *Fashioning Horror: Dressing to Kill on Screen and in Literature* (London: Bloomsbury, 2017), p. 222.
59 Katerina Clark and Michael Holquist, *Mikhail Bakhtin* (Cambridge: Belknap Press/Harvard University Press, 1984), p. 304.
60 Bakhtin, *Rabelais and His World*, p. 39.
61 Bakhtin, *Rabelais and His World*, p. 40.
62 Rozaliya Yaneva, *Misrule and Reversals: Carnivalesque Performances in Christopher Marlowe's Plays* (Munich: Herbert Utz Verlag, 2012), p. 210.
63 See Christol, 'Massacres and Masquerades'; Barbara Creed, 'Horror and the Carnivalesque: The Body-Monstrous', in Leslie Devereaux and Roger Hillman (eds), *Fields of Vision: Essays in Film Studies, Visual Anthropology, and Photography* (Berkeley: University of California Press, 1995), pp. 127–59; Angela Ndalianis, *The Horror Sensorium: Media and the Senses* (Jefferson: McFarland & Co., 2012); Robert Stam, *Subversive Pleasures: Bakhtin, Cultural Criticism and Film* (Baltimore: The Johns Hopkins University Press, 1989).

64 Jack Santino, 'Flexible Halloween: Longevity, Appropriation, Multiplicity and Contestation', in Malcolm Foley and Hugh O'Donnell (eds), *Treat or Trick? Halloween in a Globalising World* (Newcastle upon Tyne: Cambridge Scholars Publishing, 2009), pp. x, 12–13.
65 Richard Schechner, *Performance Studies: An Introduction* (London: Routledge, 2013), p. 52.
66 Schechner, *Performance Studies*, p. 52.
67 Sigmund Freud, 'The Uncanny', in *The Standard Edition of the Complete Psychological Works of Sigmund Freud* (London: The Hogarth Press, 1955), p. 219; Helen Wheatley, 'Television', in William Hughes, David Punter and Andrew Smith (eds), *The Encyclopedia of the Gothic* (Malden: John Wiley & Son, 2016), p. 677.
68 Frederick S. Frank, 'Glossary', in *The Castle of Otranto and The Mysterious Mother By Horace Walpole*, ed. Frederick S. Frank (Peterborough: Broadview Press Ltd, 2003), p. 343.
69 William Hughes, *Historical Dictionary of Gothic Literature* (Lanham: Scarecrow Press, 2013), p. 86.
70 Paul Fleming, 'Doppelgänger/Doppeltgänger', *Cabinet Magazine*, 14 (2004), www.cabinetmagazine.org/issues/14/fleming.php (accessed 28 February 2019).
71 Georges Bataille, 'The Mask', *LVNG*, 10 (2002), 63–7 (64).
72 Bataille, 'The Mask', 65.
73 Grimes, 'Masking', 509.
74 Tseëlon, 'Reflections on Mask and Carnival', p. 21.
75 Tseëlon, 'Reflections on Mask and Carnival', p. 21.
76 Grimes, 'Masking', 509, 510.
77 Grimes, 'Masking', 509.
78 Tseëlon, 'Reflections on Mask and Carnival', p. 20.
79 Tseëlon, 'Reflections on Mask and Carnival', p. 20.
80 Tseëlon, 'Reflections on Mask and Carnival', p. 21.
81 Simon Shepherd and Mick Wallis, *Drama/Theatre/Performance* (Hoboken: Taylor and Francis, 2004), p. 180.
82 Nunley and McCarty, *Masks: Faces of Culture*, p. 16.
83 Adam Lowenstein, *Shocking Representation: Historical Trauma, National Cinema and the Modern Horror Film* (New York: Columbia University Press, 2005), p. 2.
84 Lowenstein, *Shocking Representation*, p. 2.
85 Lowenstein, *Shocking Representation*, pp. 2–3.
86 Doug Bradley, *Sacred Monsters: Behind the Mask of the Horror Actor* (London: Titan Books, 1996), p. 15.

87   Clive Barker, 'Foreword', in Bradley, *Sacred Monsters: Behind the Mask of the Horror Actor*, p. 8.
88   Neale, 'Questions of Genre', 56.
89   Butler, 'Faces of Rage', pp. 197, 199.
90   Butler, 'Faces of Rage', p. 200.
91   Sipos, *Horror Film Aesthetics*, p. 63.
92   Jason Huddleston, 'Unmasking the Monster: Hiding and Revealing Male Sexuality in John Carpenter's *Halloween*', *Journal of Visual Literacy*, 25/2 (autumn 2005), 219–36 (220).
93   Carol J. Clover, *Men, Women and Chain Saws: Gender in the Modern Horror Film* (Princeton: Princeton University Press, 1992), p. 42.
94   Clover, *Men, Women and Chain Saws*, p. 42.
95   Clover, *Men, Women and Chain Saws*, pp. 62–3.
96   Tony Williams, 'Trying to Survive the Darker Side: 1980s Family Horror', in Barry Keith Grant (ed.), *The Dread of Difference: Gender and the Horror Film* (Austin: University of Texas Press, 1996), p. 17.
97   These include: *Funeral Home* (William Fruet, 1980), *Night School* (Ken Ward, 1981), *Girls Nite Out* (Anthony N. Gurvis, 1982), *Night Warning* (William Asher, 1982), *The Final Terror* (Andrew Davis, 1983), *Mountaintop Motel Massacre* (Jim McCullough Sr., 1983), *Sweet Sixteen* (Jim Sotos, 1983), *The Initiation* (Larry Stewart, 1984), *Killer Party* (William Fruet, 1986), *April Fool's Day* (Fred Walton, 1986), *Hello Mary Lou: Prom Night II* (Bruce Pittman, 1987), *Killer Workout* (David A. Prior, 1987), *Mommy's Epitaph* (Joseph Merhi, 1987), *Cheerleader Camp* (John Quinn, 1988) and *Evil Laugh* (Dominick Brascia, 1988).
98   Huddleston, 'Unmasking the Monster', 220.

1   Situating Masks and Horror Cinema

1   Ian Woodward, *Understanding Material Culture* (Los Angeles: Sage Publications, 2007), p. 3.
2   Woodward, *Understanding Material Culture*, p. 4.
3   Vivian Sobchack, *Carnal Thoughts: Embodiment and Moving Image Culture* (Berkeley: University of California Press, 2004), p. 59.
4   Sobchack, *Carnal Thoughts*, p. 62.
5   John G. Cawelti, *The Six-Gun Mystique* (Bowling Green: Bowling Green University Popular Press, 1970), p. 32.
6   Claude Lévi-Strauss, *The Way of the Masks* (Seattle: University of Washington Press, 1982), p. 12.

7   Lévi-Strauss, *The Way of the Masks*, p. 14.
8   Lévi-Strauss, *The Way of the Masks*, p. 14.
9   Claude Lévi-Strauss, 'The Structural Study of Myth', in Claude Lévi-Strauss, *Structural Anthropology* (1955; London: Penguin, 1968), p. 217; Andrew Tudor, *Theories of Film* (New York: Viking Press, 1973), pp. 135, 139. Although, as Daniel Chandler has rightly noted, that 'this begs the question about who "we" are'. See 'An Introduction to Genre Theory', *Visual Memory* (11 August 1997), *visual-memory.co.uk/daniel/Documents/intgenre/* (accessed 28 February 2019).
10 Mark Jancovich, *Horror, The Film Reader* (London: Routledge, 2002), p. 12.
11 Thomas Schatz, 'The Structural Influence: New Directions in Film Genre Study', in Barry Keith Grant (ed.), *Film Genre Reader IV* (Austin: University of Texas Press, 2012), p. 115.
12 Rick Altman, *The American Film Musical* (Bloomington: Indiana University Press, 1987), p. 340.
13 Angela Ndalianis, *The Horror Sensorium: Media and the Senses* (Jefferson: McFarland & Co., 2012), p. 29.
14 Mikhail Bakhtin, *Rabelais and His World* (Cambridge: MIT Press, 1965; Bloomington: Indiana University Press, 1984), p. 40.
15 Steve Neale, *Genre and Hollywood* (London: Routledge, 2000), p. 196.
16 Steve Neale, 'Questions of Genre', *Screen*, 31/1 (1990), 45–66 (56).
17 Neale, 'Questions of Genre', 56.
18 J. C. Crocker, 'Ceremonial Masks', in Victor Turner (ed.), *Celebration: Studies in Festivity and Ritual* (Washington: Smithsonian Institution Press, 1982), p. 81.
19 Doug Bradley, *Sacred Monsters: Behind the Mask of the Horror Actor* (London: Titan Books, 1996), p. 28.
20 Bradley, *Sacred Monsters*, p. 30.
21 Robin and Tonia Ridington, 'The Inner Eye of Shamanism and Totemism 1970', *History of Religions*, 10/1 (1970), 49–61 (50).
22 Ridington, 'The Inner Eye', 50.
23 Bradley, *Sacred Monsters*, p. 31.
24 Michael Ripinsky-Naxon, *The Nature of Shamanism: Substance and Function of a Religious Metaphor* (Albany: State University of New York Press, 1993), p. 42.
25 Also neo-shamanism, a contemporary spiritual practice linked to neo-paganism and the so-called 'New Age' movement. See Ward Churchill, 'Spiritual Hucksterism: The Rise of the Plastic Medicine Men', in Graham Harvey (ed.), *Shamanism: A Reader* (London: Routledge, 2003),

pp. 324–33; R. J. Wallis, 'Waking Ancestor Spirits: Neo-shamanic Engagements with Archeology', in Graham Harvey (ed.), *Shamanism: A Reader* (London: Routledge, 2003), pp. 402–23; Gordon MacLellan, 'Dancing on the Edge: Shamanism in Modern Britain', in Graham Harvey (ed.), *Shamanism: A Reader* (London: Routledge, 2003), pp. 365–74.

26 Margaret Stutley, *Shamanism: A Concise Introduction* (London: Routledge, 2003), pp. 2–3.
27 Stutley, *Shamanism*, p. 3.
28 Stutley also notes the complexity of the term and the difficulties of locating a single origin for it (*Shamanism*, p. 3).
29 Graham Harvey, 'General Introduction', in Graham Harvey (ed.), *Shamanism: A Reader* (London: Routledge, 2003), pp. 1, 2.
30 Harvey, 'General Introduction', pp. 5, 6.
31 Anne Marsh, *Performance Ritual Document* (Melbourne: Macmillan Art Publishing, 2014), p. 98.
32 Donald Cordry's once-foundational anthropological monograph, *Mexican Masks* (Austin: University of Texas Press, 1980) offers a key example of the dangers of cultural bias. Despite its influence, Pavel Shlossberg argues that the 'Cordry regime' was a 'screwball farce' (*Crafting Identity: Transnational Indian Arts and the Politics of Race in Central Mexico* (Tuscon: University of Arizona Press, 2015), pp. 192, 183), identifying a widespread failure of the academic process because those who validated his work did not realise that the masks in question were created precisely to suit the myths that Cordry himself was looking for evidence to support (*Crafting Identity*, p. 191).
33 Leslie J. Moran, 'Law and the Gothic Imagination', in Fred Botting (ed.), *The Gothic* (Cambridge: D. S. Brewer, 2001), p. 90.
34 Peter Brooks, *The Melodramatic Imagination: Balzac, Henry James, Melodrama, and the Mode of Excess* (New Haven: Yale University Press, 1995), pp. xv, vii.
35 Brooks, *The Melodramatic Imagination*, p. 4.
36 Brooks, *The Melodramatic Imagination*, p. 15.
37 Brooks, *The Melodramatic Imagination*, p. 18.
38 Brooks, *The Melodramatic Imagination*, p. 18.
39 Brooks, *The Melodramatic Imagination*, pp. 19–20.
40 Brooks, *The Melodramatic Imagination*, p. 20.
41 Brooks, *The Melodramatic Imagination*, p. 20.
42 Peter Hutchings, *Historical Dictionary of Horror Cinema* (Lanham: Scarecrow Press, 2008), p. 150; John Ruskin, *The Nature of Gothic: A Chapter from the Stones of Venice* (London: George Allen, 1900), p. 52.

43 Maria Beville, *Gothic-Postmodernism: Voicing the Terrors of Postmodernity* (Amsterdam: Rodopi, 2009), p. 55.
44 See Nicole Burkholder-Mosco and Wendy Carse, '"Wondrous Material to Play On": Children as Sites of Gothic Liminality in *The Turn of the Screw*, *The Innocents* and *The Others*', *Studies in Humanities*, 32/2 (2005), 201–20; Manuel Aguirre, 'Narrative Structure, Liminality, Self-similarity: The Case of Gothic Fiction', in Clive Bloom (ed.), *Gothic Horror: A Guide for Students and Readers* (London: Palgrave Macmillan, 2006), pp. 226–46; Peter Messent, 'American Gothic: Liminality and the Gothic in Thomas Harris's Hannibal Lecter Novels', in Benjamin Szumskyj (ed.), *Dissecting Hannibal Lecter: Essays on the Novels of Thomas Harris* (Jefferson: McFarland & Co., 2008), pp. 13–36; Ineke Bockting, 'The Ecstasy of the Abyss: The Voice Beyond *Dr. Haggard's Disease*', in Jocelyn Dupont (ed.), *Patrick McGrath: Directions and Transgressions* (Newcastle upon Tyne: Cambridge Scholars Publishing, 2012), pp. 51–64; Pasi Nyyssönen, 'Gothic Liminality in A. J. Annila's Film Sauna', in P. M. Mehtonen and Matti Savolainen (eds), *Gothic Topographies: Language, Nation Building and 'Race'* (London: Routledge, 2013), pp. 187–202.
45 Charles Ducey, 'The Life History and Creative Psychopathology of the Shaman', *Psychoanalytic Study of Society*, 7 (1976), 173–230 (175).
46 Victor Turner, *Ritual Process: Structure and Anti-Structure* (Chicago: Aldine Publishing, 1969), p. 107.
47 Turner, *Ritual Process*, p. 95.
48 Turner, *Ritual Process*, pp. 128–9.
49 William S. Haney II, *Postmodern Theater and the Void of Conceptions* (Newcastle: Cambridge Scholars Press, 2006), p. 131.
50 Sandor Klapcsik, *Liminality in Fantastic Fiction: A Poststructuralist Approach* (Jefferson: McFarland & Co., 2012), p. 3.
51 Stanley C. Krippner, 'Conflicting Perspectives on Shamans and Shamanism: Points and Counterpoints', *American Psychologist*, 57/11 (November 2002), 962–77 (970).
52 Krippner, 'Conflicting Perspectives', 964–70.
53 Krippner, 'Conflicting Perspectives', 970.
54 Krippner, 'Conflicting Perspectives', 970.
55 Cathleen Rountree, 'Auteur Film Directors as Contemporary Shamans', *Jung Journal*, 2/2 (spring 2008), 123–34 (123).
56 Laurel Kendall, 'Numinous Dress/Iconic Costume: Korean Shamans Dressed for the Gods and for the Camera', in Heike Behrend, Anja Dreschke and Martin Zillinger (eds), *Trance Mediums and New Media: Spirit Possession in the*

Age of Technical Reproduction (New York: Fordham University Press, 2014), pp. 116–36.

57 Nikki J. Y. Lee, 'Apartment Horror: *Sorum* and *Possessed*', in Alison Peirse and Daniel Martin (eds), *Korean Horror Cinema* (Edinburgh: Edinburgh University Press, 2013), p. 100.

58 Richard Leonard, *The Mystical Gaze of The Cinema: The Films of Peter Weir* (Melbourne: Melbourne University Press, 2009), pp. 220, 223; Jeremy Mark Robinson, *The Sacred Cinema of Andrei Tarkovsky* (Maidstone: Crescent Moon, 2007), pp. 168, 181; Brad Prager, *The Cinema of Werner Herzog: Aesthetic Ecstasy and Truth* (London: Wallflower, 2011), pp. 40, 91; James Norton, 'The Mystery, as Always: Raúl Ruiz, Klimt and the Poetics of Cinema', *Vertigo*, 3/6 (summer 2007), https://www.closeupfilmcentre.com/vertigo_magazine/volume-3-issue-6-summer-2007/makers-the-mystery-as-always-raul-ruiz/ (accessed 28 February 2019); Kelley Harrell, 'The Shamanic Narrative in Star Wars', *HuffPost* (17 December 2015), www.huffingtonpost.com/kelley-harrell/the-shamanic-narrative-in_b_8819874.html (accessed 28 February 2019).

59 See James R. Keller, *Food, Film and Culture: A Genre Study* (Jefferson: McFarland & Co., 2006). The shaman is also explored in Mike King, *Luminous: The Spiritual Life on Film* (Jefferson: McFarland & Co., 2014), pp. 37–49.

60 Tanya Krzywinska, *Sex and the Cinema* (London: Wallflower, 2006), p. 140; Tom Huddleston, 'An Interview with Richard Stanley', *Not Coming to a Theatre Near You* (20 August 2007), http://www.notcoming.com/features/richard-stanley-interview/ (accessed 28 February 2019).

61 Jason Horsley, *The Secret Life of Movies: Schizophrenic and Shamanic Journeys in American Cinema* (Jefferson: McFarland & Co., 2009), p. 1.

62 Horsley, *The Secret Life of Movies*, p. 2.

63 Horsley, *The Secret Life of Movies*, p. 2.

64 Horsley, *The Secret Life of Movies*, p. 2.

65 Horsley, *The Secret Life of Movies*, p. 3.

66 Horsley, *The Secret Life of Movies*, p. 3.

67 Horsley, *The Secret Life of Movies*, p. 3.

68 Horsley, *The Secret Life of Movies*, p. 4.

69 Horsley, *The Secret Life of Movies*, p. 4.

70 Horsley, *The Secret Life of Movies*, p. 3.

71 Mark Allen Peterson, 'From Jinn to Genies: Intertextuality, Media and the Making of Global Folklore', in Sharon R. Sherman and Mikel J. Koven (eds), *Folklore/Cinema: Popular Film as Vernacular Culture* (Logan: Utah State University Press, 2007), p. 93.

72 See Cynthia A. Freeland, 'Realist Horror', in Cynthia A. Freeland and Thomas E. Wartenberg (eds), *Philosophy and Film* (New York: Routledge, 1995), pp. 126–42.
73 See Noël Carroll, *The Philosophy of Horror: Paradoxes of the Heart* (New York: Routledge, 1990).
74 Timothy Shary, *Generation Multiplex* (Austin: University of Texas Press, 2004), p. 149.
75 Lewis Hyde, *Trickster Makes This World: Mischief, Myth and Art* (New York: Farrar, Straus and Giroux, 2010), n.p.
76 See Turner, *Ritual Process*, p. 92; George P. Hansen, *The Trickster and the Paranormal* (Bloomington: Xlibris Corporation, 2001); Alby Stone, *Explore Shamanism* (Loughborough: Explore Books, 2003), pp. 62–5.
77 Larry Ellis, 'Trickster: Shaman of the Liminal', *Studies in American Indian Literatures*, 5/4 (winter 1993), 55–68 (57).
78 Joseph Campbell, *The Masks of God: Primitive Mythology* (New York: Penguin, 1959), p. 273.
79 Carl Gustav Jung, *Four Archetypes: Mother, Rebirth, Spirit, Trickster* (London: Routledge, 2001), p. 160.
80 Jung, *Four Archetypes*, p. 173.
81 William J. Hynes, 'Mapping the Characteristics of Mythic Tricksters: A Heuristic Guide', in William J. Hynes and William G. Doty (eds), *Mythical Trickster Figures: Contours, Contexts, and Criticisms* (Tuscaloosa: The University of Alabama Press, 1993), p. 34.
82 Helena Bassil-Morozow, *The Trickster in Contemporary Film* (London: Routledge, 2012), p. 24.
83 Bassil-Morozow, *The Trickster in Contemporary Film*, p. 30.
84 Terrie Waddell, *Wild/lives Trickster, Place and Liminality on Screen* (Hoboken: Taylor and Francis, 2014), p. xi.

2 Masks and Horror in Literary and Performance Traditions and Early Cinema

1 W. Anthony Sheppard, *Revealing Masks: Exotic Influences and Ritualized Performance in Modernist Music Theater* (Berkeley: University of California Press, 2001), p. 37.
2 Sheppard, *Revealing Masks*, p. 37.
3 Sheppard, *Revealing Masks*, p. 38.
4 Sheppard, *Revealing Masks*, pp. 39, 41.

5   Sheppard, *Revealing Masks*, p. 73.
6   Sheppard, *Revealing Masks*, pp. 74–83, 86.
7   John Schechter, *Popular Theatre: A Sourcebook* (Hoboken: Taylor and Francis, 2013), p. 81.
8   John Rudlin, *Commedia Dell'Arte: An Actor's Handbook* (Hoboken: Taylor and Francis, 2002), p. 7.
9   Pierre Louis Duchartre, *The Italian Comedy* (Newburyport: Dover Publications, 2012), p. 64; Schechter, *Popular Theatre*; Rudlin, *Commedia Dell'Arte*, p. 7.
10 Steve Neale, 'Questions of Genre', *Screen*, 31/1 (1990), 45–66 (56).
11 Sheppard, *Revealing Masks*, p. 72.
12 Sheppard, *Revealing Masks*, p. 72.
13 Sheppard, *Revealing Masks*, p. 38.
14 David Wiles, *The Masks of Menander: Sign and Meaning in Greek and Roman Performance* (Cambridge: Cambridge University Press, 1991), p. 112; Benito Ortolani, *Japanese Theatre: From Shamanistic Ritual to Contemporary Pluralism* (Princeton: Princeton University Press, 1990), p. xvii.
15 Ortolani, *Japanese Theatre*, p. xvii.
16 Ortolani, *Japanese Theatre*, p. 300.
17 Ortolani, *Japanese Theatre*, p. 300.
18 Ortolani, *Japanese Theatre*, p. xvi.
19 Ortolani, *Japanese Theatre*, p. xvii.
20 Ortolani, *Japanese Theatre*, p. xvii.
21 Ortolani, *Japanese Theatre*, p. 1.
22 Ortolani, *Japanese Theatre*, p. 1.
23 Ortolani, *Japanese Theatre*, p. 2.
24 Ortolani, *Japanese Theatre*, p. 3.
25 Ortolani, *Japanese Theatre*, pp. 4, 5.
26 Wheeler Winston Dixon and Gwendolyn Audrey Foster, *A Short History of Film* (New Brunswick: Rutgers University Press, 2008), p. 87.
27 Aaron Gerow, *A Page of Madness: Cinema and Modernity in 1920s Japan* (Ann Arbor: Center for Japanese Studies, The University of Michigan, 2008), pp. 1, 4.
28 David Sorfa, '*Kurutta ichipeiji*; Sometimes *Kuruta ippejiji/A Page of Madness* (1926)', in S. Barrow, S. Haenni and J. White (eds), *The Routledge Encyclopedia of Films* (London: Routledge, 2015), p. 297.
29 Colette Balmain, *Introduction to Japanese Horror Film* (Edinburgh: Edinburgh University Press, 2008), p. 32.
30 Keiko I. McDonald, *Japanese Classical Theater in Films* (Rutherford: Fairleigh Dickinson University Press, 1994), p. 132.
31 McDonald, *Japanese Classical Theater in Films*, p. 126.

32 McDonald, *Japanese Classical Theater in Films*, p. 126.
33 Wiles, *The Masks of Menander*, p. 112.
34 Sorfa, '*Kurutta ichipeiji*', p. 297.
35 Sorfa, '*Kurutta ichipeiji*', p. 297.
36 Timothy Iles, *The Crisis of Identity in Contemporary Japanese Film* (Leiden: Brill, 2008), p. 20.
37 Iles, *The Crisis of Identity*, p. 20.
38 Marvin A. Carlson, *Theatre: A Very Short Introduction* (Oxford: Oxford University Press, 2014), p. 102.
39 Rudlin, *Commedia Dell'Arte*, p. 2.
40 Rudlin, *Commedia Dell'Arte*, p. 9.
41 Rudlin, *Commedia Dell'Arte*, p. 14.
42 M. A. Katritzky, *The Art of Commedia: A Study in the Commedia dell'Arte 1560–1620 with Special Reference to the Visual Records* (Amsterdam: Rodopi, 2006), p. 19.
43 Herbert E. Plutschow, *Matsuri: The Festivals of Japan* (Richmond: Japan Library, 1996), p. 159.
44 Robert L. Winzeler, *Anthropology and Religion: What We Know, Think, and Question* (Lanham: AltaMira Press, 2008), p. 135.
45 Carlson, *Theatre*, p. 102.
46 Christopher Frayling, *Spaghetti Westerns: Cowboys and Europeans from Karl May to Sergio Leone* (London: I. B. Tauris, 1998), p. 131.
47 Frayling, *Spaghetti Westerns*, p. 131.
48 Frayling, *Spaghetti Westerns*, p. 131.
49 Rudlin, *Commedia Dell'Arte*, p. 23.
50 Rudlin, *Commedia Dell'Arte*, p. 24.
51 Rudlin, *Commedia Dell'Arte*, p. 32.
52 Duchartre, *The Italian Comedy*, p. 48.
53 Duchartre, *The Italian Comedy*, p. 51.
54 Olly Crick and John Rudin, *Commedia Dell'Arte: A Handbook for Troupes* (Hoboken: Taylor and Francis, 2002), p. 1.
55 Schechter, *Popular Theatre*, p. 79.
56 Rudlin, *Commedia Dell'Arte*, p. 4.
57 Angela Ndalianis, *The Horror Sensorium: Media and the Senses* (Jefferson: McFarland & Co., 2012), p. 109.
58 George Kurman, 'Cultural Antecedents of Beavis and Butt-head', *The Journal of Popular Culture*, 18/1 (October 1995), 101–12; David James LeMaster, 'Charlie Chaplin and Harpo Marx as Masks of the Commedia Dell'Arte: Theory and Practice' (PhD thesis, Texas Tech University, 1995).

59　See Steve Neale and Frank Krutnik, *Popular Film and Television Comedy*. (London: Routledge, 1990), p. 21; Louise Peacock, 'Slapstick and Comic Violence in Commedia Dell'arte', in Judith Chaffee and Olly Crick (eds), *The Routledge Companion to Commedia dell'Arte* (London: Routledge, 2014), p. 185.

60　Jason Marc Harris, 'Smiles of Oblivion: Demonic Clowns and Doomed Puppets as Fantastic Figures of Absurdity, Chaos and Misanthropy in the Writings of Thomas Ligotti', *The Journal of Popular Culture*, 45/6 (2012), 1249–65.

61　While make-up such as that of the horror clown is certainly a rich site for critical analysis that may in places overlap with the concerns of this book, it is practical here to maintain my interest only in actual masks that appear diegetically in films, and not as costume elements.

62　See David Roche, *Making and Remaking Horror in the 1970s and 2000s: Why Don't They Do It Like They Used To?* (Jackson: University Press of Mississippi, 2014), p. 175; Roberto Curti, *Italian Gothic Horror Films, 1957–1969* (Jefferson: McFarland & Co., 2015), pp. 119–20; John T. Soister, *Of Gods and Monsters: A Critical Guide to Universal Studios' Science Fiction, Horror and Mystery Films, 1929–1939* (Jefferson: McFarland & Co., 1999), p. 34; Mark Goodall, *Sweet and Savage: The World Through the Shockumentary Film Lens* (London: Headpress, 2006), p. 74.

63　Schechter identifies three groups of characters: the maskless *caricati*, comic cameos by the *macchietta* and the *maschere*, 'the . . . top bananas' (Schechter, *Popular Theatre*, p. 84).

64　Schechter, *Popular Theatre*, p. 84.

65　Schechter, *Popular Theatre*, p. 84.

66　Schechter, *Popular Theatre*, p. 84.

67　Katritzky, *The Art of Commedia*, p. 102.

68　John O'Brien, *Harlequin Britain: Pantomime and Entertainment, 1690–1760* (Baltimore: The Johns Hopkins University Press, 2004), p. 119.

69　O'Brien, *Harlequin Britain*, p. 119.

70　Annette Lust, *From the Greek Mimes to Marcel Marceau and Beyond: Mimes, Actors, Pierrots, and Clowns: A Chronicle of the Many Visages of Mime in the Theatre* (Lanham: Scarecrow Press, 2000), pp. 38–40; James W. Gousseff, *Street Mime* (Woodstock: The Dramatic Publishing Company, 1993), p. 33.

71　Rush Rehm, *Greek Tragic Theatre* (London: Routledge, 1992), p. 40.

72　Rehm, *Greek Tragic Theatre*, p. 40.

73　MSU Museum, 'Mask: Secrets and Revelations: Masks on Stage', *Smithsonian Institute*, Michigan State University (2012), http://museum.msu.edu/?q=node/326 (accessed 28 February 2019).

74 John Emigh, *Masked Performance: The Play of Self and Other in Ritual and Theater* (Philadelphia: University of Pennsylvania Press, 1996), p. 35.
75 Steve Tillis, *Rethinking Folk Drama* (Westport: Greenwood Press, 1999), p. 179.
76 See Susan Harris Smith, *Masks in Modern Drama* (Berkeley: University of California Press, 1984), pp. 89–126; Harald William Fawkner, *Deconstructing Macbeth: The Hyperontological View* (Cranbury: Associated University Presses, Inc., 1990), p. 202.
77 Dani Cavallaro, *The Gothic Vision: Three Centuries of Horror, Terror and Fear* (London: Continuum, 2002), p. 8.
78 Cavallaro, *The Gothic Vision*, p. 9.
79 Cavallaro, *The Gothic Vision*, p. 8.
80 Philip Brophy, '*Arashi Ga Oka (Onimaru)*: The Sound of the World Turned Inside Out', in Jay McRoy (ed.), *Japanese Horror Cinema* (Edinburgh: Edinburgh University Press, 2006), p. 159.
81 Catherine Spooner, *Fashioning Gothic Bodies* (Manchester: Manchester University Press, 2004), p. 201.
82 Catherine Spooner, 'Masks, Veils and Disguises', in William Hughes, D. Punter and A. Smith (eds), *The Encyclopedia of the Gothic. Volume II (L–Z)* (Malden: Wiley-Blackwell, 2013), p. 421.
83 Spooner, 'Masks, Veils and Disguises', p. 422.
84 Spooner, 'Masks, Veils and Disguises', p. 423.
85 Tammis Elise Thomas, 'Masquerade Liberties and Female Power in Le Fanu's *Carmilla*', in E. E. Smith and R. Haas (eds), *The Haunted Mind: The Supernatural in Victorian Literature* (New York: Scarecrow Press, 1999), p. 44.
86 See Alex Houstoun, '"Hearken . . . I Can Tell You the Whole Story": Monologues and Confessions in the Early Works of H. P. Lovecraft and Edgar Allan Poe', in R. H. Waugh (ed.), *Lovecraft and Influence: His Predecessors and Successors* (Plymouth: Scarecrow Press, Inc., 2013), pp. 44–54; Dennis Perry and Carl Sederholm, *Poe, The House of Usher, and the American Gothic* (London: Palgrave, 2009), pp. 63–82.
87 Efrat Tseëlon, 'Reflections on Mask and Carnival', in Efrat Tseëlon (ed.), *Masquerade and Identities: Essays on Gender, Sexuality and Marginality* (London: Routledge, 2001), p. 30.
88 Dawn B. Sova, *Critical Companion to Edgar Allan Poe* (New York: Facts On File, 2001), p. 110.
89 Paul Roland, *The Curious Case of H. P. Lovecraft* (Medford: Plexus, 2014), n.p.; Shelley Costa Bloomfield, *The Everything Guide to Edgar Allan Poe Book: The Life, Times, and Work of a Tormented Genius* (Avon: Adams Media, 2007), pp. 198–9.

90 Martyn Colebrook, '"Comrades in Tentacles": H. P. Lovecraft and China Miéville', in David Simmons (ed.), *New Critical Essays on H. P. Lovecraft* (New York: Palgrave Macmillan, 2013), p. 222.
91 B. F. Fisher, 'Poe and the Gothic Tradition', in Kevin J. Hayes (ed.), *The Cambridge Companion to Edgar Allan Poe* (Cambridge: Cambridge University Press, 2003), p. 76.
92 R. A. Gilbert, 'Penny Dreadfuls', in Marie Mulvey-Roberts (ed.), *The Handbook to Gothic Literature* (New York: New York University Press, 1998), p. 172.
93 Gilbert Keith Chesterton, 'A Defence of Penny Dreadfuls', from *The Defendant*, published in The Wayfarer's Library by J. M. Dent and Sons Ltd, London (1901), republished at De Montfort University, *www.cse.dmu.ac.uk/~mward/gkc/books/penny-dreadfuls.html* (accessed 28 February 2019).
94 George Augustus Sala, *The Seven Sons of Mammon: A Story* (London: Tinsley Brothers, 1862), pp. 22–3.
95 Paul Bird, 'Writing Crime: Black Mask and the Conventions of 1920s–1930s Hard-Boiled Fiction', *Journal of the Faculty of Economics, KGU*, 22/1 (September 2012), 51–65 (51).
96 Peter Stanfield, *Maximum Movies – Pulp Fictions: Film Culture and the Worlds of Samuel Fuller, Mickey Spillane, and Jim Thompson* (New Brunswick: Rutgers University Press, 2011), p. 47.
97 Don Hutchison, *The Great Pulp Heroes* (New York: Book Republic, 2006), p. 9.
98 *The Lone Ranger* premiered on radio in February 1933 on a programme that would continue until 1955, launching a successful cross-media franchise. See Chadwick Allen, 'Hero with Two Faces: *The Lone Ranger* as Treaty Discourse', *American Literature*, 68/3 (September 1996), 609–38 (613). The figure of Zorro, first appearing in Johnston McCulley's short story *The Curse of Capistrano* (1919) – a precursor to contemporary superheroes – appeared across film, radio, pulps, comic books and television. See Kevin Starr, *Material Dreams: Southern California through the 1920s* (New York: Oxford University Press, 1990), p. 227.
99 John M. Callahan, 'The Grand-Guignol in New York City, October–November 1923: Violence Fails to Draw an Audience', in Arthur Gewirtz and James J. Kolb (eds), *Art, Glitter, and Glitz: Mainstream Playwrights and Popular Theatre in 1920s America* (Westport: Praeger, 2004), p. 162.
100 Tom Gunning, 'The Horror of Opacity: The Melodrama of Sensation in the Plays of Andre de Lorde', in J. Cook, J. Bratton and C. Gledhill (eds), *Melodrama: Stage, Picture, Screen* (London: British Film Institute, 1994), p. 60; Adam Rockoff, *Going to Pieces: The Rise and Fall of the Slasher Film, 1978–1986* (Jefferson: McFarland & Co., 2002), p. 24.

101 Richard J. Hand and Michael Wilson, *Grand Guignol: The French Theatre of Horror* (Devon: Exeter University Press, 2002), p. 139.
102 Bert Cardullo and Robert Knopf, *Theater of the Avant-garde, 1890–1950: A Critical Anthology* (New Haven: Yale University, 2001), p. 373.
103 Cardullo and Knopf, *Theater of the Avant-garde*, p. 375.
104 Robert Cunliffe, 'Bakhtin, Artaud, and Brecht', in David Shepherd (ed.), *Bakhtin: Carnival and Other Subjects* (Amsterdam: Rodopi, 1991), p. 53.
105 Cunliffe, 'Bakhtin, Artaud, and Brecht', p. 54.
106 Margaret Rogerson, *Playing a Part in History: The York Mysteries, 1951–2006* (Toronto: University of Toronto Press, 2009), p. 82.
107 Rogerson, *Playing a Part in History*, p. 57.
108 Antonin Artaud, *The Theater and its Double*, trans. Mary Caroline Richards (New York: Grove Press, 1958), p. 53.
109 Artaud, *The Theater and Its Double*, p. 93.
110 Linda Badley, *Film, Horror, and the Body Fantastic* (Westport: Greenwood Press, 1995), p. 9.
111 Badley, *Film, Horror, and the Body Fantastic*, p. 10.
112 Hand and Wilson, *Grand Guignol*, p. ix.
113 Victor Emeljanow, 'Grand Guignol and the Orchestration of Violence', *Themes in Drama 12: Violence in Drama* (New York: Cambridge University Press), p. 153.
114 Emeljanow, 'Grand Guignol and the Orchestration of Violence', p. 153.
115 Emeljanow, 'Grand Guignol and the Orchestration of Violence', p. 154.
116 Emeljanow, 'Grand Guignol and the Orchestration of Violence', p. 154.
117 Callahan, 'The Grand-Guignol in New York City', p. 167.
118 Hand and Wilson, *Grand Guignol*, p. 8.
119 Callahan, 'The Grand-Guignol in New York City', p. 168.
120 Emeljanow, 'Grand Guignol and the Orchestration of Violence', p. 154.
121 Hand and Wilson, *Grand Guignol*, p. 8.
122 Gunning, 'The Horror of Opacity', p. 56; Adam Lowenstein, *Shocking Representation: Historical Trauma, National Cinema and the Modern Horror Film* (New York: Columbia University Press, 2005), p. 47.
123 Richard J. Hand, 'Half-Masks and Stage Blood: Translating, Adapting and Performing French Historical Theatre Forms', in K. Krebs (ed.), *Translation and Adaptation in Theatre and Film* (New York: Routledge, 2014), p. 146.
124 Hand and Wilson, *Grand Guignol*, pp. 180, 244–64.
125 Rémi Fournier Lanzoni, *French Cinema: From Its Beginnings to the Present* (New York: Continuum, 2005), pp. 56–7.

126 Richard Abel, *The Cine Goes to Town: French Cinema 1896–1914* (Berkeley: University of California Press, 1994), p. 66.
127 These include *Masked Mirth* (Robin Williamson, 1917) and two versions of *Masks and Faces* – one by Lawrence Marston (1914) and a British version by Fred Paul (1917).
128 Many movies from this period feature masks in their titles alone, including *Behind Comedy's Mask* (Urban Gad, 1913), *The Gray Mask* (Frank Crane, 1915), *Behind the Mask* (Alice Guy, 1917) and *The Mask* (Thomas N. Heffron, 1918).
129 Pamela Hutchinson, '10 Great Silent Horror Films', *British Film Institute* (7 November 2016), www.bfi.org.uk/news-opinion/news-bfi/lists/10-great-silent-horror-films (accessed 28 February 2019).
130 David Robinson, *Das Cabinet Des Dr. Caligari* (London: Palgrave Macmillian/British Film Institute, 2013), p. 88.
131 Peter Selz, *German Expressionist Painting* (Berkeley: University of California Press, 1974), p. 125.
132 Ben Morgan, '*Metropolis* – The Archetypal Version: Sentimentality and Self-Control in the Reception of the Film', in M. Minden and H. Bachmann (eds), *Fritz Lang's Metropolis: Cinematic Visions of Technology and Fear* (New York: Camden House, 2000), p. 299.
133 Translations by Franck Boulègue, Julien Allen and Samuel Bréan, with thanks.
134 According to Deslandes, this story was reprinted in *L'impossible*, 5 (November 1971), which states that Gance's short story with the same title was first published in *Le miroir* #81, 12 October 1913, which Deslandes believes to be incorrect.
135 John T. Soister and Henry Nicolella, *American Silent Horror, Science Fiction and Fantasy Feature Films, 1913–1929, vol. 1* (Jefferson: McFarland & Co., 2012), p. 637.

3 Masks in Horror Film before 1970

1 Steve Neale, 'Questions of Genre', *Screen*, 31/1 (1990), 45–66 (56).
2 Harry H. Long, 'The Phantom of the Opera', in J. T. Soister and H. Nicolella (eds), *American Silent Horror, Science Fiction and Fantasy Feature Films, 1913–1929* (Jefferson: McFarland & Co., 2012), p. 461.
3 Long, 'The Phantom of the Opera', p. 461.
4 Long, 'The Phantom of the Opera', p. 461.
5 Nick Haslam, 'What is Dehumanization?', in J. Vaes, P. G. Bain and J. P. Leyens (eds), *Humanness and Dehumanization* (London: Taylor and Francis, 2013), p. 38.

6   Long, 'The Phantom of the Opera', p. 460.
7   Mark Jancovich, *Horror, The Film Reader* (London: Routledge, 2002), p. 73.
8   Jancovich, *Horror, The Film Reader*, p. 73.
9   Jancovich, *Horror, The Film Reader*, p. 74.
10 Sue Ellen Case 'Tracking the Vampire', *difference*, 3/2 (summer 1991), 1–20 (3).
11 Barbara Creed, *The Monstrous-Feminine: Film, Feminism, Psychoanalysis* (New York: Routledge, 1993); Barbara Creed, 'Horror and the Monstrous-Feminine: An Imaginary Abjection', in Mark Jancovich (ed.), *Horror, The Film Reader* (London: Routledge, 2002).
12 Creed, 'Horror and the Monstrous-Feminine', p. 75.
13 Creed, 'Horror and the Monstrous-Feminine', p. 75.
14 Mircea Eliade, *The Sacred and the Profane: The Nature of Religion* (New York: Harcourt, Brace & World, 1959), p. 105; Anat Zanger, *Film Remakes as Ritual and Disguise: From Carmen to Ripley* (Amsterdam: Amsterdam University Press, 2006).
15 Harry H. Long, 'The Bat', in J. T. Soister and H. Nicolella (eds), *American Silent Horror, Science Fiction and Fantasy Feature Films, 1913–1929* (Jefferson: McFarland & Co., 2012), p. 21.
16 S. T. Joshi, *Icons of Horror and the Supernatural: An Encyclopaedia of Our Worst Nightmares. Volume 1* (Westport: Greenwood Press, 2007), p. 298.
17 Alison Peirse, 'Bauhaus of Horrors: Edgar G. Ulmer and *The Black Cat*', in Gary Rhodes (ed.), *Edgar G. Ulmer: Detour on Poverty Row* (London: Lexington Books, 2010), p. 280.
18 Peirse, 'Bauhaus of Horrors', p. 280.
19 Tom Weaver, Michael Brunas and John Brunas, *Universal Horrors: The Studio's Classic Films, 1931–1946* (Jefferson: McFarland & Co., 2007), p. 13.
20 Aija Ozolins, 'Dreams and Doctrines: Dual Strands in *Frankenstein*', *Science Fiction Studies*, 2/2 (1975), 103–12 (104).
21 William J. Hynes, 'Mapping the Characteristics of Mythic Tricksters: A Heuristic Guide', in William J. Hynes and William G. Doty (eds), *Mythical Trickster Figures: Contours, Contexts, and Criticisms* (Tuscaloosa: The University of Alabama Press, 1993), p. 34.
22 Sarah Thomas, *Peter Lorre: Face Maker: Stardom and Performance between Hollywood and Europe* (New York: Berghahn Books, 2012), p. 3.
23 Haslam, 'What is Dehumanization?', p. 38.
24 *The Face Behind the Mask* was promoted heavily by Columbia at the time of its release as a horror film, despite being traditional crime material. See Stephen D. Youngkin, *The Lost One: A Life of Peter Lorre* (Lexington: University Press of Kentucky, 2005), p. 172.

25 Ron Backer, *Classic Horror Films and the Literature that Inspired Them* (Jefferson: McFarland & Co., 2015), p. 97.
26 Jeremy Tambling, *Opera, Ideology and Film* (Manchester: Manchester University Press, 1987), pp. 48–9.
27 Backer, *Classic Horror Films*, p. 99.
28 Mark Jancovich, *Rational Fears: American Horror in the 1950s* (Manchester: Manchester University Press, 1996), p. 1.
29 Robin Wood, *Hollywood from Vietnam to Reagan . . . and Beyond* (New York: Columbia University Press, 2003), pp. 1–2; Jancovich, *Rational Fears*, p. 2.
30 Jancovich, *Rational Fears*, p. 2.
31 Jancovich, *Rational Fears*, p. 2.
32 Jancovich, *Rational Fears*, p. 2.
33 Jancovich, *Rational Fears*, pp. 262–3, 268.
34 Jancovich, *Rational Fears*, p. 271.
35 Bruce F. Kawin, *Horror and the Horror Film* (London: Anthem Press, 2012), p. 160.
36 Joel Eisner, *The Price of Fear: The Film Career of Vincent Price in His Own Words* (Antelope: Black Bed Sheet Books, 2013), p. 138.
37 Efrat Tseëlon, 'Reflections on Mask and Carnival', in Efrat Tseëlon (ed.) *Masquerade and Identities: Essays on Gender, Sexuality and Marginality* (London: Routledge, 2001), p. 20.
38 See Steven Jay Schneider and Tony Williams, 'Introduction', in Steven Jay Schneider and Tony Williams (eds), *Horror International* (Detroit: Wayne State University Press, 2005), pp. 1–12; Steven Jay Schneider, 'Introduction', in Steven Jay Schneider (ed.), *Fear without Frontiers: Horror Cinema Across the Globe* (Godalming: FAB Press, 2003), pp. 12–13.
39 Tino Balio, *The Foreign Film Renaissance on American Screens, 1946–1973* (Madison: The University of Wisconsin Press, 2010), p. 79.
40 Richard S. Randall, 'Censorship: From The Miracle to Deep Throat', in Thomas Schatz (ed.), *Hollywood: Critical Concepts in Media and Cultural Studies. Vol. III: Social Dimensions: Technology, Regulation and the Audience* (London: Routledge, 2004), p. 216.
41 Peter Hutchings, *Historical Dictionary of Horror Cinema* (Lanham: Scarecrow Press, 2008), p. 321; Tim Bergfelder, 'The Nation Vanishes: European Co-Productions and Popular Genre Formula in the 1950s and 1960s', in Mette Hjort and Scott MacKenzie (eds), *Cinema and Nation* (London: Routledge, 2000), p. 141.
42 See Austin Fisher and Johnny Walker (eds), *Grindhouse: Cultural Exchange on 42nd Street, and Beyond* (New York: Bloomsbury, 2016).

43 Raymond Durgnat, *Franju* (Berkeley: University of California Press, 1968), p. 83.
44 Durgnat, *Franju*, p. 73.
45 Identifying features of tricksters, noted previously by Hynes, 'Mapping the Characteristics of Mythic Tricksters: A Heuristic Guide', p. 34.
46 David J. Skal, *Screams of Reason: Mad Science and Modern Culture* (New York: W. W. Norton & Co., 1998), p. 23.
47 Kate Ince, *Georges Franju* (Manchester: Manchester University Press, 2005), p. 104.
48 Joan Hawkins, *Cutting Edge: Art-Horror and the Horrific Avant-Garde* (Minneapolis: University of Minnesota Press, 2000), p. 69.
49 Hawkins, *Cutting Edge*, p. 71.
50 Adam Lowenstein, *Shocking Representation: Historical Trauma, National Cinema and the Modern Horror Film* (New York: Columbia University Press, 2005), p. 42.
51 Lowenstein, *Shocking Representation*, p. 42.
52 Lowenstein, *Shocking Representation*, p. 43.
53 Lowenstein, *Shocking Representation*, p. 48.
54 Octavia Paz, *The Labyrinth of Solitude* (1959; New York: Grove Press Inc., 1985), p. 29.
55 Alexandra Mendoza Covarrubias, 'Día de los Muertos (Day of the Dead)', in María Herrera-Sobek (ed.), *Celebrating Latino Folklore: An Encyclopedia of Cultural Traditions, Volume 1* (Santa Barbara: ABC-CLIO, 2012), p. 403.
56 Tseëlon, 'Reflections on Mask and Carnival', p. 20.
57 See S. V. Lutes, 'The Mask and Magic of the Yaqui Paskola Clowns', in N. Ross Crumrine and Marjorie Halpin (eds), *The Power of Symbols: Masks and Masquerade in the Americas* (Vancouver: University of British Columbia Press, 1983), pp. 81–92; N. Ross Crumrine, 'Mask Use and Meaning in Easter Ceremonialism: The Mayo Parisero', in N. Ross Crumrine and Marjorie Halpin (eds), *The Power of Symbols: Masks and Masquerade in the Americas* (Vancouver: University of British Columbia Press, 1983), pp. 93–101; Frances Gillmor, 'Symbolic Representation in Mexican Combat Plays', in N. Ross Crumrine and Marjorie Halpin (eds), *The Power of Symbols: Masks and Masquerade in the Americas* (Vancouver: University of British Columbia Press, 1983), pp. 102–10; Victoria R. Bricker, 'The Meaning of Masking in San Pedro Chenalho', in N. Ross Crumrine and Marjorie Halpin (eds), *The Power of Symbols: Masks and Masquerade in the Americas* (Vancouver: University of British Columbia Press, 1983), pp. 111–15; J. Brody Esser, 'Tarascan Masks of Women as Agents of Social Control', in

N. Ross Crumrine and Marjorie Halpin (eds), *The Power of Symbols: Masks and Masquerade in the Americas* (Vancouver: University of British Columbia Press, 1983), pp. 116–27.
58 Walter Sorell, *The Other Face: The Mask in the Arts* (London: Thames and Hudson, 1973), p. 213.
59 Doyle Greene, *Mexploitation Cinema: A Critical History of Mexican Vampire, Wrestler, Ape-Man and Similar Films, 1957–1977* (Jefferson: McFarland & Co., 2005), p. 8.
60 Greene, *Mexploitation Cinema*, p. 8.
61 Gabrielle Murray, 'El Santo: Wrestler, Saint and Superhero', *Refractory: A Journal of Entertainment Media* (December 2006), http://refractory.unimelb.edu.au/2006/12/04/el-santo-wrestler-saint-and-superhero-gabrielle-murray/ (accessed 28 February 2019).
62 Murray, 'El Santo'.
63 Murray, 'El Santo'.
64 Evan Lieberman, 'Mask and Masculinity: Culture, Modernity, and Gender Identity in the Mexican Lucha Libre films of El Santo', *Studies in Hispanic Cinemas*, 6/1 (December 2009), 3–17 (3).
65 *Fotonovellas* are comic books that featured actual photographs of actors/actions instead of illustrations.
66 Murray, 'El Santo'.
67 Lieberman, 'Mask and Masculinity', 3.
68 Peter T. Markman and Roberta H. Markman, 'The Mask as Metaphor', in Peter T. Markman and Roberta H. Markman (eds), *Masks of the Spirit: Image and Metaphor in Mesoamerica* (Berkeley: University of California Press, 1990), p. xix.
69 Murray, 'El Santo'.
70 Murray, 'El Santo'.
71 Murray, 'El Santo'.
72 Greene, *Mexploitation Cinema*, p. 101.
73 For example, *Santo vs. the Zombies* (*Santo Contra los Zombis*, Benito Alazraki, 1961), *Santo in the Hotel of Death* (*Santo en el hotel de la muerte*, Federico Curiel, 1963), *Santo vs. the Diabolical Hatchet* (*El Hacha diabólica*, José Díaz Morales, 1965), *Santo Attacks the Witches* (*Atacan las brujas*, José Díaz Morales, 1968), *Santo and Dracula's Treasure* (*Santo en El tesoro de Dracula*, René Cardona, 1969), *Revenge of the Vampire Women* (*La venganza de las mujeres vampire*, Federico Curiel, 1970) and *Santo and the Vengeance of the Mummy* (*Santo En La Venganza De La Momia*, René Cardona, 1971).

74 Greene, *Mexploitation Cinema*, p. 103.
75 Greene, *Mexploitation Cinema*, p. 104.
76 Lieberman, 'Mask and Masculinity', 5.
77 Murray, 'El Santo'.
78 Lieberman, 'Mask and Masculinity', 3.
79 Murray, 'El Santo'.
80 See, for instance, *Hercules and the Masked Rider* (*Golia e il cavaliere mascherato*, Piero Pierotti, 1963) and *Terror of the Red Mask* (*Il terrore della maschera rossa*, Luigi Capuano, 1960).
81 Mikel J. Koven, *La Dolce Morte: Vernacular Cinema and the Italian Giallo Film* (Lanham: Scarecrow Press, 2006), p. 6.
82 Gary Needham, 'Playing with Genre: An Introduction to the Italian Giallo', in Ernest Mathijs and Xavier Mendik (eds), *The Cult Film Reader* (Maidenhead: McGraw Hill, 2008), p. 296.
83 Koven, *La Dolce Morte*, pp. 7, 159.
84 Leon Hunt, 'A (Sadistic) Night at the Opera', in Ken Gelder (ed.), *The Horror Reader* (London: Routledge, 2000), p. 330.
85 Hunt, 'A (Sadistic) Night at the Opera', p. 330.
86 Hunt, 'A (Sadistic) Night at the Opera', p. 330.
87 Peter Bondanella, *A History of Italian Cinema* (New York: Continuum, 2009), p. 310.
88 Martyn Conterio, *Black Sunday* (Leighton Buzzard: Auteur, 2014), p. 71.
89 Conterio, *Black Sunday*, p. 71.
90 Zvika Serper, 'Shindô Kaneto's Films *Kuroneko* and *Onibaba*: Traditional and Innovative Manifestations of Demonic Embodiments', *Japan Forum*, 17/2 (2005), 231–56 (231).
91 Serper, 'Shindô Kaneto's Films', 232, 233.
92 Serper, 'Shindô Kaneto's Films', 232.
93 Serper, 'Shindô Kaneto's Films', 232.
94 Serper, 'Shindô Kaneto's Films', 247.
95 Colette Balmain, *Introduction to Japanese Horror Film* (Edinburgh: Edinburgh University Press, 2008), p. 59.
96 Lowenstein, *Shocking Representation*, p. 87.
97 Lowenstein, *Shocking Representation*, p. 87.
98 Lowenstein, *Shocking Representation*, p. 88.
99 Lowenstein, *Shocking Representation*, p. 93.
100 Neale, 'Questions of Genre', *Screen*, 31/1 (1990), 45–66 (56).

4 Skin Masks: Ritual, Power and Transformation

1. See Christina Pratt, *An Encyclopedia of Shamanism* (New York: Rosen, 2007), p. 263; Cunera Cornelia Maria Buijs, *Furs and Fabrics: Transformations, Clothing and Identity in East Greenland* (Leiden: Center of Non Western Studies, 2004).
2. See John Schechter, *Popular Theatre: A Sourcebook* (Hoboken: Taylor and Francis, 2013), p. 84; Dennis Kennedy (ed.), *The Oxford Companion to Theatre and Performance* (Oxford: Oxford University Press, 2010), p. 376; Antonio Fava, *The Comic Mask in the Commedia Dell'Arte: Actor Training, Improvisation, and the Poetics of Survival* (Chicago: Northwestern University Press, 2007), p. 15.
3. Ricki Stefanie Tannen, *The Female Trickster: The Mask That Reveals – Post-Jungian and Postmodern Psychological Perspectives on Women in Contemporary Culture* (Hove: Routledge, 2007), p. 279.
4. W. Anthony Sheppard, *Revealing Masks: Exotic Influences and Ritualized Performance in Modernist Music Theater* (Berkeley: University of California Press, 2001), p. 28.
5. Sheppard, *Revealing Masks*, p. 28.
6. John E. Parnum, '*The Abominable Dr. Phibes* and *Dr. Phibes Rises Again* (1971/1972)', in G. J. Svehla and S. Svehla (eds), *Vincent Price* (Baltimore: Luminary Press, 1998), p. 247.
7. Rick Worland, 'Faces Behind the Mask: Vincent Price, Dr. Phibes, and the Horror Genre in Transition', *Post Script*, 22/2 (winter–spring 2003), 20–33 (20).
8. Patricia MacCormack, *Cinesexuality* (Aldershot: Ashgate, 2008), p. 108.
9. Steve Chibnall, 'A Heritage of Evil: Pete Walker and the Politics of Gothic Revisionism', in Steve Chibnall and Julian Petley (eds), *British Horror Cinema* (London: Routledge, 2002), p. 162.
10. Parnum, 'The Abominable Dr. Phibes', p. 247.
11. Richard Schechner, *Performance Theory* (London: Routledge, 2003), p. 45.
12. Larry Ellis, 'Trickster: Shaman of the Liminal', *Studies in American Indian Literatures*, 5/4 (winter 1993), 55–68 (57).
13. William J. Hynes, 'Mapping the Characteristics of Mythic Tricksters: A Heuristic Guide', in William J. Hynes and William G. Doty (eds), *Mythical Trickster Figures: Contours, Contexts, and Criticisms* (Tuscaloosa: The University of Alabama Press, 1993), p. 34.
14. Karen Hollinger, *The Actress: Hollywood Acting and the Female Star* (New York: Routledge, 2006), p. 28.
15. Fernando G. Pagnoni Berns and Amy M. Davis, 'From Jigsaw to Phibes: God, Free Will and Foreknowledge in Conflict', in James Aston (ed.), *To See the*

Saw Movies: Essays on Torture Porn and Post-9/11 Horror (Jefferson: McFarland & Co., 2013), p. 79.
16 Pagnoni Berns and Davis, 'From Jigsaw to Phibes', p. 80.
17 Pagnoni Berns and Davis, 'From Jigsaw to Phibes', p. 80.
18 Pagnoni Berns and Davis, 'From Jigsaw to Phibes', p. 80.
19 MacCormack, *Cinesexuality*, p. 108.
20 MacCormack, *Cinesexuality*, p. 108.
21 Victor Turner, 'Frame, Flow and Reflection: Ritual and Drama as Public Liminality', in Michael Benamou and Charles Caramello (eds), *Performance and Postmodern Culture* (Milwaukee: University of Wisconsin-Milwaukee Press, 1977), pp. 41–2.
22 Tony Williams, *Hearths of Darkness: The Family in the American Horror Film* (Madison: Fairleigh Dickinson University Press, 1996), p. 171.
23 Claire Sisco King, 'Acting Up and Sounding Off: Sacrifice and Performativity in *Alice, Sweet Alice*', *Text and Performance Quarterly*, 27/2 (April 2007), 124–42 (125–6, 124).
24 Judith Butler, *Gender Trouble: Feminism and the Subversion of Identity* (New York: Routledge, 1990), p. 25.
25 Brian Albright, *Regional Horror Films, 1958–1990: A State-by-State Guide with Interviews* (Jefferson: McFarland & Co., 2012), p. 232.
26 Aalya Ahmad and Sean Moreland, 'Introduction: Horror in the Classroom', in Aalya Ahmad and Sean Moreland (eds), *Fear and Learning: Essays on the Pedagogy of Horror* (Jefferson: McFarland & Co., 2013), p. 14. While no sequel exists, there were rumours in 2016 of a remake. See John Squires, 'Dante Tomaselli Provides Update on *Alice, Sweet Alice* Remake', *Dread Central* (24 May 2016), www.dreadcentral.com/news/167951/dante-tomaselli-provides-update-alice-sweet-alice-remake/ (accessed 28 February 2019).
27 Tannen, *The Female Trickster*, p. 39.
28 See Peter Hutchings, *The A to Z of Horror Cinema* (Lanham: Scarecrow Press, 2009), p. 294; Mikel J. Koven, *Film, Folklore, and Urban Legends* (Lanham: Scarecrow Press, 2008), p. 113.
29 Christopher Sharrett, 'The Idea of Apocalypse in The Texas Chainsaw Massacre', in Barry Keith Grant and Christopher Sharrett (eds), *Planks of Reason: Essays on the Horror Film* (Lanham: Scarecrow Press, 2004), p. 301.
30 Pagnoni Berns and Davis, 'From Jigsaw to Phibes', p. 84.
31 Robin Wood, 'An Introduction to the American Horror Film', in Barry Keith Grant and Christopher Sharrett (eds), *Planks of Reason: Essays on the Horror Film* (Lanham: Scarecrow Press, 2004), p. 129.

32   Mircea Eliade, *The Sacred and the Profane: The Nature of Religion* (New York: Harcourt, Brace & World, 1959), p. 105.
33   Sharrett, 'The Idea of Apocalypse', pp. 315–16.
34   James Rose, *The Texas Chain Saw Massacre* (Leighton Buzzard: Auteur, 2013), p. 72.
35   Rose, *The Texas Chain Saw Massacre*, p. 72.
36   Sharrett, 'The Idea of Apocalypse', p. 308.
37   See Richard Eves, 'Shamanism, Sorcery and Cannibalism: The Incorporation of Power in the Magical Cult of Buai', *Oceana*, 65/3 (March 1995), 212–33; Charles Stépanoff, 'Devouring Perspectives: On Cannibal Shamans in Siberia', *Inner Asia*, 11 (2009), 283–307.
38   Stefan Jaworzyn, *The Texas Chain Saw Massacre Companion* (London: Titan Books, 2003), p. 79.
39   Jaworzyn, *The Texas Chain Saw Massacre Companion*, p. 81.
40   Buijs, *Furs and Fabrics*, p. 74.
41   Maria Tamboukou, *Gendering the Memory of Work: Women Workers' Narratives* (London: Routledge, 2016), p. 130.
42   Johan Höglund, *The American Imperial Gothic: Popular Culture, Empire, Violence* (London: Routledge, 2014), p. 76.
43   Rose, *The Texas Chain Saw Massacre*, p. 78.
44   Jaworzyn, *The Texas Chain Saw Massacre Companion*, p. 81.
45   Sharrett, 'The Idea of Apocalypse', p. 317.
46   Robin Wood, *Hollywood from Vietnam to Reagan . . . and Beyond* (New York: Columbia University Press, 2003), pp. 63–84.
47   Thomas Sipos (*Horror Film Aesthetics: Creating the Visual Language of Fear* (Jefferson: McFarland & Co., 2010), p. 63) and Butler ('Faces of Rage: Masks, Murderers, and Motives in the Canadian Slasher Film', in Julia Petrov and Gudrun D. Whitehead (eds), *Fashioning Horror: Dressing to Kill on Screen and in Literature* (London: Bloomsbury, 2017), p. 208) privilege this scene, describing it as a 'crone' mask, neither acknowledging the historically derogatory nature of the term (Karen Rauch and Jeff Fessler, *When Drag is Not a Car Race: An Irreverent Dictionary of Over 400 Gay and Lesbian Words and Phrases* (New York: Fireside/Simon & Schuster, 1997), p. 21; M. A. Yadugiri and B. Naidu, *Understanding Literature* (Hyperabad: Orient Longman, 1996), p. 6), although it has been reclaimed in Wicca and neo-pagan circles – see Dorothy Morrison, *In Praise of the Crone: A Celebration of Feminine Maturity* (St Paul: Llewellyn Worldwide, 1999).
48   Butler, 'Faces of Rage', p. 210.
49   Butler, *Gender Trouble*, p. 25.

50 Barbara Creed, *The Monstrous-Feminine: Film, Feminism, Psychoanalysis* (New York: Routledge, 1993), p. 2.
51 Sarah Allison Miller, 'Virgins, Mothers, Monsters: Late-medieval Readings of the Female Body Out of Bounds' (unpublished PhD dissertation, University of North Carolina at Chapel Hill, 2008), 55.
52 Miriam Bernard, Pat Chambers and Gillian Granville, 'Women Ageing: Changing Identities, Challenging Myths', in Miriam Bernard, Val Harding Davies, Linda Machin and Judith Phillips (eds), *Women Ageing: Changing Identities, Challenging Myths* (Florence: Taylor and Francis, 2005), p. 2.
53 Deborah Jermyn and Su Holmes, 'Introduction: A Timely Intervention — Unravelling the Gender/Age/Celebrity Matrix', in Deborah Jerym and Su Holmes (eds), *Women, Celebrity and Cultures of Ageing: Freeze Frame* (London: Palgrave Macmillan, 2015), p. 1.
54 Deborah Jermyn, '"Get a Life, Ladies. Your Old One is Not Coming Back": Ageing, Ageism and the Lifespan of Female Celebrity', *Celebrity Studies*, 3/1 (2012), 1–12 (4).
55 Jermyn and Holmes, 'Introduction', p. 1.
56 Roger Ebert, *Life Itself: A Memoir* (New York: Grand Central Publishing, 2011), p. 53; Ann Hornaday, 'Harvey Weinstein Embodies a Culture Whose Power is on the Wane', *Sydney Morning Herald* (10 October 2017), *www.smh.com.au/lifestyle/news-and-views/harvey-weinstein-embodies-a-culture-whose-power-is-on-the-wane-20171008-gywr20.html* (accessed 28 February 2019); Deborah Martinson, *Lillian Hellman: A Life with Foxes and Scoundrels* (New York: Counterpoint, 2005), p. 124.
57 Jim Rutenberg, Rachel Abrams and Melena Ryzikoct, 'Harvey Weinstein's Fall Opens the Floodgates in Hollywood', *The New York Times* (16 October 2017), *https://www.nytimes.com/2017/10/16/business/media/harvey-weinsteins-fall-opens-the-floodgates-in-hollywood.html* (accessed 28 February 2019).
58 Earlier in the film, one of the women's partners, Peter, wears a stocking mask over his head during their consensual 'rape-play' seduction scene: the mask here is gendered distinctly feminine (a stocking), subverted as a symbol of gendered violence and power.
59 Reynold Humphries, *The American Horror Film: An Introduction* (Edinburgh: Edinburgh University Press, 2002), p. 18.
60 Humphries, *The American Horror Film*, p. 149.
61 Julie A. Ruth and Cele C. Ontes, 'Consumption Rituals', in Daniel Thomas Cook and J. Michael Ryan (eds), *The Wiley Blackwell Encyclopedia of Consumption and Consumer Studies* (Chichester: Wiley Blackwell, 2015), pp. 187–9.

62 Cynthia Hendershot, *The Animal Within: Masculinity and the Gothic* (Ann Arbor: University of Michigan Press, 1998), p. 85; H. C. Erik Midelfort, *A History of Madness in Sixteenth-Century Germany* (Stanford: Stanford University Press, 1999), p. 7.
63 Adam Rockoff, *The Horror of It All: One Moviegoer's Love Affair with Masked Maniacs, Frightened Virgins, and the Living Dead* (New York: Scribner, 2015), p. 68.
64 Sorcha Ní Fhlainn, 'Sweet, Bloody Vengeance: Class, Social Stigma and Servitude in the Slasher Genre', in Holly Lynn Baumgartner and Roger Davis (eds), *Hosting the Monster* (Amsterdam: Editions Rodopi, 2008), p. 179.
65 Ní Fhlainn, 'Sweet, Bloody Vengeance', p. 179.
66 Ní Fhlainn, 'Sweet, Bloody Vengeance', p. 186.
67 Vera Dika, *Games of Terror: Halloween, Friday the 13th and the Films of the Stalker Cycle* (Rutherford: Fairleigh Dickinson University Press, 1990), p. 104.
68 Dika, *Games of Terror*, p. 104.
69 Dika, *Games of Terror*, p. 104.
70 Dika, *Games of Terror*, p. 105.
71 Martha Sims and Martine Stephens, *Living Folklore: An Introduction to the Study of People and Their Traditions* (Logan: Utah State University Press, 2011), p. 102.
72 Dika, *Games of Terror*, p. 105.
73 Dika, *Games of Terror*, p. 105.
74 Jason L. Jarvis, 'Digital Image Politics: The Networked Rhetoric of Anonymous', in Matthew Johnson and Samid Suliman (eds), *Protest – Analysing Current Trends* (London: Routledge, 2014), p. 218.
75 Jarvis, 'Digital Image Politics', p. 218.
76 Cole Stryker, 'Go to Bed, Tao Lin', *Rhizome* (21 March 2012), https://rhizome.org/editorial/2012/mar/27/tao-lin/ (accessed 28 February 2019).
77 Stryker, 'Go to Bed, Tao Lin'.
78 Jarvis, 'Digital Image Politics', p. 218.
79 E. Gabriella Coleman, 'Phreaks, Hackers and Trolls: The Politics of Transgression and Spectacle', in Michael Mandiberg (ed.), *The Social Media Reader* (New York: New York University Press, 2012), p. 115.
80 Bettina Kluge, 'The Collaborative Construction of an Outsider as a Troll in the Blogosphere of Latin American Immigrants to Quebec, Canada', in Kristina Bedijs, Gudrun Held and Christiane Maaß (eds), *Face Work and Social Media* (Zurich: Lit Verlad, 2014), p. 326.

81 Whitney Phillips, *This Is Why We Can't Have Nice Things: Mapping the Relationship Between Online Trolling and Mainstream Culture* (Cambridge: The MIT Press, 2015), pp. 56, 57.
82 Stryker, 'Go to Bed, Tao Lin'.
83 Phillips, *This Is Why We Can't Have Nice Things*, p. 88.
84 Dorothy M. Bollinger and Merle Horowitz, *Cyberbullying in Social Media Within Educational Institutions* (Lanham: Rowman & Littlefield, 2014), p. 84.
85 Lizbeth Goodman, *Literature and Gender* (Abingdon: The Open University/Routledge, 1996), p. 110.

5   Blank Masks: Ritual, Power and Transformation

1 Elizabeth Tonkin, 'Mask', in Richard Bauman (ed.), *Folklore, Cultural Performances, and Popular Entertainments – A Communications-centered Handbook* (New York: Oxford University Press, 1992), p. 230.
2 Ski masks are mentioned further in chapter 6 as they also intersect with the repurposed mask category. Blank masks appear in films including *Litan* (Jean-Pierre Mocky, 1982), *Edge of the Axe* (José Ramón Larraz, 1988), *Cut* (Kimble Rendall, 2000), *Cinderella* (Bong Man-dae, 2006), *The Cabin in the Woods* (Drew Goddard, 2012), *Cruel Tango* (Salvatore Metastasio, 2014), *Goddess of Love* (Jon Knautz, 2015), *Brakenmore* (Chris Kemble and J. P. Davidson, 2016), *Tragedy Girls* (Tyler MacIntyre, 2017) and *House of Sweat and Tears* (Sonia Escolano, 2018).
3 In Franco's *oeuvre*, this includes *The Awful Dr. Orloff* (1962) and *Faceless* (1988). Almodóvar cited Franju as a direct influence on *The Skin I Live In* (2011), see Gonzalo Suárez López, 'Interview with Pedro Almodóvar', *Cineuropa* (19 May 2011), *cineuropa.org/it.aspx?t=interview&lang=en&documentID=203802* (accessed 28 February 2019).
4 Catherine Russell, *Narrative Mortality: Death, Closure, and New Wave Cinemas* (Minneapolis: University of Minnesota Press, 1995), p. 194.
5 Thomas Schatz, 'Hollywood Genres: Film Genre and the Genre Film', in Leo Braudy and Marshall Cohen (eds), *Film theory and Criticism: Introductory Readings* (Oxford: Oxford University Press, 2009), p. 564.
6 Andrew Scahill, 'Serialized Killers: Prebooting Horror in *Bates Motel* and *Hannibal*', in Amanda Ann Klein, R. Barton Palmer (eds), *Cycles, Sequels, Spin-offs, Remakes, and Reboots: Multiplicities in Film and Television* (Austin: University of Texas Press, 2016), p. 322; Charles Derry, *Dark Dreams*

     2.0: A Psychological History of the Modern Horror Film from the 1950s to the 21st Century (Jefferson: McFarland & Co., 2009), p. 311.
7. Christina Pratt, *An Encyclopedia of Shamanism* (New York: Rosen, 2007), p. 396.
8. Mircea Eliade, *Rites and Symbols of Initiation* (Putname: Connecticut Springs Publications, 2003), p. 6.
9. Umberto Eco, 'Innovation and Repetition: Between Modern and Post-Modern Aesthetics', *Daedalus*, 11/4/4 (fall 1985), 161–84 (167).
10. Anat Zanger, *Film Remakes as Ritual and Disguise: From Carmen to Ripley* (Amsterdam: Amsterdam University Press, 2006), p. 16.
11. Kendall R. Phillips, *Dark Directions: Romero, Craven, Carpenter and the Modern Horror Film* (Carbondale: Southern Illinois University Press, 2012), p. 144.
12. Reynold Humphries, *The American Horror Film: An Introduction* (Edinburgh: Edinburgh University Press, 2002), p. 140.
13. J. P. Telotte, 'Through a Pumpkin's Eye: The Reflexive Nature of Horror', in Gregory Albert Waller (ed.), *American Horrors: Essays on the Modern American Horror Film* (Urbana: University of Illinois Press, 1987), p. 119.
14. Murray Leeder, *Halloween* (Leighton Buzzard: Auteur, 2014), p. 98.
15. Leeder, *Halloween*, p. 29.
16. David Roche, *Making and Remaking Horror in the 1970s and 2000s: Why Don't They Do It Like They Used To?* (Jackson: University Press of Mississippi, 2014), p. 175.
17. Adapted from Kôji Suzuki's 1991 novel, *Ringu* inspired sequels and remakes internationally such as Kim Dong-bin's *The Ring Virus* from South Korea in 1999 and a US remake *The Ring* (Gore Verbinski, 2002) and sequel *The Ring Two* (Hideo Nakata, 2005), a BBC One radio play in 2015, as well as other novels and videogames.
18. Adam Lowenstein, *Shocking Representation: Historical Trauma, National Cinema and the Modern Horror Film* (New York: Columbia University Press, 2005), p. 102.
19. Tim Cross, 'Staging the Local and Sacramental: Yamakasa as New Noh', in Andrew Cobbing (ed.), *Hakata: The Cultural Worlds of Northern Kyushu* (Leiden: Brill, 2013), p. 214.
20. Colette Balmain, *Introduction to Japanese Horror Film* (Edinburgh: Edinburgh University Press, 2008), p. 169.
21. A rich strand of Japanese film history that featured the work of filmmakers Hiroshi Teshigahara, Nobuhiko Obayashi, Toshio Matsumoto and Seijun Suzuki.

22 Celia's complex relation to genre is discussed at length in Craig Martin, 'Trust Your Instinct: An Interview with Ann Turner', *Senses of Cinema*, 81 (December 2016), *sensesofcinema.com/2016/beyond-the-babadook/ann-turner-interview/* (accessed 28 February 2019).
23 Dennis Fischer, 'George Romero on Bruiser, Development Hell and Other Sundry Matters', in Tony Williams (ed.), *George A. Romero: Interviews* (Jackson: University Press of Mississippi, 2011), p. 124.
24 Barry Keith Grant, 'Rich and Strange: The Yuppie Horror Film', in Barry Keith Grant and Christopher Sharrett (eds), *Planks of Reason: Essays on the Horror Film* (Lanham: The Scarecrow Press, Inc., 2004), p. 153.
25 Grant, 'Rich and Strange', pp. 162, 167.
26 Grant, 'Rich and Strange', p. 153.
27 Kendall R. Phillips, *Dark Directions: Romero, Craven, Carpenter and the Modern Horror Film* (Carbondale: Southern Illinois University Press, 2012), p. 47.
28 Phillips, *Dark Directions*, p. 54.
29 Steve Neale, 'Questions of Genre', *Screen*, 31/1 (1990), 45–66 (56).
30 The film's coda shows future Henry with counter-culture identifying long hair and a tie-dye t-shirt, who reveals the return of his white mask when being hassled by his boss in a new job as a mail room clerk, implying both a return to his senses of dehumanisation and his capacity to fill the 'empty' space with violence.
31 See Steve Barton, 'Stephen King Gets Loud About Hush', *Dread Central* (21 April 2016), *www.dreadcentral.com/news/162737/stephen-king-gets-loud-hush/* (accessed 28 February 2019); Scott Weinberg, '*Hush* is a Cool, Quiet, Creepy Thriller', *Nerdist* (9 April 2016), *https://nerdist.com/review-hush-is-a-cool-quiet-creepy* (accessed 28 February 2019); Eric Kohn, 'Netflix's Horror Movie Hush Proves the Effectiveness of the Blumhouse Model', *IndieWire* (15 March 2016), *www.indiewire.com/2016/03/sxsw-2016-review-netflixs-horror-movie-hush-proves-the-effectiveness-of-the-blumhouse-model-58031/* (accessed 28 February 2019).
32 Peter Brooks, *The Melodramatic Imagination: Balzac, Henry James, Melodrama, and the Mode of Excess* (New Haven: Yale University Press, 1995), p. 59.
33 Brooks, *The Melodramatic Imagination*, p. 56.
34 Linda Williams, *Playing the Race Card: Melodramas of Black and White from Uncle Tom to O. J. Simpson* (Princeton: Princeton University Press, 2001), p. 101; Christine Gledhill, 'Rethinking Genre', in Christine Gledhill and Linda Williams (eds), *Reinventing Film Studies* (London: Arnold, 2000), p. 227.
35 I discuss the relationship to muteness as a simultaneous sign of weakness and an empowering device in the case of the rape-revenge film in my monograph *Ms. 45* (New York: Columbia University Press, 2017).

6   Animal Masks: Ritual, Power and Transformation

1. Walter Sorell, *The Other Face: The Mask in the Arts* (London: Thames and Hudson, 1973), p. 9.
2. Sorell, *The Other Face*, p. 9.
3. John W. Nunley and Cara McCarty, *Masks: Faces of Culture* (New York: Harry N. Abrams, Inc. Publishers, 1999), p. 329.
4. Elizabeth Tonkin, 'Mask', in Richard Bauman (ed.), *Folklore, Cultural Performances, and Popular Entertainments – A Communications-centered Handbook* (New York: Oxford University Press, 1992), p. 228.
5. Georges Bataille, 'The Mask', *LVNG*, 10 (2002), 63–7.
6. Richard Schechner, *Performance Theory* (London: Routledge, 2003), p. 96.
7. Thomas Schatz also drew parallels between *Jaws* and slasher movies: see Thomas Schatz, 'The New Hollywood', in Graeme Turner (ed.), *The Film Cultures Reader* (London: Routledge, 2002), p. 191.
8. Michel Weemans and Bertrand Prévost, 'Introduction', in Walter Melion, Bret Rothstein and Michel Weemans (eds), *The Anthropomorphic Lens: Anthropomorphism, Microcosmism, and Analogy in Early Modern Thought and Visual Arts* (Leiden: Brill, 2014), p. 1.
9. Weemans and Prévost, 'Introduction', p. 4.
10. William Wynn Yarbrough, *Masculinity in Children's Animal Stories, 1888–1928* (Jefferson: McFarland & Co., 2014), p. 4.
11. Filippo Menozzi, *Postcolonial Custodianship: Cultural and Literary Inheritance* (New York: Routledge, 2014), p. 162.
12. Weemans and Prévost, 'Introduction', p. 1.
13. Leviticus 11:7.
14. Peter Stallybrass and Allon White, *The Politics and Poetics of Transgression* (Ithaca: Cornell University Press, 1986), p. 5.
15. Carol J. Clover, *Men, Women and Chain Saws: Gender in the Modern Horror Film* (Princeton: Princeton University Press, 1992), p. 28.
16. John Kenneth Muir, *Horror Films of the 1980s* (Jefferson: McFarland & Co., 2007), p. 111.
17. Shaun Kimber, '"Meat's Meat, and a Man's Gotta Eat" (*Motel Hell*, 1980): Food and Eating Within Contemporary Horror Cultures', in Peri Bradley (ed.), *Food, Media and Contemporary Culture: The Edible Image* (London: Palgrave Macmillan, 2016), p. 126.
18. See National Folk Museum of Korea, *Encyclopedia of Korean Seasonal Customs: Encyclopedia of Korean Folklore and Traditional Culture Vol. 1* (Seoul: The National Folk Museum of Korea, 2009), p. 71; Mauro Van Aken, 'Virtual

Water, H2O and the De-socialisation of Water – A Brief Anthropological Journey', in Marta Antonelli and Francesca Greco (eds), *The Water We Eat: Combining Virtual Water and Water Footprints* (Cham: Springer, 2015), p. 115.
19. Maggie Nolan, 'Displacing Indigenous Australians: Freud's Totem and Taboo', in Joy Damousi and Robert Reynolds (eds), *History on the Couch: Essays in History and Psychoanalysis* (Melbourne: Melbourne University Press, 2003), pp. 60–71.
20. Sigmund Freud, *Totem and Taboo* (New York: Cosimo Classics, 2009), p. 5.
21. Christina Pratt, *An Encyclopedia of Shamanism* (New York: Rosen, 2007), p. 498.
22. Pratt, *An Encyclopedia of Shamanism*, p. 498.
23. Daniel Martin, 'South Korean Horror Cinema', in Harry M. Benshoff (ed.), *A Companion to the Horror Film* (Hoboken: John Wiley & Sons, Inc., 2014), p. 424; Linda Williams, *Playing the Race Card: Melodramas of Black and White from Uncle Tom to O. J. Simpson* (Princeton: Princeton University Press, 2001), p. 16.
24. Martin, 'South Korean Horror Cinema', p. 438.
25. Ben Singer, *Melodrama and Modernity: Early Sensational Cinema and Its Contexts* (New York: Columbia University Press, 2001), p. 44.
26. Williams, *Playing the Race Card*, p. 25.
27. Cathy Rose A. Garcia, 'Meet Miffy at Hangaram Design Museum', *Korea Times* (10 July 2009), www.koreatimes.co.kr/www/art/2019/03/691_48249.html (accessed 28 February 2019).
28. *The Encyclopedia of Korean Folk Literature* (Seoul: The National Folk Museum of Korea, 2014), p. 240.
29. *The Encyclopedia of Korean Folk Literature*, pp. 362, 240.
30. *The Encyclopedia of Korean Folk Literature*, p. 336.
31. Danielle Kirby, *Fantasy and Belief: Alternative Religions, Popular Narratives and Digital Cultures* (London: Routledge, 2013), p. 35.
32. André Loiselle, 'Cinema du Grand Guignol: Theatricality in the Horror Film', in André Loiselle and Jeremy Maron (eds), *Stages of Reality: Theatricality in Cinema* (Toronto: University of Toronto Press, 2000), p. 74.
33. Loiselle, 'Cinema du Grand Guignol', p. 74.
34. Loiselle, 'Cinema du Grand Guignol', p. 74.
35. See Lesli J. Favor, *Italy: A Primary Source Cultural Guide* (New York: PowerPlus Books, 2004), p. 49; Carol King, 'Top 13 Italian Superstitions', *Italy Magazine* (31 October 2013), www.italymagazine.com/featured-story/top-13-italian-superstitions (accessed 28 February 2019).
36. Desmond Morris, *Owl* (London: Reaktion Books, 2009), p. 28.

37 Morris, *Owl*, p. 28.
38 Michael Rice, *The Power of the Bull* (London: Routledge, 1998), p. 113.
39 Michael Patella, *Lord of the Cosmos: Mithras, Paul, and the Gospel of Mark* (New York: T & T Clark, 2006), p. 12.
40 Rice, *The Power of the Bull*, p. 112.
41 Rice, *The Power of the Bull*, p. 113.
42 Rice, *The Power of the Bull*, p. 114.
43 Rice, *The Power of the Bull*, p. 112.
44 Mike Gingold, 'Q&A: *The Conspiracy* Writer/Director Christopher MacBride', Fangoria (29 August 2013), https://web.archive.org/web/20170221224609/www.fangoria.com/new/qa-the-conspiracy-writerdirector-christopher-macbride/ (accessed 28 February 2019).
45 Mr Disgusting, 'Go Down the Rabbit Hole with *The Conspiracy* Director Christopher MacBride!', *Bloody Disgusting* (6 August 2013), bloody-disgusting.com/news/3247319/interview-go-down-the-rabbit-hole-with-the-conspiracy-director-christopher-macbride/; (accessed 28 February 2019).
46 Mr Disgusting, 'Go Down the Rabbit Hole'.
47 Thom Burnett and Alex Games, *Who Really Runs the World? The War between Globalization and Democracy* (New York: Conspiracy Books, 2007), p. 1917.
48 Jack Fritscher, *Popular Witchcraft: Straight from the Witches Mouth* (Madison: The University of Wisconsin Press, 2004), p. 65.
49 Alice Von Kannon and Christopher L. Hodapp, *Conspiracy Theories and Secret Societies for Dummies* (Hoboken: Wiley Publishing, Inc., 2008), p. 343.
50 Tim Lucas, 'Matters of Life and Death', *Sight and Sound*, 21/3 (2011), 88.
51 Ian MacAllister McDonald, 'Lost Girls: A Conversation about Fantastical Filmmaker Jean Rollin', *Los Angeles Review of Books* (29 April 2017), https://blog.lareviewofbooks.org/interviews/lost-girls-conversation-fantastical-filmmaker-jean-rollin/ (accessed 28 February 2019).
52 Hal Foster, *Compulsive Beauty* (London: MIT Press, 1993), p. xvii.
53 Sigmund Freud, 'The Uncanny', in *The Standard Edition of the Complete Psychological Works of Sigmund Freud* (London: The Hogarth Press, 1955), pp. 219, 224–5.
54 Freud, 'The Uncanny', p. 245.
55 David Bate, *Photography and Surrealism: Sexuality, Colonialism and Social Dissent* (New York: I. B. Tauris, 2004), p. 39.
56 Jean Rollin, 'For an Illogical and Nonsensical European Cinema', in Ernest Mathijs and Xavier Mendik (eds), *Alternative Europe: Eurotrash and Exploitation Cinema Since 1945* (London: Wallflower, 2004), p. 12.
57 Rollin, 'For an Illogical and Nonsensical European Cinema', p. 12.

58 Budd Wilkins, 'Flesh and Blood: The Cinema of Jean Rollin', *Slant Magazine* (27 January 2012), *https://www.slantmagazine.com/features/article/flesh-and-blood-the-cinema-of-jean-rollin* (accessed 28 February 2019).
59 Rollin, 'For an Illogical and Nonsensical European Cinema', p. 13.
60 Danny Shipka, *Perverse Titillation: The Exploitation Cinema of Italy, Spain and France, 1960–1980* (Jefferson: McFarland & Co., 2011), p. 277.
61 Paul Coates, *Screening the Face* (Basingstoke: Palgrave Macmillan, 2012), p. 2.
62 Jeanne Dubino, 'Introduction', in Jeanne Dubino, Ziba Rashidian and Andrew Smyth (eds), *Representing the Modern Animal in Culture* (New York: Palgrave Macmillan, 2014), p. 2.

7 Repurposed Masks: Ritual, Power and Transformation

1 John Mack, 'Introduction', in John Mack (ed.), *Masks: The Art of Expression* (London: British Museum Press, 1994), p. 31.
2 Laura Makarius, 'The Mask and the Violation of Taboo', in N. Ross Crumrine and Marjorie Halpin (eds), *The Power of Symbols: Masks and Masquerade in the Americas* (Vancouver: University of British Columbia Press, 1983), p. 197.
3 John W. Nunley and Cara McCarty, *Masks: Faces of Culture* (New York: Harry N. Abrams, Inc. Publishers, 1999), p. 328.
4 Nunley and McCarty, *Masks: Faces of Culture*, p. 17.
5 Nunley and McCarty, *Masks: Faces of Culture*, p. 17.
6 Ski masks – which also feature qualities of blank masks, as noted in chapter 5 – appear in films including *Terrified* (Lew Landers, 1963), *Death Walks on High Heels* (Luciano Ercoli, 1971), *Torso* (Sergio Martino, 1973), *Haunts* (Herb Freed, 1977), *The Toolbox Murders* (Dennis Donnelly, 1978), *Prom Night* (Paul Lynch, 1980), *Deadly Games* (Scott Mansfield, 1982), *Iced* (Jeff Kwitny, 1988) and *Cry Wolf* (Jeff Wadlow, 2005). Gas masks appear in *The Prowler* (Joseph Zito, 1981), *Nigel the Psychopath* (Jim Larsen, 1994), *Anti Gas Skin* (*Bangdokpi*, Gok Kim and Sun Kim, 2010), *Vile* (Taylor Sheridan, 2011), *Found* (Scott Schirmer, 2012), *Avatar* (*Abatâ*, Atsushi Wada, 2011) and both *The Crazies* (George A. Romero, 1973) and Breck Eisner's 2010 remake of the same name. Masks employed in workplace contexts also appear in *Mardi Gras Massacre* (Jack Weis, 1978), *X-Ray* (Boaz Davidson, 1982), *Sweatshop* (Stacy Davidson, 2009), *Pet Peeve* (*Fuan no tane*, Toshikazu Nagae, 2013), while sport safety masks appear in *The Snorkel* (Guy Green, 1958), *Asylum of Terror* (George Demick, 1988), *Bloody Murder* (Rafe M. Portilo, 2000) and *The Unravelling* (Thomas Jakobsen, 2015).

7   Richard Nowell, *Blood Money: A History of the First Teen Slasher Film Cycle* (New York: Continuum, 2011), p. 53.
8   Caelum Vatnsdal, *They Came from Within: A History of Canadian Horror Cinema* (Winnipeg: Arbeiter Ring Publishing, 2004), p. 147.
9   Vatnsdal, *They Came from Within*, p. 148.
10 Rose Butler, 'Faces of Rage: Masks, Murderers, and Motives in the Canadian Slasher Film', in Julia Petrov and Gudrun D. Whitehead (eds), *Fashioning Horror: Dressing to Kill on Screen and in Literature* (London: Bloomsbury, 2017), p. 204.
11 Jim Harper, *Legacy of Blood: A Comprehensive Guide to Slasher Movies* (Manchester: Critical Vision/Headpress, 2004), p. 128.
12 Nunley and McCarty, *Masks: Faces of Culture*, p. 331.
13 Finis Dunaway, *Seeing Green: The Use and Abuse of American Environmental Images* (Chicago: The University of Chicago Press, 2015), p. 49.
14 Dunaway, *Seeing Green*, p. 52.
15 Mack, 'Introduction', p. 31.
16 Dunaway, *Seeing Green*, p. 52.
17 'Coal Mining', n.d. Nova Scotia Museum of Industry website, *https://museum ofindustry.novascotia.ca/nova-scotia-industry/coal-mining* (accessed 28 February 2019).
18 Ricki Stefanie Tannen, *The Female Trickster: The Mask That Reveals – Post-Jungian and Postmodern Psychological Perspectives on Women in Contemporary Culture* (Hove: Routledge, 2007).
19 Nunley and McCarty, *Masks: Faces of Culture*, p. 332.
20 Anne Balay, *Steel Closets: Voices of Gay, Lesbian, and Transgender Steelworkers* (Chapel Hill: University of North Carolina Press, 2014), p. 102.
21 Kimberly Monteyne, *Hip Hop on Film: Performance Culture, Urban Space, and Genre Transformation in the 1980s* (Jackson: University Press of Mississippi, 2013), p. 189.
22 Mary Ann Doane, 'Film and the Masquerade: Theorizing the Female Spectator', in Amelia Jones (ed.), *The Feminism and Visual Culture Reader* (London: Routledge, 2003), p. 66.
23 Mary Ann Doane, *Femmes Fatales: Feminism, Film Theory, Psychoanalysis* (New York: Routledge, 1991), p. 37.
24 Hilary Neroni, *The Violent Woman: Femininity, Narrative, and Violence in Contemporary American Cinema* (Albany: State University of New York Press, 2005), p. 95.
25 Kath Woodward, *Embodied Sporting Practices: Regulating and Regulatory Bodies* (New York: Palgrave Macmillan, 2009), p. 68.

26 Susan Birrell, 'Sport as Ritual: Interpretations from Durkheim to Goffman', *Social Forces*, 60/2 (December 1981), 354–76 (354).
27 Kendall Blanchard, *The Anthropology of Sport: An Introduction* (Westport: Bergin & Garvey, 1995), p. 51.
28 Bruce F. Kawin, *Horror and the Horror Film* (London: Anthem Press, 2012), p. 145.
29 Anne Bolin and Jane Granskog, 'Pastimes and Presentimes: Theoretical Issues in Research on Women in Action', in Anne Bolin and Jane Granskog (eds), *Athletic Intruders: Ethnographic Research on Women, Culture, and Exercise* (Albany: State University of New York Press, 2003), p. 254.
30 This can also be seen in Hannibal Lector's famous mask from Jonathan Demme's *The Silence of the Lambs* (1991), discussed in chapter 1. While not exactly a hockey mask, it shares aspects of its design but with an altogether different purpose – to literally imprison the mouth of that film's cannibal antagonist. The mask here unites the hockey mask with what appears to be an animal muzzle, the latter adding even further to the dehumanising aspects of Lector's taboo affinity for eating human flesh.
31 I discuss this film in my monograph *Rape-Revenge Films: A Critical Study* (Jefferson: McFarland & Co., 2011), pp. 64, 72.
32 David Grove, *Making Friday the 13th: The Legend of Camp Blood* (Godalming: FAB Press, 2005), p. 82.
33 Grove, *Making Friday the 13th*, p. 100.
34 Grove, *Making Friday the 13th*, p. 100.
35 Nunley and McCarty, *Masks: Faces of Culture*, p. 332.
36 Vera Dika, *Games of Terror: Halloween, Friday the 13th and the Films of the Stalker Cycle* (Rutherford: Fairleigh Dickinson University Press, 1990).
37 Michael Dylan Foster, *Pandemonium and Parade: Japanese Monsters and the Culture of Yokai* (Berkeley: University of California Press, 2009), p. 185.
38 Yoki Inagi, 'Kuchisake Onna (2007)', in Salvador Murguia (ed.), *The Encyclopedia of Japanese Horror Films* (Lanham: Rowman & Littlefield, 2016), pp. 176–8 (pp. 176–7).
39 Foster, *Pandemonium and Parade*, p. 185.
40 Inagi, 'Kuchisake Onna', pp. 176–7.
41 Alan Leddon, *A Child's Eye View of Ghosts and Hauntings* (Madison: Spero Publishing, 2014), p. 43.
42 Foster, *Pandemonium and Parade*, p. 185.
43 Foster, *Pandemonium and Parade*, p. 186.
44 Alan Dundes, *Bloody Mary in the Mirror: Essays in Psychoanalytic Folkloristics* (Jackson: University Press of Mississippi, 2002), pp. 83–4.

45 Gail De Vos, *Tales, Rumors, and Gossip: Exploring Contemporary Folk Literature in Grades 7–12* (Westport: Libraries Unlimited, 1996), p. 58.
46 See Dundes, *Bloody Mary in the Mirror*, p. 84; De Vos, *Tales, Rumors, and Gossip*, p. 67; Robin Potter, 'Bloody Mary or I Believe in Mary Worth', in Christopher R. Fee and Jeffrey B. Webb (eds), *American Myths, Legends, and Tall Tales: An Encyclopedia of American Folklore* (Santa Barbara, ABC-CLIO, 2016), pp. 129–31.
47 Inagi, 'Kuchisake Onna', p. 178.
48 Jim Harper, 'Shiraishi, Kōji', in Salvador Murguia (ed.), *The Encyclopedia of Japanese Horror Films* (Lanham: Rowman & Littlefield, 2016), p. 288.
49 Thy Phu, *Picturing Model Citizens: Civility in Asian American Visual Culture* (Philadelphia: Temple University Press, 2011), pp. 124, 123.
50 Adam Burgess and Mitsutoshi Horii, 'Risk, Ritual and Health Responsibilisation: Japan's "Safety Blanket" of Surgical Face Mask-Wearing', *Sociology of Health & Illness*, 34/8 (2012), 1184–98 (1184).
51 Burgess and Horii, 'Risk, Ritual and Health Responsibilisation', 1184.
52 Azriel Perel, 'Surgical Masks: Evidence, Image, and Art', *BJA: British Journal of Anaesthesia*, 99/6 (2007), 918.
53 Perel, 'Surgical Masks', 918.
54 Adam Lowenstein, *Shocking Representation: Historical Trauma, National Cinema and the Modern Horror Film* (New York: Columbia University Press, 2005), p. 166.
55 William Beard, *The Artist as Monster: The Cinema of David Cronenberg* (Toronto: University of Toronto Press, 2001), p. 252.
56 Lowenstein, *Shocking Representation*, p. 146.
57 Beard, *The Artist as Monster*, p. 252.
58 Steven Shaviro, 'Bodies of Fear: The Films of David Cronenberg', in Brian Massumi (ed.), *The Politics of Everyday Fear* (Minneapolis: University of Minnesota Press, 1993), p. 133.
59 Lowenstein, *Shocking Representation*, pp. 2–3.
60 Steffen Hantke, 'Germany's Secret History: Stefan Ruzowitzky's *Anatomie* (*Anatomy*, 2000)', *Kino Eye*, 1/1 (September 2001), www.kinoeye.org/01/01/hantke01.php (accessed 28 February 2019).
61 Alexandra Ludegwig, 'Screening Nazism and Reclaiming the Horror Genre: Stefan Ruzowitzky's *Anatomy* Films', in Robert von Dassanowsky and Oliver C. Speck (eds), *New Austrian Film* (New York: Bergahn, 2011), p. 287.
62 Linnie Blake, *The Wounds of Nations: Horror Cinema, Historical Trauma and National Identity* (Manchester: Manchester University Press, 2008), pp. 2–3.

63　Peter Hutchings, 'Northern Darkness: The Curious Case of the Swedish Vampire', in Leon Hunt, Sharon Lockyer and Milly Williamson (eds), *Screening the Undead: Vampires and Zombies in Film and Television* (London: I. B. Tauris, 2014), p. 62.
64　Ludegwig, 'Screening Nazism', p. 279.
65　Ludegwig, 'Screening Nazism', p. 280.
66　Ludegwig, 'Screening Nazism', p. 280.
67　Ludegwig, 'Screening Nazism', p. 281.
68　Steven P. Remy, *The Heidelberg Myth: The Nazification and Denazification of a German University* (Cambridge: Harvard University Press, 2002), p. 107. *Anatomy* also explicitly references another real-world link to the University of Heidelberg through its inclusion of medical school graduate Gunther von Hagens's 'plastination' process of solidifying real human biological samples for educational use and public display (Ludegwig, 'Screening Nazism', p. 284).

8　Technological Masks: Ritual, Power and Transformation

1　Montserrat Ginés Gibert, 'Introduction', in Montserrat Ginés Gibert (ed.), *The Meaning of Technology: Selected Readings from American Sources* (Barcelona: Edicions UPC, 2003), p. 9.
2　Heather Margaret-Louise Miller, *Archaeological Approaches to Technology* (Florence: Taylor and Francis, 2016), p. 227.
3　N. Ross Crumrine, 'Masks, Participants, and Audience', in N. Ross Crumrine and Marjorie Halpin (eds), *The Power of Symbols: Masks and Masquerade in the Americas* (Vancouver: University of British Columbia Press, 1983), p. 3.
4　Christina Pratt, *An Encyclopedia of Shamanism* (New York: Rosen, 2007), p. xiii.
5　John Bowen, 'Gothic Motifs', British Library (15 May 2014), *https://www.bl.uk/romantics-and-victorians/articles/gothic-motifs* (accessed 28 February 2019).
6　Jeffrey Sconce, *Haunted Media: Electronic Presence from Telegraphy to Television* (Durham: Duke University Press, 2000), p. 16.
7　Sconce, *Haunted Media*, p. 10.
8　Miller, *Archaeological Approaches to Technology*, p. 5.
9　Miller, *Archaeological Approaches to Technology*, p. 6.
10　Shohini Chaudhuri, *Feminist Film Theorists: Laura Mulvey, Kaja Silverman, Teresa de Lauretis, Barbara Creed* (London: Routledge, 2006), p. 34.
11　Carol J. Clover, *Men, Women and Chain Saws: Gender in the Modern Horror Film* (Princeton: Princeton University Press, 1992), p. 169.

12　Michele Aaron, 'Looking On: Troubling Spectacles and the Complicitous Spectator', in Geoff King (ed.), *The Spectacle of the Real: From Hollywood to 'Reality' TV and Beyond* (Bristol: Intellect Books, 2004), p. 216.
13　Kaja Silverman, *The Acoustic Mirror: The Female Voice in Psychoanalysis and Cinema* (Bloomington: Indiana University Press, 1988), p. 32.
14　Clover, *Men, Women and Chain Saws*, p. 169.
15　See Steve Chibnall and Julian Petley (eds), *British Horror Cinema* (London: Routledge, 2002); Ian Onley, *Euro Horror: Classic European Horror Cinema in Contemporary American Culture* (Bloomington: Indiana University Press, 2013).
16　Elana Del Ray, 'The Body of Voyeurism: Mapping a Discourse of the Senses in Michael Powell's Peeping Tom', *Camera Obscura*, 15/3 (2001), 114–49 (115–16).
17　Del Ray, 'The Body of Voyeurism', 117.
18　Vivian Sobchack, *Carnal Thoughts: Embodiment and Moving Image Culture* (Berkeley: University of California Press, 2004), p. 62.
19　Clover, *Men, Women and Chain Saws*, p. 170.
20　Quoted in Adam Lowenstein, *Shocking Representation: Historical Trauma, National Cinema and the Modern Horror Film* (New York: Columbia University Press, 2005), p. 61.
21　Caelum Vatnsdal, 'Monsters Up North: A Taxonomy of Terror', in Gina Freitag and André Loiselle (eds), *The Canadian Horror Film: Terror of the Soul* (Toronto: University of Toronto Press, 2015), p. 28.
22　Ray Zone, *3D Revolution: The History of Modern Stereoscopic Cinema* (Lexington: University Press of Kentucky, 2012), p. 250.
23　Martin Harris, 'You Can't Kill the Boogeyman: *Halloween III* and the Modern Horror Franchise', *Journal of Popular Film and Television*, 32/3 (2004), 98–109 (100).
24　Robert C. Cumbow, *Order in the Universe: The Films of John Carpenter* (Lanham: The Scarecrow Press, 2000), p. 69.
25　Tony Williams, *Hearths of Darkness: The Family in the American Horror Film* (Madison: Fairleigh Dickinson University Press, 1996), p. 218.
26　Williams, *Hearths of Darkness*, p. 219.
27　Harris, 'You Can't Kill the Boogeyman', 104.
28　William J. Hynes, 'Mapping the Characteristics of Mythic Tricksters: A Heuristic Guide', in William J. Hynes and William G. Doty (eds), *Mythical Trickster Figures: Contours, Contexts, and Criticisms* (Tuscaloosa: The University of Alabama Press, 1993), p. 34.
29　Helena Bassil-Morozow, *The Trickster in Contemporary Film* (London: Routledge, 2012), p. 30.

30 Thomas Sipos, *Horror Film Aesthetics: Creating the Visual Language of Fear* (Jefferson: McFarland & Co., 2010), p. 63.
31 Harris, 'You Can't Kill the Boogeyman', 105.
32 Harris, 'You Can't Kill the Boogeyman', 103.
33 Alexandra Heller-Nicholas, *Found Footage Horror Films: Fear and the Appearance of Reality* (Jefferson: McFarland & Co., 2014).
34 David Lyon, *Surveillance Studies: An Overview* (Cambridge: Polity Press, 2007), p. 11.
35 Lyon, *Surveillance Studies*, p. 13; Adam L. Penenberg, 'The Surveillance Society', *Wired*, 9/12 (December 2001) *http://www.wired.com/wired/archive/9.12/surveillance.html* (accessed 28 February 2019).
36 Trevor J. Blank, *Folk Culture in the Digital Age: The Emergent Dynamics of Human Interaction* (Boulder: University Press of Colorado, 2012), n.p.
37 Harold Bell, 'Social Media Masquerade: A Digital Age of Identity Masks', *Silicon Valley De-Bug* (11 June 2012), *archives.siliconvalleydebug.org/articles/2012/06/11/social-media-masquerade-digital-age-identity-masks* (accessed 28 February 2019).
38 Armina Dinescu, 'Negotiating Identities in a Randomized Video-chat', *Ethnographic Encounters*, 1/1 (2012), 27–39 (34).
39 Dinescu, 'Negotiating Identities', 34.
40 Ninja Dixon, '*Månguden* (1988)', *Ninja Dixon* blog (25 March 2010), *ninjadixon.blogspot.se/2010/03/manguden-1988.html* (accessed 28 February 2019).
41 *Cinezilla* blog, 'Månguden' (18 May 2010), *cinezilla.blogspot.se/2010/05/manguden.html?zx=89d44ba062875ab2* (accessed 28 February 2019).
42 Pidde Andersson, *Blue Swede Shock! The History of Swedish Horror Films* (n.p.: The TOPPRAFFEL! Library, 2009), unpaginated.
43 *Cinezilla* blog, 'Månguden'.
44 Walid El Khachab, 'Cinema as a Sacred Surface: Ritual Rememoration of Transcendence', *Kinephanos: Journal of Media Studies and Popular Culture* (2013), *www.kinephanos.ca/2013/sacred-surface/* (accessed 28 February 2019).
45 El Khachab, 'Cinema as a Sacred Surface'.
46 John Mack, 'Introduction', in John Mack (ed.), *Masks: The Art of Expression* (London: British Museum Press, 1994), p. 10.
47 Mack, 'Introduction', p. 10.
48 Jim Harper, 'This Carnival of Venice Mask Has a Dark Origin', *Historic Mysteries* (6 June 2016), *https://www.historicmysteries.com/plague-doctor* (accessed 28 February 2019).

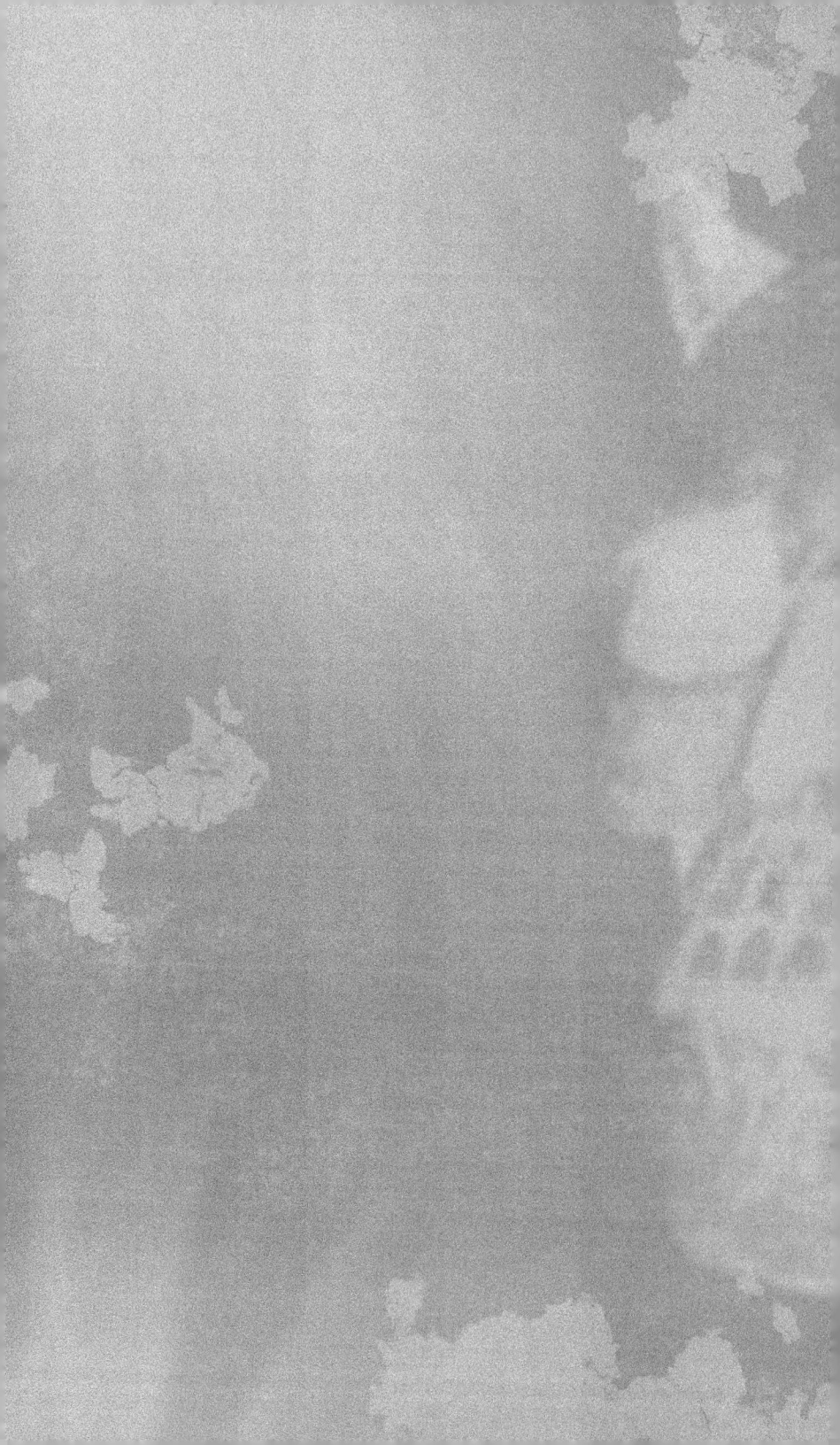

Bibliography

Aaron, Michele, 'Looking On: Troubling Spectacles and the Complicitous Spectator', in Geoff King (ed.), *The Spectacle of the Real: From Hollywood to 'Reality' TV and Beyond* (Bristol: Intellect Books), pp. 213–22.

Abel, Richard, *The Cine Goes to Town: French Cinema 1896–1914* (Berkeley: University of California Press, 1994).

Aguirre, Manuel, 'Narrative Structure, Liminality, Self-similarity: The Case of Gothic Fiction', in Clive Bloom (ed.), *Gothic Horror: A Guide for Students and Readers* (London: Palgrave Macmillan, 2006), pp. 226–46.

Ahmad, Aalya and Sean Moreland, 'Introduction: Horror in the Classroom', in Aalya Ahmad and Sean Moreland (eds), *Fear and Learning: Essays on the Pedagogy of Horror* (Jefferson: McFarland & Co., 2013), pp. 5–18.

Albright, Brian, *Regional Horror Films, 1958–1990: A State-by-State Guide with Interviews* (Jefferson: McFarland & Co., 2012).

Allen, Chadwick, 'Hero with Two Faces: *The Lone Ranger* as Treaty Discourse', *American Literature*, 68/3 (September 1996), 609–38.

Altman, Rick, *The American Film Musical* (Bloomington: Indiana University Press, 1987).

——, 'A Semantic/Syntactic Approach to Film Genre', in Barry Keith Grant (ed.), *Film Genre Reader IV* (Austin: University of Texas Press, 2012), pp. 27–41.

Andersson, Pidde, *Blue Swede Shock! The History of Swedish Horror Films* (n.p.: The TOPPRAFFEL! Library, 2009).

Artaud, Antonin, *The Theater and its Double*, trans. Mary Caroline Richards (New York: Grove Press, 1958).

Asma, Stephen T., *On Monsters: An Unnatural History of Our Worst Fears* (Oxford: Oxford University Press, 2009).

Backer, Ron, *Classic Horror Films and the Literature that Inspired Them* (Jefferson: McFarland & Co., 2015).

Badley, Linda, *Film, Horror, and the Body Fantastic* (Westport: Greenwood Press, 1995).

Bakhtin, Mikhail, *Rabelais and His World* (Cambridge: MIT Press, 1965; Bloomington: Indiana University Press, 1984).

Balay, Anne, *Steel Closets: Voices of Gay, Lesbian, and Transgender Steelworkers* (Chapel Hill: University of North Carolina Press, 2014).

Balio, Tino, *The Foreign Film Renaissance on American Screens, 1946–1973* (Madison: The University of Wisconsin Press, 2010).

Balmain, Colette, *Introduction to Japanese Horror Film* (Edinburgh: Edinburgh University Press, 2008).

Barton, Steve, 'Stephen King Gets Loud About Hush', *Dread Central* (21 April 2016), www.dreadcentral.com/news/162737/stephen-king-gets-loud-hush/ (accessed 28 February 2019).

Bassil-Morozow, Helena, *The Trickster in Contemporary Film* (London: Routledge, 2012).

Bataille, Georges, 'The Mask', *LVNG*, 10 (2002), 63–7.

Bate, David, *Photography and Surrealism: Sexuality, Colonialism and Social Dissent* (New York: I. B. Tauris, 2004).

Beard, William, *The Artist as Monster: The Cinema of David Cronenberg* (Toronto: University of Toronto Press, 2001).

Bell, Harold, 'Social Media Masquerade: A Digital Age of Identity Masks', *Silicon Valley De-Bug* (11 June 2012), archives.siliconvalleydebug.org/articles/2012/06/11/social-media-masquerade-digital-age-identity-masks (accessed 28 February 2019).

Bergfelder, Tim, 'The Nation Vanishes: European Co-Productions and Popular Genre Formula in the 1950s and 1960s', in Mette Hjort and Scott MacKenzie (eds), *Cinema and Nation* (London: Routledge, 2000), pp. 139–52.

Bernard, Miriam, Pat Chambers and Gillian Granville, 'Women Ageing: Changing Identities, Challenging Myths', in Miriam Bernard, Val Harding Davies, Linda Machin and Judith Phillips (eds), *Women Ageing: Changing Identities, Challenging Myths* (Florence: Taylor and Francis, 2005), pp. 1–22.

Beville, Maria, *Gothic-Postmodernism: Voicing the Terrors of Postmodernity* (Amsterdam: Rodopi, 2009).

Bird, Paul, 'Writing Crime: Black Mask and the Conventions of 1920s–1930s Hard-Boiled Fiction', *Journal of the Faculty of Economics, KGU*, 22/1 (September 2012), 51–65.

Birell, Susan, 'Sport as Ritual: Interpretations from Durkheim to Goffman', *Social Forces*, 60/2 (December 1981), 354–76.

Blake, Linnie, *The Wounds of Nations: Horror Cinema, Historical Trauma and National Identity* (Manchester: Manchester University Press, 2008).

Blanchard, Kendall, *The Anthropology of Sport: An Introduction* (Westport: Bergin & Garvey, 1995).

Blank, Trevor J., *Folk Culture in the Digital Age: The Emergent Dynamics of Human Interaction* (Boulder: University Press of Colorado, 2012).

Bloomfield, Shelley Costa, *The Everything Guide to Edgar Allan Poe Book: The Life, Times, and Work of a Tormented Genius* (Avon: Adams Media, 2007).

Bockting, Ineke, 'The Ecstasy of the Abyss: The Voice Beyond *Dr. Haggard's Disease*', in Jocelyn Dupont (ed.), *Patrick McGrath: Directions and Transgressions* (Newcastle upon Tyne: Cambridge Scholars Publishing, 2012), pp. 51–64.

Bolin, Anne and Jane Granskog, 'Pastimes and Presentimes: Theoretical Issues in Research on Women in Action', in Anne Bolin and Jane Granskog (eds), *Athletic Intruders: Ethnographic Research on Women, Culture, and Exercise* (Albany: State University of New York Press, 2003), pp. 247–58.

Bollinger, Dorothy M. and Merle Horowitz, *Cyberbullying in Social Media Within Educational Institutions* (Lanham: Rowman & Littlefield, 2014).

Bondanella, Peter, *A History of Italian Cinema* (New York: Continuum, 2009).

Bowen, John, 'Gothic Motifs', British Library, (15 May 2014), *https://www.bl.uk/romantics-and-victorians/articles/gothic-motifs* (accessed 28 February 2019).

Bradley, Doug, *Sacred Monsters: Behind the Mask of the Horror Actor* (London: Titan Books, 1996).

Bricker, Victoria R., 'The Meaning of Masking in San Pedro Chenalho', in N. Ross Crumrine and Marjorie Halpin (eds), *The Power of Symbols: Masks and Masquerade in the Americas* (Vancouver: University of British Columbia Press, 1983), pp. 111–15.

Brooks, Peter, *The Melodramatic Imagination: Balzac, Henry James, Melodrama, and the Mode of Excess* (New Haven: Yale University Press, 1995).

Brophy, Philip, '*Arashi Ga Oka* (*Onimaru*): The Sound of the World Turned Inside Out', in Jay McRoy (ed.), *Japanese Horror Cinema* (Edinburgh: Edinburgh University Press, 2006), pp. 150–60.

Buijs, Cunera Cornelia Maria, *Furs and Fabrics: Transformations, Clothing and Identity in East Greenland* (Leiden: Center of Non Western Studies, 2004).

Burgess, Adam and Mitsutoshi Horii, 'Risk, Ritual and Health Responsibilisation: Japan's "Safety Blanket" of Surgical Face Mask-Wearing', *Sociology of Health & Illness*, 34/8 (2012), 1184–98.

Burkholder-Mosco, Nicole and Wendy Carse, '"Wondrous Material to Play On": Children as Sites of Gothic Liminality in *The Turn of the Screw*, *The Innocents* and *The Others*', *Studies in Humanities*, 32/2 (2005), 201–20.

Burnett, Thom and Alex Games, *Who Really Runs the World? The War Between Globalization and Democracy* (New York: Conspiracy Books, 2007).

Burton, Stacy, 'Paradoxical Relations: Bakhtin and Modernism', *Modern Language Quarterly: A Journal of Literary History*, 61/3 (2000), 519–43.

Butler, Judith, *Gender Trouble: Feminism and the Subversion of Identity* (New York: Routledge, 1990).

Butler, Rose, 'Faces of Rage: Masks, Murderers, and Motives in the Canadian Slasher Film', in Julia Petrov and Gudrun D. Whitehead (eds), *Fashioning Horror: Dressing to Kill on Screen and in Literature* (London: Bloomsbury, 2017), pp. 197–214.

Callahan, John M., 'The Grand-Guignol in New York City, October–November 1923: Violence Fails to Draw an Audience', in Arthur Gewirtz and James J. Kolb (eds), *Art, Glitter, and Glitz: Mainstream Playwrights and Popular Theatre in 1920s America* (Westport: Praeger, 2004), pp. 159–66.

Campbell, Joseph, *The Masks of God: Primitive Mythology* (New York: Penguin, 1959).

Cardullo, Bert and Robert Knopf, *Theater of the Avant-garde, 1890–1950: A Critical Anthology* (New Haven: Yale University, 2001).

Carlson, Marvin A., *Theatre: A Very Short Introduction* (Oxford: Oxford University Press, 2014).

Carroll, Noël, *The Philosophy of Horror: Paradoxes of the Heart* (New York: Routledge, 1990).

Case, Sue Ellen, 'Tracking the Vampire', *difference*, 3/2 (summer 1991), 1–20.

Cavallaro, Dani, *The Gothic Vision: Three Centuries of Horror, Terror and Fear* (London: Continuum, 2002).

Cawelti, John G., *The Six-Gun Mystique* (Bowling Green: Bowling Green University Popular Press, 1970).

Chandler, Daniel, 'An Introduction to Genre Theory', *Visual Memory* (11 August 1997), *visual-memory.co.uk/daniel/Documents/intgenre/* (accessed 28 February 2019).

Chaudhuri, Shohini, *Feminist Film Theorists: Laura Mulvey, Kaja Silverman, Teresa de Lauretis, Barbara Creed* (London: Routledge, 2006).

Chesterton, G. K., 'A Defence of Penny Dreadfuls', from *The Defendant*, published in The Wayfarer's Library by J. M. Dent and Sons Ltd, London (1901), republished at De Montfort University, *www.cse.dmu.ac.uk/~mward/gkc/books/penny-dreadfuls.html* (accessed 28 February 2019).

Chibnall, Steve, 'A Heritage of Evil: Pete Walker and the Politics of Gothic Revisionism', in Steve Chibnall and Julian Petley (eds), *British Horror Cinema* (London: Routledge, 2002), pp. 156–71.

Christol, Florent, 'Massacres and Masquerades: Costume in the American Slasher Film and the Cultural Myth of the "Foolkiller"', in Julia Petrov and Gudrun D. Whitehead (eds), *Fashioning Horror: Dressing to Kill on Screen and in Literature* (London: Bloomsbury, 2017), pp. 215–31.

Churchill, Ward, 'Spiritual Hucksterism: The Rise of the Plastic Medicine Men', in Graham Harvey (ed.), *Shamanism: A Reader* (London: Routledge, 2003), pp. 324–33.

Cinezilla blog, 'Månguden' (18 May 2010), *cinezilla.blogspot.se/2010/05/manguden.html?zx=89d44ba062875ab2* (accessed 28 February 2019).

'Coal Mining', n.d. Nova Scotia Museum of Industry website, *https://museumofindustry.novascotia.ca/nova-scotia-industry/coal-mining* (accessed 28 February 2019).

Coates, Paul, *Screening the Face* (Basingstoke: Palgrave Macmillan, 2012).

Clark, Katerina and Michael Holquist, *Mikhail Bakhtin* (Cambridge: Belknap Press/Harvard University Press, 1984).

Clover, Carol J., *Men, Women and Chain Saws: Gender in the Modern Horror Film* (Princeton: Princeton University Press, 1992).

Colebrook, Martyn, '"Comrades in Tentacles": H. P. Lovecraft and China Miéville', in David Simmons (ed.), *New Critical Essays on H. P. Lovecraft* (New York: Palgrave Macmillan, 2013), pp. 209–26.

Coleman, E. Gabriella, 'Phreaks, Hackers and Trolls: The Politics of Transgression and Spectacle', in Michael Mandiberg (ed.), *The Social Media Reader* (New York: New York University Press, 2012), pp. 99–119.

Collis, Clark, 'Come Out and Play: The Mystery of the Masked Director', *Entertainment Weekly*, 25 March 2013, *ew.com/article/2013/03/25/makinov-come-out-and-play-diego-luna/* (accessed 22 February 2019).

Conterio, Martyn, *Black Sunday* (Leighton Buzzard: Auteur, 2014).

Cordry, Donald, *Mexican Masks* (Austin: University of Texas Press, 1980).

Creed, Barbara, *The Monstrous-Feminine: Film, Feminism, Psychoanalysis* (New York: Routledge, 1993).

——, 'Horror and the Carnivalesque: The Body-Monstrous', in Leslie Devereaux and Roger Hillman (eds), *Fields of Vision: Essays in Film Studies, Visual Anthropology, and Photography* (Berkeley: University of California Press, 1995), pp. 127–59.

——, 'Horror and the Monstrous-Feminine: An Imaginary Abjection', in Mark Jancovich (ed.), *Horror, The Film Reader* (London: Routledge, 2002), pp. 67–76.

Crick, Olly and John Rudin, *Commedia Dell'Arte: A Handbook for Troupes* (Hoboken: Taylor and Francis, 2002).

Crocker, J. C., 'Ceremonial Masks', in Victor Turner (ed.), *Celebration: Studies in Festivity and Ritual* (Washington: Smithsonian Institution Press, 1982), pp. 77–88.

Cross, Tim, 'Staging the Local and Sacramental: Yamakasa as New Noh', in Andrew Cobbing (ed.), *Hakata: The Cultural Worlds of Northern Kyushu* (Leiden: Brill, 2013), pp. 211–30.

Crumrine, N. Ross, 'Mask Use and Meaning in Easter Ceremonialism: The Mayo Parisero', in N. Ross Crumrine and Marjorie Halpin (eds), *The Power of Symbols: Masks and Masquerade in the Americas* (Vancouver: University of British Columbia Press, 1983), pp. 93–101.

——, 'Masks, Participants, and Audience', in N. Ross Crumrine and Marjorie Halpin (eds), *The Power of Symbols: Masks and Masquerade in the Americas* (Vancouver: University of British Columbia Press, 1983), pp. 1–11.

Cumbow, Robert C., *Order in the Universe: The Films of John Carpenter* (Lanham: The Scarecrow Press, 2000).

Cunliffe, Robert, 'Bakhtin, Artaud, and Brecht', in David Shepherd (ed.), *Bakhtin: Carnival and Other Subjects* (Amsterdam: Rodopi, 1991), pp. 48–69.

Curti, Roberto, *Italian Gothic Horror Films, 1957–1969* (Jefferson: McFarland & Co., 2015).

De Vos, Gail, *Tales, Rumors, and Gossip: Exploring Contemporary Folk Literature in Grades 7–12* (Westport: Libraries Unlimited, 1996).

Deighan, Samm (ed.), *Lost Girls: The Phantasmagorical Cinema of Jean Rollin* (Windsor: Spectacular Optical Publications, 2017).

Del Ray, Elana, 'The Body of Voyeurism: Mapping a Discourse of the Senses in Michael Powell's *Peeping Tom*', *Camera Obscura*, 15/3 (2001), 114–49.

Derry, Charles, *Dark Dreams 2.0: A Psychological History of the Modern Horror Film from the 1950s to the 21st Century* (Jefferson: McFarland & Co., 2009).

Dika, Vera, *Games of Terror: Halloween, Friday the 13th and the Films of the Stalker Cycle* (Rutherford: Fairleigh Dickinson University Press, 1990).

Dinescu, Armina, 'Negotiating Identities in a Randomized Video-chat', *Ethnographic Encounters*, 1/1 (2012), 27–39.

Dixon, Ninja, '*Månguden* (1988)', *Ninja Dixon blog* (25 March 2010), ninjadixon.blogspot.se/2010/03/manguden-1988.html (accessed 28 February 2019).

Dixon, Wheeler Winston and Gwendolyn Audrey Foster, *A Short History of Film* (New Brunswick: Rutgers University Press, 2008).

Doane, Mary Anne, 'Film and the Masquerade', *Screen*, 23/3–4 (1982), 74–87.

——, 'Masquerade Reconsidered: Further Thoughts on the Female Spectator', *Discourse*, 11/1 (fall–winter 1988–9), 42–54.
——, *Femmes Fatales: Feminism, Film Theory, Psychoanalysis* (New York: Routledge, 1991).
——, 'Film and the Masquerade: Theorizing the Female Spectator', in Amelia Jones (ed.), *The Feminism and Visual Culture Reader* (London: Routledge, 2003), pp. 60–71.
Dubino, Jeanne, 'Introduction', in Jeanne Dubino, Ziba Rashidian and Andrew Smyth (eds), *Representing the Modern Animal in Culture* (New York: Palgrave Macmillan, 2014), pp. 1–19.
Ducey, Charles, 'The Life History and Creative Psychopathology of the Shaman', *Psychoanalytic Study of Society*, 7 (1976), 173–230.
Duchartre, Pierre Louis, *The Italian Comedy* (Newburyport: Dover Publications, 2012).
Dunaway, Finis, *Seeing Green: The Use and Abuse of American Environmental Images* (Chicago: The University of Chicago Press, 2015).
Dundes, Alan, *Bloody Mary in the Mirror: Essays in Psychoanalytic Folkloristics* (Jackson: University Press of Mississippi, 2002).
Durgnat, Raymond, *Franju* (Berkeley: University of California Press, 1968).
Eagleton, Terry, 'I Contain Multitudes', *London Review of Books*, 29/12 (21 June 2007), 13–15, https://www.lrb.co.uk/v29/n12/terry-eagleton/i-contain-multitudes (accessed 28 February 2019).
Ebert, Roger, *Life Itself: A Memoir* (New York: Grand Central Publishing, 2011).
Eco, Umberto, 'Articulations of the Cinematic Code', in Bill Nichols (ed.), *Movies and Methods* (Berkeley: University of California Press, 1976), pp. 590–607.
——, 'Innovation and Repetition: Between Modern and Post-Modern Aesthetics', *Daedalus*, 11/4/4 (fall 1985), 161–84.
Eisner, Joel, *The Price of Fear: The Film Career of Vincent Price in His Own Words* (Antelope: Black Bed Sheet Books, 2013).
El Khachab, Walid, 'Cinema as a Sacred Surface: Ritual Rememoration of Transcendence', *Kinephanos: Journal of Media Studies and Popular Culture* (2013), www.kinephanos.ca/2013/sacred-surface/ (accessed 28 February 2019).
Eliade, Mircea, *The Sacred and the Profane: The Nature of Religion* (New York: Harcourt, Brace & World, 1959).
——, *Rites and Symbols of Initiation* (Putname: Connecticut Springs Publications, 2003).
Ellis, Larry, 'Trickster: Shaman of the Liminal', *Studies in American Indian Literatures*, 5/4 (winter 1993), 55–68.

Emeljanow, Victor, 'Grand Guignol and the Orchestration of Violence', *Themes in Drama 12: Violence in Drama* (New York: Cambridge University Press), pp. 151–63.

Emigh, John, *Masked Performance: The Play of Self and Other in Ritual and Theater* (Philadelphia: University of Pennsylvania Press, 1996).

The Encyclopedia of Korean Folk Literature (Seoul: The National Folk Museum of Korea, 2014).

Esser, J. Brody, 'Tarascan Masks of Women as Agents of Social Control', in N. Ross Crumrine and Marjorie Halpin (eds), *The Power of Symbols: Masks and Masquerade in the Americas* (Vancouver: University of British Columbia Press, 1983), pp. 116–27.

Eves, Richard, 'Shamanism, Sorcery and Cannibalism: The Incorporation of Power in the Magical Cult of Buai', *Oceana*, 65/3 (March 1995), 212–33.

Fava, Antonio, *The Comic Mask in the Commedia Dell'Arte: Actor Training, Improvisation, and the Poetics of Survival* (Chicago: Northwestern University Press, 2007).

Favor, Lesli J., *Italy: A Primary Source Cultural Guide* (New York: PowerPlus Books, 2004).

Fawkner, Harald William, *Deconstructing Macbeth: The Hyperontological View* (Cranbury: Associated University Presses, Inc., 1990).

Fleming, Paul, 'Doppelgänger/Doppeltgänger', *Cabinet Magazine*, 14 (2004), *www.cabinetmagazine.org/issues/14/fleming.php* (accessed 28 February 2019).

Fischer, Dennis, 'George Romero on *Bruiser*, Development Hell and Other Sundry Matters', in Tony Williams (ed.), *George A. Romero: Interviews* (Jackson: University Press of Mississippi, 2011), pp. 122–33.

Fisher, Austin and Johnny Walker (eds), *Grindhouse: Cultural Exchange on 42nd Street, and Beyond* (New York: Bloomsbury, 2016).

Fisher, B. F., 'Poe and the Gothic Tradition', in Kevin J. Hayes (ed.), *The Cambridge Companion to Edgar Allan Poe* (Cambridge: Cambridge University Press, 2003), pp. 72–91.

Foster, Hal, *Compulsive Beauty* (London: MIT Press, 1993).

Foster, Michael Dylan, *Pandemonium and Parade: Japanese Monsters and the Culture of Yokai* (Berkeley: University of California Press, 2009).

Frank, Frederick S., 'Glossary', in *The Castle of Otranto and The Mysterious Mother By Horace Walpole*, ed. Frederick S. Frank (Peterborough: Broadview Press Ltd, 2003).

Frayling, Christopher, *Spaghetti Westerns: Cowboys and Europeans from Karl May to Sergio Leone* (London: I. B. Tauris, 1998).

Freeland, Cynthia A., 'Realist Horror', in Cynthia A. Freeland and Thomas E. Wartenberg (eds), *Philosophy and Film* (New York: Routledge, 1995), pp. 126–42.
Freud, Sigmund, 'The Uncanny', in *The Standard Edition of the Complete Psychological Works of Sigmund Freud* (London: The Hogarth Press, 1955). Originally published as 'The Uncanny', in *The Standard Edition of the Complete Psychological Works of Sigmund Freud, Volume XVII (1917–1919): An Infantile Neurosis and Other Works* (London: Hogarth, 1919), pp. 217–56.
——, *Totem and Taboo* (New York: Cosimo Classics, 2009).
Fritscher, Jack, *Popular Witchcraft: Straight from the Witches Mouth* (Madison: The University of Wisconsin Press, 2004).
Garcia, Cathy Rose A., 'Meet Miffy at Hangaram Design Museum', *Korea Times* (10 July 2009), *www.koreatimes.co.kr/www/art/2019/03/691_48249.html* (accessed 28 February 2019).
Gemzøe, Anker, 'Modernism, Narrativity and Bakhtinian Theory', in Astradur Eysteinsson and Vivian Liska (eds), *Modernism* (Amsterdam: John Benjamins Publishing Company, 2007), pp. 125–41.
Gerow, Aaron, *A Page of Madness: Cinema and Modernity in 1920s Japan* (Ann Arbor: Center for Japanese Studies, The University of Michigan, 2008).
Gibert, Montserrat Ginés, 'Introduction', in Montserrat Ginés Gibert (ed.), *The Meaning of Technology: Selected Readings from American Sources* (Barcelona: Edicions UPC, 2003), pp. 9–12.
Gilbert, R. A., 'Penny Dreadfuls', in Marie Mulvey-Roberts (ed.), *The Handbook to Gothic Literature* (New York: New York University Press, 1998), p. 172.
Gillmor, Frances, 'Symbolic Representation in Mexican Combat Plays', in N. Ross Crumrine and Marjorie Halpin (eds), *The Power of Symbols: Masks and Masquerade in the Americas* (Vancouver: University of British Columbia Press, 1983), pp. 102–10.
Gingold, Mike, 'Q&A: *The Conspiracy* Writer/Director Christopher MacBride', *Fangoria* (29 August 2013), *https://web.archive.org/web/20170221224609/www.fangoria.com/new/qa-the-conspiracy-writerdirector-christopher-macbride/* (accessed 28 February 2019).
Gledhill, Christine, 'Rethinking Genre', in Christine Gledhill and Linda Williams (eds), *Reinventing Film Studies* (London: Arnold, 2000), pp. 221–43.
Goodall, Mark, *Sweet and Savage: The World Through the Shockumentary Film Lens* (London: Headpress, 2006).
Goodman, Lizbeth, *Literature and Gender* (Abingdon: The Open University/Routledge, 1996).
Gousseff, James W., *Street Mime* (Woodstock: The Dramatic Publishing Company, 1993).

Grant, Barry Keith, 'Rich and Strange: The Yuppie Horror Film', in Barry Keith Grant and Christopher Sharrett (eds), *Planks of Reason: Essays on the Horror Film* (Lanham: The Scarecrow Press, Inc., 2004), pp. 153–69.

Greene, Doyle, *Mexploitation Cinema: A Critical History of Mexican Vampire, Wrestler, Ape-Man and Similar Films, 1957–1977* (Jefferson: McFarland & Co., 2005).

Grimes, Ronald L., 'Masking: Toward a Phenomenology of Exteriorization', *Journal of the American Academy of Religion*, 43/3 (September 1975), 508–16.

Grove, David, *Making Friday the 13th: The Legend of Camp Blood* (Godalming: FAB Press, 2005).

Gunning, Tom, 'The Horror of Opacity: The Melodrama of Sensation in the Plays of Andre de Lorde', in J. Cook, J. Bratton and C. Gledhill (eds), *Melodrama: Stage, Picture, Screen* (London: British Film Institute, 1994), pp. 50–61.

Hand, Richard J., 'Half-Masks and Stage Blood: Translating, Adapting and Performing French Historical Theatre Forms', in K. Krebs (ed.), *Translation and Adaptation in Theatre and Film* (New York: Routledge, 2014), pp. 143–61.

—— and Michael Wilson, *Grand Guignol: The French Theatre of Horror* (Devon: Exeter University Press, 2002).

Haney II, William S., *Postmodern Theater and the Void of Conceptions* (Newcastle: Cambridge Scholars Press, 2006).

Hansen, George P., *The Trickster and the Paranormal* (Bloomington: Xlibris Corporation, 2001).

Hantke, Steffen, 'Germany's Secret History: Stefan Ruzowitzky's *Anatomie* (*Anatomy*, 2000)', *Kino Eye*, 1/1 (September 2001), www.kinoeye.org/01/01/hantke01.php (accessed 28 February 2019).

Harper, Jim, *Legacy of Blood: A Comprehensive Guide to Slasher Movies* (Manchester: Critical Vision/Headpress, 2004).

——, 'Shiraishi, Kōji', in Salvador Murguia (ed.), *The Encyclopedia of Japanese Horror Films* (Lanham: Rowman & Littlefield, 2016), pp. 287–8.

——, 'This Carnival of Venice Mask Has a Dark Origin', *Historic Mysteries* (6 June 2016), https://www.historicmysteries.com/plague-doctor (accessed 28 February 2019).

Harrell, Kelley, 'The Shamanic Narrative in *Star Wars*', *Huff Post* (17 December 2015), www.huffingtonpost.com/kelley-harrell/the-shamanic-narrative-in_b_8819874.html (accessed 28 February 2019).

Harris, Jason Marc, 'Smiles of Oblivion: Demonic Clowns and Doomed Puppets as Fantastic Figures of Absurdity, Chaos and Misanthropy in the Writings of Thomas Ligotti', *The Journal of Popular Culture*, 45/6 (2012), 1249–65.

Harris, Martin, 'You Can't Kill the Boogeyman: *Halloween III* and the Modern Horror Franchise', *Journal of Popular Film and Television*, 32/3 (2004), 98–109.

Harvey, Graham, 'General Introduction', in Graham Harvey (ed.), *Shamanism: A Reader* (London: Routledge, 2003), pp. 1–23.

Haslam, Nick, 'What Is Dehumanization?', in J. Vaes, P. G. Bain and J. P. Leyens (eds), *Humanness and Dehumanization* (London: Taylor and Francis, 2013), pp. 34–48.

Hawkins, Joan, *Cutting Edge: Art-Horror and the Horrific Avant-Garde* (Minneapolis: University of Minnesota Press, 2000).

Heller-Nicholas, Alexandra, *Rape-Revenge Films: A Critical Study* (Jefferson: McFarland & Co., 2011).

——, *Found Footage Horror Films: Fear and the Appearance of Reality* (Jefferson: McFarland & Co., 2014).

——, *Ms. 45* (New York: Columbia University Press, 2017).

Hendershot, Cynthia, *The Animal Within: Masculinity and the Gothic* (Ann Arbor: University of Michigan Press, 1998).

Höglund, Johan, *The American Imperial Gothic: Popular Culture, Empire, Violence* (London: Routledge, 2014).

Hollinger, Karen, *The Actress: Hollywood Acting and the Female Star* (New York: Routledge, 2006).

Hornaday, Ann, 'Harvey Weinstein Embodies a Culture Whose Power is on the Wane', *Sydney Morning Herald* (10 October 2017), www.smh.com.au/lifestyle/news-and-views/harvey-weinstein-embodies-a-culture-whose-power-is-on-the-wane-20171008-gywr20.html (accessed 28 February 2019).

Horsley, Jason, *The Secret Life of Movies: Schizophrenic and Shamanic Journeys in American Cinema* (Jefferson: McFarland & Co., 2009).

Houstoun, Alex, '"Hearken . . . I Can Tell You the Whole Story": Monologues and Confessions in the Early Works of H. P. Lovecraft and Edgar Allan Poe', in R. H. Waugh (ed.), *Lovecraft and Influence: His Predecessors and Successors* (Plymouth: Scarecrow Press, Inc., 2013), pp. 44–54.

Huddleston, Jason, 'Unmasking the Monster: Hiding and Revealing Male Sexuality in John Carpenter's *Halloween*', *Journal of Visual Literacy*, 25/2 (autumn 2005), 219–36.

Huddleston, Tom, 'An Interview with Richard Stanley', *Not Coming to a Theatre Near You* (20 August 2007), http://www.notcoming.com/features/richard-stanley-interview/ (accessed 28 February 2019).

Hughes, William, *Historical Dictionary of Gothic Literature* (Lanham: Scarecrow Press, 2013).

Humphries, Reynold, *The American Horror Film: An Introduction* (Edinburgh: Edinburgh University Press, 2002).

Hunt, Leon, 'A (Sadistic) Night at the Opera', in Ken Gelder (ed.), *The Horror Reader* (London: Routledge, 2000), pp. 330–2.

Hutchings, Peter, *Historical Dictionary of Horror Cinema* (Lanham: Scarecrow Press, 2008).

——, *The A to Z of Horror Cinema* (Lanham: Scarecrow Press, 2009).

——, 'Northern Darkness: The Curious Case of the Swedish Vampire', in Leon Hunt, Sharon Lockyer and Milly Williamson (eds), *Screening the Undead: Vampires and Zombies in Film and Television* (London: I. B. Tauris, 2014), pp. 54–70.

Hutchinson, Pamela, '10 Great Silent Horror Films', British Film Institute (7 November 2016), www.bfi.org.uk/news-opinion/news-bfi/lists/10-great-silent-horror-films (accessed 28 February 2019).

Hutchison, Don, *The Great Pulp Heroes* (New York: Book Republic, 2006).

Hyde, Lewis, *Trickster Makes This World: Mischief, Myth and Art* (New York: Farrar, Straus and Giroux, 2010).

Hynes, William J., 'Mapping the Characteristics of Mythic Tricksters: A Heuristic Guide', in William J. Hynes and William G. Doty (eds), *Mythical Trickster Figures: Contours, Contexts, and Criticisms* (Tuscaloosa: The University of Alabama Press, 1993), pp. 33–45.

Iles, Timothy, *The Crisis of Identity in Contemporary Japanese Film* (Leiden: Brill, 2008).

Inagi, Yoki, 'Kuchisake Onna (2007)', in Salvador Murguia (ed.), *The Encyclopedia of Japanese Horror Films* (Lanham: Rowman & Littlefield, 2016), pp. 176–8.

Ince, Kate, *Georges Franju* (Manchester: Manchester University Press, 2005).

James, Jonathan, 'Q&A with *Come Out and Play* Director Makinov', *Daily Dead*, at https://dailydead.com/qa-with-come-out-and-play-director-makinov/ (accessed 22 February 2019).

Jancovich, Mark, *Rational Fears: American Horror in the 1950s* (Manchester: Manchester University Press, 1996).

——, *Horror, The Film Reader* (London: Routledge, 2002).

Jarvis, Jason L., 'Digital Image Politics: The Networked Rhetoric of Anonymous', in Matthew Johnson and Samid Suliman (eds), *Protest – Analysing Current Trends* (London: Routledge, 2014), pp. 218–44.

Jaworzyn, Stefan, *The Texas Chain Saw Massacre Companion* (London: Titan Books, 2003).

Jermyn, Deborah, '"Get a Life, Ladies. Your Old One is Not Coming Back": Ageing, Ageism and the Lifespan of Female Celebrity', *Celebrity Studies*, 3/1 (2012), 1–12.

―― and Su Holmes, 'Introduction: A Timely Intervention – Unravelling the Gender/Age/Celebrity Matrix', in Deborah Jermyn and Su Holmes (eds), *Women, Celebrity and Cultures of Ageing: Freeze Frame* (London: Palgrave Macmillan, 2015), pp. 1–10.

Johnston, Claire, 'Femininity and the Masquerade: *Anne of the Indies*', in Claire Johnston and Paul Willemen (eds), *Jacques Tourneur* (London: British Film Institute, 1975), pp. 36–44.

Joshi, S. T., *Icons of Horror and the Supernatural: An Encyclopaedia of Our Worst Nightmares. Volume 1* (Westport: Greenwood Press, 2007).

Jung, Carl Gustav, *Four Archetypes: Mother, Rebirth, Spirit, Trickster* (London: Routledge, 2001).

Katritzky, M. A., *The Art of Commedia: A Study in the Commedia dell'Arte 1560–1620 with Special Reference to the Visual Records* (Amsterdam: Rodopi, 2006).

Kawin, Bruce F., *Horror and the Horror Film* (London: Anthem Press, 2012).

Keller, James R., *Food, Film and Culture: A Genre Study* (Jefferson: McFarland & Co., 2006).

Kendall, Laurel, 'Numinous Dress/Iconic Costume: Korean Shamans Dressed for the Gods and for the Camera', in Heike Behrend, Anja Dreschke and Martin Zillinger (eds), *Trance Mediums and New Media: Spirit Possession in the Age of Technical Reproduction* (New York: Fordham University Press, 2014), pp. 116–36.

Kennedy, Dennis (ed.), *The Oxford Companion to Theatre and Performance* (Oxford: Oxford University Press, 2010).

Kimber, Shaun, '"Meat's Meat, and a Man's Gotta Eat" (*Motel Hell*, 1980): Food and Eating Within Contemporary Horror Cultures', in Peri Bradley (ed.), *Food, Media and Contemporary Culture: The Edible Image* (London: Palgrave Macmillan, 2016), pp. 125–43.

King, Carol, 'Top 13 Italian Superstitions', *Italy Magazine* (31 October 2013), *www.italymagazine.com/featured-story/top-13-italian-superstitions* (accessed 28 February 2019).

King, Claire Sisco, 'Acting Up and Sounding Off: Sacrifice and Performativity in *Alice, Sweet Alice*', *Text and Performance Quarterly*, 27/2 (April 2007), 124–42.

King, Mike, *Luminous: The Spiritual Life on Film* (Jefferson: McFarland & Co., 2014).

Kirby, Danielle, *Fantasy and Belief: Alternative Religions, Popular Narratives and Digital Cultures* (London: Routledge, 2013).

Klapcsik, Sandor, *Liminality in Fantastic Fiction: A Poststructuralist Approach* (Jefferson: McFarland & Co., 2012).

Kluge, Bettina, 'The Collaborative Construction of an Outsider as a Troll in the Blogosphere of Latin American Immigrants to Quebec, Canada', in Kristina Bedijs, Gudrun Held and Christiane Maaß (eds), *Face Work and Social Media* (Zurich: Lit Verlad, 2014), pp. 323–48.

Knight, Arthur, Clara Pafort-Overduin and Deb Verhoeven, 'Senses of Cinema-Going: Brief Reports on Going to the Movies around the World', *Senses of Cinema*, 58 (March 2011), *sensesofcinema.com/2011/feature-articles/senses-of-cinema-going-brief-reports-on-going-to-the-movies-around-the-world/* (accessed 28 February 2019).

Kohn, Eric, 'Netflix's Horror Movie Hush Proves the Effectiveness of the Blumhouse Model', *IndieWire* (15 March 2016), *www.indiewire.com/2016/03/sxsw-2016-review-netflixs-horror-movie-hush-proves-the-effectiveness-of-the-blumhouse-model-58031/* (accessed 28 February 2019).

Koven, Mikel J., *La Dolce Morte: Vernacular Cinema and the Italian Giallo Film* (Lanham: Scarecrow Press, 2006).

——, *Film, Folklore, and Urban Legends* (Lanham: Scarecrow Press, 2008).

Kracauer, Siegfried, *From Caligari to Hitler: A Psychological History of the German Film* (Ewing: Princeton University Press, 1947).

Krippner, Stanley C., 'Conflicting Perspectives on Shamans and Shamanism: Points and Counterpoints', *American Psychologist*, 57/11 (November 2002), 962–77.

Kristeva, Julia, *Desire in Language: A Semiotic Approach to Literature and Art* (New York: Columbia University Press, 1980).

——, *Powers of Horror: An Essay on Abjection* (New York: Columbia University Press, 1982).

Krzywinska, Tanya, *Sex and the Cinema* (London: Wallflower, 2006).

Kurman, George, 'Cultural Antecedents of Beavis and Butt-head', *The Journal of Popular Culture*, 18/1 (October 1995), 101–12.

Lanzoni, Rémi Fournier, *French Cinema: From Its Beginnings to the Present* (New York: Continuum, 2005).

Leddon, A., *A Child's Eye View of Ghosts and Hauntings* (Madison: Spero Publishing, 2014).

Lee, Nikki J. Y., 'Apartment Horror: Sorum and Possessed', in Alison Peirse and Daniel Martin (eds), *Korean Horror Cinema* (Edinburgh: Edinburgh University Press, 2013), pp. 101–13.

Leeder, Murray, *Halloween* (Leighton Buzzard: Auteur, 2014).

LeMaster, David James, 'Charlie Chaplin and Harpo Marx as Masks of the Commedia Dell'Arte: Theory and Practice' (unpublishsed PhD thesis, Texas Tech University, 1995).

Leonard, Richard, *The Mystical Gaze of The Cinema: The Films of Peter Weir* (Melbourne: Melbourne University Press, 2009).
Lévi-Strauss, Claude, 'The Structural Study of Myth', in Claude Lévi-Strauss, *Structural Anthropology* (1955; London: Penguin, 1968), pp. 206–31.
——, *The Way of the Masks* (Seattle: University of Washington Press, 1982).
Lieberman, Evan, 'Mask and Masculinity: Culture, Modernity, and Gender Identity in the Mexican Lucha Libre films of El Santo', *Studies in Hispanic Cinemas*, 6/1 (December 2009), 3–17.
Loiselle, André, 'Cinema du Grand Guignol: Theatricality in the Horror Film', in André Loiselle and Jeremy Maron (eds), *Stages of Reality: Theatricality in Cinema* (Toronto: University of Toronto Press, 2000), pp. 55–81.
Long, Harry H., 'The Bat', in J. T. Soister and H. Nicolella (eds), *American Silent Horror, Science Fiction and Fantasy Feature Films, 1913–1929* (Jefferson: McFarland & Co., 2012), pp. 21–4.
——, 'The Phantom of the Opera', in J. T. Soister and H. Nicolella (eds), *American Silent Horror, Science Fiction and Fantasy Feature Films, 1913–1929* (Jefferson: McFarland & Co., 2012), pp. 455–61.
Lowenstein, Adam, *Shocking Representation: Historical Trauma, National Cinema and the Modern Horror Film* (New York: Columbia University Press, 2005).
Lucas, Tim, 'Matters of Life and Death', *Sight and Sound*, 21/3 (2011), 88.
Ludegwig, Alexandra, 'Screening Nazism and Reclaiming the Horror Genre: Stefan Ruzowitzky's Anatomy Films', in Robert von Dassanowsky and Oliver C. Speck (eds), *New Austrian Film* (New York: Bergahn, 2011), pp. 279–91.
Lust, Annette, *From the Greek Mimes to Marcel Marceau and Beyond: Mimes, Actors, Pierrots, and Clowns: A Chronicle of the Many Visages of Mime in the Theatre* (Lanham: Scarecrow Press, 2000).
Lutes, S. V., 'The Mask and Magic of the Yaqui Paskola Clowns', in N. Ross Crumrine and Marjorie Halpin (eds), *The Power of Symbols: Masks and Masquerade in the Americas* (Vancouver: University of British Columbia Press, 1983), pp. 81–92.
Lyon, David, *Surveillance Studies: An Overview* (Cambridge: Polity Press, 2007).
MacAllister McDonald, Ian, 'Lost Girls: A Conversation about Fantastical Filmmaker Jean Rollin', *Los Angeles Review of Books* (29 April 2017), https://blog.lareviewofbooks.org/interviews/lost-girls-conversation-fantastical-filmmaker-jean-rollin/ (accessed 28 February 2019).
MacCormack, Patricia, *Cinesexuality* (Aldershot: Ashgate, 2008).
McDonald, Keiko I., *Japanese Classical Theater in Films* (Rutherford: Fairleigh Dickinson University Press, 1994).

Mack, John (ed.), *Masks: The Art of Expression* (London: British Museum Press, 1994).
MacLellan, Gordon, 'Dancing on the Edge: Shamanism in Modern Britain', in Graham Harvey (ed.), *Shamanism: A Reader* (London: Routledge, 2003), pp. 365–74.
Makarius, Laura, 'The Mask and the Violation of Taboo', in N. Ross Crumrine and Marjorie Halpin (eds), *The Power of Symbols: Masks and Masquerade in the Americas* (Vancouver: University of British Columbia Press, 1983), pp. 191–203.
Markman, Peter T. and Roberta H. Markman, 'The Mask as Metaphor', in Peter T. Markman and Roberta H. Markman (eds), *Masks of the Spirit: Image and Metaphor in Mesoamerica* (Berkeley: University of California Press, 1990), pp. xix–xxi.
Marsh, Anne, *Performance Ritual Document* (Melbourne: Macmillan Art Publishing, 2014).
Martin, Craig, 'Trust Your Instinct: An Interview with Ann Turner', *Senses of Cinema*, 81 (December 2016), sensesofcinema.com/2016/beyond-the-babadook/ann-turner-interview/ (accessed 28 February 2019).
Martin, Daniel, 'South Korean Horror Cinema', in Harry M. Benshoff (ed.), *A Companion to the Horror Film* (Hoboken: John Wiley & Sons, Inc., 2014), pp. 423–41.
Martinson, Deborah, *Lillian Hellman: A Life with Foxes and Scoundrels* (New York: Counterpoint, 2005).
Mazur, Eric Michael (ed.), *Encyclopedia of Religion and Film* (Santa Barbara: ABC-CLIO, 2011).
Mendoza Covarrubias, Alexandra, 'Día De Los Muertos (Day of the Dead)', in María Herrera-Sobek (ed.), *Celebrating Latino Folklore: An Encyclopedia of Cultural Traditions, Volume 1* (Santa Barbara: ABC-CLIO, 2012), pp. 403–13.
Menozzi, Filippo, *Postcolonial Custodianship: Cultural and Literary Inheritance* (New York: Routledge, 2014).
Merrifield, Ralph, *The Archeology of Ritual and Magic* (London: B. T. Batsford, 1987).
Messent, Peter, 'American Gothic: Liminality and the Gothic in Thomas Harris's Hannibal Lecter Novels', in Benjamin Szumskyj (ed.), *Dissecting Hannibal Lecter: Essays on the Novels of Thomas Harris* (Jefferson: McFarland & Co., 2008), pp. 13–36.
Metz, Christian, *Film Language: A Semiotics of Cinema* (New York: Oxford University Press, 1974).

Midelfort, H. C. Erik, *A History of Madness in Sixteenth-Century Germany* (Stanford: Stanford University Press, 1999).

Miller, Heather Margaret-Louise, *Archaeological Approaches to Technology* (Florence: Taylor and Francis, 2016).

Miller, Sarah Allison, 'Virgins, Mothers, Monsters: Late-medieval Readings of the Female Body Out of Bounds' (unpublished PhD thesis, University of North Carolina at Chapel Hill, 2008).

Monteyne, Kimberly, *Hip Hop on Film: Performance Culture, Urban Space, and Genre Transformation in the 1980s* (Jackson: University Press of Mississippi, 2013).

Moran, Leslie J., 'Law and the Gothic Imagination', in Fred Botting (ed.), *The Gothic* (Cambridge: D.S. Brewer, 2001), pp. 87–110.

Morgan, Ben, '*Metropolis* – The Archetypal Version: Sentimentality and Self-Control in the Reception of the Film', in M. Minden and H. Bachmann (eds), *Fritz Lang's Metropolis: Cinematic Visions of Technology and Fear* (New York: Camden House, 2000), pp. 288–310.

Morris, Desmond, *Owl* (London: Reaktion Books, 2009).

Morrison, Dorothy, *In Praise of the Crone: A Celebration of Feminine Maturity* (St Paul: Llewellyn Worldwide, 1999).

Mr Disgusting, 'Go Down the Rabbit Hole with *The Conspiracy* Director Christopher MacBride!', *Bloody Disgusting* (6 August 2013), *bloody-disgusting.com/news/3247319/interview-go-down-the-rabbit-hole-with-the-conspiracy-director-christopher-macbride/;* (accessed 28 February 2019).

MSU Museum, 'Mask: Secrets and Revelations: Masks on Stage', *Smithsonian Institute*, Michigan State University (2012), *http://museum.msu.edu/?q=node/326* (accessed 28 February 2019).

Muir, John Kenneth, *Horror Films of the 1980s* (Jefferson: McFarland & Co., 2007).

Mulvey, Laura, 'Visual Pleasure and Narrative Cinema', *Screen*, 3/1 (1975), 6–18.

Murray, Gabrielle, 'El Santo: Wrestler, Saint and Superhero', *Refractory: A Journal of Entertainment Media* (December 2006), *http://refractory.unimelb.edu.au/2006/12/04/el-santo-wrestler-saint-and-superhero-gabrielle-murray* (accessed 28 February 2019).

National Folk Museum of Korea, *Encyclopedia of Korean Seasonal Customs: Encyclopedia of Korean Folklore and Traditional Culture Vol. 1* (Seoul: The National Folk Museum of Korea, 2009).

Ndalianis, Angela, *The Horror Sensorium: Media and the Senses* (Jefferson: McFarland & Co., 2012).

Neale, Steve and Frank Krutnik, *Popular Film and Television Comedy* (London: Routledge, 1990).

——, 'Questions of Genre', *Screen*, 31/1 (1990), 45–66.
——, *Genre and Hollywood* (London: Routledge, 2000).
Needham, Gary, 'Playing with Genre: An Introduction to the Italian Giallo', in Ernest Mathijs and Xavier Mendik (eds), *The Cult Film Reader* (Maidenhead: McGraw Hill, 2008), pp. 294–300.
Neroni, Hilary, *The Violent Woman: Femininity, Narrative, and Violence in Contemporary American Cinema* (Albany: State University of New York Press, 2005).
Ní Fhlainn, Sorcha, 'Sweet, Bloody Vengeance: Class, Social Stigma and Servitude in the Slasher Genre', in Holly Lynn Baumgartner and Roger Davis (eds), *Hosting the Monster* (Amsterdam: Editions Rodopi, 2008), pp. 179–96.
Nolan, Maggie, 'Displacing Indigenous Australians: Freud's Totem and Taboo', in Joy Damousi and Robert Reynolds (eds), *History on the Couch: Essays in History and Psychoanalysis* (Melbourne: Melbourne University Press, 2003), pp. 60–71.
Norton, James, 'The Mystery, as Always: Raúl Ruiz, Klimt and the Poetics of Cinema', *Vertigo*, 3/6 (summer 2007), *https://www.closeupfilmcentre.com/vertigo_magazine/volume-3-issue-6-summer-2007/makers-the-mystery-as-always-raul-ruiz/* (accessed 28 February 2019).
Nowell, Richard, *Blood Money: A History of the First Teen Slasher Film Cycle* (New York: Continuum, 2011).
Nunley, John W. and Cara McCarty, *Masks: Faces of Culture* (New York: Harry N. Abrams, Inc. Publishers, 1999).
Nyyssönen, Pasi, 'Gothic Liminality in A. J. Annila's Film Sauna', in P. M. Mehtonen and Matti Savolainen (eds), *Gothic Topographies: Language, Nation Building and 'Race'* (London: Routledge, 2013), pp. 187–202.
O'Brien, John, *Harlequin Britain: Pantomime and Entertainment, 1690–1760* (Baltimore: The Johns Hopkins University Press, 2004).
Onley, Ian, *Euro Horror: Classic European Horror Cinema in Contemporary American Culture* (Bloomington: Indiana University Press, 2013).
Ortolani, Benito, *Japanese Theatre: From Shamanistic Ritual to Contemporary Pluralism* (Princeton: Princeton University Press, 1990).
Ozolins, Aija, 'Dreams and Doctrines: Dual Strands in *Frankenstein*', *Science Fiction Studies*, 2/2 (1975), 103–12.
Pagnoni Berns, Fernando G. and Amy M. Davis, 'From Jigsaw to Phibes: God, Free Will and Foreknowledge in Conflict', in James Aston (ed.), *To See the Saw Movies: Essays on Torture Porn and Post-9/11 Horror* (Jefferson: McFarland & Co., 2013), pp. 73–85.
Parnum, John E., '*The Abominable Dr. Phibes* and *Dr. Phibes Rises Again* (1971/1972)', in G. J. Svehla and S. Svehla (eds), *Vincent Price* (Baltimore: Luminary Press, 1998), pp. 247–57.

Patella, Michael, *Lord of the Cosmos: Mithras, Paul, and the Gospel of Mark* (New York: T & T Clark, 2006).

Paz, Octavia, *The Labyrinth of Solitude* (1959; New York: Grove Press Inc., 1985).

Peacock, Louise, 'Slapstick and Comic Violence in Commedia Dell'arte', in Judith Chaffee and Olly Crick (eds), *The Routledge Companion to Commedia dell'Arte* (London: Routledge, 2014), pp. 185–62.

Peirse, Alison, 'Bauhaus of Horrors: Edgar G. Ulmer and *The Black Cat*', in Gary Rhodes (ed.), *Edgar G. Ulmer: Detour on Poverty Row* (London: Lexington Books, 2010), pp. 275–87.

Penenberg, Adam L., 'The Surveillance Society', *Wired*, 9/12 (December 2001), *http://www.wired.com/wired/archive/9.12/surveillance.html* (accessed 28 February 2019).

Perel, Azriel, 'Surgical Masks: Evidence, Image, and Art', *BJA: British Journal of Anaesthesia*, 99/6 (2007), 918.

Perry, Dennis and Carl Sederholm, *Poe, The House of Usher, and the American Gothic* (London: Palgrave, 2009).

Peterson, Mark Allen, 'From Jinn to Genies: Intertextuality, Media and the Making of Global Folklore', in Sharon R. Sherman and Mikel J. Koven (eds), *Folklore/Cinema: Popular Film as Vernacular Culture* (Logan: Utah State University Press, 2007), pp. 93–112.

Phillips, Kendall R., *Dark Directions: Romero, Craven, Carpenter and the Modern Horror Film* (Carbondale: Southern Illinois University Press, 2012).

Phillips, Whitney, *This Is Why We Can't Have Nice Things: Mapping the Relationship Between Online Trolling and Mainstream Culture* (Cambridge: The MIT Press, 2015).

Phu, Thy, *Picturing Model Citizens: Civility in Asian American Visual Culture* (Philadelphia: Temple University Press, 2011).

Plutschow, Herbert E., *Matsuri: The Festivals of Japan* (Richmond: Japan Library, 1996).

Potter, Robin, 'Bloody Mary or I Believe in Mary Worth', in Christopher R. Fee and Jeffrey B. Webb (eds), *American Myths, Legends, and Tall Tales: An Encyclopedia of American Folklore* (Santa Barbara, ABC-CLIO, 2016), pp. 129–31.

Prager, Brad, *The Cinema of Werner Herzog: Aesthetic Ecstasy and Truth* (London: Wallflower, 2011).

Pratt, Christina, *An Encyclopedia of Shamanism* (New York: Rosen, 2007).

Pušnik, Maruša, 'Cinema Culture and Audience Rituals: Early Mediatisation of Society', *Anthropological Notebooks*, 21/3 (2015), 51–74.

Quinn, Michael L., 'Self-Reliance and Ritual Renewal: Anti-theatrical Ideology in American Method Acting', *Journal of Dramatic Theory and Criticism*, 10/1 (fall 1995), 5–20.

Randall, Richard S., 'Censorship: From *The Miracle* to *Deep Throat*', in Thomas Schatz (ed.), *Hollywood: Critical Concepts in Media and Cultural Studies. Vol. III: Social Dimensions: Technology, Regulation and the Audience* (London: Routledge, 2004), pp. 215–36.

Rauch, Karen and Jeff Fessler, *When Drag is Not a Car Race: An Irreverent Dictionary of Over 400 Gay and Lesbian Words and Phrases* (New York: Fireside/Simon & Schuster, 1997).

Rehm, Rush, *Greek Tragic Theatre* (London: Routledge, 1992).

Remy, Steven P., *The Heidelberg Myth: The Nazification and Denazification of a German University* (Cambridge: Harvard University Press, 2002).

Rice, Michael, *The Power of the Bull* (London: Routledge, 1998).

Richardson, Michael, *Surrealism and Cinema* (Oxford: Berg, 2006).

Ridington, Robin and Tonia, 'The Inner Eye of Shamanism and Totemism 1970', *History of Religions*, 10/1 (1970), 49–61.

Ripinsky-Naxon, Michael, *The Nature of Shamanism: Substance and Function of a Religious Metaphor* (Albany: State University of New York Press, 1993).

Riviere, Joan, 'Womanliness as Masquerade', in Hendrick M. Ruitenbeck (ed.), *Psychoanalysis and Female Sexuality* (New Haven: College and University Press, 1966), pp. 121–41. Originally published in *The International Journal of Psychoanalysis*, 10 (1929).

Robinson, David, *Das Cabinet Des Dr. Caligari* (London: Palgrave Macmillian/British Film Institute, 2013).

Robinson, Jeremy Mark, *The Sacred Cinema of Andrei Tarkovsky* (Maidstone: Crescent Moon, 2007).

Roche, David, *Making and Remaking Horror in the 1970s and 2000s: Why Don't They Do It Like They Used To?* (Jackson: University Press of Mississippi, 2014).

Rockoff, Adam, *Going to Pieces: The Rise and Fall of the Slasher Film, 1978–1986* (Jefferson: McFarland & Co., 2002).

——, *The Horror of It All: One Moviegoer's Love Affair with Masked Maniacs, Frightened Virgins, and the Living Dead* (New York: Scribner, 2015).

Rogerson, Margaret, *Playing a Part in History: The York Mysteries, 1951–2006* (Toronto: University of Toronto Press, 2009).

Roland, Paul, *The Curious Case of H. P. Lovecraft* (Medford: Plexus, 2014).

Rollin, Jean, 'For an Illogical and Nonsensical European Cinema', in Ernest Mathijs and Xavier Mendik (eds), *Alternative Europe: Eurotrash and Exploitation Cinema Since 1945* (London: Wallflower, 2004), pp. 12–13.

Rose, James, *The Texas Chain Saw Massacre* (Leighton Buzzard: Auteur, 2013).
Rountree, Cathleen, 'Auteur Film Directors as Contemporary Shamans', *Jung Journal*, 2/2 (spring 2008), 123–34.
Rudlin, John, *Commedia Dell'Arte: An Actor's Handbook* (Hoboken: Taylor and Francis, 2002).
Ruskin, John, *The Nature of Gothic: A Chapter from the Stones of Venice* (London: George Allen, 1900).
Russell, Catherine, *Narrative Mortality: Death, Closure, and New Wave Cinemas* (Minneapolis: University of Minnesota Press, 1995).
Rutenberg, Jim, Rachel Abrams and Melena Ryzikoct, 'Harvey Weinstein's Fall Opens the Floodgates in Hollywood', *The New York Times* (16 October 2017), *https://www.nytimes.com/2017/10/16/business/media/harvey-weinsteins-fall-opens-the-floodgates-in-hollywood.html* (accessed 28 February 2019).
Ruth, Julie A. and Cele C. Ontes, 'Consumption Rituals', in Daniel Thomas Cook and J. Michael Ryan (eds), *The Wiley Blackwell Encyclopedia of Consumption and Consumer Studies* (Chichester: Wiley Blackwell, 2015), pp. 187–9.
Sala, George Augustus, *The Seven Sons of Mammon: A Story* (London: Tinsley Brothers, 1862).
Santino, Jack, 'Flexible Halloween: Longevity, Appropriation, Multiplicity and Contestation', in Malcolm Foley and Hugh O'Donnell (eds), *Treat or Trick? Halloween in a Globalising World* (Newcastle upon Tyne: Cambridge Scholars Publishing, 2009), pp. 9–15.
Scahill, Andrew, 'Serialized Killers: Prebooting Horror in *Bates Motel* and *Hannibal*', in Amanda Ann Klein, R. Barton Palmer (eds), *Cycles, Sequels, Spin-offs, Remakes, and Reboots: Multiplicities in Film and Television* (Austin: University of Texas Press, 2016), pp. 316–33.
Schatz, Thomas, *Hollywood Genres: Formulas, Filmmaking and the Studio System* (New York: Random House, 1981).
——, 'The New Hollywood', in Graeme Turner (ed.), *The Film Cultures Reader* (London: Routledge, 2002), pp. 184–205.
——, 'Hollywood Genres: Film Genre and the Genre Film', in Leo Braudy and Marshall Cohen (eds), *Film theory and Criticism: Introductory Readings* (Oxford: Oxford University Press, 2009), pp. 564–75.
——, 'The Structural Influence: New Directions in Film Genre Study', in Barry Keith Grant (ed.), *Film Genre Reader IV* (Austin: University of Texas Press, 2012), pp. 110–20.
Schechner, Richard, *Performance Theory* (London: Routledge, 2003).
——, *Performance Studies: An Introduction* (London: Routledge, 2013).

Schechter, John, *Popular Theatre: A Sourcebook* (Hoboken: Taylor and Francis, 2013).
Schneider, Steven Jay, 'Introduction', in Steven Jay Schneider (ed.), *Fear without Frontiers: Horror Cinema Across the Globe* (Godalming: FAB Press, 2003), pp. 12–13.
—— and Tony Williams, 'Introduction', in Steven Jay Schneider and Tony Williams (eds), *Horror International* (Detroit: Wayne State University Press, 2005), pp. 1–12.
Sconce, Jeffrey, *Haunted Media: Electronic Presence from Telegraphy to Television* (Durham: Duke University Press, 2000).
Selz, Peter, *German Expressionist Painting* (Berkeley: University of California Press, 1974).
Senf, Carol, *The Vampire in Nineteenth Century English Literature* (Madison: University of Wisconsin Press, 1988).
Serper, Zvika, 'Shindô Kaneto's Films *Kuroneko* and *Onibaba*: Traditional and Innovative Manifestations of Demonic Embodiments', *Japan Forum*, 17/2 (2005), 231–56.
Sharrett, Christopher, 'The Idea of Apocalypse in *The Texas Chainsaw Massacre*', in Barry Keith Grant and Christopher Sharrett (eds), *Planks of Reason: Essays on the Horror Film* (Lanham: Scarecrow Press, 2004), pp. 300–20.
Shary, Timothy, *Generation Multiplex* (Austin: University of Texas Press, 2004).
Shaviro, Steven, 'Bodies of Fear: The Films of David Cronenberg', in Brian Massumi (ed.), *The Politics of Everyday Fear* (Minneapolis: University of Minnesota Press, 1993), pp. 113–35.
Shepherd, Simon and Mick Wallis, *Drama/Theatre/Performance* (Hoboken: Taylor and Francis, 2004).
Sheppard, William Anthony, *Revealing Masks: Exotic Influences and Ritualized Performance in Modernist Music Theater* (Berkeley: University of California Press, 2001).
Shipka, Danny, *Perverse Titillation: The Exploitation Cinema of Italy, Spain and France, 1960–1980* (Jefferson: McFarland & Co., 2011).
Shlossberg, Pavel, *Crafting Identity: Transnational Indian Arts and the Politics of Race in Central Mexico* (Tuscon: University of Arizona Press, 2015).
Silverman, Kaja, *The Acoustic Mirror: The Female Voice in Psychoanalysis and Cinema* (Bloomington: Indiana University Press, 1988).
Sims, Martha and Martine Stephens, *Living Folklore: An Introduction to the Study of People and Their Traditions* (Logan: Utah State University Press, 2011).
Singer, Ben, *Melodrama and Modernity: Early Sensational Cinema and Its Contexts* (New York: Columbia University Press, 2001).
Sipos, Thomas, *Horror Film Aesthetics: Creating the Visual Language of Fear* (Jefferson: McFarland & Co., 2010).

Skal, David J., *Screams of Reason: Mad Science and Modern Culture* (New York: W. W. Norton & Co., 1998).

Smith, Susan Harris, *Masks in Modern Drama* (Berkeley: University of California Press, 1984).

Sobchack, Vivian, *Carnal Thoughts: Embodiment and Moving Image Culture* (Berkeley: University of California Press, 2004).

Soister, John T., *Of Gods and Monsters: A Critical Guide to Universal Studios' Science Fiction, Horror and Mystery Films, 1929–1939* (Jefferson: McFarland & Co., 1999).

—— and Henry Nicolella, *American Silent Horror, Science Fiction and Fantasy Feature Films, 1913–1929*, vol. 1 (Jefferson: McFarland & Co., 2012).

Sorell, Walter, *The Other Face: The Mask in the Arts* (London: Thames and Hudson, 1973).

Sorfa, David, '*Kurutta ichipeiji*; Sometimes *Kuruta ippejiji/A Page of Madness* (1926)', in S. Barrow, S. Haenni and J. White (eds), *The Routledge Encyclopedia of Films* (London: Routledge, 2015), pp. 296–8.

Sova, Dawn B., *Critical Companion to Edgar Allan Poe* (New York: Facts On File, 2001).

Spooner, Catherine, *Fashioning Gothic Bodies* (Manchester: Manchester University Press, 2004).

——, 'Masks, Veils and Disguises', in William Hughes, D. Punter and A. Smith (eds), *The Encyclopedia of the Gothic. Volume II (L–Z)* (Malden: Wiley-Blackwell, 2013), pp. 421–4.

Squires, John, 'Dante Tomaselli Provides Update on *Alice, Sweet Alice* Remake', *Dread Central* (24 May 2016), www.dreadcentral.com/news/167951/dante-tomaselli-provides-update-alice-sweet-alice-remake/ (accessed 28 February 2019).

Stallybrass, Peter and Allon White, *The Politics and Poetics of Transgression* (Ithaca: Cornell University Press, 1986).

Stam, Robert, *Subversive Pleasures: Bakhtin, Cultural Criticism and Film* (Baltimore: The Johns Hopkins University Press, 1989).

Stanfield, Peter, *Maximum Movies – Pulp Fictions: Film Culture and the Worlds of Samuel Fuller, Mickey Spillane, and Jim Thompson* (New Brunswick: Rutgers University Press, 2011).

Starr, Kevin, *Material Dreams: Southern California through the 1920s* (New York: Oxford University Press, 1990).

Stépanoff, Charles, 'Devouring Perspectives: On Cannibal Shamans in Siberia', *Inner Asia*, 11 (2009), 283–307.

Stone, Alby, *Explore Shamanism* (Loughborough: Explore Books, 2003).

Stryker, Cole, 'Go to Bed, Tao Lin', *Rhizome* (21 March 2012), https://rhizome.org/editorial/2012/mar/27/tao-lin/ (accessed 28 February 2019).

Stutley, Margaret, *Shamanism: A Concise Introduction* (London: Routledge, 2003).

Suárez López, Gonzalo, 'Interview with Pedro Almodóvar', *Cineuropa* (19 May 2011), cineuropa.org/it.aspx?t=interview&lang=en&documentID=203802 (accessed 28 February 2019).

Tambling, Jeremy, *Opera, Ideology and Film* (Manchester: Manchester University Press, 1987).

Tamboukou, Maria, *Gendering the Memory of Work: Women Workers' Narratives* (London: Routledge, 2016).

Tannen, Ricki Stefanie, *The Female Trickster: The Mask That Reveals – Post-Jungian and Postmodern Psychological Perspectives on Women in Contemporary Culture* (Hove: Routledge, 2007).

Telotte, J. P., 'Through a Pumpkin's Eye: The Reflexive Nature of Horror', in Gregory Albert Waller (ed.), *American Horrors: Essays on the Modern American Horror Film* (Urbana: University of Illinois Press, 1987), pp. 114–28.

Thomas, Sarah, *Peter Lorre: Face Maker: Stardom and Performance between Hollywood and Europe* (New York: Berghahn Books, 2012).

Thomas, Tammis Elise, 'Masquerade Liberties and Female Power in Le Fanu's *Carmilla*', in E. E. Smith and R. Haas (eds), *The Haunted Mind: The Supernatural in Victorian Literature* (New York: Scarecrow Press, 1999), pp. 30–65.

Tillis, Steve, *Rethinking Folk Drama* (Westport: Greenwood Press, 1999).

Tonkin, Elizabeth, 'Mask', in Richard Bauman (ed.), *Folklore, Cultural Performances, and Popular Entertainments – A Communications-centered Handbook* (New York: Oxford University Press, 1992), pp. 225–32.

Tseëlon, Efrat, 'Reflections on Mask and Carnival', in Efrat Tseëlon (ed.), *Masquerade and Identities: Essays on Gender, Sexuality and Marginality* (London: Routledge, 2001), pp. 18–37.

Tudor, Andrew, *Theories of Film* (New York: Viking Press, 1973).

Turner, Victor, *Ritual Process: Structure and Anti-Structure* (Chicago: Aldine Publishing, 1969).

——, 'Frame, Flow and Reflection: Ritual and Drama as Public Liminality', in Michael Benamou and Charles Caramello (eds), *Performance and Postmodern Culture* (Milwaukee: University of Wisconsin-Milwaukee Press, 1977), pp. 41–2.

——, 'Introduction', in Victor Turner (ed.), *Celebration: Studies in Festivity and Ritual* (Washington: Smithsonian Institution Press, 1982), pp. 11–32.

Twitchell, James, *Dreadful Pleasures: An Anatomy of Modern Horror* (New York: Oxford University Press, 1985).

Van Aken, Mauro, 'Virtual Water, H2O and the De-socialisation of Water – A Brief Anthropological Journey', in Marta Antonelli and Francesca Greco (eds), *The Water We Eat: Combining Virtual Water and Water Footprints* (Cham: Springer, 2015), pp. 103–22.

Van Wert, Bill, '*The Exorcist*: Radical Therapy', *Jump Cut: A Review of Contemporary Media*, 1/4–5 (1974), *www.ejumpcut.org/archive/onlinessays/JC01folder/exorcist.html* (accessed 28 February 2019).

Vatnsdal, Caelum, *They Came from Within: A History of Canadian Horror Cinema* (Winnipeg: Arbeiter Ring Publishing, 2004).

——, 'Monsters Up North: A Taxonomy of Terror', in Gina Freitag and André Loiselle (eds), *The Canadian Horror Film: Terror of the Soul* (Toronto: University of Toronto Press, 2015), pp. 21–9.

Von Kannon, Alice and Christopher L. Hodapp, *Conspiracy Theories and Secret Societies for Dummies* (Hoboken: Wiley Publishing, Inc., 2008).

Waddell, Terrie, *Wild/lives Trickster, Place and Liminality on Screen* (Hoboken: Taylor and Francis, 2014).

Wallis, R. J., 'Waking Ancestor Spirits: Neo-shamanic Engagements with Archeology', in Graham Harvey (ed.), *Shamanism: A Reader* (London: Routledge, 2003), pp. 402–23.

Weaver, Tom, Michael Brunas and John Brunas, *Universal Horrors: The Studio's Classic Films, 1931–1946* (Jefferson: McFarland & Co., 2007).

Weemans, Michel and Bertrand Prévost, 'Introduction', in Walter Melion, Bret Rothstein and Michel Weemans (eds), *The Anthropomorphic Lens: Anthropomorphism, Microcosmism, and Analogy in Early Modern Thought and Visual Arts* (Leiden: Brill, 2014), pp. 1–18.

Weinberg, Scott, '*Hush* is a Cool, Quiet, Creepy Thriller', *Nerdist* (9 April 2016), *https://nerdist.com/review-hush-is-a-cool-quiet-creepy* (accessed 28 February 2019).

Wheatley, Helen, 'Television', in William Hughes, David Punter and Andrew Smith (eds), *The Encyclopedia of the Gothic* (Malden: John Wiley & Son, 2016), pp. 677–83.

Wiles, David, *The Masks of Menander: Sign and Meaning in Greek and Roman Performance* (Cambridge: Cambridge University Press, 1991).

Wilkins, Budd, 'Flesh and Blood: The Cinema of Jean Rollin', *Slant Magazine* (27 January 2012), *https://www.slantmagazine.com/features/article/flesh-and-blood-the-cinema-of-jean-rollin* (accessed 28 February 2019).

Williams, Linda, *Playing the Race Card: Melodramas of Black and White from Uncle Tom to O. J. Simpson* (Princeton: Princeton University Press, 2001).

Williams, Tony, *Hearths of Darkness: The Family in the American Horror Film* (Madison: Fairleigh Dickinson University Press, 1996).

——, 'Trying to Survive the Darker Side: 1980s Family Horror', in Barry Keith Grant (ed.), *The Dread of Difference: Gender and the Horror Film* (Austin: University of Texas Press, 1996), pp. 15–34.

Winzeler, Robert L., *Anthropology and Religion: What We Know, Think, and Question* (Lanham: AltaMira Press, 2008).

Wood, Robin, *Hollywood from Vietnam to Reagan . . . and Beyond* (New York: Columbia University Press, 2003).

——, 'An Introduction to the American Horror Film', in Barry Keith Grant and Christopher Sharrett (eds), *Planks of Reason: Essays on the Horror Film* (Lanham: Scarecrow Press, 2004), pp. 107–41.

Woodward, Ian, *Understanding Material Culture* (Los Angeles: Sage Publications, 2007).

Woodward, Kath, *Embodied Sporting Practices: Regulating and Regulatory Bodies* (New York: Palgrave Macmillan, 2009).

Worland, Rick, 'Faces Behind the Mask: Vincent Price, Dr. Phibes, and the Horror Genre in Transition', *Post Script*, 22/2 (winter–spring 2003), 20–33.

Yadugiri, M. A. and B. Naidu, *Understanding Literature* (Hyperabad: Orient Longman, 1996).

Yaneva, Rozaliya, *Misrule and Reversals: Carnivalesque Performances in Christopher Marlowe's Plays* (Munich: Herbert Utz Verlag, 2012).

Yarbrough, William Wynn, *Masculinity in Children's Animal Stories, 1888–1928* (Jefferson: McFarland & Co., 2014).

Youngkin, Stephen D., *The Lost One: A Life of Peter Lorre* (Lexington: University Press of Kentucky, 2005).

Zanger, Anat, *Film Remakes as Ritual and Disguise: From Carmen to Ripley* (Amsterdam: Amsterdam University Press, 2006).

Zone, Ray, *3D Revolution: The History of Modern Stereoscopic Cinema* (Lexington: University Press of Kentucky, 2012).

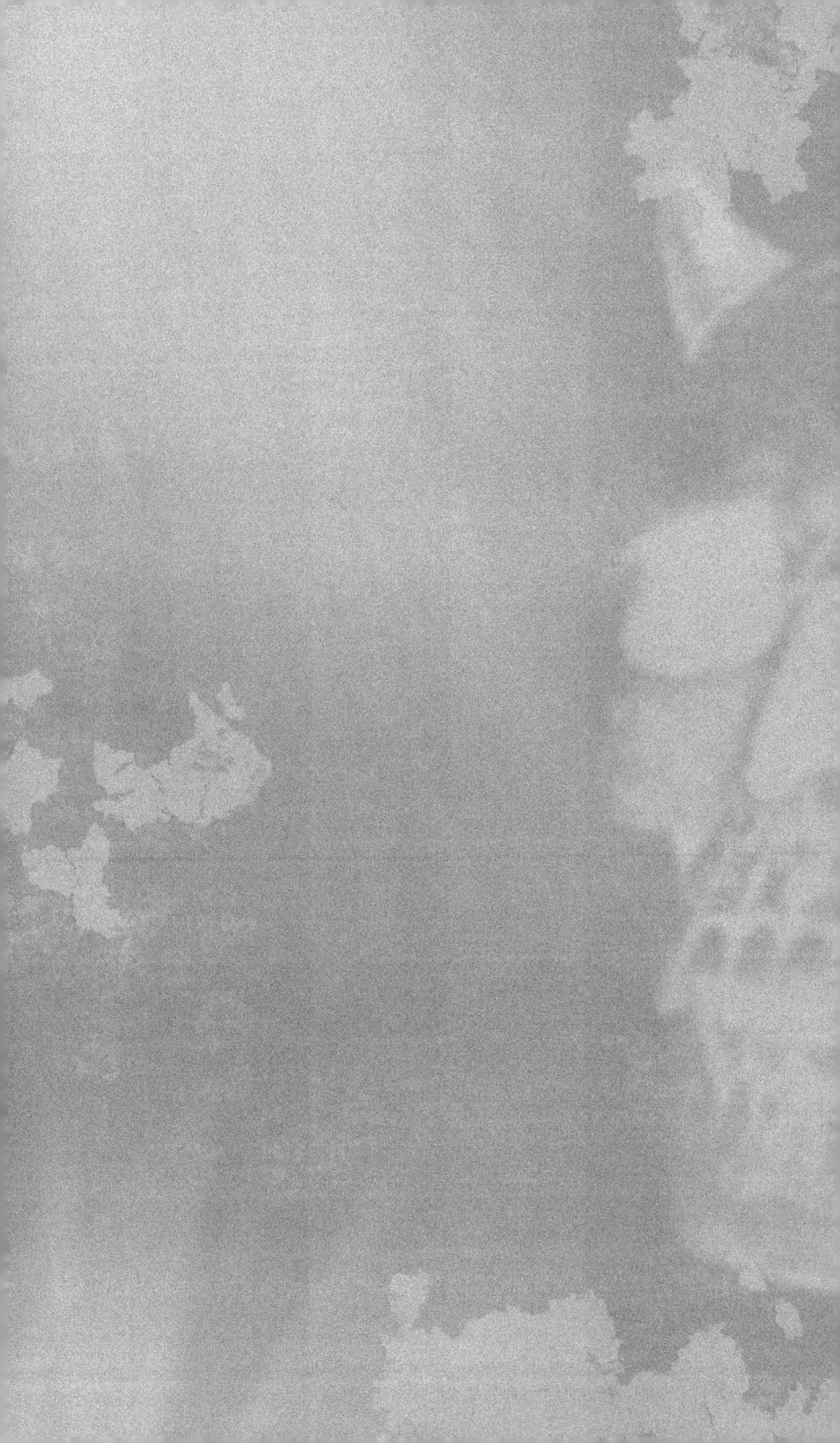

Index

3D 74, 157, 172, 175–6, 187
4chan 106, 107, 108
9/11 attacks 139, 179

The Abominable Dr. Phibes (Robert Fuest, 1971) 4, 90–4, 97, 103, 108, 126, 131
Act of Vengeance (1974) 156
Alice Sweet Alice (Albert Sole, 1976) 4, 90, 91, 92, 94–7, 100, 102, 103, 108, 153, 187
All the Colors of the Dark (1974) 8
Almodóvar, Pedro 112, 225n
Altman, Rick 25
Anatomy (2000) 5, 149, 159–65,
Anonymous 106–8, 194
anthropomorphism 130–1
Artaud, Antonin 3, 37, 48, 54–5, 61
avant-garde movement 41, 44, 54

Bakhtin, Mikhail 7, 11, 13–14, 17, 26, 47, 55, 192, 200, 203
    see also carnivalesque

Barker, Clive 17
The Bat (1926) 67
The Bat (1959) 67
The Bat Whispers (1930) 67
Bataille, Georges 15, 130
Batman (comic book) 67, 81
Black Death (plague) 10, 185
Black Mask (magazine) 53
Black Sunday (1960) 4, 27, 82–3, 85
Blood and Black Lace (1963) 82–3
Bloody Reunion (2006) 4, 131–7, 141, 146
Bradley, Doug 17, 27
Brooks, Peter 29–30, 125
    see also melodrama
Bruiser (George A. Romero, 2000) 4, 49, 112, 123–4, 127
Butler, Judith 96, 101

The Cabinet of Dr. Caligari (1920) 44, 58
    see also German expressionism
Campbell, Joseph 35–6

cannibalism 90, 99
Carmilla (novella) 51
Carnival 8, 13, 14, 17, 26, 46–8, 50, 52, 55, 72, 76, 79, 82, 85, 94, 132, 186, 191
carnivalesque 4, 7, 11, 14–15, 17, 47–8, 91, 97, 121, 186, 192
Carved: The Slit-Mouthed Woman (2007) 5, 149, 158–60
Castle, William 4, 73–76
The Castle of Otranto (novel) 50
Cawelti, John G. 24
Celia (Ann Turner, 1998) 4, 13, 42, 113, 118–23, 127, 227n
Chaney Sr., Lon 1, 4, 17, 53, 65, 71
Chaplin, Charles 42
Christianity 42, 79, 95–7, 161, 162
    Christian theatre 41
    see also religion
Chomón, Segundo de 57
Christie, Agatha 49, 104
The Circular Staircase (novel) 67
class 4, 11, 53, 80, 90, 100, 103–9, 126, 135, 144, 151 153–6, 164,
Clover, Carol J. 19, 66, 82, 91, 105, 132, 172–3, 174
Collins, Wilkie 51
Come Out and Play (2012) 1
comic books 54, 67, 81
commedia dell'arte 3, 13, 37, 42, 46–9, 50, 54, 57, 76, 82, 85, 116, 191, 192
conspiracy theories 138–40, 163,
consumerism 5, 99, 176–81, 187
Corman, Roger 52–3, 74
Creed, Barbara 12, 66, 123
Cronenberg, David 159–62, 175
The Curse of the Crimson Altar (1968) 8, 131

Curtains (1983) 4, 18, 19, 90, 91, 97, 100–4, 108, 109

Dark Night of the Scarecrow (1981) 27
De Lorde, Andre 55–6, 60
    see also Grand Guignol theatre
Dead Ringers (David Cronenberg, 1988) 5, 149, 159–62
dehumanisation 12, 65, 70, 75, 90 101, 113, 129, 131, 152, 155, 186, 227n, 233n
Demons (1985) 10
The Den (2013) 5, 107, 170, 176, 179–81, 184, 185, 187
Dika, Vera 10, 105–6, 157
disguise 2, 5, 6, 12, 14, 15, 46, 51, 52, 53, 65, 67, 68, 69, 77, 82, 84, 90, 91, 92, 94, 95, 103, 105, 106, 116, 118, 119, 129, 150, 152, 154, `56, 159, 182, 187
Doane, Mary Ann 12, 154
domestic violence 158, 160, 165
doppelgänger 15, 44, 58, 67, 68, 69, 77, 81, 91, 93, 106, 161
Dr. Phibes Rises Again (1972) 91

Eco, Umberto 24, 115
El Santo 4, 79–82
Eliade, Mircea 67, 98, 114–15
Englund, Robert 17
Ensor, James 13
Euripides 50
Evidence (2013) 5, 12, 149, 153–5, 164
exhibition 24
Eyes Wide Shut (1999) 8
Eyes Without a Face (1960) 4, 27, 60, 77–9, 84, 112

The Face Behind the Mask (1941) 64, 71, 215n
Feast of Flesh (1967) 115
Feuillade, Louis 60
Final Girl 105, 117, 135, 137, 145, 156
   see also Clover, Carol J.
Flashdance (1983) 154
folklore 34, 35, 48, 102, 120, 136, 137
   see also urban legends
Franco, Jesús 112
Franju, Georges 60, 77–8, 141
   see also Eyes Without a Face (1960)
Frankenstein (novel) 77
Frankenstein (1931) 64, 69, 81
Freud, Sigmund 15, 66, 133, 141, 183
   see also the uncanny, totemism
Friday the 13th (film franchise) 1, 2, 17, 18, 114, 155
   Friday the 13th (1980) 19
   Friday the 13th Part II (1981) 156
   Friday the 13th Part III (1982) 5, 149, 155–7, 165, 174

gender performativity 94, 96–7, 154
   see also Judith Butler
genre theory 24–7
German expressionism 44, 58, 67, 55–6, 57, 67, 70, 73, 74, 76, 92, 170, 171,
giallo cinema 82–3, 129, 138
gothic 15, 29, 31, 51
   gothic imagination 29–30, 37
   gothic literature 3, 37, 42, 50, 51, 53, 55, 60, 192

Grand Guignol theatre 3, 37, 42, 50, 54–7, 59–60, 69, 76, 77, 141, 192
Greek theatre 13, 41, 42, 48, 50, 116
grotesque 14, 51
   see also Bakhtin, Mikhail
Gurozuka (Yoichi Noshiyama, 2005) 4, 42, 113, 118–20, 122, 127

Halloween (film franchise) 1, 2, 3, 18, 24, 34, 111, 112, 114–18, 119, 123, 126, 127, 150
   Halloween (1978) 10, 18–19, 24, 89, 103, 112, 116, 157
   Halloween (2007) 113, 116, 135
   Halloween (2018) 118
   Halloween II (1981) 118
   Halloween II (2009) 113, 116
   Halloween III: Season of the Witch (1982) 5, 23, 170, 176–9, 180, 181, 187
   Halloween IV: The Return of Michael Myers (1988) 115
Halloween (holiday) 3, 8, 14, 71, 89, 95, 170, 194
Hansen, Gunnar 17, 99
Happy Birthday to Me (J. Lee Thompson, 1981) 4, 10, 19, 82, 90, 103–6, 107, 108. 126, 136, 137, 146
Hawkins, Joan 78
Hellraiser (film series) 17
   see also Bradley, Doug
Hiroshima (attack) 85
Hodder, Kane 1, 7
Holocaust 78, 164
House of Wax (1953) 74, 92, 93
Hush (Mike Flannagan, 2016) 4, 49, 57, 113, 123–7, 143, 144

Identity 1, 2, 4, 6, 7, 9, 22, 13, 15, 36, 46, 51, 52, 58, 60, 66, 68, 70, 73, 74–6, 78, 79, 82, 85, 91, 94, 95–6, 97, 100, 111, 112, 113, 114, 16, 117, 120, 123–7, 134, 141, 150, 151, 153, 154, 155, 156, 163, 180, 185, 187, 188
The Iron Mask (1929) 67, 70

J-horror 83–5, 113, 118–20, 158–60
Jancovich, Mark 25, 65–6, 73–4
The Johnsons (1992) 8
Johnston, Claire 12
Jung, Carl Gustave 6, 36, 54

Karloff, Boris 17, 69
Keaton, Buster 42, 57–8
Kitses, Jim 25
Kneale, Nigel 177
Kristeva, Julie 12, 66
Ku Klux Klan 122, 194

labour 4–5, 150–5, 160–5
Leatherface (character) 17, 98–100, 108
    see also *The Texas Chain Saw Massacre*
Leone, Sergio 47
Lévi-Strauss, Claude 25–6,
liminality 3, 28, 29, 31, 35, 37, 45, 66, 68, 73, 93, 94, 96, 108
Lorre, Peter 4, 69, 71
Lovecraft, H.P. 3, 27, 51–3, 60
Lowenstein, Adam 16, 56, 78, 84–5, 161–2
lucha libre 79–82

Mad Love (1935) 64, 69
Makinov 1

Månguden (1988) 5, 119, 170, 181–5, 188
The Mask (1961) 5, 169, 170–6
The Mask (1994) 16
The Mask of Diijon (1946) 70
Masks (2011) 9
Le Masque d'horreur (1912) 58–60, 77
The Masque of the Red Death (short story) 52
The Masque of the Red Death (1964) 52, 74, 93
    see also Roger Corman, Vincent Price, Edgar Allan Poe
materiality 23–4
Méliès, George 57
melodrama 29–30, 44, 56, 70, 125
    melodramatic imagination 29–30, 37, 134, 135
Méténier, Oscar 56
Metz, Christian 24
mime 11, 49
modernism 13, 41, 53,
monsters and monstrosity 12, 51, 69, 102, 109, 119, 123, 130, 151, 153, 164
Motel Hell (1980) 4, 129, 131–6, 137, 141, 146
Motokiyo, Zeami 41, 84, 119
Mr. Sardonicus (1961) 75–6, 91
Mulvey, Laura 12, 172
muteness 125–6, 227n
My Bloody Valentine (1981) 4, 10, 18, 103, 149, 150–2
My Bloody Valentine (2009) 150
Myers, Michael (character) 2, 7, 24, 34, 37, 68, 114–17, 123, 130, 135, 176, 177
    see also *Halloween*

Mystery of the Wax Museum (1933) 74, 81
myths and mythology 2, 4, 23, 24–6, 44, 47, 106, 114, 118, 126, 130, 131, 136–40, 143, 146, 191, 192

Nazism 73, 162–3, 164
Ndalianis, Angela 26, 48
Neale, Steve 4, 18, 26, 42, 57, 64, 72, 76, 85, 90, 112, 115, 124, 126, 127, 177, 192–3
    see also genre theory
A Nightmare on Elm Street (film franchise) 17, 114
Noh theatre 3, 5, 11, 13, 27, 41–6, 49, 57, 60, 84–5, 111, 113, 118–22, 127, 192
Nolde, Emil 13, 58
The Nude Vampire (Jean Rollin, 1970) 4, 129, 131, 140, 141–3, 144, 146

Old Dark House films 4, 57, 67–8, 192
Onibaba (1964) 4, 56, 84–5, 118
opera dei pupi (puppetry) 47

A Page of Madness (1926) 44–6, 58, 83, 113, 118, 120
pantomime 48
Paz, Octavia 79
Peeping Tom (1960) 5, 169, 170, 171–4, 182, 187
penny dreadfuls (literature)
performance 53
The Phantom of Crestwood (1932) 68
The Phantom of the Opera (novel) 4
The Phantom of the Opera (1925/1930) 4, 26, 53, 64–7, 85, 92, 192

The Phantom of the Opera (1943) 4, 71–2
Picasso, Pablo 13, 25, 42
Poe, Edgar Allan 3, 27, 51, 52–3, 54, 55, 60, 74
Possessed (2006) 32
postmodernism 13, 32, 35, 97, 115, 153, 177
The Poughkeepsie Tapes (2007) 5, 10, 27, 170, 181, 182, 184–8
Price, Vincent 1, 4, 17, 64, 67, 73–6, 92–3
Psycho (1960) 74, 132
pulp literature 53–4, 60, 69
puppari (puppetry) 47
Pussy Riot 194

Rabelais, François 13–14
    see also Mikhail Bakhtin
religion 2, 3, 4, 6, 10, 28, 31, 41, 42, 43–4, 60, 63, 64, 67, 79, 80, 92–7, 98, 107, 108, 115, 121, 130, 138–9, 161, 162, 170
    see also Christianity
remakes 1, 4, 64, 67, 71, 74, 98, 113, 114, 115, 116, 117, 119, 127, 135, 150
Ring (film franchise) 114
    Ringu (1998) 113
Riviere, Joan 12
Rollin, Jean 141–2
    see also The Nude Vampire (1970)
Roman theatre 48
The Rose Garden (short story)
Ruskin, John 30

Sanskrit epics 50
Saw (film franchise) 93, 114
Scared to Death (1947) 64, 72–3, 75

Schatz, Thomas 25, 26, 114
Scream (1996) 25, 178
sensory experience 24, 26, 54, 55, 65, 173, 192
sequels 35, 98, 113, 114, 116–17, 127
sexual harassment 102–3
Shakespeare, William 50
shamanic imagination 3, 23, 27–37, 41, 45, 46, 47, 49, 55, 61, 63–4, 75, 90, 94, 101, 109, 113, 122, 124, 126, 127, 143, 150, 153, 157, 162, 171, 178, 186, 191, 192
shamanism 3, 23, 25–37, 43, 75, 94, 99, 111, 130, 153, 178, 191
  see also shamanic imagination
Shepard, Sam 1
Silence of the Lambs (1991) 27, 233n
slasher films 1, 2, 7, 10, 12, 18, 19, 68, 82, 89, 97, 100, 103, 104, 105, 117, 130, 132, 134, 137, 138, 143, 151, 152, 177, 182, 198
Smiley (2012) 4, 90, 91, 103, 106–8, 109, 179
Sobchack, Vivian 24, 26, 173
social media 176, 179, 180, 181, 188
sport 155–7, 165, 231n
Stagefright (1987) 4, 129, 131, 136–8
Stanley, Richard 32
Steele, Barbara 4, 83, 85
Strange Case of Dr Jekyll and Mr Hyde (novel) 51, 103
Strange Impersonation (1946) 70
surrealism 9, 13, 54, 141, 143
surveillance 179–81, 185
Suspension (2015) 7

Terror Train (1980) 18, 91
The Texas Chain Saw Massacre (film franchise) 18, 36
  The Texas Chain Saw Massacre (Tobe Hooper, 1974) 4, 8, 17, 89, 90, 91, 97–100, 102, 103, 108, 132, 132
Theatre of Cruelty 3, 37, 42, 48, 54–5, 61, 192
The Three Masks (1921) 49
The Three Masks (1929) 49
The Tingler (1959) 75
totemism 4, 66, 93, 130, 132–6
  see also Freud, Sigmund
Tourneur, Jacques 70
Tourneur, Maurice 60
tricksters 3, 27, 35–7, 42, 47, 66, 69, 70, 73, 74, 77, 90, 92, 93, 94, 95, 97, 101, 106–7, 108, 126, 143, 153, 157, 177–8, 186
Tudor, Andrew 25
Turner, Victor 8, 31, 94
Twitchell, James B. 10

the uncanny 15, 66, 71, 75, 107, 125, 141, 142, 146
  see also Freud, Sigmund
Universal Studios monster films 4, 53, 64, 65, 67, 69, 71, 74, 192
urban legends 107, 137, 158, 158–60, 165

V for Vendetta (2005) 106, 194
Voorhees, Jason (character) 2, 7, 17, 37, 68, 69, 130, 155
  see also Friday the 13th

The Wailing (2016) 32
War of the Worlds (radio play) 170

Who Can Kill a Child? (1976) 1
The Wicker Man (1973) 8, 131
Wood, Robin 73, 98
The Woman Who Came Back (1945) 71

Wright, Will 25

You're Next (Adam Wingard, 2011) 4, 57, 126, 129, 131, 140, 143–6